An Eager God

M.J. Lindemann

For my husband
Who dragged me kicking and screaming into the world of travel
Who buys me the things I don't buy for myself, and then sends
me the bill
Who has supported me unceasingly through this journey

I love you

Contents

A Moment of Your Time

A short story was written as a companion to this novel. You can claim it by signing up for my newsletter at mjlindemann. com. It stars one of the characters, Kiko, as she grows into the empress she would one day become. All short stories set in the world of Kohru are 100% unnecessary for understanding the plot of the main novels, but I do highly recommend reading them. They're both fun AND free!

Recommended reading order:

The Eye

The Will of The World

The Princess

An Eager God

Thank you for your time, intrepid reader, and may the will of the world guide your path!

-M. J. Lindemann

Prologue

Kohru blesses those with and without. She embraces those meek and hungry, those mighty and prosperous. Her gentle light shines on all.

Carula Rashee recited a prayer to herself while bouncing on a wagon down a cobblestone street leading out of The Glittering City. She wore the color red to feign support for the National Party, a red blouse with red earrings imprinted with a bold letter R. She did not wear these things because she believed in their Egal First philosophy or because she shared their hatred for immigrants and refugees, she wore them because if she did not, they would fine her, jail her, or worse. The short woman sitting behind her, underneath the wagon's canvas, wore a green blazer over a white, linen shirt and scowled at the floor, muttering something about justice and pride. She refused to wear splashes of red, and so Carula demanded she sit under the canvas until they were safely away from the city.

They were fleeing to Nakonipol under the pretense of a pylon maintenance team for The Guild of Commerce. It wasn't much of a lie, either. The Guild hadn't sent a team since the coup, and the oceanside city sorely needed their expertise. The danger was that they had no intention of returning, this was an escape attempt, one made all the more difficult due to Oji's obstinance regarding her clothing.

Earlier in the day, Carula had prepared by packing every belonging she saved from the sale of the Rashee mansion. This included traveling clothes, *The Book of Kohru*, a comb given to her by her mother before she died, and a small book of terrible poetry written by her son, Seffin. He'd gifted it to her as a birthday present when he was eleven. The intensity in his eyes as he'd handed it to her weighted the gift heavily in her heart.

The Seffin she knew now would never make something so sentimental. Not because he lacked sensitivity, but because through the years, she and her late husband, Pulpin, had stamped those impulses out. A Rashee was to be intellectual and pragmatic above all else. Stoicism tempered by power. Even at eleven, her son's face barely moved, trying his best not to react as his father scoffed at the gift. She would have liked if she had told her husband off for being so cruel, she would have loved if she had grabbed her son's hand and told him to keep at it, that the gift meant everything to her. But instead, she gave a thin smile and nodded before putting it in a box in a closet not to be found again until now, many years later. She read through some of it before leaving but could only make it a few pages. It truly was dreadful. A project best done over time... perhaps quite a long time.

A checkpoint jostled into view at the city's northeast gate. Six guards stood in a line wearing red bandannas and red armor. Blocking Prolivgrad's main exit was a throng of travelers, merchants, and couriers queued up and filing through. Carula put the cart in line and turned back to Oji, still scowling at the wooden floor of the wagon. "Please, at least take my earrings and put them on, or take a scarf out of my pack, *something.*"

"I am free by divine right. My liberty cannot be taken from me, and no *New National Government* is gonna demand my obedience. I wear what I choose."

Kohru embraces those meek and hungry and mighty and prosperous... and stupid.

Followers of Svoboda acclimated poorly after the coup. Their dogma could not reconcile itself with the new order, even if their philosophies used the same words. Svoboda's sect within Prolivgrad believed in freedom from. Freedom from oppression, from fear, from cruelty. The New National Government believed in freedom to. Freedom to dictate, to enforce, and to rule.

Oji believed The Nationals had left her alone because of her faith, but truthfully, she was just lucky. Svoboda claimed to protect those who fiercely adhered to their freedoms, and in Oji's mind, that explained all the close calls she'd had with The National Party thus far. Party enforcers who kept clear of Oji's office during a check had been evidence of Svoboda's blessing, not because of Boris, her supervisor, steering them away. An angry mystic who skewered a patrol with ice lances just as they were to arrest her wasn't dumb luck, it was Svoboda's wrath on those who deserved it.

To protect his best engineer, Boris, the division head of operations at the Guild, assigned Oji to a permanent placement in Nakonipol, and Carula signed on to protect herself. Prolivgrad may be the safest place from the husk, but since the coup, death had become a constant backdrop. She's lost count of the murders she witnessed from Nationals attacking anyone they suspected of supporting the Resistance.

Foolishness. A few good people helping out their fellow citizens from the Nationals' crackdown does not mean there's a resistance.

They came closer to the checkpoint as the line marched on. Carula tried once more, "Please, this isn't a patrol on the street or some overzealous party member. They will arrest you."

Oji looked up at Carula, fire in her eyes. "They can try."

"What in Kohru's name does that mean?"

"The pursuit of my goals alone will grant us Svoboda's protection. Watch, you'll see."

They're going to arrest her, and then they're going to arrest me for trying to hide her.

Carula closed the flaps of the canopy. "Lay down and don't speak. If we make it out of this, it will be by our wits and a healthy dose of luck."

The horse signified a certain level of wealth which Carula hoped would encourage the guards to let her pass. Wealth meant power here after all, and between the animal and the clothing, she looked like nobility. She was also an actual noble, which helped. The Rashees were—had been—a noble family with a long history of supporting the National Party. Between the cart, the clothing, her job, and her name, the six guards should, theoretically, wave them past with little more than a greeting.

The queue moved quicker than she expected, and before long Carula pulled her horse to a stop next to the guards and put a smile on which she hoped didn't betray her anxiety. "Good afternoon."

A boy who looked to be in his early twenties with short hair and a warm, beige skin tone walked up to her. "Afternoon ma'am." He held a spear with a red scarf tied just beneath the metal of the blade. "What is your name and what are you transporting?"

"Carula Rashee, we're a maintenance team from the Guild heading up to Dunburough to catch a ship to Nakonipol. Just carrying rations and pylon materials. My engineer is asleep in the back."

The young man arched an eyebrow and eyed the canvas flaps. "You have someone in the back?"

"Yes, she had a late night preparing everything for the trip, so I told her she could nap while I drove for the first part of the day. She has a problem sleeping at night anyway and this will be the first maintenance team to go to Griela since the..." *I'm talking too much. Shut up, Carula. Shut up.* "... the..."

She swallowed. "Since the liberation of our country from the Labor Party."

The guard's arched eyebrow lowered, and his face took on a bored expression. "Very well, go through."

Carula let out a breath and nodded. "Thank you, sir. Have a nice day."

She flicked the reins and the horse lurched forward. Behind her, she heard arguing. They'd gone no more than thirty paces before one of the other guards, an older woman with red hair, jogged up. "Sorry to bother you, but we have to take a look at your wagon."

Kohru help me.

The woman went around back and Carula held her breath, listening intently. There was a gasp muffled by the canvas material followed by choking and a crashing of metal on stone.

"Go!" Oji's voice sprang from the canvas flaps. "Now!"

Carula whipped the reins as hard as she could, and the horse lurched forward. The clanging of guards' boots on cobblestone rushed after them, accompanied by shouts of "Halt!" and "Stop!". She whipped the reins again frantically as the blur of an arrow hissed past her head. The archer's aim was true, it was only by luck her head bounced to the side from the jostling of the cart. The back of the wagon started shaking violently. The young guard from earlier had leapt inside and grappled with Oji.

Forgive me.

Carula stood and created a shield of ice just in time for another arrow to glance off it with a scrape. She broke the shield apart with her will, formed the pieces into small lances, and shunted all but one toward the archer. Then she made a wall of ice behind the cart to stop the remaining guards from following. Ducking into the back of the wagon, she saw Oji's hand with a dagger in it, slick with blood, and the guard holding her wrist to prevent the blade from lodging in his throat. "Please, stop," he grunted the words out with panic-stricken eyes.

"Oji!" Carula yelled. "Drop the dagger."

The cart hit a bump and the dagger tip sliced his throat. He fell to the floor, his hands around his neck while Oji brought the weapon up to stab him again. Carula shunted her final lance at Oji's dagger. The engineer fell backward, holding her hand while Carula jumped onto the young soldier, met his frantic eyes with her own, gently put one hand on his cheek, and the other on his hands covering his throat. While she had never formally trained in healing, she had been taught first aid techniques in her youth as a traveling mystic. Blood oozed out between his fingers and dripped down the sides of his neck, seeping between the floorboards of the wagon. He would pass out soon.

"Koth's asshole, what did you do that for?" Oji shouted.

"Grab the reins and guide the horse," she yelled behind her, then focused her attention on the young guard again. "I need you to let go in order to stop the bleeding."

Carula tugged on the guard's hands, but he held firm.

"If you don't let me close the wound you'll die."

His eyes darted around like a caged animal before finally resting back on her again. With tears streaming down the side of his face, he nodded and croaked out, "Please."

She ripped his hands off the wound and pinched the artery shut before focusing a stream of will-fire to cauterize the cut. He screamed for only a moment before passing out, likely from the pain and blood loss. Luckily, the blade only sliced open the side of the vessel, it didn't pierce through. With the guard unconscious and mostly out of danger, she took a length of rope, wrapped his hands behind his back, and tied his legs together. Then she cleaned the blood off his neck to ensure the cauterization was done properly.

Out the back of the wagon, Prolivgrad shrank into the horizon. Her wall of ice had stopped the pursuit cleanly, and regardless, any sane person wouldn't chase beyond the city's barrier. They were safe for now, at least from the Nationals. Sighing, she hopped up to the front of the wagon and sat next to Oji who had a look on her face that could kill a husk.

"Mind explaining why you just saved a Nationalist pig?"

"Mind explaining why you killed that woman without so much as *trying* to talk our way out?"

"They kill or jail anyone who disagrees with them and you're asking me why I slit her throat?"

"And how'd that work out for us? They'll mark us as murderers. We'll never—"

"They're the murderers."

"We didn't know if those guards were. Not all of them—"

"I don't want to hear how *some* of them have a conscience. I've seen enough to know that each and every member of that cult can rot. In fact, bring her dead body outside the barrier. She can turn husk and I'll kill her again. Just like we should kill that pig in the back."

"He's only a boy. He wasn't trying to kill you; he was trying to arrest you."

"So they could kill me later."

Carula thought for a moment. Oji wasn't wrong that being sent to The Pit was as good as a death sentence, but... still. "True enough I suppose, but I'm not killing someone unless I absolutely have to."

"And what are you going to do with him? We're going to Dunburough, remember? That's still in Egal. I doubt the Nationals are going to let us waltz through there with an injured National guard in our wagon."

"Once he's recovered, we can let him go."

"Carula, the husk hordes have been surging around Prolivgrad. If we let him go, I might as well have stabbed him. It would have been an easier death."

"Then we try and convince him to keep his mouth shut when we get to Dunburough."

Oji grunted. "I know of a surefire way we can convince him to keep his mouth shut forever."

"Enough, we'll wait until he wakes and then we'll see what kind of person he is. I heard a lot of the city guards weren't too happy with the Nationals taking over. Maybe he's one of them."

"If he didn't like them taking over then he might have tried quitting."

Carula decided not to respond to that, the argument was headed toward well-trodden territory between them, and she didn't feel like walking down that particular path again. Instead, she reached back into the wagon, into her bag, and pulled out Seffin's book of poetry to see if she could get through a couple more pages. Opening where she left off, she suffered through an entry about a husk and a turtle making friends. The next one seemed to just list things that were red.

Did no one teach him how to rhyme?

She snapped the book shut and took in the scenery. Spring was here, and with it came wildflowers and bird songs and a warm wind. She took a deep breath in and enjoyed the fresh smell of the wilds. In the last twenty years, she could count on one hand the number of times she'd left the city and its malodor. A tingling sensation cascaded down her arms at the excitement of being out in the world again, and something about seeing so much green, even under a cloudy sky, tickled her. Despite the violence and excitement from earlier, she couldn't contain the joy she felt at finally, after so many years, seeing the world again. *I am the ship that travels these treacherous waters and Kohru's light is the beacon by which I am guided.*

A groan from the back of the wagon ruined the moment. She peeked behind her. The boy didn't struggle against his bonds so much as test them, and when he saw her watching, he stopped, fear writ upon his face.

"You won't get out of those knots. I may not look it, but I'm not new to this sort of thing," she warned.

Before Pulpin, she worked for the Guild, traveling around to different contracted hubs and townships recharging their pylons, taking care of roaming hordes, and handling amalgamations that strayed too close to roads or villages. On more than a few occasions, she stopped in villages that needed help not with husk, but with humans.

"What are you going to do with me?"

"I'll tell you what we should—"

"Oji!" Carula glared at the engineer. "Drop it." She stepped into the back of the wagon and sat across from her prisoner. "What do *you* think we should do?"

He gave her a quizzical look before his eyes drifted out the back of the cart. Prolivgrad had long since faded from sight. If he asked her to let him go, she would, but his chances of surviving the trek alone were low. He had a simple spear which meant he probably couldn't use a willed weapon, and even with a willed weapon, stumbling onto a horde would likely kill him unless he was very, very good. But he'd already proved he wasn't.

"You said you were heading to Nakonipol?" he asked, finally.

"Dunburough, and then to Nakonipol. What do you think we should do?" she pressed.

With a forlorn look on his face, he kept his gaze out the back of the cart while he said, "I've always wanted to go to Nakonipol."

Carula's eyes went wide at that.

"Nope! Nuh-uh." Oji said from the front of the wagon. "I'm not escorting some bootlicker to Nakonipol after he tried to kill me."

"I wasn't trying to kill you," he said.

"The spear you thrust at me said differently."

"I was trying to knock the knife out of your—"

"Stop it," Carula said. "What is your name?"

"Yufei."

"Well, Yufei, you have two weeks to convince us that bringing you to Nakonipol is worth the risk. If you can do that then we'll discuss how you can pay us back for the rations and coin we'll have to waste on keeping you alive."

She climbed up over their supplies to the front of the wagon and sat next to Oji.

"I want it on record that this is the stupidest idea I've ever heard."

"Does Svoboda not encourage second chances?"

"Svoboda teaches that you make your own second chance."

"Well, Kohru teaches that a seed of mercy now can grow into a field of peace later."

"Well, if this seed grows into a weed, I'll be pruning it."

Carula looked back into the wagon. Yufei's expression was pitiful, scared. She turned and met Oji's eyes. "If that happens, I'll yank it out myself."

Ren

Orbs of fire and water spun around each other so quickly they blurred together. Ren froze and unfroze the water to flex and work at his kinetics while Seffin stood across the room doing the same exercise with orbs three times in size, though only with half the speed. In the month since arriving, Ren spent most of his conscious hours drilling control exercises while Seffin trained with Ka to learn the wild elements, earth and wind.

Ren was just thankful he could practice at all; the will reserves he lost after his poor attempt at flickering took a while to return. The Caretaker explained that he had never learned the proper applications of force for each of his cells, so the technique taxed his pathways of intention more than it should, whatever the hells that meant. Ka sat him down afterward to explain, but it didn't help. Everyone was made up of the pieces and parts he used for elementalism, and while he knew the structure of the pieces in a person mattered, he hadn't realized just how much. Eventually, Ka got to talking about organs and she lost him. He wasn't a healer, and he wasn't going to try flickering again, not without a trainer, and thanks to some vague clues from The Caretaker, he knew the chances of encountering a flicker teacher were low. The technique originated in Karm, a place he didn't intend to go anytime soon.

Finished with practice, he melted the ice, enveloped his fire orb with water, and detonated it, billowing steam outward. Seffin did the same, but to much more dramatic effect. After the initial shock wave, the training area transformed into a steam room.

A shadowy shape in the proportions of Seffin came toward him through the steam. Each wore nothing besides smallclothes while they practiced since the humidity from combining their fire and water elementalism made clothing sticky and uncomfortable. As he approached, Seffin brought his arms up and wrapped them around Ren, pulling their bodies in close, their skin slick and warm against one another. He returned the embrace and rested his hands on Seffin's lower back, making small circular motions with his fingers. Ren brought his head down and kissed his neck, then went lower and kissed his chest, and then the small scar by his belly button, before—

"Here?"

Ren looked up at Seffin, obscured by vapor. "Why not?"

Seffin fanned his fingers through Ren's short, soft hair and massaged the back of his head, "What if someone sees?"

"We're in Nari'ko. Even if they see, they won't care."

"What if I care?"

Ren shucked Seffin's smallclothes down.

A short—but not too short—while later, Ren returned to standing and they both laughed between kisses. With their lips still touching, he felt Seffin smile and whisper, "Your turn."

Ren gave him a peck and slapped his bare ass. "You can get me later. We have our meeting with Shaia."

Seffin let out a disappointed grunt.

"I'd pull your shorts up if I were you," Ren said.

"Why?"

Ren raised his hand to will all the steam in the room into a floating river of water that terminated into the corner basin. Within a few seconds, the cloudy obscurity granting them privacy cleared away to reveal Seffin, frantically pulling his shorts up and laughing.

"You asshole."

"Gods, Seffin. Cover yourself up you perv, what if somebody sees you?"

Seffin chuckled while he tried to get the waist of his shorts over his backside. "It was your idea."

"I'm not the one with my ass hanging out."

Ren moved toward the door of the practice room; a large wooden cube hollowed out in one of the massive trees the Nari'ko Wilders used as buildings. They were sprinkled throughout the city and free to use, just like most things here. He opened the door and held it with a smug face, waiting for Seffin to catch up. In the dressing room, they put on their new traveling clothes. Ren's blue coat had a collar with a golden leaf pattern sewed into it that continued down the front, and

Seffin had a matching green one. The linen shirts they wore underneath were fitted, and the pants were leather lined with thick cotton to withstand the harsh, snowy conditions they would march through in Kori'ko. Ren smiled at how they looked like a matched set, and how the high collar on Seffin's coat framed his jaw in a way that kept Ren's eyes on his face. After straightening out his coat, Seffin ran his fingers through his hair to push it off to the side, hardly styled, but it fell in an effortlessly handsome way.

Outside, they navigated the bridge network toward Shaia's sanctum. By now it was midday, and they were to be at the sanctum no later than one. Columns of light pierced through the canopy and shifted with the waving of the trees as they walked over swaying bridges, smiles on both their faces. The break from the road was relaxing, and Poppy had been right when they told Ren he'd be sad to go. But, as sad as tomorrow's parting would be, it did not mean he wasn't ready. Far from it. He wanted to get back on the road. The itinerary had them stopping in Kelsig, a place few mainlanders were even allowed. Then on to Nakonipol, a tropical city almost as populace as Prolivgrad. Other than Karm and Garvelle City, he couldn't think of anywhere else he'd rather visit.

"Do you think Polk will be there?" Seffin asked.

Since meeting the small boy who seemed to know every-thing, Seffin worried after him. The Caretaker, Shaia Tekk, said he'd *made* the boy for the express purpose of becoming the new vessel for Koth. They insisted the child could say no if he wanted to, but Ren wondered how much free will a creation could have. Shaia was The Voice of Kohru though, and Kohru supposedly gave life to this world, including humans, ages ago. Humans had free will, so if Shaia said the boy could choose whether or not to sacrifice himself, then he decided to take The Caretaker at their word.

The Sanctum Tree was easy to spot with its thicker trunk, taller crown, and densely packed, luminescent vines hanging from its branches, but finding the correct bridges to get to the damned thing was decidedly less easy. Trees had wooden balconies around their circumference, some with external ramps to change levels, some with internal stairs, and others without any way to travel up or down, simply stopping at a specific level on a seemingly random tree. Furthermore, routes weren't intuitive, taking a bridge in the direction of a destination often ended in disappointment, standing on the wrong balcony with no clear options outside backtracking. The maze of Nari'ko had ceased to confound either Ren or Seffin at this point though. They spent the first week after Ren's recovery exploring the treetop city and committing important paths to memory.

When they arrived at the large, circular balcony outside the entrance to Shaia's sanctum, it held only Poppy, Ka, and two guards standing on either side of the massive wooden doors leading inside. Ka waved them over. "About time you two showed up. How was practice?"

"My reserves are back to what they were, so that's good."

"Shaia said we'll finally learn how the crystal functions, and then wrap up plans to go through Kori'ko. Hopefully, they can last long enough to go over everything," Poppy said.

The meetings the four had with Shaia were always frustratingly short. Nari'ko sat on the location where Kohru implanted herself into the world, and The Voice of Kohru needed to meditate at the site for almost sixteen hours a day. Breaks from meditation lasted an hour at most.

"As long as they go over how to kill Koth this time," Seffin said.

Ka grimaced. "They don't seem to think that's the route we should take. Polk may be a child, but he's been adamant he wants to be the next vessel."

"So he can spend a thousand years—"

"It's *his* choice, Seffin," Poppy interjected. "It's also the safest option for the world right now."

"He's a child."

"He's more than that and you know it. He may appear as a child, but he has never once acted like one. I've never met a child with the depth of knowledge he possesses nor the maturity and strength of character. He may come off as naive at times, but I don't see that as an example of his immaturity. It's more likely a result of living his entire life in one place."

"Exactly."

"Exactly?" Poppy gave a confused look.

"He's only ever known Nari'ko. Who's to say he won't want to live if he sees more of the world? Who's to say something won't change his mind? He's only ever known his duty and what Shaia tells him. I know that with my parents—"

"Shaia is not your parents, Seffin," Poppy snapped, but their voice softened before they went on, "I *know* this strikes a nerve for you, and believe me, I don't love how Shaia does things either. But Shaia offered Polk a choice and he made it. We have to respect that."

"What if he changes his mind?"

"If that happens then we'll cross that bridge when we get to it." Poppy looked out at the city with its interconnected ropeways crisscrossing like a spider's web they'd all been caught in. "We've had plenty of practice by now."

The doors leading into Shaia's sanctum groaned as they opened enough for Polk to slip out, his big green eyes peering at them. "Hey." His high voice pierced through the creaking of the doors. "Come in. They're ready to see you."

Shaia sat at the large, circular wooden table in the center of the room, bubbling with energy the way they always did at the beginning of these meetings. Bouncing up from their seat with a smile plastered on their face, they waved. "Voiceless, I promise you I didn't influence him at all, but thank you for worrying after him. It means he'll be in good hands." They went to sit back down but paused for a moment. A frown formed and their voice hardened. "You'll have your answers, but I don't appreciate your accusation."

They all turned to Seffin. Shaia could sense a person's intentions, but Seffin didn't have an internal voice, so his thoughts were very close to pure intention, which meant that to Shaia, Seffin's thoughts were the same as speaking was to everyone else. *What is he thinking to cause that kind of reaction?*

"Best not to wonder that right now, Ren. We have much to discuss, and I wouldn't waste our limited time with argument."

They filed down the stairway to the lowered pit in the middle of the room and took their seats at the table. Luminescent vines hung down the walls tinting everything a pale blue, but the wood grain and soft edges still managed to project warmth and hominess.

Shaia started, "I'm sending a unit with you as an escort to Kori'ko, Kelsig, and finally to Nakonipol. At that point, they'll break off and continue on their own assignments. I told you of the pacts with Kelsig and Karm we made to aid at the end of a cycle, that piece of business may be thornier than I let on. The current leader of Kelsig, Leif Gjorn, has no intentions of honoring the pact his ancestors made to aid at the end of a cycle. You should have more luck with his son, Bjorn."

Ren couldn't help himself. "Bjorn Gjorn? Really?"

"Yes, it rhymes. How novel." Shaia said, his mood more serious than—, "It's not my mood, Ren. It's simply not that funny. Moving on. The dark-hued crystal. Polk already told you its purpose was to house Koth while the new vessel can bind him. What he didn't tell you is that Koth's..." He put his finger up to his lips, thinking. "We'll go with core. You could call it a base or soul or spirit among other things. The point is, after you kill Lana, you must transfer his core into the crystal—it is a simple thing, Polk can show you. And yes, before you ask, Lana is still technically alive, it's one of the benefits of being a vessel." Shaia gestured to themself. "Polk will then charge the crystal, forming a connection with Koth. Having nowhere else to go he will be forced to take up residence in Polk's will reserves, at which point Polk begins his time as the Vessel of Kohru."

Seffin's mouth moved to speak, but Shaia cut him off.

"Importantly!" Shaia held his finger out to shush Seffin. "Lana's mind will have been corrupted by Koth, becoming a living husk. She will attack you. Having known her in life I promise you it will not be an easy fight." Shaia spun to face Seffin. "You are wearing on my nerves, but fine. If no one becomes a vessel after Lana, the only way to stop Koth is to force the entirety of his portion of the Sea of Intention into the crystal and destroy it."

"That's it?" Ren asked.

"No," Shaia said ominously. "The point of The Vessel is to limit Koth's connection between his core and his Sea. Think of the core like Koth's brain, and his portion of the Sea of Intention like his body. Once you start pulling in his Sea you will make a direct connection between the two. He'll have access to all the will he has accumulated from every cycle. Without a living body, he can't perform any will techniques, but with access to all of the will he's accumulated over the ages, he'll have the ability to reanimate the corpse of every person who's ever died almost immediately. He'll be able to make amalgamations in seconds. Not to mention the damage any of his dreadworms would do."

Ka leaned forward. "What do you mean?"

"Dreadworms were his creation in the same way humans and everything else were Kohru's, but free will wasn't a priority for him. He'll be able to take direct control while he's free. It will take an army just to install a new vessel. To stop him from converging all those monstrosities on your location would need an overwhelming force."

Poppy's eyes grew wide. "Jessica's Gogallo Initiative."

"Just so," said Shaia. "Unfortunately, and it pains me to have kept this from you, but the champion I spoke of that died, was Jessica Saunders. Your home country has undergone a coup."

Poppy's shocked expression quickly turned to anger. "You absolute piece of—"

"I know you're angry, and you have every right to be. But Polk needs your protection, and you all needed the rest, especially Ren. I couldn't be sure you'd stay if I told you everything."

"Still," Ka said, "you took that choice away from us."

Poppy stood from their chair. "I am just about done with your machinations. Are we finished here, or do you have some other important news you've been keeping secret?"

Shaia nodded. "We are done, and again, I'm sorry it had to be this way."

Poppy walked toward the door. They all began to follow before Shaia spoke up again, "Seffin, please stay a moment."

"Why?" he asked.

"Because what I have to tell you is an answer to a question you've been asking since you first came." Shaia's gaze shifted to Ren. "The words are for him alone. He'll be out in a moment."

Ren met Poppy, Polk, and Ka on the wooden landing outside the sanctum. Poppy paced back and forth, muttering profanities Ren rarely heard them say out loud, and Ka leaned on the railing, her eyes panning back and forth over the city with a stony gaze. Polk simply stood by the door, watching them with that same flat affect he always had, similar to the way Seffin used to be, but also different in a meaningful way. Seffin's stoicism hid anxiety and insecurity, but Ren sensed nothing behind Polk's facade.

What is he telling Seffin that we're not supposed to know?

Standing next to Ka by the railing, Ren looked down at the forest floor. It was so very far down. He scanned for a laranee, the locals said they stalked through from time to time, but only a few deer bounded through, and an elk stood just at the edge of his sight range.

"This is bad," Ka said. "Without Jessica's initiative..." She shook her head. "Well, regardless. You remember what Kiko said when she visited us?"

"That she would go to war with Egal if Winnow won the election?"

"She was serious when she said that. If Winnow truly did take over, then he has to know the other nations aren't going to like his lockdown on focus crystals."

"She'll already be marching to Nakonipol by now." Poppy stopped their pacing. "Her army will resupply there and then move on to Egal. I know Kiko well. She's decisive, unrelenting, and ruthless. Our stop in Kelsig must be brief. We need to talk to her before she turns Prolivgrad into rubble."

Worry flashed on Ka's face. "You really think Auntie Kiko would destroy the city?"

"I'm afraid it's worse than that. The empress is not someone you want backed into a corner, and that's exactly what's happening right now."

"Doesn't she want peace? She always seemed so concerned for common people," Ren said.

"Peace means nothing if there's no world left to enjoy it. That fact drove Jessica to do the things she did, and in that regard, Kiko isn't much different. We're talking about a woman who killed her own father. She'll leave Prolivgrad a smoking pile of ash and stone if she thinks it's what's best for the world, and the truth is, I don't disagree with her. I only want to encourage exhausting all other options first."

The door to the sanctum opened and Seffin stepped out. He had a vacant expression not unlike Polk's as the two walked over to join the group.

"Bad?" Ren asked.

Seffin set a hand on Polk's head and gave Ren a meaningful look. "Let's... talk about it later. Polk will travel with us going forward."

"Just so," Ka said. "We should get some rest. We'll have plenty of time to talk on the march north."

They made their way back, through the maze of rope bridges and finally to the inn they stayed at, Kara'o's Rest, greeted by a cozy fire and a friendly waiter. They ordered some dinner and ate in silence. Polk barely touched his spiced venison, seeming content to simply watch each of them in turn with an unsettling, blank expression. Normally a rather talkative bunch, the small, silent watcher changed the dynamics of the meal. When they were done, Poppy pointed at him. "You're bunking with us. Come on, I'll get you set up."

He hopped off his chair and dutifully followed through the hallway that led to the inn's few rooms. Ka swallowed the final bit of her stew. "This is going to take some getting used to."

"Yes, it is."

"Yup"

Ren and Seffin answered at the same time. Ka stood, and before walking off, she said, "I'll see you two in the morning. Remember, we meet the escorts at nine. Be packed and ready to go by then."

Ren and Seffin retreated to their room as well. They checked and rechecked their packs. Ren had stocked up on enough jerky to ensure he wouldn't have to suffer through salted fish rations. After going through every nook and cranny in the room to ensure they didn't leave any of their belongings, they climbed into bed and let sleep take them.

***

Kalli'a and Sori'o were the two leaders of the escort Shaia charged with bringing their group to Nakonipol. Twin brother and sister who always had smiles on their faces so big they seemed on the verge of laughter. Weeks ago, Sori'o helped with Ren's recovery drills on Shaia's recommendation. His will reserves would have returned either way, but the drills helped improve his control in the meantime, and exercising his will would restore his reserves faster than simply resting.

With his short brown hair, dark green eyes, and muscular physique, Ren didn't mind working with the wilder. Not until he tried to *make friends* with him anyway. It was flattering, and if Ren was honest with himself, more than a little tempting, but he had no intention of betraying Seffin's trust. In Nari'ko, these types of advances were as notable as going out for a drink, but his relationship with Seffin was new, and mostly out of awkwardness, they'd never really discussed their feelings on that particular custom.

They all stood at the base of the northernmost tree in the city. Polk looked cute with his large pack on like a kid getting ready for his first day of school. Except they were headed to a deadly, frozen wasteland with an endless blizzard.

"We're hiking twelve-hour days until we rendezvous with the Kori'ko. Once we hit snow we'll slow our march, but we've been asked to keep a fast pace." Kalli'a set her hand on Poppy's shoulder when she said the word "asked". She looked exactly like her brother but without hair. "Let's get a move on."

The last time Ren went through the Nari'ko Wilds he was in and out of consciousness, lying on a litter hastily made by Ka and Poppy. He thought the trees in Nari'ko City were intentionally grown large as homes for the people living there, but as they hiked north, the trees never got smaller, only more numerous.

The hike took more effort than expected. The denser the trees the more giant roots they had to climb over or duck under, and he had to watch his feet to make sure he didn't trip over any foliage. He worried Polk might not be able to keep up, but the physical exertion didn't have any visible effect on him. In front of the pack with Kalli'a, he scaled giant roots and hopped down the other side with the ease of an afternoon stroll.

As the day wore on into evening, the sun faded and the luminescent vines hanging from the trees took over as their light source with a pale blue glow, casting thin shadows around them. A herd of deer led by a large stag crossed their path, his antlers fanned out on top of his head. Sori'o stopped the group by putting his hand up and motioned everyone to get down.

The deer all froze.

From behind a tree, a laranee leapt through the air, the stag shifted his head to catch the laranee with his antlers, but it might as well have been a pin prick to the massive cat. The herd bolted away as a snapping sound pierced the silence. As quickly as it came, the laranee was gone, stalking away with the stag hanging from its mouth, its head lolling unnaturally with each step.

Ren's heart raced. It didn't warp around like the amalgamated laranee he and Seffin had fought while they were preparing for their final, but the cat's speed and size made it impossible not to be intimidated. *And how did Sori'o even know it was there?* Regardless, he hoped they didn't see another one during their trip. It was one thing to hope for a glimpse while safely looking down from Nari'ko's walkways, and quite another to see one hunting less than a hundred feet away. Kalli'a got everyone going again and they continued their trek north, further into the unforgiving wilds.

Troy

The researchers Troy required to restart production of controlled amalgamations either fled the city, died from the Nationals' overzealous brand of law enforcement, or languished in the very cells he'd been plucked out of not less than a week ago. Carula might have helped him, but signing off on her reassignment with Oji was the only risk he'd allowed himself since emerging from The Pit. After everything Seffin went through in the last year, he couldn't bring himself to trap the boy's mother in the city just to save his own skin.

With Winnow breathing down his neck, he racked his brain for a solution. Troy's will reserves were below that of a wielder, and far below that of a mystic. His education exclusively applied to business, and business school had exactly zero classes that covered will techniques or the mechanics of intentioned will. If this were a logistics issue, he could handle it, but science? He'd never learned much science save for what little Ka taught him during their excursion to Oleksandra's Harbor, and knowing fire fuel floated around him at all hours of the day didn't really apply here. He shuddered at the thought. *How do mystics walk around knowing the air could explode at any moment?*

He massaged his aching left arm stump. The healer he saw after getting out of The Pit called it a "residual limb", but that felt too polite. Too clean for what happened. He held it aloft. An anger he never had before that night seethed and rippled in his chest. He clenched his teeth because if he didn't, he would scream. *This is what happens when you make deals with monsters.* A deep breath in and a slow release out brought him back to the here and now. To the papers on the desk in front of him containing a myriad of words he didn't know the meaning of, and to the explicit threat on his life from Winnow.

He called Tia into his office. His mother's old assistant landed on her feet after the coup and was the first person to apply when he posted the position for his own assistant. It made him nervous that someone who worked so closely with his attempted murderer, his mother, wanted to work for him, but Tia knew things about the Gogallo Initiative no one else alive or not in jail did. Winnow killed or locked up all the smart people, and without smart people, science didn't get done, and without science getting done, he couldn't help Winnow produce amalgamations, and without amalgamations, he'd be thrown back in The Pit or made an example.

"Yes?" Tia said, strolling into the office.

"We need smart people," Troy said. He realized how stupid that sounded, but it didn't stop it from being true. She only stared at him blankly. "I mean we need scientists. Researchers."

"The Guild's research teams were thrown in The Pit for conspiring with Jessica."

"I don't know how we're going to pick the research back up without them."

"I agree," she said, shortly. "Your meeting with Winnow is at three today."

Tia gave him a meaningful look, but for the life of him, he couldn't figure out the meaning. She did this frequently in the few days she'd worked for him, and he couldn't shake the feeling he was missing something about the expression. Like a ball being tossed to him that he couldn't manage to catch. Just then he had a thought, though he didn't like it.

"I could ask him to release the teams to help me restart the labs."

Tia smiled, seemingly pleased with herself. He couldn't tell what for. Winnow demanded results, and instead of results, he was about to ask for more help. Not a good start to their arrangement. "Do you think he'll go for that?" he asked. The few times he met the man his mood shifted dramatically from moment to moment. He could never tell what Winnow's reaction to anything would be.

Tia's smile vanished and... *did she just roll her eyes?*

"Winnow is an idiot, but he knows damn well you're not a scientist. Do you have anything to give him that might make the medicine go down easier? Lead with something he wants and then ask for something you need."

The pained expression on her face told him everything he needed to know. Winnow would need something good in exchange for letting the scientists out to help him. All the man talked about during their last two meetings was more weapons to secure Egal's freedom. Weapons of war. But the Guild didn't make weapons of war, or at least they weren't supposed to. The Guild handled crystal trade and distribution. Negotiating prices, balancing costs, and standardizing mining processes, like what to do with all the crystal dust produced by the—

Tender's explosives.

The overeager engineer had told him the recipe for their grenades when he'd expressed interest on their way back from Oleksandra's Harbor, and if he thought hard enough, he could probably remember the ratios.

"I've got an idea of what we can give him."

Tia's voice sounded exasperated, "Perfect, let me know if you need anything else to prepare for the meeting."

"Thank you, Tia."

Why does she always seem so annoyed?

He set the thought aside, best to focus on how to pitch freeing his science team.

***

Troy stepped into the office of the president where Winnow sat behind a large, oak desk eating a sandwich. Sauce dripped down onto a plate resting in front of him when he took a bite. Still chewing, he waved Troy into a chair across from him and swallowed. "What progress do you have?"

Troy put on his best smile and acted pleased with himself to hide his fear. "First, I have something you might find interesting."

Winnow's face contorted. "Unless it's a new amalgamation you can bind to me, I don't want to hear it."

"It's better than that." *Nope, too much of a lie.* "Well, almost. The good news is it's something you can use without will reserves."

His nostrils flared. "This better be fucking good."

"Explosives."

"...go on."

"An engineer discovered how to make hand-held explosives with crystal dust last year."

A wolfish grin split Winnow's face. "That... is excellent. Good job."

A pit formed in Troy's stomach; he tasted acid in the back of his throat. Something about Winnow's reaction just now gave him the impression he'd made a grave error.

"Now, Troy. The amalgamations."

Yes, right. What I came here for.

"Unfortunately, we haven't had much progress, but I know what I need to start."

"And?"

"The scientists from the Guild that were locked up. I need them released."

"Sure."

"I know they were loyal to—wait a minute. Did you say yes?"

"Yes, yes. I don't care." Winnow waved his hand dismissively. "Just get me my amalgamations, and if you need to do human trials feel free to take some of the refugees we have in there as well."

Troy was stunned. He shouldn't be surprised, after everything, but the man had a way of casually horrifying him no matter how desensitized he became.

Winnow quickly scratched something onto a piece of official stationery and slid it across the desk. Troy grabbed it and skimmed the contents. It gave him free rein to release any prisoner he wanted. The president went back to eating his sandwich and Troy was left wondering if he should leave or if Winnow had more to say. After watching him chew for what felt like a full minute, Troy hesitantly stood and started walking out of the office. When he made it to the door Winnow called after him. "Tell the science team failure is not an option."

"Yes, sir."

Troy hurried through the capitol building, the hallways decorated in all manner of red, pictures of past presidents removed and replaced with pictures of Winnow or Nationalist propaganda. Outside, on the streets, he finally felt like he could breathe again. The teams of red-garbed patrols and citizens doing their best not to stand out may not have relaxed him, but it was a good sight better than sitting across a desk from someone who wouldn't think twice on having him killed. Helping a man who gleefully murdered people made his stomach turn, but he couldn't refuse, the last time he did something brave he lost his hand, his mother, and his freedom.

The Pit wasn't too far from the capitol, he summoned his coach, hopped in, and told his driver to head that direction. Freeing his science team was his top priority. He hoped they'd be grateful enough for their freedom they wouldn't balk at the idea of starting immediately.

Prolivgrad had never been an overly friendly city, but the people had always been lively. Now, out the carriage window, the streets were mostly abandoned, haunted sparsely by party members and meek laborers with fear on their faces. Turning a corner to put the entrance of The Pit in view, he turned his gaze inside the carriage. The street had high walls on either side covered in hanging bodies. He'd already seen their battered and bloated faces when Winnow brought him out of The Pit. Once was enough.

Nationalists always went on about the Resistance, but he'd yet to see any opposition organized enough to call itself that. Once in the last week, he saw two women wearing blue use ice lances and fire elementalism to kill a group of Nationalists harassing an elderly woman, but that didn't mean there was a resistance. That just meant two pissed off mystics had it out for Nationalists. It would be nice if there *were* an organized effort. At least then he'd have a little hope.

The carriage came to a stop, and he hopped out, careful not to pay attention to the human shapes floating in his peripheral vision. The small, brick building that led down into The Pit had a set of six guards stationed at the entrance. Scowls and evil grins slipped onto their faces at the sight of him. The front one, with a golden badge on his chest and a smug smile on his face, stepped forward. "Stumpy, back so soon?" The other guards laughed.

Troy handed over the document Winnow gave him along with another slip of paper containing the names of all the scientists he needed. That wiped the smug look off his face. The head guard handed the papers to one of his subordinates and whispered into his ear. A small argument broke out between them, but a slap so hard it could have dislocated his jaw ended it. Stricken, the subordinate grabbed two of the others and retreated down the stairs, into The Pit, while Golden Badge turned back to Troy and glared daggers.

"One of these is dead," he said. "The others will be up shortly."

"Tell them to report to the outer lab immediately."

"I'm not your fucking secretary, Stumpy."

"No, you're a fucking guard that just got a direct order from an agent of the president. If the remaining people on that list aren't at the lab by tonight, Winnow will know about it, and he won't be happy."

Golden Badge's face blanched. Good. Acting meek didn't suit Troy, and even as small as this was, it felt good to stand up for himself again. He left The Pit via carriage and had the driver take him to the Guild's outer lab; built after Sharon destroyed their first one by releasing the mutated laranee. All the previously bound amalgamations had been rounded up and brought there for extermination, they were useless now, but the binding process mutated them, preventing Prolivgrad's barrier from turning them into ash. This was part of what he needed the scientists for. He needed help killing the amalgamations in order to make room for their replacements. The team may not be trained or skilled in combat, but at least two were elementalists and the rest should be able to use willed weapons or shunt sharp objects if needed. Far more than he could manage on his own with only one arm and will reserves shy of classifying as a wielder.

His carriage rolled to a stop at a building outside Prolivgrad's walls. The outer lab was a typical Guild structure shaped like a large, brick box. Focus crystal infused building materials caused it to glitter in the waning dusk light as he unlocked the reinforced, metal door. The creaking of its hinges echoed around the empty entrance. *Winnow didn't even leave support staff here.* The door slammed behind him when he let it go, creating a cacophonous reverberation throughout the building. Distant, twisted cries called out in answer. Troy's right hand instinctively gripped the sword at his hip, the same one Sharon used to kill Clem, not that it would do him much good. In the few drills he'd attempted since regaining his freedom, he could tell his swordplay suffered for the loss of his left hand. He could overcome the small change in balance, but it would take time and effort, two things he couldn't spare right now.

Further into the building, there was a second-floor entrance to the demonstration area his mother had set up to show her creations off to the other world leaders. A stench of decay assaulted his nose when he entered, and a sea of cages lay spread out below him, the twisted cries from earlier restarted in earnest as the creatures heard him enter. He stepped out onto the metal grating that passed for a balcony. The screeching and howling stopped at once, and every eye on every amalgamation shifted to regard him hungrily.

Knowing their cages kept him safe didn't help, panic pumped through his veins, and breath caught in his throat. Every hair on his body stood on end. Something deep in his mind insisted he was in danger. He walked to the metal stairway leading down to the floor of the room and unlocked the safety barrier, hundreds of eyes following him silently as he worked.

Down on the floor was a locker room which held a variety of will-weapons. None he had the skills to use, but hopefully some of the wielders had enough combat training to use the will-blade or will-spear. They wouldn't have to be skilled. Just proficient enough to produce an edge to cut up the amalgamations in their cages. He laid an assortment of weapons out on the stone floor of the demonstration area. Eyes continued to watch him, peering out from behind their bars. The werewiller and gorilla amalgamations, in particular, possessed an intelligence in their expressions that troubled him. He made his way back to the front, waiting for the science team to arrive.

Night fell on the facility while he lingered, but eventually, the stumbling, tired forms of twenty-three people came into view. Sumiko Thompson, Pulpin's understudy, was the first to reach him. She was tall with short, black hair and warm, dark tan skin. An exhausted smile rested on her face as she shook his hand.

"I'm sorry I couldn't give you a day to recover, but this needs to be taken care of now," he said.

"Anything is better than sitting in The Pit."

"Let's see if you feel that way after you find out what I need you for."

The tired smile shifted to an exhausted frown. "Exactly what do you need us for?"

He gestured inside the building, so they walked and talked with the rest of the team trailing behind. "The first batch of mutated amalgamations were all bound to my mother. I've been led to believe that without her they essentially function as normal amalgamations now, seeking out anything with will to kill and eat."

Sumiko nodded, hesitantly. "Once bound, their masters cannot be changed."

"I had them all brought here so we can dispose of them. I'd also like to repurpose this lab to start up production again." He opened the door to the demonstration area.

"We're continuing with The Initiative?" Her eyes grew wide.

"Not exactly."

This time, the amalgamations didn't cry out when the science team entered. They only watched as everyone spread out to listen to Troy go on about their new job, more at ease with so many people in the room. The eyes had more than just him to follow now.

"Winnow has requested we produce more amalgamations to bind to him." The entire team shifted around uneasily with doubt, fear, and frustration clear in their eyes. "I realize how you all must feel, but completing this will grant us our freedom."

"I didn't know Winnow was a wielder," said a man with shockingly red hair who looked to be in his early twenties.

And here we have the problem. "He's not."

"Impossible," a woman said. She fidgeted with a dirty braid of blonde hair.

"Cillian O'hare and Klara Thorson." Sumiko pointed to each of them in turn, naming them for Troy's benefit.

"Well, we need to figure out a way or Winnow will be furious."

Troy wanted to be clear. Winnow said failure wasn't an option. It didn't take much imagination to guess what would happen if they couldn't complete their task.

"You should have left us in there," said a boy who couldn't be any older than Ren.

"Tyler Chen," Sumiko provided.

Troy nodded. "Tyler, I'm not going to try and soften the reality of the situation. If you request to go back to The Pit, I have no idea what Winnow will do. He may not care, or he may make you an example. It would depend on the mood he's in at the time."

"If he can't wield, he won't be able to give specific orders to his bound amalgamation. It requires intentioned will, and that takes deep reserves. The training—"

"Don't you think I know that?" he snapped, interrupting Cillian. He took a deep breath and let it out. "Look, I *know* this is impossible, but controlling an amalgamation was impossible until it wasn't. And regardless, it's not like we have a choice."

"We could run," Cillian said. "We're on the outskirts of the city, beyond the wall. There aren't any guards around."

Sumiko stepped forward. "The guards spoke constantly of the hordes surging around Prolivgrad, but if any of you want to take your chances out in the wilds with no traveling crystal be my guest. I wouldn't bet on you." Her eyes were bloodshot, and she looked on the verge of sleep. "Troy, tell them what we're doing here so we can get started."

"We have to dispose of these tonight and have a barrier dead zone ready by tomorrow for a shipment of husk I have coming in. I have some hoarwolf colossi scheduled for delivery next week. I know you're all tired, but your reserves should be full. Kill the mutated amalgamations, stage the cages in the yard out behind the building for the husk shipment and we can call it a night."

He gestured at the lineup of will-weapons on the ground. "If you can use a weapon, do so. If you can burn them or kill them with ice, feel free. If you can't do either of those things, please use the lifts and stage the empty cages out in the yard. Anyone that can help set up the dead zone follow me. I've got the keys to the crystal room."

Screeches from all the amalgamations pierced their ears as Cillian and Klara threw ice lances into the cages. Tyler grabbed the will-spear and Sumiko came to stand next to Troy while everyone else split off, focused on the duties they'd been given. Sumiko touched his shoulder. "Let's get the dead zone set up so we can get out of here. I'm exhausted and I haven't seen my family in a month."

They ascended the metal staircases up to a closed-in room hanging from the ceiling of the demonstration area. The floor was made of the same metal grating used in the walkway that encircled the room, large windows on each side peered down to the cages below. In the middle of the room, a crystal the size of a wagon wheel sat floating in a pylon encasement. Sumiko grabbed some tools that were resting on the wall and checked the machinery. All the while, the screams of amalgamations dying echoed around them. Troy yawned as he leaned out one of the windows.

"There," Sumiko said. "It should be ready for tomorrow."

"How much can we trust them?" he asked flatly.

"Excuse me?" Sumiko's tone pitched up, both questioning and offended.

"One of them already mentioned running away, and another wanted to go back into The Pit."

She walked over and leaned out the window, gazing down on their team. "What makes you think you can trust me?"

Because I have to trust someone, and if I'm to pick a random person it might as well be the smartest one in the room.

He shrugged. "I need to know if they're going to do anything dangerous. Winnow needs to be handled with care, if one of them were to report to him behind my back it could affect all—"

Sumiko laughed. "Cillian, the one who asked about running away, wouldn't do anything to put his mother at risk. Likely, he just wants to get her out of Prolivgrad. And Tyler is young, but he's smart. He's the one who said you should have left him in The Pit. He may not be the bravest person I've met, but he wouldn't do anything to harm someone he likes, and he likes our team. No, they're far from perfect, but you don't need to worry about any of them going to Winnow behind your back."

Troy started to respond, but a flurry of activity on the floor caught his eye. Tyler was clutching his spear. No, he was pulling on it and yelling for help. The amalgamation must have grabbed the weapon. Both his feet pushed against the side of the cage as he desperately yanked at the weapon. He lost his grip and fell to the floor. A flurry of scrapes and clangs flew out of the cage before...

Oh, gods...

Tyler sprang to his feet and bolted away. Everyone sprinted from the cages as the werewiller, holding the will-spear, leapt from its sliced-up cage. It slammed and whipped the spear around as pieces of all the remaining cages on the floor started cutting away. Impossibly, it had figured out how to put will into the weapon. The scientists barely had time to funnel into the locker room before every surviving amalgamation burst from their confines and stampeded out the open back door, into the forest surrounding Prolivgrad.

Sumiko faced Troy wearing a mask of exhaustion.

"Well, fuck," she said.

Sharon

The stand sat on a residential block and contained an assortment of vegetables along with a short stack of this week's *Egal Gazette*. The man behind the counter was short, no taller than Sharon, and had a curly mustache extending off the side of his face; he absentmindedly stroked the tips as he followed her every movement while whining about the number of thieves lately. The turban Sharon wore to the riot before the coup sat on her head now, with a longer, red cloth that draped down to her waist, covering the right side of her face and body. Garb that was out of place in Prolivgrad, but it matched the color of the National Party, so she rarely received comments. Wearing the head accessory wouldn't bother her during the spring months, but if she had to keep up the disguise into summer, she would have to find something that didn't hold in so much heat. She reached over to grab a gazette and read the cover:

GLORIOUS WINNOW DOES IT AGAIN

The article went on to discuss some type of nonsense regarding a device Winnow came up with that could cause explosions. She turned the paper to face Hugo, the street vendor. "You think this is real? Devices that explode like a fireball?" she asked. His eyes flicked over the writing on the paper at the same time her hand flitted over the onions and peppers. The sack she carried with her now hung a little heavier.

"If he says he did then he did. He saved us from that bitch, Saunders."

No, stupid. That was me.

A boy came up to the stand and sized up some produce while Sharon grabbed a tomato and slipped it into her bag, setting a coin down to pay. As she walked away Hugo yelled at the boy, accusing him of theft. He was taking the fall for the onion and pepper she'd just pilfered.

Stealing from Hugo was a necessary risk for Sharon. Noah couldn't return to his mining job after his injury, the few mystic healers left in the city after the coup weren't up to the task of fully healing him, and she couldn't work anywhere without significant risk of someone figuring out her identity. Hugo was a natural mark, too. He was a true believer in the Nationalist cult's philosophies, paranoid, and chatty which made him easy to distract. All she had to do was mention Winnow or something about Nationals, and she could grab multiple days' worth of food. Eating away at the scumbag's profit margins was a bonus as far as she was concerned. Unfortunately, she might have dipped from this well a few too many times. Hugo accused the boy of stealing all the missing produce she'd taken in the last few weeks. Hearing a ruckus, she turned to see him break the boy's nose. He fell backward into the street, dazed and bleeding. Sharon clenched her fists.

That was a mistake.

Hugo walked around the stand and brought his leg back to kick the child. Sharon shoved him away. "Stop it," she said calmly, standing over the boy.

"This thief has been taking from my stand for weeks."

"Do you have proof of that?"

"The thieving didn't start till he showed his grubby little face a month ago. I *know* it was him."

Lies, I've stolen from you for longer than that.

She reached down, grabbed the boy's hand, and pulled him to standing. "Not a very convincing argument."

The noise drew the attention of some passersby, two of whom were National guardsmen who decided to make the disagreement their business. They started in the direction of Hugo's stand. Sharon fell back into the assassin training taught to her while she'd worked for The Eyes of Koth, taking in the entirety of her situation.

An alleyway opened thirty feet away from her location. A small girl kept turning to watch the excitement while two men holding each of her hands pulled her away, making for the street corner. A window shutter snapped shut in the building across from the stand while Hugo waved over the two Nationals. She would have to solve this peacefully or she'd have to trust the citizens to keep quiet. A few other pedestrians milled about a few blocks down, but otherwise, they were alone. The only witnesses would be Sharon, the boy, Hugo, and with the girl and her dads now safely around the corner, the two Nationals.

"What's your name, kid?" Sharon asked, still holding the boy's hand.

"Hassan." He looked up at her with big, brown eyes clutching his nose. Children always looked odd with their heads too big for their bodies and their eyes too big for their heads.

She leaned down to his ear and whispered, "Well, Hassan, if I tell you to run, you head for the alley over there."

He nodded as the two Nationals approached. "What seems to be the problem, Hugo."

"This kid is a thief."

They immediately reached for Hassan, prompting Sharon to step in their way. "Now, don't tell me you're going to take him to The Pit based on a single claim from a paranoid vegetable seller."

"Step aside or you'll be joining him," the bigger of the two said.

Hugo held a self-satisfied look on his face while the guard reached for Hassan again. *Godsdamnit.* She gripped the guard's wrist. "You have no proof other than what this—"

He didn't let her finish. Instead, he stupidly reached for her neck. Possibly to grab her by the collar, or maybe to choke her. Regardless, he caught hold of the fabric hanging off her turban and ripped it off. They all gasped at the waxy burn scars on the right of side her face.

"You're the one that—"

She threw some will into her hand and knocked most of his teeth out. "Killed Pulpin Rashee. I know." While the guard coughed out blood and broken teeth she turned to Hassan. "Run."

The boy bolted away while she pulled the guard's sword out from its sheath and shoved his own blade through his chest in a fluid motion. He made a dying gasp as Hugo let out a scared yelp before turning to run down the street. The other guard raised his hand up to make an ice lance.

Not fast enough, though.

As he finished forming the pointed spear, Sharon pulled his dead friend's sword from his chest and chucked it at his head. The blade lodged into his skull and his body crumpled. Sharon caught his ice lance with kinetics before it hit the ground, raised it into an aiming position, and shunted it at Hugo who was halfway to the corner.

Another yelp sprang from his mouth, this one more pained and pitched up, as the lance pierced through his back and out his chest with enough force to lift his feet off the ground. He landed and slid on the cobblestones a ways before coming to a stop, his lifeblood oozing onto the ground while his mouth whispered out some final words no one would ever hear or care about.

Sharon sighed, picked up her turban, and walked over to the stand. She grabbed a copy of the gazette, filled her sack to bursting with produce, and pouched Hugo's earnings for the day before heading over to the alley. Hassan stood in an alcove, shaking like a leaf.

"You're fine now. Here." She fished out some coin and a squash and handed it to him. "Do you live near?"

"Three blocks up, in the basement of an abandoned pub."

"Blackbill's?"

He nodded. The owners of that pub were taken to The Pit for refusing to support the National Party. They'd only just reopened, too.

"Do exactly as I say. From here, go to Patterson's bakery. Buy something with the money I gave you. Then head directly home. If anyone stops you, just tell them you were out running errands." She popped the turban back on her head and adjusted the cloth to cover her burns again. "Now go."

She watched Hassan jog away and make a turn in the direction of Patterson's before she walked off toward Noah's apartment. This is the third time in two weeks she saved someone from the Nationals. Truly, the least she could do after causing the problem in the first place. Killing Jessica had ripple effects far beyond what Sharon ever considered. The destruction of the Lodge, wanton murder of refugees, political murders... the focus crystal tariffs alone would kill off smaller towns across the world.

Just like Gull Harbor.

The little villages would get priced out of maintenance fees, the Guild would send someone to collect their pylon, and the villagers would either have to relocate or take their chances against the husk. But with the husk population continuing to grow so far out of bounds, that would be suicide. Many would come to Prolivgrad as "refugees" and Winnow would throw them in The Pit or hang them on the wall. Her revenge came at too great a cost, creating a debt she could never repay. Her conscience had formed into a knife and carved away pieces of her, leaving guilt, regret, and little else.

She came upon Noah's building and walked past it. Instead, she turned into an alley and rubbed her right side. The aching rarely bothered her now, but it tended to flare up after she fought. She compensated for her injury as best she could, but choosing between overexerting herself or dying wasn't much choice. After four deep breaths, she held it in, listening for the footsteps of whoever had been following her for the last four blocks. The soft scuffs of his boots approached, and when the man turned the corner, he came face to face with Sharon. He made a choking sound as she grabbed him by the neck and slammed him up against the wall.

"Why are you following me?"

He made indiscernible throat noises that sounded like... mother? She slackened her grip.

"You saved my brother." The words burst from his mouth followed by deep, gulping breaths. She dropped her grip on him completely and took a step back, eyeing him suspiciously.

"I *just* did that."

He gasped in between each statement. "The woman across the street. In the window. Ethel. She came to get me as soon as trouble started. I found Hassan on the way. He told me who you were—what you did."

Uh oh, did he tell him everything?

Something on her face must have clued him in.

"I'm from the Resistance," he said, still gulping air. "I don't care that you killed Rashee. He was a National anyway. We could use your help."

"What resistance are you talking about?"

She hadn't noticed anything resembling a resistance before, but neither had she left Noah's apartment much since the day the Lodge was destroyed.

"I'll show you."

"No, you'll meet me. Give me the address and I'll be there in an hour."

"Great!"

"I wouldn't celebrate. I haven't said anything about helping you."

Ahmad was his name. She could see the resemblance with his brother now that she took a moment to look. He gave her the address and went on his way. Doubling back to the apartment, she considered his words. This could be a chance to help right the wrong she committed, but if the Resistance members were as clumsy as this Ahmad had been in following her, then overthrowing Winnow was a fool's errand. She popped in to check on Noah who lay sleeping in bed, she left the groceries and a note saying she would be back in a few hours, and then went down to the café on the bottom level to order a coffee.

As she sipped at her drink, she flipped through the gazette she took earlier and frowned. It looked like Winnow's claims of making an explosive weren't an exaggeration. Not that *The Gazette* could be trusted, but they tended to twist the truth rather than fabricate it, which was honestly worse in a way. It gave them an appearance of legitimacy they didn't deserve. She dropped the paper on the table and made to leave when a name caught her eye. Troy Saunders. It was a small headline in the lower corner of the paper. Something like relief settled in her chest. Troy didn't deserve what she did to him. It's good he'd landed on his feet.

The fastest route to the hideout would take her past the scene of her crime, so she took a slower, more circuitous path instead. Ahmad was standing by the door when she arrived. *Idiot.* He waved at her excitedly, because why wouldn't he? She grabbed him by the back of the neck and shoved him through the door, closing it behind them.

"Are you *trying* to get caught?" she hissed.

"No."

"Then maybe don't stand outside your hideout and wave your arms around like a fool."

She finished chewing Ahmad out and looked around the room she'd burst into. It was lit by candlelight with tables and chairs strewn haphazardly. Like someone just moved them in and set them down in the first spot they could. Stepping deeper inside, she saw one of the tables had a map of Prolivgrad laid out with some pins and an assortment of garbage on it. Little blue circles dotted the map, some of them with red x's on them. She pointed. "Are these hideouts that were destroyed?"

Ahmad nodded. "We've been unlucky."

"No, you've been careless. Whoever your leader is they don't know what the hells they're doing. First off, you tried to recruit me by tailing me to my home. You *knew* I was an assassin and you somehow thought that was a good idea?"

"You saved my brother, I assumed—"

"Secondly, with only the knowledge of who I am and the fact that I killed some guards to protect a *child*, you gave me the location of one of your hideouts and *left the map of all your other hideouts* in plain view."

"We only bring people here that we know we can—"

"Trust me when I say that your processes are going to get you and your brother killed. What if someone saw you waving me into this place? What if someone saw our—"

"Will," he shouted over her, "you help us? We clearly need it, and despite what you say I get the feeling you would have said no straight away if you planned to."

"A lack of a no is not a yes." She looked at the map again. The sheer amount of hideouts *was* kind of impressive. "But I'm willing to meet with your leader."

Seffin

The Kori'ko people were not as friendly as Seffin had hoped, especially compared with their cousins to the south. Not that it mattered much, the endless blizzard made talking prohibitively difficult.

Mystics in the group kept everyone warm with small fireballs strewn about the walking party. The fire turned snow into stinging rain with the gales as strong as they were, so Seffin used his deep reserves to divert it, though it did nothing for the whipping wind.

Knut, the Kori'ko guide, marched at the front of the pack with a scowl on his face. He clearly disliked these trips, but as Shaia spoke of a pact with Kelsig and Karm, so too did they have a pact with the Kori'ko to guide travelers north through their snowy plateaus and valleys.

Seffin moved up to walk alongside Ren, his face a dark spot in the middle of the endless white surrounding them. Ren leaned in. "Knut says we should come up on Klion in the next couple hours."

Seffin furrowed his brow. "Really? He told you that?"

"Yes? Is that weird?"

"Yes... no... I don't know. He never answers any of my questions."

"That's because you ask too many."

Ren sealed the statement with a smile and a light touch on his shoulder, but it didn't remove the sting. Seffin knew he asked too many questions, but how was he to learn otherwise? And anyway, he'd come a long way since his days of relentlessly pestering Troy on their contract to Oleksandra's Harbor. He put the thought out of his mind. Everyone agreed Knut was a bit of an asshole; he shouldn't let himself get bent out of shape just because one person didn't like him.

Polk's head bobbed up and down between Ka and Tender, bounding through the snow with his short legs, like a black-haired snow rabbit. He never tired, but he also never helped with anything. Shaia had said his reserves were even deeper than Seffin's, but a person could never tell because the boy never used them. He didn't help keep the group warm, he didn't help divert the sleet like Seffin did... he hadn't even used simple kinetics since joining. Fortunately, what he lacked in usefulness he made up for in knowledge, and unlike Knut, Polk never tired of answering questions, or at least he never complained about them.

Time ticked by as they crested drift after drift until a trembling light behind a curtain of snow marked their destination, Klion. An hour later, they funneled into the small settlement where Seffin noted the lack of a pylon and almost, *almost* asked

Knut how that could possibly be safe, but decided to leave it a mystery. He'd had enough of the guide's withering looks and grunts of dismissal to last him a lifetime.

A ship awaited at the dock with Kori'ko Wilders milling about on its deck, tying ropes and lugging boxes and doing whatever it was sailors did to prepare for a journey, Seffin didn't know. He'd never been on a ship before, only tried and failed to keep one from sinking. Tender hobbled up next to him. "We're boarding the ship immediately."

Seffin glanced around the town. Seventeen huts made of ice with only a handful of dour-faced Kori'ko people. He gestured at the pure white landscape around them. "I was hoping we could stay for a bit. See the sights."

Tender gave an amused smile. "A captivating view to be sure, but you'll be surprised to learn they don't particularly love visitors."

He placed a hand on his chest dramatically. "I'm shocked. Knut has been an absolute beacon of hospitality."

A huffing sound had him spinning around to see Knut, his gray-brown face quickly turning red. The guide stormed off before Seffin could apologize.

"Good to see you haven't lost your knack for making friends," Tender said.

They all boarded the ship and found cabins to put their things in. Seffin's skin needled as his body adjusted back to a more humane temperature. The calm of the ship's interior was a welcome change from the pelting snow of the blizzard outside. Exhausted and sleepy, he flopped onto the cabin's cot to take a nap, but a grumbling started in his belly. The battle between hunger and sleep was an old one with a storied history, rife with changing allegiances and consequences that could last anywhere between six to eight hours, but today's skirmish had a clear winner. Sleep's tempting call faltered against hunger's gnawing revolt.

Seffin stood back up and went in search of food. Surely, they'd have some options on board besides the salted fish he'd eaten for the past two weeks. It wouldn't have been so bad if he had some variety, like Ren's jerky, but Ren guarded his jerky stores like a laranee over a fresh kill.

In the room the sailors referred to as the mess, Ka and Polk sat on a bench, chatting. Through a serving window, a blonde-haired, friendly-looking man darted around in a room Seffin had always called a kitchen, but not here. Here, it was a *galley.* It was adorable how these boat people liked to make up special names for everything.

"Where's Ren?" Ka asked as Seffin sat next to them.

"Hells if I know. He dropped his stuff in our cabin and walked off."

"Oh? I would have assumed you two had business to attend to after so long on the march."

"Business?"

"Sex," Polk offered. The high pitch of his voice made the word sound dirtier than it was.

Seffin's face went hot. "N-no. He left before... err... just no."

"Well, you'll have plenty of time over the next week," Ka said.

"What's Kelsig like?" Seffin reached for a change in topic.

"Never been."

"They're violent but friendly," Polk said.

Seffin leaned forward. "What does that mean?"

"Honor and bravery mean everything to them, but they'll sometimes fight to the death over minor disagreements. They even decide who their king is by a duel to the death."

Seffin thought for a moment. "That seems like a really bad way to decide a ruler."

Polk shrugged. "That hasn't happened for a while. Leif Gjorn's family has ruled for the last few generations, and no one has challenged them."

"Why?" Ka cocked her head.

"Shaia said the Gjorns have been good leaders. They keep their people fed and their coastal villages protected from ocean husk."

"Ocean husk?" Seffin almost couldn't believe his ears.

"Yes, husk can't get to Kori'ko because they freeze—" That answered Seffin's question on why Klion didn't have a pylon. "—but they can go in the water just fine. They don't need to breathe."

"So, they what? Walk on the ocean floor?" Seffin asked.

"No. Husks have a lot of gas inside their bodies so they float or amalgamate with other things that can swim easier."

The idea of a husk shark popped into Seffin's head, and a chill went down his spine. "Don't they have pylons?"

"Just one, but it's massive." Polk said, "In Strothjem. It's the same one they were given for helping Lana at the end of the last cycle. It used to cover a huge portion of the island, but without maintenance and replacement crystals their barrier only goes out to the edge of Strothjem Castle now."

Seffin's belly rumbled.

"Hungry?" Ka asked.

"Can he make us some food?" Seffin pointed to the man flitting around the galley.

"He said to give him an hour."

Seffin frowned, the hunger pangs were taking on a torturous quality. "I'll just have some rations."

He trudged off back toward his cabin, anticipating an unsatisfying meal of salted fish followed by a nap he'd been wanting for days. Stumbling awkwardly with the rocking of the ship, he navigated the thin, wooden hallways and happened upon Ren, standing in front of their cabin holding hands with Sori'o. Ren flashed a wide-eyed, help-me-out-of-this-conversation look, so Seffin stomped toward the pair and put some edge into his tone as he said, "Are you kidding me, Ren? I've been looking everywhere for you."

Ren's worried expression was convincing enough that it almost fooled him. "What? What did I do?"

Seffin put a hand on Sori'o's shoulder. "I'm sorry, I need to speak with him. Privately."

"I hope it's nothing major," the wilder said.

He glared at Ren. "No, just a few questions I need answered. Now." He opened their door and pulled Ren into the cabin. After closing it behind them, Seffin immediately dove into his pack and started munching on fish rations.

Ren took his jacket off. "Thanks."

"You're welcome," Seffin said. Except his mouth was full of fish, so it came out a muffled mess. Ren seemed to get the idea though. He swallowed. "Do I need to ask what Sori'o wanted?"

"No. He's being nice about it, but I can tell he wants more."

Their eyes met and that alone said plenty. Neither wanted to discuss the Nari'ko way of making friends, how they didn't view sex in the same way everyone else did. In some ways it was more precious, and in others less. Regardless of that knowledge, it felt too overwhelming right now. Seffin swallowed the rest of his fish and climbed into the cot.

"You're going to sleep?"

Seffin gave a questioning look. "You're not?"

"I'm starving. I'm gonna go check the kitchen."

"It's called a galley."

"Whatever, I'll see you in a bit." Ren leaned down and gave him a goodbye kiss. "Yuck!"

"What?"

"You taste like fish!"

"Maybe consider sharing some of your jerky if you don't want fish kisses."

"Absolutely not. I warned you to pack something other than fish. Besides, didn't you just get back from the kitchen? What are you eating fish rations for?"

"I went to the mess for food, but the cook wasn't ready yet, so I had some rations instead."

"The kitchen's a mess?"

"No, the dining area is a mess."

"What?"

Seffin massaged his temples. "The kitchen is called the galley, and the dining area is called the mess."

"Oh." Ren scratched his head. "These names are a mess."

"Agreed."

***

The trip from Kori'ko to Kelsig went quickly, but Seffin still ached to get off the ship as soon as possible. He couldn't occupy himself with wielding practice for risk of damaging the hull, which only left playing cards with Ren and the crew or reading through the books Ka brought along.

On a boring, lazy afternoon as Seffin paged through Ka's copy of *The Parts of Air*, the crew sighted land. He rushed to the deck. On the horizon, a huge island sprouted up from the ocean. Its geography came into focus as the ship sailed closer; snow-capped mountains, rocky hills, and cliffs towering over the water. As they sailed closer, a herd of goats hanging off the nearest cliffside came into view, one wrong step and they would tumble into a watery grave.

The ship dropped anchor, and they all piled into a dinghy to row ashore. High waves made the short trip more perilous than they would have liked, but between Ka, Ren, and Seffin all using elementalism they managed to calm the waters around their little vessel.

The shore was all stones and pebbles with none of the fine sand like the beaches of Oleksandra's Harbor and Lanneshire. The landscape was even harsher up close, with boulders and rocks wedged into the ground and sparse vegetation outside of short grass. The overcast sky that accompanied their ship the whole way here still loomed; it had begun to feel like a permanent fixture for this part of the world.

After his time at sea, Seffin fought not to sway as he stepped onto the beach, but before their group made it more than a few feet on land, a unit of soldiers emerged from the nearby village and marched toward them. Shockingly, two hoarwolves—one gray and one white—with riders astride, trotted at the front of the group.

No one had said anything about Kelsigans domesticating hoarwolves.

The two riders were clearly related, one older and one younger. Leif and his son, Bjorn, Seffin surmised. Leif was light-skinned with greying, blonde hair hanging in locks and a matching, braided beard down to his big belly. His eyes were so blue they seemed inhuman, and his arms were as thick as Seffin's thighs, something he had in common with his son. Bjorn was a younger version of Leif with a smaller belly and a beard that only went down to his chest, which bulged underneath a leather coat. The monarch and his retinue came to a stop in front of them. Bjorn kept a wide smile and happy eyes that fixed themselves on Ren and Seffin. When he nodded a greeting, Seffin blushed, and Ren simply stared with a breathless look.

Leif hopped off his mount and strode over to shake Tender's hand. "Welcome to Kelsig. Shaia sent word ahead of your arrival. It is good to see new faces. We have prepared rooms for your party, and tonight there is a feast planned to celebrate the arrival of the Hammer of Garvelle, along with their legendary children who walked through a sea of husk and survived to tell the tale."

"Thank you for your hospitality. Not to be too forward, but once we settle in, might I insist upon an audience?" Tender asked.

Leif chuckled and waved his hands. "If you have come to convince me that I should send my warriors to the mainland, you will find a better listener in a deaf man. These pacts are old promises made by someone who is not me. Come, bathe in our hot springs, take in the beauty of our home, enjoy the feast, but leave this talk of war behind you."

Bjorn watched his father intently. Seffin couldn't read his expression, it seemed both loving and critical. It reminded him of his relationship with his mother.

Tender pressed. "We'll take you up on your offer, but I would still beg an audience. I'd like a chance to convince you of the pact's importance."

Leif waved his hand dismissively. "Bah, very well. Out of respect for Shaia and out of respect for our ancestors who made this foolish promise, I will call a summit. But this is a formality. I am king, and I tell you I am immovable on this. Now come, we have half a day's ride to the castle. That will leave you little time to bathe before dinner, and after so long on a ship, you will need it." He chuckled again before turning to mount his wolf.

Bjorn and his black wolf trotted over to the group. "I must apologize, we were not prepared for such a large group to accompany you here. We have few horses, but my father and I can take a couple riders each. This is Skygge." He scratched the massive, black hoarwolf behind its ears and then pointed to his father's grey, "And that is Regnsky." Bjorn gave Ren and Seffin an expectant look.

"Polk and Ka go with Leif, Ren and Seffin go with Bjorn. I'll take a horse on my own if you please. I'm a bit large to be sharing a mount," Tender said as they hobbled up to Ren and Seffin, then whispered in their ears, "See if you can't talk the son into convincing the father. He seems to have taken a liking to you two."

"A bit too much of a liking," Ren said back.

"Regardless, if you can convince him to talk to his father on our behalf..."

"We'll try," Seffin said. He had butterflies in his stomach.

Tender mounted their horse and Seffin walked up to Bjorn and Skygge. He startled when the wolf went in for a sniff, his snout was almost as big as Seffin's body. Bjorn laughed. "You jump from him as a rabbit does, mainlander. Show him confidence or he will walk all over you."

"Sorry," Seffin said, reaching out to rub the wolf's muzzle, the fur was soft and warm, so different from the slimy, blood-clotted coat of the last hoarwolf he had the displeasure of meeting. Skygge opened his giant maw and his tongue swiped over Seffin with such force he fell to the ground and laughed. The licks kept coming until Bjorn yelled a command he couldn't make out. "See, he is walking all over you now." He gave the wolf two pats on the shoulder, and it dropped to a crouching position. "Come, rabbits. Hop up here and we can be on our way."

Seffin made to hop up behind Bjorn, but the prince put his hand up. "You will sit in front. I do not want Skygge's drool all over my clothing." Bjorn reached down and pulled him up with one arm. "Yuck. See?" He wiped his hands off on Skygge's fur before reaching down to pull Ren up behind him.

This was the first time Seffin had ever been on a mount. "What do we hold on to?"

Bjorn reached around him and put his palm on Seffin's chest. The butterflies in his stomach fluttered harder. "You will lean into me." Seffin gulped. "And you," Bjorn said as he reached behind and grabbed Ren's arms, wrapping them around his torso, "will hold onto me, tightly. If you two do this, I can promise you will reach Strothjem safely. If not, then I hope there are no rocks where you fall." He chuckled afterward.

He was joking, surely.

The man smelled like fresh earth, and his breath warmed the back of Seffin's neck. Bjorn grabbed the reins that were resting in Seffin's lap, his biceps so large they boxed him in. When he flicked them, the wolf stood, and Seffin instinctually flexed his legs and grabbed its fur. Bjorn tapped his thigh lightly. "No. Do not squeeze." Then put his palm on his chest again. "Lean back into me. I do not bite." He wiped wolf drool off his hands again. "Unless you get more of Skygge's drool on me." Then he shouted a command and they trotted away.

Seffin dutifully leaned back into Bjorn's chest and felt Ren's arms on his lower back, gripping Bjorn's abdomen. A kind of rhythm developed between the bouncing trot of the hoarwolf and the steady breaths of its rider. Hours passed in relative silence as Seffin swiveled his head back and forth, taking in the views the best he could to distract from the awkwardness of his current position.

"So, little rabbits, you are here to convince my father he should send our warriors to Gogallo?" Bjorn spoke so only Ren and Seffin could hear.

"We're here because it's the only safe path to Prolivgrad," Seffin said.

"Nonsense, you are here on a mission from The Caretaker. The Voice of Kohru. Shaia Tekk themself has tasked you with convincing my father to honor the commitments our ancestors made."

"That's not wrong," Ren said, "but truthfully, we're on our way to Prolivgrad. If Egal and Garvelle cannot unite against Gogallo then Kelsig's assistance won't mean much."

"You think so little of Kelsigans." Seffin felt him take a deep breath in and exhale. "I do not blame you. We have cut ourselves off."

"It's not that at all. We need your help, it's just... not enough on its own," Seffin said.

Skygge crested a hill, bounded over a rock, and Strothjem came into view. A castle built into the side of a rocky mountain made of grey stone, its towers tore at the clouded sky. The wolf trotted steadily up the path to the gate.

"Would you two care to join me in cleaning for the feast? In ancient times my personal bath was intended to entertain diplomats, but in our isolation, it has become nothing more than a hot pool for me to float in alone. Besides, I would relish the chance to speak with you more."

The invitation left Seffin's head buzzing. This aligned perfectly with their goal, the time and privacy they would need to make their case for Kelsig's participation in the push to Gogallo, but Bjorn was the prince, not the king, and he clearly wanted more than just talk. Seffin knew he could be aloof, but this much was obvious. He didn't want to answer without talking to Ren first.

"We would be glad to," Ren said.

"Wonderful. I'll inform the servants of your intentions." That decided that, then. Bjorn's large hands squeezed Seffin's thigh. If that was suggestive or friendly, he couldn't tell, but his heart rate wasn't concerned with the distinction. Seffin didn't know how he felt about Ren deciding these things unilaterally, but he couldn't deny his own excitement.

The gates to the castle opened as they came near. Regnsky trotted in behind them with Leif, Ka, and Polk astride, and behind that came Tender on horseback with the rest of their group containing Kalli'a, Sori'o, and a small escort of Nari'ko Wilders. Bjorn instructed them to stay put while he stabled Skygge after they all dismounted and shouldered their packs.

Ka and Tender strolled over with Polk toddling between them. "Well, he likes you two," Ka said with a mischievous smile on her face.

"I get the feeling he wants to help us. He just has to convince his father," Ren said.

"That's great news, but I don't know how," Ka said. "Leif spent the ride here swearing up and down that Kelsig's only concerns are its own borders."

"Maybe Bjorn knows something we can use against Leif at the summit," Tender said. "They are a society preoccupied with honor. Shaming him in front of his lords could convince him."

"It could also turn him against us," Polk said.

"How is that worse than now?" Seffin asked.

"They are a nation of violent warriors," Polk spoke with the gravity of someone far more wizened than the small boy he appeared as. "I'll leave your own imagination to fill in the gaps of what could happen."

"We'll talk with Bjorn and go from there," Seffin said.

"Ok, but how much talking are you *really* going to be doing?" Ka teased.

Ren punched her in the shoulder. "As much talking as it takes."

She punched him back. "It'll be hard to talk with your mouth full of—"

"Kulelika!" Tender said.

She grinned. "Just be careful. It's a nation of warriors, remember? Don't overstep."

"We will be," Seffin said.

Ka and Tender both chuckled. "Taking care isn't exactly a strong suit for either of you, but we'll hope for your success." Tender nodded behind them. "Here he comes."

Bjorn put a hand on each of their shoulders. "I am borrowing these two until dinner," he proclaimed. "Come, little rabbits."

He turned and walked off without looking to see if Seffin or Ren followed. Ka leaned into Seffin and whispered, "Little rabbits?" Seffin only shrugged before following the prince.

The castle hallways were lit with wall sconces and hung with detailed tapestries displaying illustrations of events Seffin didn't recognize. They made their way to a secluded wing, down a hallway that ended in a set of sturdy, wooden double doors. Bjorn pushed them open to reveal a spacious bedroom with a massive bed covered in furs and pillows. Off to the side, an opening led onto a terrace with a pool fed by steaming water pouring off the mountain, blue and white flowers drifted around on its surface.

Seffin and Ren immediately walked out to marvel at the inviting scent of the flowers and the swirling warm vapor floating off the water. Bjorn stepped in between them, completely naked, and lightly tugged at their jackets.

"Take these off and come in. Unless they bathe with clothes on where you come from?" He jumped into the pool, splashing water onto the stones around the side. When he surfaced, he wiped his eyes and looked at them. The water was clear and left nothing to the imagination.

Seffin stared wide-eyed until Ren grabbed his hand. "We'll be right back."

Bjorn shrugged. "Don't be long. There are only a few hours before the feast. While you're out there, tell my servant to bring us some wine. He should be just outside the door." Then he pushed himself off the bottom of the pool and floated on his back. They both gawked far longer than was appropriate before retreating to the bedroom and informing the servant of the prince's request for wine.

"I know I'm the one that agreed to this, but I thought we'd have some time before..." Ren swallowed hard. "We can still leave."

"Maybe he just wants to talk?"

Ren cradled Seffin's face and gave him a quick kiss. "I know you're not that dumb."

"I know."

Ren scratched at his finger, something he did when he got nervous. "Well, what do you think?"

"I think we need to talk him into convincing his father."

"I wasn't asking about—"

"I know what you were asking about." Seffin let out an anxious sigh and looked down at the ground. "You think he's attractive."

"You think he's attractive."

"I know."

Ren put his hand on Seffin's waist. "We don't have to."

"No, we don't." He thought for a moment. "Let's just talk for a while and see what happens."

Ren gave him another kiss. "Laranee."

"Laranee?"

"Use it in a sentence and I'll know what you mean. Then we leave."

"What if he's not convinced by then?"

"Then we'll find another way."

The servant returned with a wineskin in their hands. Seffin took the wine and, together, he and Ren walked back out to the terrace. Bjorn rested up against the side of the pool, lazily plucking petals off one of the flowers that floated by. They stripped and jumped in. The water stung as Seffin acclimated.

"My rabbits are back. Come here. And bring the wine."

They walked over and all took drinks from the wineskin.

"Now. I ask you to speak the truth. What are the consequences if you fail in your task?"

"Koth wins and everyone dies," Seffin said simply. No use beating around the bush. "If we don't start a new cycle the surges of husk will get worse and worse until everyone is dead."

Bjorn's gaze drifted up to the grey sky. "So, the pact is true." He took several more gulps of wine. "My father isolates us on these islands as if it will protect us. This is foolish. Our shore patrols already struggle to keep up. And if you speak the truth, it is all for naught, the husk will still surge and kill us all if you fail."

"Could you not talk to him?" Ren asked.

"I have tried. I love him, but he cares naught for the struggles of mainlanders. Even if those struggles bleed over into our lands. His only concern is for the wellbeing of our people, but our honor and pride are sacrificed at the altar of peace while a looming threat promises to devour us."

"Doesn't he have advisors? Councilors? Is there anyone else that could help to convince him?" Seffin asked.

"Some of our tribal leaders disagree with his actions, but they do not press him. To do so would be to accuse him of cowardice, and he would—"

"Protect his honor by dueling them to the death," Seffin said. "Polk gave us a brief lesson on your traditions."

Bjorn brought the skin back to his lips, wine spilled down his chin as he gulped. He finished and wiped his face with his forearm. "That is right. It would mean the cost of going to war starts with my father's life." For the first time since meeting Bjorn, the seemingly permanent smile and joy he held in his face failed to reach his eyes.

"Do you think he might reconsider if there were more dissenters? Could you convince more of the tribal leaders?" Ren offered.

"Most would follow him into a volcano if he asked. Even if I convince them, open criticism at a summit is a risk. I can try, though. Perhaps they could change his mind in private."

Bjorn took yet another swig of his wine and handed the cask to Seffin. "Here. Enjoy what wine is left my little rabbits. I have ears to bend, and with some luck, minds to change."

Seffin's eyes opened wide in surprise as he glanced between Ren and Bjorn.

Bjorn gave a sly smile. "If my rabbits are looking for a tumble, I would be happy to oblige... at a later time. The first of our tribal leaders will be arriving for the feast shortly, and I should start pleading my case. Besides, I prefer partners to be eager." He shifted his body to stand between them, and a huge arm dropped around each of their shoulders. "You two are beautiful, but the quickening of your hearts is more out of fear than passion. Even if your eyes can't seem to peel themselves away from me."

He let out a mirthful laugh before he ruffled their hair then pulled himself out of the pool. Water flowed off his body and splashed onto the tiles. Beads of moisture made his blonde chest hair sparkle and drips fell from his beard below a wide smile. "Take all the time you need. The servant at the door will show you to your quarters once you are finished relaxing." Then he sauntered back to his room, watched closely by Seffin and Ren who—despite just being called out for doing so—could not peel their eyes from him.

"Gods," said Ren.

Seffin took a drink of wine and passed it over. "I know."

Ren

Ren's eyes opened in the morning light. Last night's feast was a blur of dancing and laughing and wine, so much wine. As the first visitors other than Nari'ko Wilders in many lifetimes, the Kelsigans couldn't get enough of their guests' attention.

The king, drunk on mead, forced everyone to dance. Kelsig's version of dance was distinct in how close everyone stood together, more a mass of people jumping up and down than dancing, but Ren couldn't get enough. Even Polk—as detached as he always seemed—took a turn, he was almost knocked to the ground with all the bumping before a large, red-haired Kelsigan by the name of Sten threw him on top of the crowd where everyone held him up and cheered.

After the song, the crowd set Polk back on the floor and Sten joined the mainlanders at their table. He was a childhood friend of Bjorn's who took a distinct interest in Ka as she recounted their trip to Nari'ko. His lips twisted in disgust when she mentioned the giant amalgamation outside the forest's border.

Whenever Ren had searched for Bjorn, he was standing over a rapt audience telling a story or dancing or leaning up against one of the many stone columns in the hall, talking with important men and women. He remembered feeling jealous. That faint echo of jealousy shifted to confusion as his eyes focused, the room he was in was *not* the quarters they'd been assigned.

Seffin was there, lying beside him on the right, snoozing underneath folds of warm furs and piles of pillows. The bed they were in stretched out well beyond Ren's reach, and... was he naked? To his left, where Seffin wasn't, his foot hit something solid. It was warm and hairy. Turning his head, he found Bjorn, his bare, muscled chest gently rising and falling with his breath.

Did we? Really?

He recounted the night back in his head. The dancing. The wine. Seffin was a little free with his hands while they danced, and then Bjorn was there smiling and moving to the music with them. Then he put his hand on Bjorn's chest and said something in his ear. Whatever he said caused the prince, with all his muscles and joy, to scoop both of them up in his arms and squeeze, laughing and saying something about rabbit hunting. Ren gazed at Seffin sleeping innocently, with his soft snoring and a peaceful expression on his face. *Far from innocent.* The night's events began to coalesce into a clearer picture. Less than an hour after the bear hug on the dance floor, they were in this bed, a whirlwind of limbs and warm flesh and moans and kisses.

A massive arm fell over Ren, gripped him, and pulled him into a warm, furry chest. "Good morning my eager little bunny."

The bass of Bjorn's voice vibrated through him, breath touching the back of his neck with each word. Across the bed, Seffin's eyes blinked sleepily as he stretched and yawned. Bjorn leaned over Ren, pushing him into the bed as he reached to grab Seffin whose eyes popped open. A surprised yelp sprang from his mouth while Bjorn yanked him over, bringing them all together. Seffin laid his head back down, easing his body back into Ren's as Ren relaxed back into Bjorn's. They lay like that for a while, dozing in and out of consciousness until Seffin—*Again!*—turned around and reached for Bjorn. This time it was less a whirlwind of limbs and more a calm ebb and flow of warm embraces and tender connection.

When they were finished, they all jumped into the hot spring pool to wash the sweat and remnants of lovemaking from their bodies. A small needle of doubt slid its way into Ren's heart at the thought of the conversation he and Seffin *didn't* have before they drunkenly fell into bed with Bjorn. Is this what Seffin wanted? Was this going to be a regular thing? What about Sori'o? What did this mean for their relationship? Did it mean anything at all?

Seffin's easy smile as he saw the worry on Ren's face did a lot to assuage his fears. Whatever this was, it had already happened, and they would deal with it. They would have to have a conversation before next time, though.

Next time?

"I am glad it is you two that are with me on this morning," Bjorn said, his eyes gazing up to the top of the hill the terrace was carved into. "Today I do my part to save the world."

"It sounds dramatic when you say it like that," Ren said as he moved up behind Seffin and grabbed him from behind, he giggled and splashed him in the face. "Did you have any luck with the tribal leaders?"

"Yes." Bjorn brought his eyes back down to the two of them and flashed his perfect smile. "I implored upon them the importance of honoring our pact and explained the consequences of abandoning our duty. They all agreed."

Seffin's eyes went wide. "All of them? That's great news!"

"What did your father say?" Ren asked.

"He is weighing our words. We will find out his decision today at the summit." Bjorn dropped his head under the water's surface. Distorted through the waves of the pool, he shook out his hair and combed his fingers through his beard, cleaning himself. When he popped up, he rung out his locks and moved closer, putting a massive hand on each of their cheeks, he said, "Thank you for helping me with this. You two brought clarity to my path."

Clarity? All we did was ask you to talk to some people.

"You're welcome." Ren tried to sound as if he knew what he was talking about.

They exited the pool and dressed. Bjorn's outfit was formal, black leather with furs over the shoulder and a war axe on his waste. Seffin and Ren donned their jackets and left to scurry back to their own quarters. The prince had more he needed to do before the summit and Ka, Poppy, and Polk would be wondering about the results of their—*Oh gods, we're never going to hear the end of this from Ka.*

As if reading his mind as they walked through the castle, Seffin asked, "What do you think Ka is going to say?"

"Oh, I'm sure it's going to be something along the lines of—"

"If it isn't the two little rabbits hopping back to their warren." Ka's voice echoed through the hall behind them.

Ren rolled his eyes. "Good morning, Ka."

"Did you two have some fun?"

"You're one to talk, I saw how Sten was looking at you."

She put her hand on her chest dramatically. "Me? Sten is a married man. I would never." The faux offense she took dropped off her face and an evil grin slid on to replace it. "Sori'o is going to be *so* jealous."

"You didn't tell him," Seffin said in disbelief.

"Of course not, but it's not like you three were subtle."

It wasn't exactly fair to their Nari'ko Wilder friend that they went to bed with Bjorn on a whim when Sori'o only wanted to deepen their friendship, but fair didn't really matter in this case. What happened was between him and Seffin. Still, an emptiness yawned in the pit of his stomach. Guilt never seemed to care whether it was justified or not.

"Bjorn said all the tribal leaders agreed with him, but Leif is supposed to announce his decision at the summit." Ren decided to move the conversation along instead of allowing Ka to needle him.

Ka's eyebrows went up in surprise. "Does Poppy know?"

"We're on our way to tell them."

"Well, you're headed the wrong way. The summit is in the same hall we were in last night."

"The summit is right now?" Seffin asked.

"It may have already started. Didn't Bjorn tell you?"

Seffin and Ren exchanged a confused look. "No. He only said he had things to prepare," Ren said.

Ka shrugged her shoulders. "Maybe he assumed you two knew?"

They doubled back up the hallway and climbed two sets of stairs which brought them to the entrance leading to the main hall. Shouts clamored out the doors, drowning out all other noise except the unmistakable clanging sound of metal on metal. *A battle? Is there some sort of ceremony we didn't know about?* They quickened their pace and slipped into the room. Everyone was yelling and cheering.

Ren's heart pounded.

In the middle of the hall, standing in a perfect battle stance with a blood-soaked axe, was Bjorn, a cutting wound on his chest, open and weeping. The bodies of seven others lay around him. Seffin's hand went to his mouth. As they entered, King Leif shrugged out of his cloak and picked up his own axe.

"Like a snake, you sought to poison my people against me. You betrayed your father for what? For the safety of mainlanders?"

"For *our* safety." It came out as a wail. Raw and sorrowful and filled with grit. "For *our* honor."

"Our highest honor has always come from safeguarding our lands. One night in bed with these soft, pathetic—"

I'll show you soft and pathetic. Ren moved to help Bjorn, but Ka grabbed his arm and shook her head. She was right, this wasn't his fight. He'd only make things worse.

"I have killed your councilors in fair combat." Bjorn's face was a mask of blood, his blue eyes piercing out behind the crimson. "You talk of snakes, but you welcomed me into this summit knowing your councilors coiled around my feet, prepared to challenge me one by one."

"You are my son! Can you blame me for not wanting your blood on my hands?"

"It already is! Your axe may not have made these cuts, but it was your command that put them there. Do you not have shame? First, you hide from the duty we are honor-bound to perform, and now you cower behind your councilors because you lack the conviction to strike me down? If you stand by this decision, then have the strength to see it through yourself."

Leif pointed his axe at Bjorn. "You have always had more muscles than sense—"

"Duel me and let this be done. One of us dies today and I would not have our last words as father and son wasted on meaningless insults."

The king nodded. "Let it begin."

In a flash, Bjorn threw his axe at Leif's head. The king deflected the weapon as his son dropped down and grabbed two more axes from the fallen councilors at his feet. Bjorn let out a rage-filled howl that sounded more beast than man. King Leif rushed forward, but Bjorn was already spinning as he stood up. He used the momentum to release another axe at his father's head. This time Leif ducked the throw, but as he did, Bjorn put both hands on his second axe and slammed it into his father's weapon. Leif held fast, but the full weight of Bjorn's strike unbalanced him. The prince dropped his axe, a dagger flashed into his hands, and before his father could recover from the strike, he plunged the blade into his neck. Bjorn hopped back, out of reach of his father's final death swing. Leif's axe clattered to the ground, he dropped to his knees, disbelief on his face as his hands found the dagger in his throat. He met his son's eyes. With no wasted movement, Bjorn picked up his father's weapon and, in a single cut, removed Leif's head from his body.

The room erupted in shouts and wails. Bjorn dropped the axe and raised his hands, victorious and howling like a wolf. The delight of victory evident only in his yell; his face was pained, and his eyes glistened with tears.

Poppy's voice came in a hushed tone from behind Ren, "Coruscare burn me where I stand, what in Kohru's name did you say to him?"

Ren rounded on Poppy defensively. "This isn't his fault. All he did was talk to people."

"He asked us about our mission. We told him the truth. That's all," Seffin said.

Poppy put one of their large hands on Ren's shoulder. "Easy. I didn't mean to accuse. I thought this outcome might be a possibility, but... to see a man kill his own father."

"Awful," Ka said.

"Shaia said this would happen," Polk's voice cut through the cheering with its high pitch.

Poppy's face twisted in anger. "What did you just fucking say?"

"They said the only way Kelsig would honor their pact was if Bjorn became king. Bjorn was on the edge of challenging his father, and they wanted you to talk to him to ensure he followed through."

"That damnable spider. We are not their puppets to dance at their whim, and why in hells didn't you mention this before?"

"But he didn't challenge his father. The king challenged him, and only after he sent all his councilors after him," Seffin said.

Polk put his hands in his pockets, but his face remained its usual, unreadable self. "Reading people's intentions isn't seeing the future. Shaia can only tell what people want to do, not what will happen." He looked up at Poppy. "I'm sorry. I wanted to say something, but Shaia made me swear not to."

"Is there anything else they made you *swear?*"

"No. They only told me to follow my gut after this."

"Tell your gut that transparency is the best policy going forward." Poppy turned and poked Ren in the chest. "I'm not stupid enough to believe you two won't talk to him again, but be careful. Killing your own blood does something to a person. I watched it happen with Kiko."

"Would you rather he died? He didn't have a choice, Poppy," Ren said, frustrated at his guardian's unwillingness to see the truth for what it was. "He didn't *ask* to kill his father. He only asked him—"

Bjorn's voice boomed over the crowd, silencing everyone save for a few men and women weeping over their dead, "Hear me, Kelsig! Our isolation is over. We will honor the pact we made with Kohru. Mainlanders! Tell your leaders that when you march on Gogallo, Bjorn Gjorn, Son of Leif, King of Kelsig, will join you with his army."

"Long live King Bjorn!" Sten shouted from the crowd of people.

The room erupted in noise once more. Poppy's frown deepened their wrinkles, showing their age as they stalked from the room. Sten put a wineskin in Bjorn's hand and whispered something in his ear. The new king's eyes alternated between Ren and Seffin—a vacancy behind them that wasn't there before—as he nodded at whatever the northern tribal leader said before raising the wine in the air. "Mainlanders! Come, share a drink with me."

Seffin, Polk, Ren, and Ka all came forward, stepping over the dead and around their mourners, to stand next to Bjorn who handed them the wine. "To our allies across the sea. Together may we fight back the undead horde, and together may we live to see a world without the husk!" More cheers erupted and Bjorn leaned down. "I hoped to spare you this sight, my little rabbits."

"I'm not a rabbit," said Polk.

"And I'm not little," said Ka.

Amusement flashed on his face, and he let out a light chuckle. "To me, you are all little. And if you are not a rabbit then why did you hop up here at my command?"

It was true. Bjorn was as tall as Poppy but made completely of muscle. Even other Kelsigans, most of which towered over Ren, appeared small standing next to him.

"Did you know this would happen?" Seffin asked.

His eyes softened momentarily before the simulacrum of a smile leapt back onto his face. "I suspected. We will talk tomorrow before you leave. One more wolf ride before you go, eh?"

"We'd like that," Ren said.

Ka made a choked noise and grabbed the wineskin.

Bjorn straightened his back. "You may take the wine. I will have to apologize for my poor hospitality, but I must ask you to leave us while we burn our dead and mourn our losses. I will leave a servant with you. Feel free to ask for wine or food at your leisure, but please keep away from the main hall. Emotions are high and my brethren may say something indelicate to the visitors that inspired such upheaval."

We didn't do anything. Why does everyone think we had a hand in this?

The mainlanders left the hall accompanied by jubilant cheers and calls of death to the undying. Outside, in the entrance, the subdued din of the main hall echoed around them as they walked toward their rooms. The stairs they climbed ended in a grey, stone hallway with windows opening out onto a cloudy sky. A servant jogged up behind them and maintained a healthy distance. Present, but not intrusive.

Ren shivered at a sudden, cool breeze. This was the longest he'd gone without drinking, bathing in a hot spring, or warming himself under the sheets with a lover since entering the castle. The wind whistled through the windows, and it reminded him a little of Polk which, in turn, reminded him of Tom Kerrick, the old wielder with a tremulous, high-pitched way of speaking, who took up residence in his doomed hometown only a few short years before it was destroyed.

"I'm sorry." Polk's voice was almost lost in the wind. He looked at them with a flat affect. An even flatter affect than Seffin would put on in the early days. The kid was like if Seffin combined with a brick wall, combined with a canary... combined with a book of forbidden knowledge. Combined with a—

"For what?" asked Seffin.

"I think I should have told you. Even though Shaia said not to. It was a mistake."

Ka set a hand on his back. "You didn't know what would have happened if you did tell us. Poppy's mad for good reason, but their anger is more for Shaia than you."

"Still. I'm sorry. It won't happen again."

"Just so," said Ka.

The rest of the day was rather boring, which made it all the more disturbing after the morning's violence. Sori'o and Kalli'a stopped by to confirm the plan for tomorrow's departure. Sori'o attempted to linger but Kalli'a tugged him away. Otherwise, Ren and Seffin spent the day lazily dipping into hot spring-fed pools, eating, drinking, reading, and dozing. The place would count as paradise if the sun ever decided to peak out from the clouds.

A starless night fell on the castle, music echoed through the wind, strange and mournful. Out the window in their bedroom, a funeral pyre flickered out on a cliffside adjacent to the castle. The silhouette of a hulking man stood, straight-backed and staring into the yellow-orange flames.

***

Skygge and Regnsky sat panting in the yard when the group wandered in. Sten fussed with Regnsky while Bjorn issued orders to some of his men who were bringing out the horses. Notably, the sun was out. Ren hadn't seen it without treetops or clouds obscuring its rays since entering Nari'ko. Its warmth balanced out the chill wind blowing over the island and made the morning downright pleasant.

Bjorn waved them over upon seeing their group. "Good morning! You are lucky to see the sun after only two days here. It doesn't grace us with its presence often." He pointed to Sten. "My friend will help us transport you to the shore. I will be sad to see my rabbits leave, but we shall be reunited when I bring my troops to fight against the husk hordes."

"If we make it that far," said Ka. "This business in Prolivgrad will be a major obstacle."

"I hope for your success," he said. "It would grieve me to learn yesterday's events were for naught."

Ka's face flushed. "I didn't mean to—"

"It is fine. It is a careful balancing act the world is doing right now." He gave two quick, firm pats to Skygge who dropped prone. "Let's make for the shore and use the sunshine while we have it."

In a repeat of the day they arrived, they all climbed on their mounts. The only difference was Leif's replacement, Sten. The wolves trotted out ahead, through the gates of the castle with the horses following behind. The island's mood was different with the sun hitting it. The sparse grass seemed to glow like rivers of green flowing between the slate grey and black rocks bursting out of the hills. Herds of goats grazed up on the mainland, chewing on shrubs, and rabbits bounced between the rocks, seeking shelter from the giant predator they rode upon.

Ren hugged close to Bjorn as Skygge bounded over a boulder. He had hoped he could sit in front this time after hearing Seffin talk about how easy the ride to the castle had been. In the back, he had to hold on for dear life whenever the wolf decided to leap over obstacles instead of going around them.

"I wanted to thank you two again."

"We didn't do anything," Ren said, annoyed at having to repeat himself so often. "You asked us about our mission, and you made your decision."

"But you did do something," Bjorn insisted. "Before you came, mainlanders were more myth to my people than anything. We speak to no one besides the Nari'ko and the Kori'ko. Even then, it is rare to see one further inland than the shore. You put a face to your struggle—*our* struggle." He corrected himself. "You convinced me the threat you face is just as much ours as yours. My father guarded information from the mainland greedily. Your candor was... needed."

"Yesterday morning, before we left your room, were you already planning to challenge your father?" Seffin asked.

A long silence passed. The wind whipped at their clothing and the grass waved with it in a pattern that made it seem more creature than plant.

"Yes," he said, finally. "If he did not change his mind, I was prepared to fight him, but I did not expect him to use the summit as a trap to send his councilors against me. I loved the man in life, but I am trying to reconcile these actions with who I knew him to be, and I cannot. It was dishonorable. Still, it was helpful, in its own way. After yesterday's events, the remaining councilors and tribal leaders have all pledged to me completely."

The dock came into view along with the oceanside village, Bjorn had called it Vedheim. The ride was almost over.

"Your sister tells me it could be some time before the battle with Gogallo."

Ren clutched Bjorn as the wolf landed a jump over a boulder. "A lot is riding on Prolivgrad. If there is a war, it could set us back. According to Shaia, we have ten years before the husk overrun everything, but they hoped to install Polk as the new vessel far sooner than that."

Bjorn shook his head. "Tender explained it all during the feast on your first night. That boy is brave. Strange, but brave."

"He's learning," Seffin said. His tone was defensive. "He's been isolated in Nari'ko his whole life."

Most wilders are isolated in Nari'ko, but only Polk behaves like Polk.

Bjorn only made an affirming grunt.

At the beach, they hopped off the mounts and made their goodbyes. Bjorn picked Ren and Seffin up in a big bear hug. "Thank you again, and take care of yourselves, my little rabbits." He dropped them and hopped back on his wolf. "Good luck in Prolivgrad, and if the wait for our battle in Gogallo is long, don't hesitate to visit. I said our isolation was over and I meant it." He waved and bounded off on top of Skygge. Ren didn't know when they would find the chance to visit what with the world ending, but the thought was nice.

Soldiers guided the extra horses back inland while their group took turns ferrying to the ship with the dinghy. The crew pulled anchor just before clouds covered the afternoon sun, and Kelsig shrank into the horizon as they set a course for Nakonipol.

Sharon

Noah chopped vegetables at the counter while some fat melted in a nearby pan. He hummed while he worked, a cute little quirk he kept hidden until they'd lived together for almost a month, probably because he couldn't carry a tune to save his life. The fat popped as he lowered some strips of salted meat into the pan while butchering a song. She couldn't be any more specific than that. *A song.* Whatever song it was had died and now spent its time flipping around in its grave as Noah's throat produced notes that had no business being next to each other. And, for some reason she couldn't figure out, the scene comforted her, deeply. Sitting on a wooden chair and watching him work filled her with so much contentment she didn't know if she'd ever leave the apartment again. After all, why leave?

I caused a coup. People are dying. My son's home is here, and I made the place a living hell. How can I live with myself knowing what I've done? How can I look at my son knowing what I've done?

She ticked the reasons off in her head to remind herself that falling into a domestic life would cause a war with her own conscience. The Winnow problem needed fixing, and the Resistance member she'd met didn't inspire confidence in their organization's ability to manage him. The problem was she'd just finished a ten-year mission, one that exacted a heavy toll, and she desperately needed a break.

A memory of Cullen coming home with a new rattle in hand for baby Ren flashed through her mind and a pit opened in her chest. A yawning chasm of numbness and despair rumbled and formed and the entirety of what made her who she was collapsed inside. She snapped her eyes back open to see Noah's smiling face, with his dumb, happy eyes. He set a plate of vegetables and meat down in front of her. How he procured the meat? Sharon didn't know and promised not to ask. Meat was a rarity now, and next to ale, it was Noah's favorite type of food.

The *Egal Gazette* claimed all the rationing was for the safety of the nation. Another half-truth. The state of their food supply was a domino effect of The New National Government's stupidity. Winnow forced the Guild to increase costs on their pylon maintenance contracts. Lighton, the breadbasket of the West, took a hit to their food production as a result of straining their pylon network and subsequently stopped trade with Egal. Farmers couldn't harvest or distribute with husk at their throats.

With its primary source of grain cut off, Prolivgrad's own farms and stockpiles couldn't keep up. Then, in his infinite wisdom, Winnow killed or jailed half the mystics in the city during his coup. The city's famous master pylon no longer had the charge necessary to extend its barrier to the farms outside its walls. A clearer cause and effect didn't exist, yet the Nationals still supported their glorious leader. They bought his lines blaming refugees from country towns for the shortage and ate up his claims that immigrants were nothing but lazy leeches. It nauseated Sharon that so many people could be duped by someone so cruel, self-interested... and stupid.

"Your meeting with the rebel leader is today?" Noah stopped his tortured humming to ask.

Sharon swallowed her bite of hopefully-pork and answered, "Yes." She left it at that. Obviously, he wanted to know if she would join them, but she hadn't made up her mind yet. That could put him in danger too, and Noah had already stuck his neck out enough for her. The thought of leaving him for his own protection crossed her mind so many times she lost count, and the first time, when the Lodge was destroyed, she almost followed through.

"You know, when I got injured in the mine. I didn't know if you'd be here when I got back."

Get out of my head. "What makes you say that?"

"I know you think I'm dumb."

"I do not," she lied.

"Yes, you do. You must. You think I don't notice when you're hiding something from me? You give short answers, and I can practically see you drawing up a chart of all the possible directions the conversation will go. You lie to me all the time—"

"I do not," she lied again.

"—and that's fine. I don't care. I know who you are, and I know what you did for work in the past, and if I asked you not to hide things from me it would be like asking a hoarwolf not to howl at the moon. But stop treating me like I'm stupid."

She paused for a long moment to consider whether coming clean was the best idea for the situation. She never focused on the relationship. Noah did all of that. And he wasn't dumb. She *knew* he wasn't dumb, but for some reason, she couldn't stop treating him like an idiot. Probably because it helped her keep some distance between them.

Oh, shit. I'm doing it again. Analyzing the conversation instead of having it.

"You're right," she said, looking down at the food he'd made her while making off-pitch throat sounds she'd grown to cherish.

"So, when I asked about your meeting today..."

She sighed. *Fine.* "I haven't decided. Helping them exposes you to danger."

"We're in danger every day."

"Exposes you to *more* danger."

"I'm fine with that."

"You don't know what kind of danger I'm talking about."

"I know a little bit, and you didn't seem to care how little I knew when you assassinated the president."

"That was different."

"It wasn't."

"The goal for that was one person—"

"Winnow is one person—"

"But the Nationals are not. The *Nationals* were nearly half the city even before the coup. Now, they run everything and killed everyone foolish enough to stand up to them."

Noah gestured broadly. "The entire city isn't safe right now. If I have to be in a little extra danger so you can do your part to fix that, then I say go for it. Actually, let me help. I'm getting bored sitting around all day."

She had to admit, the idea of letting him help was appealing, and leaving him at this point would be unfair. He proved he could keep his mouth shut, his presence comforted her, and if he was fine taking on the danger, who was she to tell him no? Still, the thought of losing him to violence put a fear in her heart she hadn't had since Gull Harbor. She would rather they never met than live with someone else she cared about dying.

Why did I do this to myself?

"You're doing it again."

She was, in fact, doing *it* again.

"Fine. You're right. But I still haven't made up my mind. I need to see what we're dealing with. If they're beyond help, I may just say we should sneak out of the city and set up in a town somewhere."

"I'd be fine with that."

I wouldn't. I fucked this up and I should help fix it.

"Let's just see how today goes."

That mollified Noah, for now. He sat next to her at the table and dug into his meal. The conversation drifted to the increased patrols in the area due to Sharon killing Hugo. They agreed he had it coming, but he'd been their chief source of food for the last months and finding someone else as easy to steal from proved difficult.

The portion of the meal came where he listed off old colleagues who'd been injured or died in the mines that day. Only one injury from his circle of friends. Lucky. When Sharon was out this morning, she'd heard there were five deaths. With food costs so high and so few jobs to go around, people were desperate for work. The mining companies were taking advantage of that fact.

The state of the city worsened by the day.

She finished up, kissed him goodbye, and left for her meeting. The streets were dead save for a few pedestrians, and for that reason, she kept herself on high alert. Fewer people on the streets meant fewer targets for the National patrols to pick from, and they would pick on you for the simple fact of being alone, separated from a pack. Not that she had anything to fear from a simple patrol, but disposing of the bodies was cumbersome and combat wasn't an exact science. There was always a chance someone could kill her with a lucky hit, and then who would listen to Noah's terrible croaking?

Two tiers up the city and a fifteen-minute walk brought her to a part of Prolivgrad she rarely visited. Large, brick warehouses lined the streets, and while the residential area had only a few people milling about, the street she walked on now was all but abandoned. A door slammed half a block down as a woman with tan skin and a stocky, muscular build walked out of a box-shaped building, leaned up against its side, and lit a cigarette. Struggling to start the flame, she had a look of desperation Sharon only ever saw on the faces of marks before she killed them. Despite the complete absence of people in the area other than Sharon, the woman never even glanced at her. That alone would mark her as suspicious, but she approached anyway. "Jacinda?"

"Yes?" she said, staring off into nothing.

"I'm here for the meet with you and Cal."

Finally, her eyes flashed to Sharon and appraised her from top to bottom, pausing momentarily on her red turban and, notably, on her stance. Noticing Sharon never left a balanced stance, even while at ease, wasn't something normal people did; Jacinda was either a merc or an assassin.

"You killed Rashee."

"Yes."

"Do The Eyes know?"

The assassin's guild doesn't make a habit of keeping their former employees informed.

"I gave up my coins over twenty years ago. I don't know what The Eyes know."

Jacinda's thick eyebrows knitted together, and she gave her a meaningful look. "You know what I'm asking."

"They wouldn't come after me for killing Rashee, but I sacrificed my immunity during my mission."

Killing an eye, Cara Soledar, made sure of that.

Jacinda dropped her spent cigarette on the ground and stomped her boot overtop it. "Are you saying they may target you even *after* you served a full term? I thought they only took immunity from someone if they killed another assassin."

"That's correct. I don't know if they're aware it was me who did it, but if they do know, they may send someone."

"What do you mean 'may'?"

"I was their top assassin before I finished. There's a chance they simply won't risk it."

"What if they do?"

"If an eye comes just stay out of the way. They'll only target me."

She nodded. "Good enough. Follow me."

Jacinda knocked on the metal door leading into the warehouse—long, short, long, very long, short, short—the door opened to reveal a man with a mess of white hair on his head that matched an equally messy set of white teeth when he smiled. He had a warm, beige skin tone and a single, cheerful eye. A patch covered the spot where his other eye should be.

"What's the password?" he asked.

"Oh, fuck off, Cal."

"Correct! How'd you know?"

Jacinda rolled her eyes and pushed past him. Sharon nodded more politely but also pushed past him as his eye darted up and down her body, lingering on her stance just like Jacinda had. Maybe she was getting too obvious.

The warehouse opened onto a room full of shelves filled with military supplies. Red body armor, red sashes, boots, socks, swords, bows, arrows... everything a fresh National recruit would need. Inside the back office, Jacinda pushed a shelf aside to reveal a staircase leading down. A din of voices echoed up. *How many people did they call together for this?* Jacinda disappeared into the unlit stairwell with Sharon close behind. They descended two levels toward a door with warm, yellow light spilling out the cracks. The noise of conversation died as it opened.

Sharon wasn't prepared for what she saw.

The room was made of packed dirt and given the sharpness of the corners, the smoothness of the surfaces, and rigidity of the walls and floor, was clearly the work of an earth elementalist. A bar ran the length of the left wall with barrels of ale and bottles of spirits behind it. In the back, a hallway with wall sconces led off somewhere, and throughout the room, at over a dozen wooden tables, sat at least forty people. Most were drunk or well on their way.

They all turned and stared. Ahmad, with glassy eyes and flushed cheeks, gave a wave when he caught her attention.

"Sharon, everyone. Everyone, Sharon." Jacinda's introduction left a lot to be desired. "You'll likely be taking orders from her soon, so be on your best behavior."

Sharon gave a disapproving glance. *I haven't agreed to anything, and why would I be giving any 'orders'?*

Jacinda led her down the hallway in the back. They passed several doors before coming to a small office with an old, wooden desk and two mismatched chairs sitting on either side. Jacinda sat and willed the door closed after Sharon came in.

A wielder? Or just enough will to close a door?

"I really wish you wouldn't have introduced me to the entirety of your resistance before I decided whether I'd like to join or not."

"Cal and I aren't cut out for this," Jacinda said. She stared at a map lying on the table and frowned.

Obviously.

She went on, "Merc work and running a Lodge requires a lot of skills, but this underground bullshit is work for The Eyes. Sneaking around, secret networks, identifying valuable targets, neither of us can handle that, at least not anymore. I hate to say it, but we were on the verge of giving up before Ahmad found you. We'd drawn up plans on how to get everyone out of the city. We were going to caravan to Nakonipol."

"Even with enough traveling crystals the hordes are far worse than they were, and I'm sure the Tychon Land Bridge is completely blocked off by Nationals. Your chances would have been—"

"We would have been fine. We have enough wild wielders and mystics to keep a horde at bay. The only thing that could have thrown a wrench into it is if we met one of Saunders' special pets, but she's dead."

At the word 'dead' Jacinda gave Sharon a searching look. She must be operating off a hunch. There's no possible way the woman could have figured out she killed Jessica. Winnow claimed that one himself, which was part of her plan. Her stupid, selfish, piece-of-shit plan. The look went on for a beat too long. Did she want her to admit it? To admit to the thing that caused all this?

"Your meaningful looks are getting old."

"Fine. Regardless, I'm glad you've decided to help clean up this mess."

"I haven't decided anything."

"Yes, you have. In Lodge leadership, part of my job was reading people, and I was very, very fucking good at my job. I'll admit you're not easy. You walk around with your asshole clenched and your eyes dart around every room and over every person as if the whole world is trying to kill you, but... you're not assessing threats. You're judging our readiness. I know you've found it lacking, and I know you want to make this right—"

"I don't know what you're implying."

"You saved a kid from The Pit and almost blew your cover doing it, and when you saw Ahmad in the other room your eyes softened. Strange, considering he said you thought he was an idiot."

"He is."

"Agreed, but you helped his brother, and you were relieved to see him, that tells me you have a desire to help."

Ok, captain deduction, nice call, but a compulsion to fix my mistake doesn't mean I'm signing on. I need to know you can do what it takes. I'm not exposing myself for a gang of hopeful incompetents who just got done daydreaming about escape.

"What if I say no?"

"You already know."

"Humor me."

"You wouldn't make it out of this basement. You know too much now. Our wild elementalist has already sealed the entrance behind you, and if you attempt to escape we'll collapse the entire base. Best I could offer is confinement until we won or decided to cut our losses and leave."

That's why they brought everyone here. Because she knew they'd need muscle to keep her from escaping if she said no. *Maybe they do have what it takes.*

"I'm in."

"Good. You've been promoted to commander, congratulations. We can't pay you in anything other than food and alcohol."

Sharon chuckled. "Well, that'll make Noah happy."

Troy

Science is a process that takes time. Testing hypotheses, analyzing data, modifying processes, testing again, more analysis, and eventually, hopefully, results coalesce that can keep a person out of The Pit. Eventually hadn't come yet, however, and Winnow was on his way to the lab to check on all the progress Troy's team hadn't made. The truth is, Winnow would never command amalgamations. Sumiko spent days with Troy to explain why, but it all came down to the president's shallow will reserves. A binding could be done, but he'd never have the ability to control it.

They switched strategy to a stalling method and came up with enough data to make Winnow's request seem plausible. The science team was understandably anxious. The Pit wasn't safe, but it was safer than working directly for Winnow, it was better to live beneath the president's notice.

After today, the science team may not stick around. He couldn't blame them, braving the wilds just might make more sense than working for a murderous dictator with a labile mood. He pitched the idea of helping the team flee the city.

Sumiko and Tia both thought it a bad idea for different reasons. Sumiko thought the team wasn't skilled enough to make it through the hordes, and Tia thought Winnow would hunt them down no matter where they went. Both had good points.

Tia had her hair tied back into a tight bun; thick glasses rested on her nose above her permanent scowl. She stood on the metal grating and looked out over the lab. The team milled around beneath her. They were busy trying to look busy, writing down observations on their clipboards to fool whatever inspectors Winnow would bring with him. Troy stopped beside her. "I don't know how we get out of this."

"You could make actual progress," she said before meeting his eyes. "So far, you've only learned why you *can't* make this happen. None of you have even attempted to come up with a solution."

"I'm not a scientist, and I'm no wielder. This whole project is well outside my area of expertise."

"And yet you still promised Winnow you could bind amalgamations to him."

Tia was supposed to be his assistant, but her tone was always pointed, accusatory. Condescending, even. *I have no idea how my mother put up with her for so many years.*

"It's not like I had a choice. And I'm not the one saying it's impossible." He gestured to the team of scientists below them and said, "They are, and they know what they're talking about."

Her gaze drifted back to the floor. "You give up too easily."

"I haven't given up. I just don't want people to die working on an unsolvable problem, and right now the best I can do is stall."

"Well, I hope he's as dumb as you think he is."

A nervous chuckle forced itself out of his throat. "He is. I'm sure about that."

"He'll be here soon. We should head out front to greet him."

Troy nodded and they left the scientists to their science. The appearance of science anyway. Footsteps reverberated off the stone hallways leading to the front of the building, it reminded him of The Pit. His mind went back to the month he spent huddled in a cell, cradling his arm and feeling sorry for himself.

Never again.

Once outside, he took a deep breath. The lab's subjects kept it smelling like a rotting corpse and the spring air was a welcome reprieve. He had only a few minutes of contentedness before Winnow's carriage, guards flanked on either side, rolled up.

The president stepped out and walked right past him, into the building. Troy scrambled to match his pace. Winnow's hand immediately went to his nose.

"It smells like a fucking outhouse in here."

"Amalgamations have an odor, I'm afraid," Troy confirmed.

"Next time we do the meeting outside."

"Very well," Tia said.

Inside the demonstration area, the team lined up to receive the president. Everyone bowed as armed guards encircled them. Winnow looked down from above, his nose wrinkled and a frown on his face so deep his lips threatened to fall off. "Which ones are you binding to me today?" He studied the various cages with different husk hybrids.

"The binding will take a while to work, but we can get a blood sample and start the process with a couple hoarwolves."

"What makes you think I'd give you any of my blood?"

Tia and Troy exchanged a panicked look.

"B-Because that's how binding works. I thought I included that in the report?"

Something shifted in Winnow's demeanor then. Like an oil lamp sprang to life and was then summarily smashed on the ground. "Right. Well, no blood. Come up with something else."

Troy's mouth was suddenly very dry. His eyes flicked down to his team, lined up like pigs waiting for slaughter. Their survival hinged on what he said next. "That's a line of research we haven't explored yet, but w-with enough time I can see what the team could come up with."

Winnow brought his hand up and pointed. "That one. I want that one to be my first."

He'd pointed at an amalgamation of a gorilla. The choice was poetic in its absurdity. The gorilla was the most difficult to bind. They'd only done it once before with his mother, and even with her training in intentioned will, the thing fought her commands. Worse, they weren't very useful. Other than the extra set of arms, the mutation process gave them no special traits to speak of, very little differentiated their mutated amalgamated gorilla from a normal amalgamated gorilla. The only reason they kept this new one in the lab was as a control. Not only was he asking them to rethink the binding process from the ground up, but he'd picked the amalgamation with the least utility and the highest will requirement to start with.

"Are you sure—"

"That will be fine, sir," Tia said. She flashed Troy a look of warning.

"Great. How long will you need?"

A wave of relief washed over him. *At least he won't expect anything today.* "We'll need time to come up with a new method for binding. A few months?"

Winnow chuckled. "You have one." Then he took a breath and shouted, "Which one of you is Sumiko?"

Sumiko stepped forward from the lineup. Winnow snapped his fingers. A guard stepped forward and punched her in the face so hard she fell to the ground, limp. Gasps from the other scientists filled the room. Troy noticed Cillian's clenched fist and taut face; he was fighting not to step in.

Be smart, Cillian.

"If any of you feel it's important to mention my will reserves in a report again, you'll have worse than that to look forward to." With that, Winnow turned around and left. The guards on the lower floor filed after him. As soon as the last guard left, the team rushed to check on Sumiko. Blood flowed out her nose freely, and her left eye had started to swell shut. No missing teeth though. No broken nose. A miracle from what Troy could tell. She'd practically flown into the air with the punch. They pulled her to a standing position where she wobbled unsteadily, dazed but conscious, while everyone began talking at once.

Chatter around taking their chances in the wilds started anew, and Sumiko, her face a bloody mess, still managed to throw a disapproving look at her colleagues while Tia's scowl intensified. Troy didn't know whose side to take. Continuing the project would kill them all. He'd made a promise he couldn't keep, and they'd all pay the price for his stupid mistake. More people dying on his watch.

No, enough of this.

He'd been acting out of fear ever since they threw him in The Pit. He couldn't take it anymore. Time to take control. "We need to come up with a plan."

"No shit," Tia said, unhelpfully.

"I don't care whether we all try to escape or whether we decide to keep stalling, but we need to—"

"If we can't use his blood for binding there's no point in stalling." Cillian's red hair almost glowed in the low light of the lab. "It's not possible."

"It won't make a difference. Mystics have a hard enough time with binding and he's not even strong enough to call himself a wielder," Tyler, the youngest on the team, said between gritted teeth. His blonde hair lay in tight curls on his head and stood out against his flushed, anger-twisted face. "We're going to die unless we do something."

"Is there nothing else you can give him?" Tia asked, her hand waving dismissively as if the solution was so simple it was barely worth talking about. "I've interacted with that oaf enough to know if you give him something shiny enough it'll distract him."

"Shiny like a knife I could slide between his ribs maybe," Cillian said. A few others in the crowd murmured agreement. Tyler only frowned.

"You'll get us all killed if you try," Sumiko said. "He's the president. His guards are always with him."

Troy stepped into the middle of the group and raised his hands. "Listen to me. You're all dismissed for the day. Spend the night brainstorming. I don't care if your ideas are bad or dumb or suicidal. Bring every stupid idea you have to me tomorrow. We'll go from there." As they all dispersed, Troy added, "Sumiko. Tia. A word."

They met in the control room for the dead zone above the lab floor. The crystal hummed quietly as it floated in the center, a single sustained note adding to the tension. A thing unique to dead zone crystals and the master pylon, or so Sumiko had told him. The two women stared at him with expressions somewhere between annoyance and hostility.

"How did he know what Sumiko said about his will reserves? I know that wasn't made explicit in the report."

"The entire team has made reference to it. He may have just picked me because I was Pulpin's assistant." She held a white cloth to her nose that was slowly turning red.

"That seems the most likely," Tia added.

"He definitely found your name somewhere," Troy said. "I grew up around politics. He was one of my mother's worst rivals, and I know how he operates. He's impressionable and reactive."

"Pot meet kettle," Tia said with a look of boredom as she fidgeted with her glasses and a cleaning towel.

Troy's finger was in her face before he even knew what he was doing. "What the fuck is your problem with me? You've antagonized me at every turn since I hired you."

She put her glasses back on and calmly pushed his finger out of her face before saying, "You're flailing, and you've been flailing since I got here. Honestly, you're no better than Winnow. You just have morals."

I would think that makes me better than Winnow.

"How in Kohru's name could you say that?" Sumiko said. "All he's done is try and help us."

"Yes, after he pulled you out of the relative safety of The Pit and set you up to wager your lives against how fast you can appease our Dear Leader. He might as well have tied the noose himself."

"You're right," he admitted. "I have been flailing, but that's why we need to come up with ideas. What we've been doing won't work. Your constant needling isn't helpful, though. Stop it."

She hesitated before giving a curt nod.

"If someone gave him Sumiko's name, we need to find out who, and we need to find out why."

"Can we leave now?" Tia asked.

"Sumiko can. I have one last thing to discuss with you."

His chief scientist left while Tia held back and gave him an unreadable look.

"Are you working for Winnow?" he began.

Her lips twisted in disgust. "Why the fuck would I work for that cretin?"

"I think it's a fair question. You sold my mother out to him, after all."

Realization dawned on her face. "That has nothing to do—"

"Oh, I think it has *everything* to do with why you're here. I may not be the most intelligent person you've ever worked with, but I'm not as big an idiot as you think I am." He circled her like a predator sizing up his prey. "I have a theory. Tell me if I'm wrong. You tried to make a little extra money and thought you were doing my mother a final favor. You tipped off Winnow about the assassination as long as he promised not to retaliate. That way my mother could keep the presidency even after her mistake. But you miscalculated. Winnow doesn't return favors and he doesn't keep his word. He set up the coup anyway."

"I never meant for her—"

"You started working for me out of a guilty conscience. You got my mother killed, and our country turned into a nightmare. If you hadn't tipped him off—"

"I'm sorry, ok. I didn't mean to get her killed." *You didn't, that was me.* "I didn't think he'd stoop so low as sedition and treason."

"Did you give him Sumiko's name?"

"I *don't* work for him... But he approached me, and Sumiko came up. He knew who she was beforehand, I *swear*. He'd read the report for once. That's how he got her name."

He looked her in the eyes. Bright green with steel and grit piercing back into his own. She was telling the truth. "Fine. Dismissed."

The indignance on her face shifted to guilt and she turned to leave, pausing in the doorway, she said, "How did you know?"

"I've met an eye before. Someone like Winnow wouldn't have survived an attack from one unless he knew it was coming. You're the only person my mom would have trusted with her plan."

Then she was gone. The soft, metal clanging of the grating below her feet faded into silence until it was just him, alone. He locked up the lab and left to start his hour-long walk home. The cobblestones were wet, and the air was cool and humid. A rain shower must have passed by not long before. It left a pleasant smell on the outskirts of the city.

Once inside the gates, however, the stench of Prolivgrad invaded his nose. He massaged his aching stump as he walked, the constant pain served as a reminder that he wasn't allowed to enjoy his days anymore. Every moment needed to focus on survival now. What were they going to do? Escape was unlikely. The binding procedure was impossible. Retaliating against Winnow was suicidal. He already handed over the recipe for explosive crystal dust.

Nothing came to him.

He entered his home and closed the door behind him. It wasn't until he was setting his jacket on the coat rack that he noticed Sharon's lover, Noah, standing in the hallway.

"Hey, Troy."

"Godsdamnit."

Ren

The Lodge in Nakonipol paled in comparison to Prolivgrad's. For starters, it had two levels instead of four. Secondly, by midday, Ren's home Lodge would bustle with over two hundred people looking for contract work or taking a load off at Mallory's, but here fewer than thirty mercs were rambling about. Seven perused the merc board, ten sat at the Lodge's pub getting day drunk, and the remainder languished in the queue at the payout window. The boards themselves held hundreds of unfilled contracts, pinned and fluttering in the warm draft of the always-open Lodge door.

Where are all the mercs?

Poppy made a beeline to the Lodge manager's office and knocked on the door. Ren had just finished reading the name Kristal Tiev when it swung inward revealing a short woman with dark brown, tightly curled hair, fair skin, and a missing eye. Her brows knit together for only a moment before she recognized Poppy which caused her arms to spring out from her sides, pulling them into a hug. Poppy was too big to return the hug normally, so they bent down and patted Kristal's back instead.

She broke off and arched an eyebrow. "You have a child traveling with you?"

"That can wait. Has the empress come through yet?"

"How did you—" She shook her head. "No. She's still a month out. The husk are surging everywhere. She's left much of her army behind to safeguard our cities."

"Good. I need to speak with Sim Larkin."

"He's preoccupied trying to keep our pylons up and running." Kristal squinted her eyes. "Wait, how is that good?"

Poppy knitted their brows. "What's wrong with your pylons?"

"Nothing, now that we have a Guild mystic and engineer here to help. Sim conscripted most of our mystics to keep the pylons charged, and without an engineer to perform maintenance, the charging efficiency degraded to—wait, answer my question, how is it a good thing that our army is delayed?"

"Because I'm trying to avoid a war." They said it as if it was the most obvious thing in the world.

Kristal laughed in disbelief. "The war has started, old friend. Egal's mutated amalgamations are running around our region causing havoc, *and* since we can't pay their new prices, they've completely cut off replacement crystal shipments."

"Didn't you just say a Guild mystic and engineer were here? Why would they send a maintenance team if they'd stopped crystal shipments?"

"Yes, they *escaped* here."

If they had to escape that means things were worse than Ren imagined. What was happening to his home? "Are things really that bad in Prolivgrad?" he asked.

She reached a hand out to him. "Hi, I'm Kristal. Our rude friend hasn't deigned to introduce us yet."

"Ren Bolin."

"Bolin?" Everyone paused while Kristal's brain filled in the gaps of what that meant. Her eyes darted between Poppy, Ren, and Ka. "You don't look like a Bolin."

"I'm adopted."

Kristal used both hands to point one at Seffin and one at Polk, a questioning look on her face.

Ka gave a tired expression. "Adopted. They're all adopted. Everyone's adopted. We love adopting things. Now tell us what's going on in Prolivgrad... please."

Kristal huffed and shot Ka a withering look before shaking her head. "It's bad. Thousands have been killed, even more have been jailed. The good news is Kiko's coming to liberate the city."

"Her version of liberation will look like conquering to the Egallan people." Poppy flexed their jaw. "Where can I find Sim?"

"Today? Larkin will be at one of the eastern pylons with Oji, I heard him talking about it last night at Semma Jen's."

Poppy's face contorted in an interesting, new way Ren had never seen. The edge of their lip curled up and their eyes darted down to the floor with eyebrows raised. Disbelief mixed with disgust mixed with relief and a sprinkling of annoyance. "Gods, that's a person I hoped to never work with again."

Ka smiled. "Why? Because she's better than you?"

"Her abrasive nature and need to be right about everything were what I was thinking, but sure, we'll go with 'because she's better than me.'" Poppy pointed to Ren and Seffin. "These two can handle your mutated amalgamations."

Kristal's face seemed to have run out of surprised looks, so instead, a sort of exhaustion settled on it. "Sure, why not? Let me grab the contracts." She walked back into her office and leafed through some papers on a desk.

"Ka. Polk. You're with me. Ren and Seffin, I'll send the twins to help you with the contracts. Four mystic-level wielders should be enough to handle whatever's out there. We'll meet back up at Semma Jen's tonight."

Poppy, Ka, and Polk left while Kristal came back with four sheets of paper. "I'm only doing this because of who Tender is, but just so you know, this would be suicide for most mercs. If you *do* survive, though, you're about to be very wealthy. Larkin commissioned these himself, and he put a lot of money on the bounties."

Seffin grabbed the contracts and looked them over. Three nods and a frown. The frown had him worried. Ren peaked at the contracts: a hoarwolf, a rafadon, and a laranee. The hoarwolf would be easy as long as they could find it. Rafadons were giant, slow-moving tortoises, how hard could that be? With two other wielders and so much combat experience under their belt, he didn't imagine the laranee would be a problem. But the last one was...

Ren's blood froze in his veins.

A werewiller. The same type of amalgamation that destroyed his hometown. The same one his mother sacrificed herself to kill. If it truly did have the same mutation as the one that killed everyone in Gull Harbor—completely soundless movement—it would be difficult to find it before it found them. Almost impossible.

Success would ride on taking each of the amalgamations down separately, as well as their ability to get the drop on them. For good or for ill, though, all four had been spotted in the same area. That meant they'd be easier to find, but it also increased their chances of engaging more than one at a time.

"Thanks for the contracts," he said, swallowing his fear.

This is merc work. This is exactly the type of job I signed up for, what I wanted.

"Check in at registration before you go." She turned around and closed the door behind her. Ren thought he heard her mumble the word *insane* from inside her office.

Out on the street, the morning heated up. From a tree paradise to an endless winter blizzard to chilly, rainswept islands, and now to a tropical, heat-blasted city on the northern edge of the empire. It's all the adventure and sightseeing Ren ever dreamed of. It wasn't dissimilar to the stories he'd heard, but the stories always glossed over the hard parts. He still thought of Sorca from time to time, the murderer he murdered. He remembered his iron grip on the pommel of his will-blade as he pushed it through Sorca's neck, the blinding orange of the fire and the watery red tears streaming out of the rogue's eyes, and above all, the sickening satisfaction that made his heart sing. Dangerous or not, killing amalgamations didn't haunt him the way Sorca did, and for that he was grateful.

The crew had brought their belongings to Semma Jen's, a local inn, and with the heat ticking upward, they'd decided to stop and change out of their cold-weather gear. Seffin had already taken off his undershirt, his bare, tan skin showing in a line down his center, the scar on his belly peeking out from the open, flapping coat. Ren copied him. It didn't stop his profuse sweating, but at least he didn't have the shirt clinging to his skin.

On their way to the inn, they stopped by a fruit stand to grab a couple bananas and two wedges of pineapple. Ren took a bite of the pineapple; his tongue prickled and tingled with its sweet tartness. Far more flavorful than the dried variety he could get in Prolivgrad. Guards patrolled around in pairs of two wearing light, sleeveless leather armor, stopping to chat now and then with the stand owners. In Prolivgrad, guards were rarely around, and when they were, they barely spoke outside of barking orders at people. Here, everyone smiled at them.

Sori'o and Kalli'a walked out of Semma Jen's as they approached, both wearing lighter clothing. Leathers exchanged for linens, and both had almost nothing on their upper bodies.

Kalli'a ran up to them. "Tender told us you were killing some amalgamations?"

"We are. Are you two already prepared?" Seffin asked.

"Just so," Sori'o said and came in for a sweaty embrace.

Kalli'a came in for a briefer, but equally sweaty, hug before Ren and Seffin went off to change. They regrouped back outside and made for the southern entrance. The contract said the amalgamations were last sighted an hour and a half walk south of the city. Within minutes of leaving, they were in dense jungle. Flies buzzed around their ears while they walked through unrelenting heat. Green vines snaked their way up and down the trees, hung off branches, and clung fast to anything they touched. More a nuisance than anything, but both Kalli'a and Sori'o kept a healthy distance anyway.

It dawned on Ren that he'd never even asked what mission Shaia had sent the twins on; he'd been too wrapped up in his own worries to spare a thought for them. Also, if he was honest with himself, the Nari'ko version of friendship had put a wedge between them. Sori'o never overtly pressured, but an expectation loomed over their interactions. And after Kelsig, Ren felt guilty. In his head, he knew what happened with Bjorn had nothing to do with their friendship with Sori'o, but it still agonized him like a betrayal. With that betrayal came a sense of guilt, compounded by the fact that Sori'o seemed completely unbothered by the event. He had to know by now, but he showed no outward sign he cared. Why wasn't he mad? Or jealous? Ren would have been.

But that's just it. They view it differently than I do.

He decided he'd let this linger too long. He should talk to Sori'o, address the porcine in the room. A chance came when Seffin and Kalli'a paired off to chat about air elementalism and the light skinned Nari'ko Wilder fell back to keep pace with Ren. *Now or never.*

"Hey, Sori'o. I wanted to say sorry."

He cocked his head. "For?"

Good question. I'm not actually sorry we didn't sleep with you. Then what am I sorry about?

"I feel like we've been ignoring you lately."

"Oh? I... didn't think so."

Ren got the distinct impression he should have thought more about this conversation before attempting it. Poppy did say the Nari'ko were aware of how odd that part of their culture was.

"Well, no. Not intentionally I guess," Ren said.

This is going terribly.

"You two are busy. Your mission is important."

"Right, but... I just know that we all wanted to be friends."

"Are we not?"

"Yes, but—"

"Oh!" Sori'o chuckled. "Who is it that told you about Nari'ko friendships? Tender?"

"Yes," he said.

Ren racked his brain, when had Poppy ever been wrong about something like this? They were a near-perfect encyclopedia of knowledge, and he'd never known them to say anything they weren't sure of.

Sori'o looked amused. "Tender is a wonderful person, and they are a powerful ally to the Nari'ko people. But I don't think I'm speaking out of turn when I tell you they are somewhat uncomfortable talking about intimacy."

Ren nodded. "Fair."

"Touching, talking, enjoying each other's company, consideration. I'm just as close with my female friends as I am with my male friends, but I have no interest in seeing them naked. Sharing yourself deeply is all that's required, but that doesn't need to involve sticking things into each other."

Ren laughed. He'd been holding the tension and pressure this whole time for nothing, and now he knew what to apologize for. After catching his breath, he said, "I'm afraid I—"

A wall of ice burst up next to them, followed by a deafening crash as something heavy slammed against the other side. Up ahead, Seffin had his arm forward with his hand facing the wall while Kalli'a had her bow out, loosing arrows at whatever crashed into the other side. Sori'o gave Ren a pat on the back and earth slipped into the ground. Ren pulled out his blade and threw some will into it as the ice wall shattered, pelting him with shards.

He dodged the largest of the ice chunks and took in the creature standing before him. It had sixteen legs, though it only used half of them to stand, the remaining eight ended in paws or claws, jutting out at odd locations as if sewn on. There were three rotting heads: one rafadon, one hoarwolf, and one laranee; all poking out of the rafadon's shell. The laranee and hoarwolf heads were twisted upside down. The spiked tale of the rafadon had a thin, jittering tail and a wagging, bushy tail on either side of it. Except for the werewiller, every creature on their list had amalgamated with each other. The whole thing flickered back and forth erratically. Ren pulled in some of the ice scattered on the ground with his will, shaped it into a lance, and shunted it at the laranee head. With the creature's flickering the lance missed and hit the Rafadon shell, which started to glow faintly.

Seffin's voice was frantic. "Get clear!"

Ren sprinted away as a fireball slammed into its side. The shockwave from the blast threw him into the air, but he tumbled into a recovery and jumped behind a nearby tree. Sori'o popped out of the ground next to him.

"Kalli'a got the hoarwolf head with an arrow. The other two pulled into the shell after Seffin's fireball."

Ren stole a glance, the wolf head hung limply with an arrow in its eye, its fur smoldering as the laranee head let out a warped roar and turned its attention to Seffin. For an amalgamated spider tortoise with decaying legs, it skittered toward him with impressive speed. The shell's glow brightened with each step it made, and trees exploded in proximity from its compulsive flickering. Ren extended the edge of his will-blade and rushed toward it. He swung for the main body, but the blade bounced off.

The shell's glow became blinding.

The world fell away, and he was plunged into darkness. A muffled, discordant tone rippled through his body followed by a sudden shake that made his bones vibrate so hard they threatened to shatter. The world reappeared as fast as it went away, leaving all four of their group prone in the dirt a good distance away from the creature. The Nari'ko Wilders had both used their earth slipping to get everyone clear of whatever the amalgamation just did, but the toll of bringing a passenger along left them exhausted and panting. The shelled creature stood in a clearing of splintered trees, spinning around and scanning for its prey. *Without the hoarwolf head, it's having a hard time finding us.* "We need to take out the laranee head next," Ren said.

"I want to know what the hells happened while we were underground," Seffin's voice was hushed.

"The shell—," Kalli'a started.

"Can't be pierced by a willed weapon," Ren finished. "My blade bounced right off it."

"No," she gave him a tired look. "The glow. It's gone."

Seffin and Ren turned their attention to the amalgamation. Sure enough, the shell looked normal now, as normal as an amalgamated tortoise shell could look anyway. *Does that mean my blade will get through? No, it's better to assume it won't work.*

Ren felt Seffin's hand grip his shoulder. "Our final."

Our final?

It took a moment for him to understand. The showcase they'd prepared for graduation, but never had the chance to perform. "I know I've said it before, but you're insane."

"Got a better plan?"

"No."

As if that was all the answer he needed, two of Seffin's giant, unwieldy fireballs burst into existence, drawing the attention of the amalgamation. Ren ran parallel to the creature at first, and then he took a circuitous path around its back. Once in position, Seffin chucked the first of the fireballs. The creature pulled both remaining heads inside its shell, but the sphere of flame didn't connect, it passed overtop. Ren caught it using kinetics. Together, Seffin and Ren threw their fireballs at the same time. The moment he released his sphere, Ren pulled in moisture from the air around him, then pushed it into Seffin's range.

Both fireballs collided with the amalgamation simultaneously. The limp hoarwolf head flailed around as the blast launched the creature into the air, flickering in short bursts as it flew. Ren dropped focus on the water he'd gathered when he felt Seffin's will reach for it. Almost too fast to see, the stream turned into a floating pool. On its way back to the ground, the rafadon plunged into the water. Seffin made a fist to flash freeze the pool and opened his hand as a flurry of ice needles exploded out. They pierced through the two remaining heads and the flailing limbs, then popped the top and bottom halves of the shell apart.

A gruesome ice sculpture now rested in the middle of the jungle.

Ren jogged toward Seffin and the Nari'ko siblings with a smile on his lips from their victory. A smile that was quickly replaced with frenzied shouting as he saw it.

"Run!" he screamed at Seffin as loud as he could. "Run!"

He watched in horror as Seffin turned to face an eight-foot, heaving, bipedal monstrosity with fetid flesh, matted fur, and long claws—one of which held a will-spear. It glared down at him, soundless and terrible.

Troy

A man with a shaved head and eyes that always looked lost stood in Troy's hallway. The last few months hadn't been kind to Noah, thin and overstretched, his clothes hung off him. He flashed an unassuming smile, but Troy knew better. This man's allegiance was to Sharon, Flicker of the Eyes, and no one else.

"I haven't said a word to anyone about what happened, what are you doing in my house?" He fought the overwhelming urge to reach for his sword.

"Sharon thought you'd be more open to listening if it was me who talked to you."

Troy put a finger to his temple and rubbed, confused and frustrated. "Skip to the part where you tell me why you're here, Noah."

The miner motioned into the dining room. "Can we sit?"

"Absolutely fucking not."

Noah frowned. "Sharon's in the Resistance and wants your help."

The words were nonsense. Sure, they formed together to make a complete sentence, and, sure, Troy knew the meaning of each word—even the name, Sharon—but put together as a single thought the man was speaking gibberish.

Troy's mind raced. "I need to sit down." He pushed past Noah, into his dining room and sat, almost fell, into one of the chairs. He gripped the edge of the wooden table, fighting the impulse to scream or puke or both. Noah walked in as if he'd been invited, then sat in a chair as if he was welcome. *He always did know how to make himself at home.* The creak of the wood as Noah's weight settled into his seat snapped Troy to attention.

"She betrayed me. She killed my mother and framed me for the crime. She single-handedly set our country on a path of self-destruction, and now that she's turned everything to shit, she joins the Resistance? And she wants *my* help?"

Noah stared at the floor. "Those aren't the words I'd use, but—"

"Can I say no? Or will she kill me if I do?"

He met Troy's eyes. "You can say no."

"How am I supposed to believe that? How can I believe anything you say? You lied to me, you *let* her kill your friend."

Noah shook his head like he was trying to shake free a thought from his mind. *Did he not realize she killed Clem?* He brought a big hand up to his scalp and rubbed, what little stubble was there made a scratching noise as his calloused palm brushed over it. He looked older than only a moment ago.

A sigh burst from his mouth like he'd been holding it back. "You don't have to trust us. Meet with the Resistance. Trust them instead."

"I have my own people to worry about now."

"They can join too."

"So you can betray them like you did me? Seriously, is there something about my face that says 'walk all over me'?" He paused for breath and used the moment to think. Helping the Resistance would be dangerous, even if an unhinged former eye wasn't connected to them, but at the same time, with Winnow taken care of, his team would be safe. "What is it the Resistance thinks I can help with? I'm the president in name only right now. My power is limited."

"They want you to send a message to the Western countries. See if they can set up some sort of alliance to unseat Winnow."

I do have ways of reaching them, and foreign officials wouldn't ignore a letter from the president of The Guild of Commerce. The Guild still had some envoys traveling between Lighton, Nashow, and Estaba. Adding three more letters to the pile wouldn't be too difficult.

"Fine. Get me some letters and I'll forward them to Mitchell, Kimberly, and Rahal."

Noah made a pained expression.

Troy leaned forward in his chair. "What is it? Isn't that what you wanted?"

"Sharon insisted I ask if you would meet with—"

"No."

"—she said she didn't like how she left things."

Troy didn't respond. What was he supposed to say to that anyway? *I didn't like how you killed my mom and framed me for it either, but why don't we just let bygones be bygones? Water under the bridge. Let's get some tea later. Maybe we can go knife shopping, so you have a fresh one to stab me in the back with later.'*

Noah looked at him expectantly. Troy remained silent; he'd already given his answer.

"Ok, then." Noah stood from his chair.

Troy couldn't help himself. "Aren't you worried she'll do the same to you? I saved her life, let her stay in my house for months, fed her, found a healer for her. And she still set me up. What makes you think she wouldn't throw you to the wolves on a whim?"

"Maybe she is using me, but I'm using her too. And every time she's had the chance to toss me aside, she hasn't." He started to walk out, paused, and turned his head toward Troy again, "And she doesn't do anything on a whim."

Troy scoffed. "Get out... and knock next time."

He nodded and left, the latch on the door clicked shut. Troy rushed to the lock. *Stupid.* He hadn't changed them when he got out of The Pit. Noah must have kept his key. He added changing locks to his chore list, jammed the door with a nearby chair, and sat on a bench to start the process of doffing his boots. Everything took so much longer with one hand, especially knots, but he was getting better each day. He finished pulling them off, and with his feet free, he flexed and stretched his toes before padding into the kitchen to grab a bite before bed.

She joined the Resistance?

It still made no sense. The woman cared for no one but herself. She said only what she needed in order to manipulate people, and after she was done, she tossed them aside like garbage, or if your name was Clem, she killed you. He grabbed a sandwich from the day before, half-eaten and stale, resting on his kitchen counter. The bread was a dried sponge on his tongue, but the cheese and meat tasted fine. A little extra chewing and it was no different than yesterday. The maid had left him a pitcher of water, so he poured himself a glass to wash it down. As he thought about his science team, and now about the secret letters he just agreed to send, he ambled around the kitchen and into the dining room, then back to the kitchen and then again into the dining room. A habit he'd had since he was a boy. Moving about, pacing, helped him clear his head.

He started with the easiest problem first. The letters. It would be a simple thing to slip them into the envoys' stacks of mail without drawing attention, but he wanted assurances the letters would remain unopened until they reached their intended recipient. Envoys, as a rule, kept to their code of ethics, but they were still human. All it would take is one to peek at a letter and... Well, he'd have to pick the right people for the job. Ones who took the position seriously, or ones he knew and trusted. Tomorrow, before heading to the lab, he'd stop by Guild headquarters and check with Boris, the head of operations, about the envoy rotation.

Next problem, how to keep the science team alive. Still pacing, he ambled into the hallway containing Sharon's old room. He hadn't been inside since the day of the coup. He walked past her door and came to his study which sat empty save for whatever sparse furniture was required to call the room an office. An empty wooden desk stood in the center with a plushly upholstered, gray, high-backed chair resting next to it. That was it. The room was lonely. He sat in his desk chair for the first time in over a year and looked around the dim, empty space with its bare walls, trying to come up with something, anything to help his team.

Nothing.

He stood and left the useless study to collect dust for another year. Footsteps and the creaking of wooden floors echoed through the hallway as he paced up and down it, keeping his eyes off Sharon's door every time he went by. It chafed him to think of it as her room, that a part of his home had become hers, but the room had never been used for anything before and probably never would again. She'd spent more time in it than he ever would, so in a real sense, it was more her room than his. Which is why he kept it shut. If he could cut it out of the house and—*science team. Solutions. I need to focus.*

What could he do to keep Winnow at bay? Giving him the recipe for Tender's explosive crystal powder bought him less time than he would have liked, and while Winnow's reticence to part with any of his own blood presented a challenge, it ultimately changed nothing. The man had shallower will reserves than Troy did. Not to mention he was untrained. He would never, in a million years, have the ability to command one of their mutated amalgamations even if they bound one to him. Frustration settled in as he continued to come up empty on ideas.

Troy trudged upstairs to prepare for bed, unbuttoning his shirt and unfastening his pants with one hand, he almost fell over pulling free of the pant leg clinging to his left ankle. Then he unwrapped his stump. He didn't *need* to wrap it; he just didn't like to look at it. Before he went to The Pit, a healer had been assigned to knit the flesh back together. They could have found his hand and put it back on if they wanted, but in the flurry of the coup, the Nationals didn't think it a priority. They cinched his arm with a tourniquet, dragged him to the only healer they'd brought—some toothless old mystic—and after they closed the flesh, he was thrown in a cell and forgotten for a month.

He held the stump out in front of him, staring hatred and grief for his loss into it. A rounded nub where a hand should be, too smooth and soft for normal skin. He could swear he still felt it there, that he could wiggle his thumb and point with his fingers. He wondered where his hand ended up. Did they throw it in the trash? Was it rotting in a garbage pit outside the city?

He hated this. He used to be in tune with his body. Now he felt off, lopsided. He pulled the blankets back with his will and climbed into bed. It was the extent of his will training—basic kinetics. His mother had started him on control exercises as soon as she could, but stopped just as quickly when she learned his reserves were "pathetically shallow". She'd been wrong. His reserves weren't at the level of a wielder, but they were a good sight deeper than the average person. Maybe Ka could help him with his control... if he ever saw her again.

Gods, I hope I see her again.

Half a year had passed since they last spoke. On one hand, he was happy she hadn't been in Prolivgrad for the coup, and on the other... limb... he wished she was here. Ka always knew what to do, always knew what to say. She would probably have ten different ideas to save the science team by now, and if anyone could stand up to Sharon, she could. Also, he missed her. He tried not to, but during the worst days in The Pit, she was all he could think about. The more he thought about her the more it hurt to think about her, and he couldn't shake the feeling like he was just whipping himself.

Still, as he lay staring up at the ceiling, her visage came to him. He thought about how her cheeks turned red when she drank too much or got embarrassed. How self-assured and kind and also so very, extremely cutting she could be. How they both danced around the feelings they both knew they had. Troy's eyes grew heavy thinking of Ka standing over him on the highway outside Oleksandra's Harbor, her long, black hair whipping in the wind as she saved him from hoarwolves. The gentle touch of her hand on his cut and the feeling of her will closing the wound, fixing him. Her voice filled with both worry and strength, asking if he was ok.

No. He thought. *I'm not.*

Seffin

A fleeting memory of a mundane day at Danver's Academy came to Seffin. Of Professor Dunreedy standing at his podium, a frown on his face, annoyed that they'd tapped him to do this year's lecture on colossi when his specialty was elementalism. A depiction of a werewiller had been pinned to the board while he droned on.

"Werewillers are mostly bipedal," he'd said. "When they run, they hunch over and incorporate their upper limbs, but for the most part, they walk around like a large, furry human with a cat-like face and a stubby, brown puff of fur that counts as a tail. The thing to worry about is their claws, which extend out their fingertips, kind of like a cat." He'd pointed directly at the claws on the picture but then shifted up toward the creature's head. "But they can tear a person apart with their teeth almost as easily."

"They look kind of cute." Kaylee had said. She wasn't wrong. The pictured creature possessed a certain unassuming passivity.

The reading they'd done for the day had said that, generally, werewillers left humans alone. Humans made for difficult prey, and outside of feeding, werewillers tended toward docility and laziness. Experts considered them to be the most intelligent animal, second only to humans. A fact usually cited as an explanation for why they were one of only two other animals known to wield will, which is how they got their name. According to the textbook, they wielded for convenience. Pulling objects to themselves that were out of reach or bending a far branch of a tree to better see their targets. They also, like apes, were known to use tools.

The memory flitted away as fast as it came and Seffin's mind came back to the here and now, to the rotting amalgamation standing fifteen paces from him, holding a will-spear in its right claw. The vacant, cat eyes scanned him over while its pointed ears, one of which was half torn off, flicked and fidgeted. Behind, Ren frantically implored him to run. That wouldn't do Seffin any good, though. Werewillers were lightning fast, and through his description of the one that destroyed his village, Ren had instilled in him a deep, paralyzing fear of the beast. The blink of an eye is all it would take for the left claw or the spear in the right claw to whip through his body.

The silence was the most terrifying part. No sounds of breath, no growls, no cracking of twigs or shuffling of leaves when it approached. It was just suddenly behind him. If it weren't for the smell, he would have doubted his eyes. All he could make out was the sound of his heartbeat, blood rushing in his ears.

The creature should be lunging at him. He was frozen in fear well within reach of it, yet miraculously, it hesitated. If he ran it would provoke an attack, wielding meant moving which would provoke an attack, if he shifted at all it would provoke an attack, so he did none of those. Instead, he focused on the sphere of influence his deep will reserves afforded him in an attempt to, without moving a muscle, enact his will. Theoretically, this should be as easy as someone using their body to focus. Attaching techniques to hand movements was, by all logic, a crutch, a way to trick the mind into enacting will in the same way someone would decide to raise their hand or shrug their shoulders. He'd have to drop his crutch now if he wanted to live.

If he wanted to save Polk.

The werewiller lunged. With an instinctual impulse, a desperate wish, a thin, half-moon sheet of ice coalesced between himself and the beast, Seffin's focus strained with the effort. The creature stopped short of bisecting itself on the ice blade, the eerie silence disturbed only by some tremors in the ground from the hulking amalgamation's pounding steps. It swung the lance in its right hand and, again, with only a thought, another blade of ice burst forth to cut the attack. The werewiller stopped the swing, though its wrist clipped the ice. Thick, black blood oozed out of the wound.

Seffin never noticed how long throwing his arm up or motioning with his hands took until this moment. Wielding unassisted by movement may only save half a second, but that half-second had become the difference between life and death. It's what put him on even footing with the monster, but the trade-off was an immense strain on his focus. The werewiller threw its left arm out to shunt a rock in his direction. Seffin modified its trajectory with his will to target the werewiller who ducked under the projectile with inhuman speed.

He'd have to disarm it or kill it, and with its strikes coming so fast he didn't have a chance to go for the body. He was on the defensive. It struck out with the spear again. Seffin opted for an earth pillar, blasting out of the ground to stop the swing. The rock broke the werewiller's arm which hung limply at its side now, still clinging to the will-spear with a tight grip.

Then it did something unexpected.

Using its left hand, it raised the spear with its will and pointed it at Seffin's head. Humans would do this and throw as much will as they could into the weapon, rapidly extending the willed edge of a blade like a projectile, but animals shouldn't know how to do that. Especially dead ones. He had to dodge, but he was using all his focus on elementalism, and telling his body to move now felt like trying to reverse a ship's course in the middle of a storm. He couldn't. He was going to die here, and if he was going to die, he'd use his last moments to stop this thing.

With the telltale hiss of air elementalism, he made a wind blade and shunted it toward the werewiller. Upon its release, a rock the size of a small child smashed into his side. His body went flailing, bouncing on the ground like a stone skipping across water. The world turned into a blurred whirlwind of ground and sky and vegetation, the hanging, clinging vines of the jungle grabbed hold of him, stretching and fighting his velocity as he careened between the trees until, finally, he slammed into a trunk. His vision flashed white before everything turned to darkness.

When he opened his eyes, he was looking at the forest floor, suspended in the air a little ways off the ground by vines, coiled and stuck to his clothing and skin. Where they had caught hold of his skin it was fire, like someone pinched up his flesh and held him aloft by it. Blood, warm on his face and smelling of iron, streamed from his right ear, down his cheek, and dripped off the tip of his nose with a steady, rapid pace. Pearls of red shifted in and out of focus on their quest downward to join a wet spot of soil hungrily soaking in the moisture his body was all too happy to give up.

"Seffin!" came a muffled voice on his left. Ren's voice, unmistakably.

He made to open his mouth to respond and then realized he couldn't. To do that he'd need to produce sound and, no doubt from the rock that sent him bouncing and the tree that stopped him, he'd broken some of the parts that managed the task. Breathing hurt terribly; his throat felt... thick? And his jaw hung slack like a door hanging on by a single hinge. His meager attempt did produce a weak cough, however; the consequence of which was a resplendent cornucopia of pain. Stabbing in his chest, aching in his head, a resurgence of the burning and tearing where vine clung to skin, a needling and stinging sensation drilled deeper into his right temple with every passing moment, and a buzzing vibration down his left leg that made his muscles flex and seize. Tears streamed from his eyes, joining the blood dripping from his nose and falling to the soil which now seemed malevolent with how much of his moisture it eagerly stole.

The ground swelled upward. He couldn't tell whether he was being lowered or if the ground rose to meet him in the air, but the result was the same. The soft soil met his body and released the tension from the vines, his face pressed into the now-bloody dirt and, after a jolt of pain from all his broken bones shifting, there was a bit of relief. The vines released and fell around him, cut by something he couldn't see. The ground shifted again. With one eye swollen shut and pressed into the soil, Seffin watched with the other as Sori'o's worried expression came into view, followed shortly thereafter by Ren's, signs of panic clear in the crease by his eyes.

"I didn't know what else to do." Ren sounded far away, even though he stood right next to him. "You were about to die."

Sori'o put a hand on Seffin's back, and he felt his will bump into his own. He allowed the Nari'ko Wilder's will into his body. "You succeeded," he said solemnly. "You killed it."

Sori'o's will spread out from his hand like a wave of soothing, warm water leaving numbness in its wake. It passed over his ribs and the stabbing stopped, the burning tenderness of torn skin from the vines subsided, the bones in his legs ceased their buzzing, the needling in his ear disappeared, and when the relief reached his broken jaw, his vision clouded. The last thing he remembered was Ren's smiling, worry-stricken face before he faded to unconsciousness.

***

Of all the injuries, it took the longest to heal Seffin's ear. Growing new took far longer than fixing old, and few even knew how to perform that particular miracle. Outside of some healers living in Nari'ko, one person in Garvelle City, and one in Estaba no one else could besides Ka. To his surprise, the bones and muscles only took a day. As long as all the parts were there it didn't take much skill to make those right again, even a mystic healer could handle it. The muscles themselves needed some stretching and a bit of usage to get back to normal, but he could walk within forty-eight hours, and by three days, with help from Sori'o, he was back to normal save for his ear nub. A nub, Ka promised, that would look far more like an ear within the week, though it had been weeks already.

Presently, he lay in bed next to Ren who wouldn't stop fingering the nub. Pressing it down and then letting it spring back. Lightly flicking it like a dog playing with a new toy. He pinched the cartilage rather hard when Seffin finally sat up and turned on him. "Are you finished?"

A wide smile split Ren's face. "Oh, am I bothering you?"

"Am I bothering you?" Seffin said back in a mocking tone which left Ren chuckling in an aggravatingly infectious way. "I can't wait till your sister is done with it."

"Why? I like your nub." Ren reached for it again, but Seffin smacked his hand away.

"Stop it. Leave my nub alone." He tried to sound serious, but he couldn't. Truthfully, it was endearing.

"You ready for dinner with your mom?"

Seffin laid back down, grabbed a pillow, and covered his face with it. "Yes," he said definitively, but in a way that meant, *I'm not too terribly happy about it though.*

"Come on. I'm kind of excited to finally meet her."

"You already met her."

"I don't count the day we brought you back half-dead as meeting her."

"You told me you cried in each other's arms."

Ren sighed. "I would have cried in the arms of a stranger off the street at that point. Doesn't count."

Seffin blindly reached a hand out and landed on Ren's shoulder, then his cheek, and then the back of his head, where he'd intended to touch originally. He started massaging his scalp. "She's not going to be happy when we tell her the plan is to go back to Prolivgrad."

Seffin felt Ren's shrug shift the bedding. "That's your problem. Not mine." Then he hopped out of bed. "Come on, let's get going."

Groaning, he pulled the pillow off his face. "Fine." He rolled out of bed onto his feet. The room they'd been assigned was massive. It had its own washing tub, a vanity, and large windows looking out onto the sprawling city. He splashed water on his face, pulled on his clothes, and tamed his hair, careful to cover his ear nub.

Ren stood by the door, looking at him with impatience as he finished up. In the last few months, especially after the horde in Lighton, the bulk of their communication had evolved into simple gestures or facial expressions Seffin could now decipher. He could tell Ren's mood by the way he breathed now, which was nice. For most of Seffin's life, he struggled to understand people, to navigate the nonverbal dance everyone seemed so insistent in making a part of their conversations. He'd learned a few of the steps; a look down could mean someone was unsure, a wrinkled nose meant disgust, repeatedly looking away from the other speaker meant they wanted out of the interaction. Like Seffin, Polk had a hard time with these rules, but that actually made him easier to talk to. There was no risk of misinterpreting the young boy's statements, he never hid behind amiable framing when he spoke.

Every person has their own way of dancing. With time he had learned Ren's way—and Ka and Tender's too. Even when Ren stood by the door giving a look that practically screamed

'Why are you taking so long?' it put a smile on Seffin's face that they understood each other in a way he'd never understood any other person in his life, not even Kent knew him this well, and he'd practically raised him. Ren's impatience turned to confusion—an arched eyebrow and a slightly turned, slightly cocked head.

"What are you so pleased about?" Ren asked.

"Nothing," Seffin said, "let's go."

They met Carula at a tavern specializing in pork. The only request Ren had for the meal was that they find a place that served something besides fish. A request even Seffin could get behind at this point. His mother, always elegant, even in the sticky heat of Nakonipol, sat sipping an ale wearing a tightly fitted, purple blouse and practical slacks. Her dark brown hair, thick and soft, was back in a loose pony and her eyes looked thoughtfully into the middle distance. When they entered, her elegance evaporated. She stood and frantically waved at them, and as soon as they sat it was all questions. How was Nari'ko? How did you get past the horde? You went to Kelsig? The prince did what? How long are you going to be in Nakonipol?

Dinner arrived and slowed her tongue.

"We're waiting for the empress to arrive. She should be here in a week." Ren answered her last question before taking a bite of pork chop.

"Oh? How is it you have business with Empress Zollinger?"

This is the part he wasn't looking forward to. "Tender is going to request she hold off on attacking Prolivgrad while we sneak in."

Carula didn't react. Which surprised him. The mother he knew would have told him not to go, would have begged him to reconsider.

She finished chewing, swallowed, and set her hand on his. "Do be careful. Oji, Yufei, and I barely made it out of there alive." She sat back and sipped her ale. "You should check in with Troy when you get there. He was just reinstated as the Guild's president when I left. He's the one that signed off on my transfer here which, now that I think about it, didn't help our escape as much as I would have liked, but it was still a kind gesture."

Apparently, when Troy's mother died, he'd lost a hand in the scuffle and was thrown in The Pit for conspiring with her. Given what Seffin knew about their relationship, though, he was convinced there was more to that story. He thought back to the last time he saw Troy, in the café before their band left for Nari'ko. He'd acted weird that day, withholding.

"I'm sure we will," he said.

"An army couldn't keep Ka from checking in on him," Ren said. "She can hide it all she wants, but she's been worried about him since we learned there was a coup."

"I would have bet my good ear you'd try to stop me going back to Prolivgrad... and who's Yufei?" Seffin asked.

She gave a tight smile and flexed her jaw. "I..." Her fingers gripped the edge of the table, and her words came quickly. "I *don't* really want you going back, but I also don't want you to be angry with me for trying to keep you away and it's not like I could stop you anyway, and besides, you're not helpless. I mean you could do some real good and... oh" His mother touched her left cheek and shook her head. "Sorry. I haven't seen you in half a year and I don't know when I'll see you next and... I don't want to argue. Yes, I'm worried, but I'm trying to—"

"Mom," Seffin interjected, "it's ok." She'd clearly built up this meeting in her head more than she let on. He reached over to take her hand; the one gripping the side of the table. The gesture still made him uncomfortable, even after six months of separation, but he forced himself to do it. She was trying, so he would, too. "We'll be careful, I promise."

Her eyes glistened as she squeezed his hand.

Ren chuckled. "Careful? You? The one who pitched the idea of stealing the pylon in the first place? The one whose idea it was to light an entire Lodge building on fire?"

Seffin had left those parts of the stories out for a reason. Carula's eyes went wide before she regained her composure. "Anyway, Yufei is Oji's new apprentice, but she almost slit his throat when he tried to stop us leaving the city."

Ren choked on his sip of ale. "She almost killed her apprentice?"

"He was one of the gate guards. During the fight, he ended up in the back of our wagon, but after I tied him up, we talked, and I decided to spare him. Though Oji wanted to kill him then and there."

A thrill went down Seffin's back. It was hard to reconcile the woman sitting before him with the person who raised him. The same person who cowed to his father so readily. Hard to reconcile, but good to see. "Why *did* you spare him? That's risky."

"Maybe the apple doesn't fall far from the tree," Ren said with a smirk.

Carula used a cloth napkin to dab sweat from her neck, visibly ignoring Ren's comment. Her face turned serious. "I didn't want to become just like them. I've killed in the past and I'd do it again if needed, but it's not something I enjoy doing. He's just a boy, and not one that's particularly skilled at violence. Though he does have wielder-level reserves, and once Oji found out he was never formally trained, she took it as a personal affront, so she brought him on. The woman is a nightmare to work with, but if you can crack her shell, she's quite the bleeding heart."

Carula looked between Ren and Seffin and gave an expression he'd never seen her make before, an evil grin. She brought out the book of awful poetry he made her as a child.

"No..." he said with entirely too much desperation. Even if he could convince her to put it away, Ren would never let her now. But it wouldn't have mattered, his protestation only made her grin wider.

"What is that?" Ren asked with growing interest.

"I have read this entire thing, twice, since leaving Prolivgrad." Her tone made it sound like she'd rolled a boulder up a mountain as she waved the little book in front of her. "It was the sweetest thing you've ever done for me, and I *do* cherish it. But! I realized while reading through the *second* time that I've been denied the opportunity to perform one of my sacred, motherly duties."

"Please, don't." He couldn't help himself from begging, even knowing there was no way out of this.

"And that duty is to embarrass my wonderful, talented, intelligent son in front of his significant other. Prepare yourself, Ren. I have selected the piece that impacted me the most. I suspect you'll enjoy it as well."

She read aloud a poem of two husk falling in love, and Seffin's mortification had no comparison. For the few minutes it took her to read it, and for Ren to finish laughing at it, he wished the werewiller had succeeded in taking off his head. Surely, that would have been preferable.

"I can't believe you wrote them having sex," Ren said between gulping for air and uncontrollable fits. "And you *gave* it to your mother! How *old* were you?"

"Okay, alright." Seffin pushed his chair back. "I think we're done. Thank you for dinner, mother. Feel free to leave that book behind at our next one... or throw it into a fire."

"No, you have to bring it," Ren said. "We can do a reading at the end of every meal."

"Like a little dessert," she said, wickedly. "I quite like that idea."

Despite it all, Seffin had to laugh. This was fun. He'd actually *enjoyed* a meal with his mother. They said their goodbyes with promises to meet up as much as possible before he and the Bolins left for Prolivgrad.

It struck him that it would be hard to say goodbye to her when the time came, but she had her duties here now. According to her, the pylon network in Nakonipol was on the verge of collapsing before she and Oji had saved it. She was also the strongest mystic in the city now, with deeper reserves than any of the local mercs. There wasn't any possible way she could leave without putting the city at risk. Besides, she'd *escaped* The Glittering City. Seffin wasn't about to ask her to return.

On their way back to Semma Jen's they walked the beach with the evening sun blaring orange over the water. Sand and frothy waves tickled Seffin's toes. Sori'o, standing knee-deep in the waves with a serene look on his face, raised his hand in greeting and waded over to them.

"This place is wonderful," the Nari'ko Wilder said as he came in for an embrace.

Ren scoffed. "Too hot for me."

They all held hands as the water lapped at their feet. The grit from the sandy water entangled with the hair just above his ankles.

"I'm glad you told me your worries about sex," Sori'o said. "I didn't feel like you were ignoring me, but... you seem more relaxed than before."

Seffin frowned. "I think we just built it up in our heads. We didn't want to offend you, but we also didn't want to take that step, and then we felt like hypocrites for sleeping with Bjorn—"

Sori'o chuckled. "No one would blame you for sleeping with Bjorn. No one who saw what he looks like naked anyway. Besides, as you know now, sex isn't required for friendships in Nari'ko, and we don't view it as a slight if someone isn't eager to hop into bed. There's nothing to be worried about."

Ren cocked his head. "When did you see him naked?"

"This isn't my first time leaving the Wilds. I've been to Kelsig before. We're friends." The smirk on Sori'o's face told them everything they needed to know.

Ren started laughing, and then Seffin joined in. The awkwardness had been absurd and juvenile. Easily solved with honest conversation.

"You're off to Estaba after this?" Seffin asked. "If you like heat, that's the place to be."

"There's heat and then there's burning," Sori'o said. "But I've heard it's not so bad within Medahd."

"I'd love to see Medahd someday," Ren said while staring into the waves. "It's not exactly top of the list, though. The laws in Estaba are..."

"Brutal," Sori'o finished Ren's thought. "Luckily, we're not being sent to do anything illegal. Only to collect information. Rahal may have no love for the Lodge system, but he's quite accommodating to Nari'ko Wilders."

Ren and Seffin gave him a questioning look.

"We train their healers for them. That's why they have some of the best in the world." Sori'o took a deep breath and closed his eyes, basking in the sun.

Seffin squeezed his hand the way the Nari'ko liked. "Well, we'll miss your company."

He smiled wide but kept his eyes shut. "Just so," he said.

They all stood there while the sun set. Gulls squawked, waves crashed, and an evening wind blew off the ocean to cool them down. It was peaceful and perfect and fleeting and all the more precious for it.

***

"The strategy is sound, Tender." Empress Kiko Zollinger sat in front of a large, wooden table between Sim Larkin on her left and Knight Bahati on her right. A map of Prolivgrad sprawled before them beneath an assortment of tokens shaped to signify all the different nations' armies. "I can only wait so long, though. Lighton and Estaba have not indicated their allegiance, so we must assume they are taking the side of the

Nationals. I would march on Prolivgrad before Rahal and Mitchell can muster armies and march them to Egal."

"Isn't it a little presumptuous to assume they'd ally themselves with the Nationals against the empire?" Tender asked.

"Yes." Kiko's voice was flat. "It is, but we act on what we know, not on what we hope to be true. I can give you a three-week head start, but then my army marches. It's your job to make sure we know friend from foe when we get there."

"Or what?" Seffin said a little too aggressively to the leader of half the known world.

"Or, young Rashee, we assume any combatants are enemies. Brinidor Mountain and its mines are far too important to take any chances."

"I was hoping they were exaggerating when Tender told me what you'd do."

The empress gave a resolute look. "If you'll allow me to give you a bit of advice. Never doubt Tender's word, and never underestimate my convictions. The two of us will do what needs to be done. Always."

The meeting had only just begun, but Seffin already felt like it was over. Kiko seemed to have made up her mind on the matter the second she saw Tender. Now the only decision to make was who to bring to Prolivgrad. Obviously, Seffin and the Bolins would go, but Polk insisted on coming too. The empress didn't approve. Losing him would mean losing the best chance they had against the husk, or so she thought. Seffin knew better. There were other options he hadn't, and wouldn't, discuss with them. He preferred everyone to think Polk was irreplaceable. Even Polk.

"The boy should stay here, in Nakonipol. We can watch over him."

"I don't need to be watched over." Polk's small voice cut in just after Kiko's.

"No offense, child, but you're too important to make this decision on your own."

"No offense, Empress, but you don't get to make that decision for him." Seffin was mad. Why wasn't Tender backing him up? They were livid when choices were taken away from them, and here Kiko was trying to tell a member of their crew what to do.

Kiko chuckled in disbelief. "He is the key to—"

"His decision is his own, and that's final," Tender finally said. "If he wants to come with us to Prolivgrad, he is welcome."

"Not if I say—"

"But you won't say, Kiko. Didn't you just tell Seffin not to doubt my word? Take your own advice. Unless you're willing to kill us all—" Kiko's mouth dropped open in shock at the statement. "—he will remain under our protection, as it is both the request from The Caretaker and his own choice."

"The same caretaker that you say speaks with the planet?"

"They don't *speak* with Kohru. They commune with her," Polk said. "And if you doubt Shaia on that then I don't know why you believe them on me."

"That's a fair point." Kiko pursed her lips. "Fine. Do as you please. I'm not going to start this chapter in our history by killing a child's protectors, especially when my closest friend numbers among them, but I'm warning you all. Keep him safe at all costs."

"You don't need to worry about that," Seffin said, though the empress' casual mention of murdering them all made the hairs on the back of his neck stand on end.

Sim Larkin, the minister of Burgston, spoke, "The Nari'ko siblings will hop on a boat to head down the Kanning Strait, crossing by Nashow and then on to Estaba, where they will send word on what they find regarding Rahal and Mitchell's intentions for the war. Tender and their band will head to Prolivgrad ahead of the Garvellian army to assess the situation, and hopefully link up with any dissenters or resistance that still live there. In three weeks, Empress Zollinger will follow with her armies at which point she will attack Prolivgrad and wrest control of Brinidor Mountain from the Nationals. Did I miss anything?"

"No, you didn't." Kiko set her hand on his shoulder. "Tender, Sim. I've ordered some lavan and ale brought to us. Join me for a few drinks. The rest of you may go."

Ren, Polk, Ka, and Seffin filed out of the meeting room inside the minister's mansion and exited back out onto the sun-blasted cobblestone roads of Nakonipol. A man holding his daughter's hand walked past, both were overly tanned and wearing a colorful assortment of clothing. That's something

Seffin had noticed since coming to Nakonipol, the amount of color people wore reminded him of Prolivgrad. Especially after Nari'ko and Kelsig, where everyone seemed to wear nothing but brown leather and furs. Seffin looked down at Polk wearing his pale white shirt and pale white pants.

"You need different clothes," Seffin said. "Something red." Then he thought for a moment. "And how has your wielding practice been going."

It may have just been the juxtaposition of his usual white clothing, but Polk's face turned red as a beet. "I can do some kinetics."

Ka frowned. "I'm sorry to tattle on you Polk, but we should be honest. He categorically does *not* have a handle on kinetics. I asked him to pluck a palm off a tree and he turned it, and the three surrounding it, to splinters with the wave of his hand. We can do some practice on the way to Prolivgrad, but it's going to take a while. He has all your problems, Seffin, with none of the training."

Polk stared at the ground. "I wanted to learn, but Shaia didn't see the point." Then he looked up at all three of them. "But I'd like to help if I can."

Ren chuckled. "Well, if we need a wall taken down, we know who to talk to."

Sharon

Running the Resistance was awful.

Especially running it with so few people trained in espionage. Jacinda and Cal had plenty of merc recruits from the Lodge, which was nice—combatants were important for what they were doing—but they all whined about Sharon's underhanded tactics. Tactics that, they were all too quick to remind her, didn't match their skill set. They made more noise than lumbering colossi. Any missions requiring subtlety were in a failure state before she finished drawing up plans.

The Resistance's numbers were fewer, their experience less, and their organization chaotic compared to the Nationals. Running around and saving people from patrols was well and good, but it wouldn't win them the city. To do that they needed to instill some bravery into the people themselves, and to do that they'd need to have some big wins. Something symbolic.

Something like blowing up the *Egal Gazette*.

"You're asking us to kill innocent people." Don Rellins, one of the many merc band leaders recruited by Jacinda, had a rigid moral compass.

"I don't remember asking *you* to do anything, Don," Sharon sniped back. "You're not a mystic." She sat in a high-backed chair with red cushioning at the head of the table looking over a map of the tiered city. A hodgepodge of objects signifying important locations cast flickering shadows over the table. She looked on with one eye, the other covered by the red cloth draping down from the turban she wore.

"There are office workers and receptionists and janitors that work there," he continued, making clear his abundance of concern for the lives of everyone except his fellow Resistance members.

"Armies have cooks and janitors and office workers as well."

"But those people *choose* to join the army."

"These people *chose* to work at a propagandist rag that has, since it was founded, published nothing but conspiracy theories and attacked anybody who dared run against a Nationalist. Since the coup, they've continued to target and publish the names of labor party leaders, most of whom are now dead or rotting in The Pit. I won't lose a wink of sleep over them, and it sends a clear message to the Nationals. Work with the enemy, burn with the enemy."

Don turned his attention to Cal. "Is this who we are now? Blowing up news outlets."

Sharon stood from her seat. "Don't you *dare* call them news. Even the morons that read that drivel don't think of it as news, it's their marching orders. Nothing more. I'm not asking you to go after the *Prolivgrad Times* or—"

"That's because the others are on our side!"

"Stop. It." Sharon let some danger creep into her voice. "The other news outlets aren't *on our side*. Facts aren't *on our side.* They are simply facts, and if you've let the *Egal Gazette's* propaganda rot your brain so thoroughly you can't see that, then maybe you don't belong sitting with us at the big kids' table. There aren't two sides to this issue. There is only truth, and the truth is the *Egal Gazette* kills people."

Don's face twisted in disgust. His hand went to his chin, and his eyes fell to the table in thought. A long moment passed before he said, "This will make the other news outlets a target."

"That's their problem. If they want protection, they can join us. If not, they can burn."

"You can't be serious," he said.

"I'm actually with Sharon on this one," Jacinda said, finally. She'd saddled Sharon with masterminding their plans and thus far did fuck all to back her up. "We're not going to win by being nice. *The Gazette* is their voice. If we take that, they'll be left scrambling to get clear messaging out. And, while it doesn't bring me joy to say it, Sharon is right about the other agencies too. If they want to help us, we can work to protect them, but the repercussions of their neutrality are their problem. Not ours."

"Why aren't we going after the Guild? We know they're helping the Nationals," Don said.

"We do not." Sharon's voice lost its edge, but there was a tightness she couldn't stifle. "That is a far more complicated issue than you know. Leave it for now."

It wasn't just that she knew Troy hated working for Winnow—as guilty as she felt, she wouldn't let her impulse to make things right with him get in the way—but the Guild snatched up the bulk of the mystic academy graduates. Mystics she'd prefer to convert to her side. They also handled both pylon maintenance and the crystal trade which still kept people safe. Disrupting the Guild had further-reaching consequences than destroying *The Gazette*. Sharon pointed at Farah. "Your cell is being assigned to this. I'll brief you after the meeting, and don't worry, I'll tag along to make sure everything goes according to plan."

Farah was a tall woman with brown skin and wavy, dark brown hair which hung to her shoulders. Despite being a pretty miserable person, she smiled constantly; not that she could help it. Some prick had cursed her to smile forever despite her best efforts to the contrary. As if to prove how miserable she was, she rolled her eyes and let out a tired sigh, but she ranked as the most powerful wielder at the table, she had to know this was coming.

Sharon sat back in her seat and let the remainder of the meeting run without fuss. They'd taken her advice on creating cells and partitioning off intel, so only the people at this table knew the locations and members of the other cells. Safety and security processes had been bolstered as well. Gone were the days of Ahmad stupidly waving people into his hideout.

The meeting adjourned and everyone went back to their normal lives except for Farah and Sharon who spent a few hours going over the details of the attack. It would happen during the day to ensure editors and writing staff were present and also to make sure as many people witnessed it as possible. The message needed to be clear: signing up with The Nationals meant making yourself a target. When they finished, Farah left in a huff. Sharon's insistence they kill any survivors rankled her, but they compromised. They'd only kill the writing staff, editors, and management if they tried to escape. It wouldn't matter either way though, and Farah had known before she left. With Sharon's plan, the likelihood of anyone making it out the door was low. Very low.

Part of the reason she chose *The Egal Gazette* as her first target was because it would be the hardest on her, personally. Blowing it up wouldn't be difficult, but of all the targets she had in mind, it was the one that would take the greatest toll on her already broken and battered conscience. These were all non-combatants after all. Just a bunch of evil writers writing their evil little words. She told herself they deserved what was coming to them, which was true, but she knew it had little to do with what they *deserved*. *The Gazette* was foundational to the National Party, and that was the only thing that mattered.

She'd hoped she could be done with all this after Jessica. Her whole life had revolved around death. First it was The Eyes, then Gull Harbor, then her revenge, and now the Resistance. When would it be over? Were those precious few years in Gull Harbor, frantically trying to keep her hometown afloat, the closest to peace she'd ever know?

Sharon snuffed out the candles and left for home, to Noah, to the coziness and warmth of her lover. The streets of Prolivgrad were dead at night. There hadn't been a curfew for a while, but the citizens still kept a healthy fear of National patrols. Sharon knew how to keep out of sight, though, and so she snaked her way through smelly back alleys and leapt over walls to avoid patrol routes. The city's focus crystal infused structures gave off a pale, ethereal light at night, but without the din of patrons filtering in and out of taverns or the bustle of people milling about in the streets, the light was unsettling, eerie. Like it didn't matter how quietly she stepped or how cleverly she hid, the city always knew where she was, knew what she'd done. There was no shadow dark enough to escape it.

***

The Gazette was a bloody affair.

Against all odds, a head writer defenestrated himself, breaking his leg in the fall, only to die skewered with ice lances from Farah's cell. Richard Silks was his name. He'd written a piece questioning the necessity of leaving political prisoners alive, claiming they were a waste of resources when the country was already stretched so thin. The drastic increase in bodies coming from The Pit to be hung on the walls proved that words have power, and he'd abused his. *Good riddance.* The remainder of the staff, all of them down to the interns, died in the inferno.

Every other news outlet condemned the attack. Though most made sure to note *The Egal Gazette* was targeted due to its "unique affinity for Nationalist ideals". It was the closest thing to support they could give to the Resistance without drawing the ire of Winnow and the military.

Sharon was pleased, the results from the attack spoke for themselves. Burning it to the ground doubled recruitment. Before, people weren't aware there even *was* an organized re-sistance, but now they practically tripped over each other to sign up. That meant vetting and training new recruits, which would take time, but that was all well and good. Acquiring targets wasn't a fast process, hopefully she could find ones that didn't weigh on everyone's conscience so heavily.

A week passed after the attack, and the base in the warehouse district now bustled with activity when Sharon stepped in. Noah sat behind the bar serving drinks, chatting with Don. He'd wanted to help, and this was the best option for keeping him out of danger. Strong though he may be, he was a lover, not a fighter.

Most of her captains sat drinking and complaining good-naturedly about the influx of fresh recruits. Farah sat alone at the bar with a grin, an expression that, on her face, only meant she was mildly perturbed for the moment. For what reason, Sharon couldn't say, and she didn't stick around to find out. When she walked through the door of the back office, the hairs on her neck stood straight out. Nessa, the late Pulpin Rashee's bodyguard, stood in front of Jacinda and Cal with a brand-new will-blade on her hip. Upon seeing Sharon, the hulking woman's mouth dropped open and her face blanched.

So, no one told her I was one of the leaders.

"Good afternoon, Sharon. This is Nessa…" Cal trailed off when he saw the reaction on Sharon and Nessa's faces.

"I didn't know," Nessa said.

"How could you?" Sharon took a relaxed posture leaning up against the door frame to show she wasn't a threat. It pained her. She'd spent her whole life poised for an attack. To intentionally drop out of a readied posture felt like putting her head on a chopping block. Every instinct she had told her to reach for the blade on her hip, but that was an instinct for Flicker, and Flicker was dead. She was Sharon now, and Sharon knew Nessa only took the job with Pulpin for money and the only reason she'd be standing in this room, with these people, was if she'd gained the Resistance's trust. Nessa's eyes dropped to Sharon's will-blade; the one Nessa gave in exchange for her life. Sharon smiled. "I'll keep it if you don't mind."

"That thing's yours as far as I'm concerned."

"Is this flirting? What's happening." Jacinda wasn't amused.

"It's nothing to be concerned about." Sharon's eyes met Nessa's, they were so bloodshot she hardly noticed their color, a rusty brown. "Right?"

"Agreed."

"Good. I don't need the only two will-blade wielders in our ranks at each other's throats." Jacinda knocked on the table, drawing their attention. "So, if you're done with your little exchange, I'd like to talk about—"

Farah burst through the door, a strained smile on her lips. "Come. Quick. There's been an attack."

"Here?" Cal leapt out of his chair.

"No, just... come. Now!"

They followed into the now-empty common room, even Noah was gone. Up the stairs, through the warehouse, and out onto the street they found the captains of the rebellion all gathered together, looking out over the city. Some were crying. The rest looked ready for murder. The warehouse district was on the second highest tier of Prolivgrad which made it easy to see what happened. Six plumes of smoke billowed up into the sky. Sharon didn't need to cross-check their map.

Six of their safe houses had been destroyed.

Ren

The glittering walls of Prolivgrad rose before them, beyond which six plumes of smoke wafted into the sky, darkening the sun.

Poppy had ensured everyone they could talk the group's way into the city. They gave strict instructions to keep quiet and make sure whatever red they wore was clearly visible. Six guards stood at the entrance, splashes of red dotting their forms like angry blisters, two wore smug smiles while the rest were perfect examples of military stoicism, all duty.

Poppy strolled up, odd only for the fact that, due to their cursed leg, Ren had never seen them stroll anywhere before. They were masking the pain it caused them. If he looked closely, he could spot signs of strain, but only because he was so familiar with Poppy's normal, affable expression, these guards would never know the difference.

"Afternoon," the front one said, his stony gaze oscillating between members of their group. "State your name and business."

"Erond Wilkes. We're a Guild team out of Oleksandra's Harbor. Returning for resupply."

One of the smug ones on the end walked over to a wooden guard station and returned with a stack of papers he began to leaf through.

"Guild teams are usually two or three people. Why are there five of you?" The first guard asked.

"Additional envoys recalled for redeployment. Is there something happening in the city?" Poppy's eyes stared at the ground, only flicking up to meet the guard's while they spoke, projecting deference.

Since when were they such a good actor?

"Nothing you need to worry about. Just doing some pest control."

Smug Guard whispered into the other's ear.

"Erond. Welcome back to Prolivgrad. I'm sure Boris will be happy for your safe return."

Who's Boris?

"Just so," Poppy said.

Stoic guard's eyes widened. "Just so? You been spending time in Nari'ko?"

That was a blunder. 'Just so' was a Nari'ko Wilder tic.

"Actually, there was one staying in the harbor while we were there. He introduced me to the most amazing drink, lavan. Have you heard of it?"

"Ah, err, no."

"It's a floral wine infused with the petals of a flowering vine found only in—"

"That's quite alright." The guard stepped aside and motioned them through. "I'm an ale man myself. Not much interest in floral wines."

As soon as the guards were out of sight, Poppy groaned in pain and their limp came back more pronounced than before. Ka came over to ease it, but the curse made it impossible to treat so she could only do so much.

Polk's head swiveled around with his mouth agape. The tiered structure and twinkling buildings of Prolivgrad had caught his attention. "Everything is so big," he said.

"That's what I said when I saw Nari'ko." Ren moved to stand next to him and gave him a pat on the back. "We'll see how much you like it after a few weeks."

"None of us will be happy after a few weeks," Poppy said, the strain in their voice making the words sound ominous.

Finished with Poppy, Ka took a few steps away from the group. "Will you be ok? I want to see how Troy is doing."

Called it.

"We'll be fine." Poppy waved her off. "We've got two mystics, a pint-sized demolitionist, and I have enough grenades along to blow up half this district if I wanted to."

"Maybe don't say that so loudly," Ka said, smiling as she jogged off.

"Where to?" Seffin asked.

"I want to see what all that smoke is about. That guard's reaction made it sound rather sinister. After that, we'll stop home. I want to see what's left of the Lodge, too, but that can wait."

Poppy's limp drew attention. Prolivgrad always had plenty of mystic healers, and between Ka and a semi-frequent rotation of Nari'ko healers that passed through, even the more complex injuries didn't last long. It made them recognizable, especially to anyone familiar with Poppy's history. The few pedestrians ambling about kept their distance, even the guards. It was bizarre to see the city so abandoned. Prolivgrad had never been friendly, but it had always been busy and noisy. The place had turned into a red-speckled simulacrum of their home.

At least the smell was the same.

They strolled in the direction of the closest plume. More than a few storefront windows had been smashed open. Halfway there, a streak of blood trailed into the street, originating from the open door of a house. Polk's eyes lingered. Shadows inside made it difficult to see, but a cut in the door frame and a broken vase just over the threshold indicated a struggle.

I imagined a curfew and some people getting arrested, but this? How could the people let this happen?

A block away from the plume, the concentration of guards increased. Ren recognized the building, Blackbill's Brews, a tavern that had closed down when last he was here. With guards buzzing around the place like hornets protecting a nest, they didn't dare go any closer. Poppy pulled a pair of freshly made looking glasses out to peer down the road, then made a grunting noise and pocketed the tool.

"What is it?" Ren asked.

"It's what I expected. We should get moving. Lingering here is dangerous."

After climbing up two tiers, they began their twenty-minute walk west to their home. A pair of day-drunk guards stumbled by, noticed Poppy's limp, and said some insult about a lame dog. They ignored them and continued walking, though that didn't stop the heckling. The guards, a man and a woman, had changed direction to continue hurling insults. *Why won't they leave us alone?* Every other citizen in the area vanished, turning down an alley, side street, or, in the case of one young woman, doing a complete turn and speed walking away in the opposite direction. After three blocks of taunting, the guards finally slurred out a command.

"Stop!" the woman said.

They did.

The man walked up. "Hello, brother."

"Sibling," Poppy corrected.

"Shut up. You know what I meant." The man giggled like they were all old friends. Like Poppy was just giving them a hard time.

"Is there something we can do for you?" Ren asked, he'd had enough of these two for a lifetime.

The woman shifted to stand on the other side of the group, flanking them, and managed to string together a poorly worded inquiry, "Why in hells does they walk like that?"

"It's obviously an injury." Polk's tiny, sharp voice dripped with condescension. The woman cuffed him on the back of the head, and he fell to his knees.

"Be respectful."

"Don't touch him," Poppy said.

"What are you going to do about it, gimpy?"

What the hells is even happening? This level of cruelty was new, even for Prolivgrad. She shoved Poppy to the ground.

"You should say you're sorry." The man made it sound like he was just giving friendly advice.

The woman unsheathed her sword and held it to Poppy's neck. "Say you're sorry or I'll slit your throat."

"I'm sorry," Poppy said, though for all their acting earlier it was clear to everyone present they were in fact, not sorry.

"Hmm, not good enough," she said, the corner of her lip turned up in a smirk. Her boot made a scraping sound on the stone and the muscles in her shoulder flexed. She was about to shove the blade through Poppy's throat.

Before Ren could even think, the woman was in three pieces, a half-moon of ice swiped into existence through her extended arm and kept going through her stomach, separating the top half from the bottom. Her face was still smirking, but there was no light of life behind her eyes as her torso flopped forward onto the ground at the same time as her sword clattered onto the cobblestones, bouncing a few times before coming to rest a few feet away, her severed hand still gripping the hilt. The man turned and bolted almost before his partner's limb hit the ground. Ren pulled out his will-blade and hesitated. *Fuck. Fuck. Fuck.* He put some will into it and threw it, piercing the National through the back. His legs gave out and he crumpled.

Ren's heart raced. He'd just killed someone as they ran *away* from him. Reflexively. He'd been trying to run to *safety*. No longer an immediate threat—

Seffin puked.

"I didn't know what to do," Seffin said between the heaving. "She was going to kill you."

Poppy stood. "Your instincts were right. Both of you." Their eyes darted between all the different points of interest and lingered on the severed hand still gripping its sword. "But you'll forgive me if I'm surprised. I didn't think you two had it in you."

Polk looked down at the woman's face with interest. Like she was a dead animal he happened across. "We need to hide the bodies."

Ren always viewed Polk as a child. It was hard not to. He walked like a child, his voice sounded like a child, and his relentless curiosity was childlike, but this reaction shifted everything. He was not a child. Not in Ren's mind. Not any longer. A child doesn't look at dead bodies and immediately think to hide them. They also didn't offer themselves up on a sacrificial altar, nor did they possess the knowledge he did. Ren, Seffin, and Poppy all exchanged looks, unnerved. No one gave voice to the feeling, not even Seffin. Poppy agreed to help Polk hide the guards while Seffin and Ren busied themselves gathering water out of the air to wipe the blood and viscera from the street.

A vision of the guardsman's face contorting in fear before he turned to run flashed in Ren's mind. *He would have reported us. He saw our faces. I had to do it.* A thought occurred to him as Polk and Poppy rejoined them on the street. Murders happened in Prolivgrad all the time, and hiding a body was far less conspicuous than burning it. How many bodies rotted away in the cracks and seams of the Glittering City?

Polk grabbed Seffin's hand—*odd*—while Poppy squeezed Ren's shoulder and coaxed them all away from the scene. "Change of plan. We're going to a pub. I don't want to lead anyone back to our home on the off chance we were seen—though I doubt we were. Everyone ran away the second they saw trouble. But we could use a drink after that anyway." A few blocks went by in silence before they added, "You two did the right thing, as awful as it is. I want you to know that."

I had to do it. I had no choice.

"That's the part I hate," Seffin said. "I didn't even think about it. I just did it. I cut her down like she was a husk."

"I'm sorry, I didn't expect her to take things so far."

"Prolivgrad really is beautiful," Polk said, peering down on the city.

What in the hells is wrong with you?

Dusk was well on its way which was, admittedly, the best time of day to appreciate Prolivgrad's twinkling. Seffin put his hand on the boy's back and hurried him along; Polk's head swiveled back and forth between all the buildings as they walked. They found the tavern they were looking for around the next corner.

The Pickaxe was a miner hangout Poppy frequented when they wanted to be alone. The sign, depicting a poorly painted pickaxe embedded in a poorly painted vein of focus crystals, hung on chains, and swung back and forth with the breeze, a red cloth tied to it swayed beneath. Sounds of conversation burst through the door when they stepped through, and the group swam into the din, searching for an open booth or table that would allow them to talk privately. A few seconds into the endeavor, Ren spotted Don Rellins, Seffin's merc friend, sitting in a corner, a full ale in front of him which he stared at blankly.

They shuffled into the seats next to him. Annoyance flashed on his face followed by recognition, but his usual, inebriated charm was nowhere to be found. Instead, he gave a weak smile and offered a hello that sounded like 'lo.

"What's wrong?" Seffin asked.

Don's eyes scanned the room. Everybody wore red like it was a uniform, as did Don, but that might be a good sign in this situation. No one had a full outfit of the National's color, nor did anyone decorate their weapons or belongings with red like the guards did. Only the barest amount of the Nationals' required obedience.

He must have judged the crowd safe to speak around. "Where have you all been, and who's the kid?"

"This is Polk. We were on a contract to the Nari'ko Wilds," Seffin said.

"And you came back?"

"Obviously."

"I mean *why* did you come back?"

"Why were you crying?"

Don's cheeks flushed red, and his eyes fell to his drink which he then grabbed and drew several gulps from. "They're dead. All of them. Teepo, Jarrod, Knecka."

Those must have been the names of his bandmates.

"How?" Seffin asked. He'd reverted to his more tactless version of conversation, but either Don didn't notice or didn't care.

Don's voice dropped low. "You seen the smoke around the city?"

That said enough, and it was all the confirmation they needed to discern Don wasn't with the Nationals. If they'd murdered his friends, he wouldn't be working with them. It had been a pretty safe assumption from the beginning. They all knew the Nationals burned down the Lodge and Don was as committed to the Lodge as anyone could be.

Poppy whispered their next words, "We're here to help the resistance. If there is one."

Don nodded. "Jacinda and Cal are running it with the help of..."

His eyes met Seffin's, and he froze.

"With the help of who?" Poppy pressed.

"She... uhh." He clearly didn't want to say.

"With the help of who? Don." Seffin asked.

The words came out pained, like each was a rotten tooth he needed to pull out. "She's an assassin. The one that killed your father. Her name is Sharon Adegast."

No.

He was lying. He had to be. Ren's mother was dead. She died in Gull Harbor fighting the mutated werewiller amalgamation. She had to be dead. If she was alive, she would have come to get him. Whoever this person was they were an impostor. That must be it. An impostor trying to hide from... something. At the edge of his awareness, Ren heard yelling that sounded like Seffin.

Oh gods. 'The one that killed your father'. The impostor killed Pulpin and Kent.

"Sit down!" Poppy yelled. The entire tavern turned their attention to their table. Seffin sat obediently, though rage still twisted his face. The crowd restarted their chatter as if nothing happened, aggressively ignoring them, almost like they were trained to do so.

"You're sure of the name," Poppy asked.

"I'm sure. She goes by Sharon Adegast. She used to go by Flicker."

No!

"That's not true," Ren said. "That can't be..."

Poppy put one of their large hands on his shoulder. "We'll get to the bottom of this, but you have to keep it together." They squeezed hard, too hard. It was a warning. Ren shook his head. *No. There's no need to worry. Whoever this person is it isn't my mother.*

"Take me to her," Seffin said.

Poppy grabbed Seffin by the jacket and pulled him next to their face. "Seffin." Their tone was dangerous.

He glared daggers back up at them. "What?"

"Sharon. Adegast."

Seffin's head whipped around to Ren. "No," he said. "No, she's dead. You said she was dead."

"She is," Ren said honestly, though with less confidence than he'd like. Something wet dripped down his cheek. "It can't be her. She would have come for me, and she wouldn't have killed... she wouldn't have done that."

A long moment passed before Poppy gave Don a pointed look. "I'll want a meeting."

"I can arrange that, but not today."

"Not today is perfectly fine with me." They shifted their attention to Seffin and then to Ren who was drowning in thought, only coming up for air long enough to give Poppy a nod of understanding. They would meet with the Resistance to see if they could help, and then they would find out who this was that posed as his mother.

Polk watched them with that indiscernible expression he seemed to have stolen from Seffin. They drank in silence, a table filled with broken people trying to fix the world.

Troy

The weeks went by mostly without incident. Winnow left Troy alone, and amalgamation production accelerated steadily. The lack of progress on binding to someone with will reserves as shallow as the president's was unsurprising. The team had dumbed the science down to Troy's level and explained enough times that he had long since accepted its impossibility. They'd have to think outside the box, or run, or join the Resistance. A series of light knocks sounded through the room while he mulled the conundrum over at his dining table. This was uncommon. Other than Tia and Sumiko from time to time or the weekly check from Winnow's staff, no one visited. He approached his front entrance with caution. Another knock came, rapid and soft.

It can't be.

He cracked the door to peek out. A woman a foot shorter than him, with black hair and beige skin, peered back through the opening with her beautiful, dark brown eyes. He threw the door open and pulled Ka inside. He barely had a chance to shut the door before she grabbed him by the hair on the back of his head and tugged his face down to hers for a kiss. Her lips were soft, and her grip was strong as iron. Reaching to her lower back, he pulled her in close, lifting her off the ground with his hand. It always amazed him how strong she was while being so light. She wrapped her legs around his waist, and he used the front door to support her while they continued kissing with a desperation he'd been fooling himself into believing he didn't have. Tears fell down his cheeks. *Gods, what am I doing? She's finally here and I'm crying?*

Ka pulled away to meet his eyes, the slightest of frowns and a searching look on her face. Releasing his waist, she dropped to the ground and grabbed his chin between her forefinger and thumb, stubbly from lack of shaving. Her other hand gripped his left shoulder. *No, don't.* She let the hand slide down his bicep, past his elbow, and along his forearm where she gingerly cupped his wrapped limb. Ashamed for reasons he couldn't put into words, he tried to turn his head to look away, but she held his chin firm with only her finger and thumb. Forcing him to look her in the eyes.

"Who did this to you?" she asked.

He blinked his eyes closed and more tears fell.

"Who, Troy?"

"I think we should sit down."

They sat next to each other at the dining room table, two chairs pulled close so they could hold hands, he recounted everything that happened after coming back from Oleksandra's Harbor. Clem coming to him about a union member housing an assassin, meeting Sharon, moving her into his spare bedroom to heal, the plot to force some accountability on his mother, the betrayal, The Pit, and now his project as the Guild's president again. She took it in stride like he knew she would, but that didn't mean she wouldn't be mad. In fact, she had every right to be mad. Ren's mother, the same person who killed Seffin's father and friend, had been recuperating in his spare bedroom while everyone thought she was dead, and he'd said nothing. Ka let go of his hand, leaned back in her chair, and sighed.

"You can be so unbelievably stupid."

"I know."

"No, I don't think you do."

He felt his cheeks get hot.

"There is no reason to mull over running away or working on the project or joining the Resistance."

"What do you mean?"

"Winnow is giving you an army. Bind the amalgamations, join the Resistance, and use them to take him down."

"The science team has done enough. They shouldn't have to get wrapped up in this."

"That's not your decision to make. I know you're trying to protect them, but honestly, Troy. Part of the reason you had such a poor relationship with your mother was because she withheld information from you, and here you are doing the same thing to your team." She paused and a smirk slipped onto her face. "I should be slapping you silly for hiding Sharon without telling us."

"I thought I could—"

"What's done is done." She pulled his arm, the handless one, over to her and began unwrapping it. "I can probably replace this if you want, but it's going to take an uninterrupted year at least." She let the wrapping drop to the floor and the soft, pale limb sat resting in her palms, naked and exposed. Using both thumbs, she massaged the scar, he sucked in his teeth at a twinge of pain when one of her thumbs reached the internal side of his limb. "I was wondering about that. Mystic healers will do in a pinch, but they miss these little details more often than not. Hold still."

Her will bumped up against his own, and he let it flow in. A cooling sensation overtook the limb, concentrating on the part that hurt him, and then it was gone. Months of aching and she fixed it in a moment. She pressed in with her thumb a final time to confirm the pain had subsided.

"You should be able to wear a prosthetic if you want now. With enough control training, it could even work as well as a regular hand. With your permission, I can have Poppy make something when they get a chance, though that might take a while what with..." She gestured broadly. "...everything."

"I think I'll just leave it for now."

"Nonsense. I know this is hard, but you have the reserves, and everyone should know simple kinetics. Even people with the shallowest reserves would benefit from floating a glass or pushing shut a door."

"So, you're saying it comes in handy."

She snorted. "Oh ha ha. But honestly, even before this, I had planned on browbeating you into learning some control maneuvers."

He wanted to ask when he would get a chance, now of all times, to work on control exercises, but she stood before he got the chance. He knitted his brows. "What? Now?"

She scoffed. "No. Now, we have sex. Afterward, I'll teach you a control exercise that you will have mastered by the time I come back tomorrow evening. Then, I'm going home to tell my brother and his boyfriend that you lied to them."

"Maybe I should be the one to tell—"

"Ah, ah." Ka was already walking away, to the stairs leading up to the bedroom. "I didn't ask for your opinion. It's been over six months and I'm not waiting a second longer."

I do not deserve this woman.

***

Sumiko wasn't happy.

"Let me get this straight. You've *already* done a favor for the Resistance, they asked specifically to recruit us, and after a talk with your girlfriend, you finally deigned to let us know?"

"She's not my girlfriend."

"Of all the parts in my last statement that's the one you chose to respond to?"

"I didn't want to put you in danger."

"How unbelievably patronizing. Troy, half the team already works for the Resistance."

Half the team?

"That's not the danger I was talking about."

"Then what in Kohru's name *are* you talking about?"

It shouldn't surprise him that some of his team had joined. Winnow himself had shown up to the lab to abuse them. But how did they even know there *was* a resistance? If Noah hadn't visited, Troy wouldn't have known until *The Egal Gazette* burned. A ruthless move. Sharon's orders, no doubt.

None of them had a clue who Sharon truly was. That she alone was responsible for the situation they were all in. It's why he'd never said anything in the first place. If he brought the offer to the table, he'd feel responsible for warning them of the retired assassin and how she operated, but if he told anyone the whole truth, she'd kill him. His heart was in his throat and his mouth was dry as sand. There would be no going back if he did this, but he'd rather die before letting them walk blindly into the clutches of the former eye.

"Fine. We'll have a meeting. Call everyone together once Tia gets here. I'll tell them everything, and after they've heard what I have to say, we'll see if they want to commit themselves to the Resistance."

They gathered in the locker room adjacent to the lab's demonstration area. The reactions on their faces ranged from appalled to fearful, especially when he got to the part where Sharon murdered the former president. Tyler Chen, the youngest on the team, spoke first.

"So, if this gets out, she'll kill you?"

"That's what she implied, yes."

He looked around at his colleagues. "Then why did you tell us?"

"Because I know what she's really like, and if we're going to pledge our cooperation you should know how dangerous she is. I'd rather leave my life in your hands than leave your lives in hers."

Everyone looked stunned, even Sumiko. Even Tia. For a while, no one said anything, and Troy began to worry. Had he blundered? Did she have someone on his team waiting for him to slip up? Tia stood from the bench she sat on. Her eyes were glassy.

"I need to apologize."

He shook his head involuntarily. "For what?"

"For underestimating you."

A flurry of apologies was suddenly hurled at him from all sides. He hadn't understood the severity of their doubts in him. *Of course they don't have faith in me. I work directly under Winnow, and I'm forcing them to work on a project they repeatedly explained was impossible.*

"It's ok," he said. "I wouldn't have trusted me either, but that's not why I sat you all down. We need to figure out if we're going to work with the Resistance or not, and I, for one, think we should. With bound amalgamations on their side, it'll increase their chances, and it beats working on a dead-end project. We should vote."

"We don't need to vote," Cillian said, his blazing red hair easily setting him apart from the crowd.

"Like I said before, half of them already work for the Resistance. What I didn't say is that the other half were picking up the slack in order to let them," Sumiko said. "You'll find everyone here would rather kill Winnow than work for him."

"My mom's even helping out," Cillian said, a mix of pride and worry on his face.

Troy had almost hoped they'd disagree. Joining with the Resistance meant he'd have to sit down with Sharon sooner or later.

Just the thought of it made his skin crawl.

Ren

The meeting Don set up was in a warehouse on one of the upper tiers of Prolivgrad. Cal, sporting an eye patch now, stood just inside the entrance with a bored expression which quickly brightened upon seeing Poppy. The five of them—Polk, Ka, Poppy, Seffin, and Ren—peered at shelves piled high with Nationalist supplies and turned to each other with concern.

"Relax," Cal said, "it's safe. The warehouse is mine under a different name. As far as the Nationals are concerned, I'm a simple business owner."

He led them to a back office with a door behind a shelf which led down a carved-out stairwell and opened onto an empty bar. Ren's hands sweat and his finger itched something fierce. *It can't be her, but Ka said she confirmed it with Troy.* His sister had shown up late last night and spoke with Poppy alone for what seemed like hours before she came up to Seffin and Ren's room to deliver the news. Sharon Adegast, Ren's mother, was both alive and a commander in the Resistance. At the back of the common area, beyond a mess of dirty tables, was a hallway leading to the room where they were to meet. The thought made the walls close in on him and his breath stopped until a hand slipped into his own.

Seffin interlaced his fingers and gripped, giving a tight smile. This meeting would be fraught for both of them. In speaking with Ka, Seffin had agreed to hold off on confronting Ren's mom about Kent. He didn't trust he could control himself if the discussion went poorly, and saving the city came before his vendetta, no matter how justified.

Cal shepherded the group back, into the gentle curve of the hallway. It ended at a simple, wooden door which he pushed through without hesitation. Standing next to Jacinda, whose broadsword sat resting against the wall, stood someone Ren never thought he'd see again. A part of him worried he might not recognize her after eleven years, but no, even with half her face covered, the intense eye, the sharp cheekbone, skin only a couple shades darker than his own, the way her lips pursed together when she was thinking, how all her movements flowed one into another as if every single thing she did was thought through, intentional. It was unmistakably her.

But it also wasn't.

Behind the intensity in her eyes there was no warmth, and her movements, while mesmerizing to him in this moment, read as dangerous.

Was she always this way?

She peeled her eyes from the map laid out on the table in front of her and looked at him. "You're shorter than I expected," she said.

"Mom..." was all he could manage.

She turned her attention to Poppy. "Thank you for caring for him. It's a debt I can never repay."

Poppy's face scrunched up and they shook their head. "Ren is a gift. I won't hear talk of debts."

"Why didn't you come for me?"

Everyone turned to him. He was sure some of the looks they gave screamed *"Not right now, not here,"* but he didn't care. She'd left him for eleven years, and now she shows up out of nowhere after murdering Seffin's dad. He wanted answers, and he wasn't going to wait.

She stiffened. "I had hoped we could have that conversation later, but..." She waved everyone toward the door. "Would everyone mind if I spoke with my son a moment? We'll join you in the common room afterward."

Seffin gave his hand another quick squeeze and turned for the door. Everyone else followed except Ka, who paused to put her hand on his shoulder and whispered, "We'll be just outside if you need us."

Once they were gone, she removed her head covering to reveal the left side of her face. It was lumpy and scarred with splotches of white. A gentle smile that radiated on one side trembled and twisted on the other.

"You asked why I didn't come for you. This is why. It was too dangerous. I couldn't have done what I needed to if you were with me."

"That's not what I meant, and you know it."

A near-imperceptible flash of frustration twitched across the uninjured side of her face. Ren doubted anyone else would recognize the expression, but a son who made a hobby out of getting caught stealing had no trouble spotting the tiniest squint of her eyes and an ever-so-slight cock of her head. Oddly enough, it comforted him. It meant at least part of his memory was accurate. Nostalgia told him what would happen next, a play he knew by heart but hadn't seen in a long while. She would sigh, shake her head, meet his eyes, and launch into brutal honesty. Whether that meant laying out consequences for stealing buttons or whether that meant laying out the truth of where she'd been these last eleven years.

She sighed, shook her head, met his eyes, and like an actor reciting lines from a script, she said, "You were a liability. I'm sorry. To tell you the truth, if I could do it all again, I would change everything, but... I just couldn't. My whole life was destroyed."

"I wasn't. I was alive. In Prolivgrad. *Waiting* for you."

"I know, Ren. I can't say anything other than I'm sorry."

"You still haven't said what you were doing."

A scowl cracked her face and she stabbed at the table with her finger as she spoke, "I hunted down every single person that was responsible for what happened and killed them."

"Pulpin?"

"Pulpin was the one who recalled the Guild's team."

A sudden urge to run around the table and hug her bubbled up. He wanted to say it was fine, all was forgiven, she was here now and that's all that mattered, but he stopped himself. He had mourned this woman. The loss of her had shaped part of who he was, and to find she'd been alive this whole time? That she *chose* not to see him? It rewrote his childhood. It added terrible context to his memories. The mother he knew would have cut through anyone or anything to get to him, to be with him, but the person standing on the other side of the table, her eyes sizing him up, she'd spent her energy chasing revenge. A revenge that swallowed over a decade of time that belonged to him. Whoever this woman was now, it wasn't the person he remembered.

"What about Kent?"

"Who?"

"Their family butler."

"Oh. That was... unfortunate. He got in the way."

He couldn't respond to that. Silence stretched as they watched each other, studied one another.

She leaned on the edge of the table. "Don tells me you tried flickering?"

A spark caught kindling in his chest and rage coursed through his body, but he controlled it. All that manifested was a sigh, his disappointment clear. He'd hoped she'd offer some wild excuse that could help him understand, but no.

Nothing. If this creature, this uncaring, unfeeling monster of a woman wanted to change the topic because fessing up to her failings made her uncomfortable, he'd let her. She spent a decade avoiding this conversation. Who was he to insist upon it? Certainly no one important. Not to her anyway.

As best he could, he made his voice calm, unbothered. "It was an accident the first time. The second time I was desperate. Both times it felt like I was going to die."

"You're lucky you didn't. The depth of your reserves makes flickering quite dangerous, even with training. Your control must be impressive."

Trying to downplay her responsibility by complimenting his skills wouldn't work to distract him from the real question. "Why did you teach me a technique that could get me killed?"

"I didn't teach you the technique. I taught you the first form of the technique. It's an excellent control exercise by itself, but its purpose is to prime your body for flickering. For advanced practitioners, you don't even need the first form to fall into it, but for beginners, like you, it should be impossible to flicker at all. If you could explain what happened, I might be able to shed some light."

"All I can say is I put all of my effort into the form. As if my life depended on it."

It really did outside Nari'ko.

The corner of her mouth flexed the way it did when she was thinking, and the more he recognized these little tics the angrier he was for missing her so much. How could she leave him knowing how much he loved her?

"The first form is supposed to help you become aware of your will and its movement through and around your body. Maybe if you're focusing on power instead of control it could jump you into the flicker state? I'm not sure. Either way, with your will reserves, your control will need to be even higher to properly perform the technique. The good news is that if you can master it, you'll be strong. Far stronger than me. Can you wield without using your body to focus yet?"

"No."

"Have you tried?"

"Also no."

"Try."

Mastery, wielding without using bodily movement to focus, wasn't common. Technically, anyone could achieve it, from the most powerful mystic down to a lowly wielder, or even lower still. It was a measure of control and technique, not power. Its difficulty meant most masters were in their thirties or older, seasoned wielders who honed their skills for decades. Seffin had done it twice, but that had been more instinct than anything, and he couldn't reproduce it. Ren had only met one true master in his lifetime, and she was standing on the other side of the table.

A small, carved figurine of a horse sitting on the map hovered up and took position in the airspace between them. His mother hadn't moved a muscle. She did this all the time when he was a child, mostly with pens for writing to spare her hand from cramping. At the time, he thought it was mostly to show off.

"How?" he asked.

"For now, pretend you're using your fingers to focus your will, but don't actually move them. Just imagine you're moving them and use that thought to hang your focus on. Try your best to stay relaxed."

I am everything but relaxed right now.

He did as she said. Visualizing his fingers moving, he reached for the figurine with his will and bumped into it. She turned her head a few degrees and stepped to the side, watching the figurine at an angle. Probably worried he'd shunt it at her. Again, visualizing that he was using his hand to focus, he brought his will around the figurine. The amount of concentration required was beyond taxing. It was like keeping track of a single pin tumbling in a box of pins that someone was shaking. He realized he wasn't breathing and pulled air into his lungs, the figurine dropped.

Fuck.

"Good job."

"What do you mean? I dropped it."

"That was your first try and you held an object without moving your body at all. Even if it was for only a second while you held your breath. I was right. You do have excellent control," she said, and then added, "for a mystic anyway. We'll work on it." He almost mistook the smug look on her face for pride, but it was just the look of someone happy they'd been right about something.

"You're offering to train me?"

Her face scrunched up, offended. "Why wouldn't I?"

What a profoundly stupid question.

"We should get back to the group." Ren went to open the door, putting his hand on the knob.

"Wait." She used her mom voice. The one for when he was in trouble. His body betrayed him and froze on instinct. It made him furious. This woman didn't deserve that kind of respect. The kind that, through repetition, and care, and kindness, and love, obeyed without question. Not out of blind obedience, but out of trust. She shouldn't have that, but yet here he was, freezing because she said *wait.*

"What?" he said angrily, still looking at the door.

"Answer my question: Why wouldn't I?"

It might not have been the best timing, but gods he just didn't care anymore. "Eleven years," he said through gritted teeth. He spun around to face her. "Eleven. Godsdamned. Years. I thought you were dead. Not one letter. Not one sign. Not a visit. Nothing. Now, I find out you've not only been alive, but you've done it all so you could run around and fucking *murder* people without the *burden* of a child. I'm a *liability?* You'll have to forgive me for not immediately assuming you'd jump at the chance to spend time with me. You'll have to—are you crying? Are you godsdamned crying? Give me a break." Tears streamed down her face, but she didn't look away. "You don't *get* to cry over me. You don't *get* to act like you care now. Did you even spare a thought on how much this would hurt me? Did you take even a second to think about me at all?"

"I *did* care. I *do* care."

"Liar!" he screamed so loud it made his ears ring, so forceful it made his lungs burn.

She stared down at the map splayed out on the table, tears sprinkling along the edges of the surface. She elevated her voice to match his own, "Would you rather they all got away with it? Would you rather the snakes that killed Shorda and Kord and Connie go free?"

A reaction at last. He couldn't understand it, but he wanted to see her angry, to see her scream at him, to say something she would regret so he didn't have to care anymore, so he didn't have to think about her anymore.

"Yes!" he yelled back. "They're *gone*. They've *been* gone. There's no one to appreciate your revenge, Mom. Do you feel better? Was it godsdamned worth it?"

She sniffed and brought her eyes back up to meet his. "This isn't going how I expected."

"That makes two of us." He pulled the door open, walked out, and slammed it so hard the wood splintered.

The hallway curved into the gathering area. He stalked over to the bar and poured himself a drink, taking several gulps before finally acknowledging the presence of the many other people in the room. Jacinda and Cal kept their eyes on anything but him. Everyone else, his family, watched with varying degrees of concern, except Polk, who peered at him with awe like he was a volcano that just erupted in front of them. He took several more gulps and tried to will the alcohol to work faster, to dull the sharpness of his feelings. He downed his mug of ale and poured another while scratching his finger on the rough bar top.

"Whoa, there. You may want to slow down," Poppy said with a lighthearted tone. "I don't want to carry you back home."

They were walking on nails in order not to set him off. He appreciated it and complied. Not just because it was good advice, but because it felt like an act of rebellion against his mother. To obey Poppy over her. To love Poppy more than her. They'd earned it after all, not her.

As if summoned by his hateful thoughts, his mother, the assassin, strolled into the room with her head covering on. She stopped directly adjacent to him, leaned down to grab a mug from under the counter, and said in a low voice, "Training starts tomorrow morning at sunrise. Be here. Don't make me come find you." She poured her ale. "You need to be taught so you don't kill yourself. You will let me do at least that much." Three gulps later she addressed the room, "We shouldn't waste this meeting. Let's talk targets."

Poppy jumped right in, "I think we should talk targets after we discuss how best to win the public over. Burning down *The Gazette* wasn't a bad move, but now that you have the attention of the populace it would be best to gain their trust." Poppy sat across the bar and tapped Ren's mug. He relinquished it and they took a drink. "Winnow has been rationing lately, yes? We should feed people. If your food suppliers can manage it that is, and if they can't," they said and turned to Sharon, "then we have our next target. Winnow's stockpiles."

Sharon nodded. "Sure, striking back at the Nationals can wait, but we're exposed right now. We still don't know where they got the locations of our hideouts, nor do we know how they caused the explosions. They don't have the people for that. There are precious few elementalists left in Prolivgrad and the Resistance only has ten—erm..." She looked at Ka, Seffin, and, with obvious reluctance, Ren. "...thirteen of them on our side."

Gods, just how many people have died? Among its mystic population, Prolivgrad had the highest concentration of elementalists in the world barring Nari'ko and Karm. When he'd left there were hundreds of them.

Poppy grimaced. "I know what caused the explosions. Confirmed it yesterday before we even found Don. Unfortunately, as long as the Nationals control the mines, there's nothing we can do about it."

"What's that supposed to mean," Jacinda called over from a nearby table.

"I'll explain later, but we're better off focusing on finding whoever or whatever the leak in your system is. Beyond that,

I think the best course of action is to get our future army fed and motivated."

Ren's mom spoke through gritted teeth, "The system is solid. If there's a leak, it's a person. Either through ignorance, carelessness... or treachery."

Sharon

The dirt-packed training room they stood in had been made by Farah the day before. She'd whined over the short notice, but the woman whined over every task assigned to her. Besides, few wild elementalists could make a room of this size so quickly. There was Ka, but Sharon wasn't about to ask Ka to do anything so mundane. Her son's little band hated her, Ka in particular. She could tell, because she hadn't stopped staring daggers since she and Ren arrived for his training session this morning. They insisted her presence was only to provide healing in the event of an injury, but it was clearly to chaperone.

Do they think I'd harm my own son?

Ren stood several paces in front of her, pushing his boot into the packed dirt floor. *Is he nervous?* She'd have to train that out of him. It's fine to be afraid, it's not fine to show it, and it's certainly less fine to waste movement on it.

"Stop that," she tried to say it flatly, as an instruction.

Ren's gaze moved up to meet her own. With a grin she took as contempt, he said, "Then start teaching."

Oh? Not nervous then. Just boredom and a bad attitude.

She leveled her practice blade and fell into the starting position of the Adegast family's first form. He mirrored her perfectly. Slowly, she made a fluid step forward and dropped her stance low, a stable power position, but more importantly, it lined up the will pathways within her body to prime the flicker state. Mirroring her again, he stopped and held the position in the same way she did. His head cocked.

"You feel it?"

"It's strange," he said. "I didn't notice that before."

The awareness of one's own pathways felt like the entire body taking a breath. Refreshing, but unsettling if it's all a person is paying attention to. Pathways connect and break off as a matter of course when a person moves their body, but the first form brings everything into alignment and locks every path open until they move again. The flow of will becomes impossible to ignore.

"Sit here for a while and get used to the feeling. You'll want to move, but don't."

The room fell silent save for Ka over in the corner, the shush of paper on paper as she turned a page in her book.

"The next two forms are to get you into and out of the flicker state. They release your will from their pathways and then confine it again once you're done. The more will in your reservoir the more difficult the third form will be. Willed punches and kicks are a modification of these forms, releasing in specific areas and confining it again after the strike."

"What's the second form?" A bead of sweat dripped down the side of his face.

You won't be learning that for a while.

"Stand."

Sharon shifted to a standing position, but Ren didn't move.

"What's the second form?" he asked again.

"Stand up this instant."

Ren's lips pursed and flexed to the left side of his face. The same way they did as a child when he was concentrating hard on something. The same way they did when he shot a rock through a werewiller.

My brave, stupid boy.

"Stand up, now. Or I will knock you out of—"

His body shifted out of focus; he'd dropped into the flicker state. Sharon will-kicked her son hard enough that he slammed into the wall and dropped unconscious. Ka's book flew out of her hand and a rock shield burst into place around both herself and Ren. The placement of the rocks and the speed with which she brought them into place confirmed Sharon's suspicions, Ka could mop the floor with her.

"What the hells is wrong with you?"

"He was going to burn himself out. We don't have time to wait a month for him to recover again."

"So you *kicked him into a wall?*"

Sharon squeezed her eyes shut and massaged her temples. "A full body flicker also affects your mind. Without proper training, it's impossible to drop out of it until you go unconscious."

She pointed her practice sword at Ren. "He also deserved it for disobeying me."

"I don't care what he deserves." The rock shield fell to the ground. "Don't hurt him again."

"That's entirely based on *him*."

"It wasn't a request." Ka kneeled next to Ren and put her hands on his chest. "I can't believe this. Aren't you supposed to be his mother?"

He isn't making it easy.

"If I knew of another way to get him out of the flicker state I would use it, and with will reserves like his, he can't sit in it for long without serious injury. I'm impressed he discovered how to strongarm his way into it without training, but this method puts him at a disadvantage. He does it by burning his will as fast as possible. A few more seconds and we'd have been waiting a week for him to recover."

Ka shook her head as Ren groaned and came to. The disoriented expression on his face gave her a fluttering of guilt. *Be nicer, Sharon. Remember how to be a mother. You were good... well, you were ok at this once. Lead with understanding.*

Ren sat up, less dazed than she would have guessed. "You're a shit instructor."

"You're a shit student."

Godsdamnit.

"Ren," Ka said, her voice taking on a dangerous tone, "she may be a terrible teacher, but she's the only one you've got. There's no point in training with her if you're not going to listen, and if she's to be believed, your antics would've burned you out."

Ren snapped to attention and made a throaty noise that sounded like agreement. She should be thankful, but instead it frustrated her that Ka only had to get cross for the boy to listen.

"Thank you, Ka. Ren, if you—"

"And Sharon, if you lay a finger on him again, I'll make sure the left side of your body matches the right." Ka went to her corner and picked up her thrown book. "If you need him knocked out, I'd be glad to help." Ren's eyes widened. "Wild healers are quite skilled at knocking out their patients for pain control, and if he won't let me touch him—" A chair made of packed dirt burst from the wall. She sat down and opened her book. "—then we'll see how long he lasts without breathing."

She didn't ask how Ka would achieve that. Ren and Sharon locked eyes, a shared acknowledgment to do better at this whole training thing. At least while his demon of a sister was in the room.

"I'm... sorry," Sharon said, though she struggled with the words. "I should have explained better before we began. You *must* learn the third form before you learn the second. Or else you'll get stuck, and then... well now you know what we'll have to do."

She waited, expecting him to make his own apology. He only nodded, walked over, and picked up his sword. *I was hoping he'd have more of Cullen in him, but he's just me, through and through. A little asshole, just like I was.* Sharon leveled her practice blade and started from the finishing stance of the second form before flowing into the third, jolting with the final movement. It broke all the major will pathways in the body, forcing a person out of the flicker state. Ren mimicked the movements closely with Sharon making corrections as he attempted. He'd have to be perfect, close wasn't good enough. A half-hour passed on the one movement before he had it down well enough to practice on his own.

"You know what it should look like, now. We'll pick it up tomorrow."

He nodded and began to put his sword away. *Did he become mute?*

"We're not done," she said as gently as she could manage. "You may be a skilled mystic, but your swordplay and will-blade focus need a lot of work. Especially if you plan to use your will-blade *while* you flicker."

Morning turned into afternoon while they drilled, only breaking briefly for lunch. Even with the room's size, it became hot and muggy with their panting and sweating until Ka became annoyed and cooled the room down using some kinetics. Ren picked up the different techniques quickly. He'd be a prodigy by now if he'd focused solely on the blade. His Estaban duelist style was particularly polished, probably from practicing with Troy.

The thought brought a twinge of guilt. The Guild's president hadn't deserved what she did to him. Sure, he'd made dumb mistakes, mistakes that cost lives, but he was a wind-up toy crafted by his mother and set on a fixed course. If Jessica had only supported him instead of exploiting him—Sharon's gaze fell on Ren as he ran through the eight different parries of the Estaban style.

"Enough." She clapped her hands. "For tonight, forget drilling swordplay. I want you to drill the third Adegast form. *If* you have it perfect, I'll consider starting you on the second form tomorrow."

He smiled for the first time since coming into the room. Not a big smile, but it lightened something in her chest. Anyway, it was better than the stony face he'd had on since she'd booted him into a wall, which might have been a mistake. In fact, it probably was, but she wasn't about to admit that to herself right now.

Ka stood from the small, earthen chair she'd created and strolled toward the exit.

She's the only one in the city who can help. I need to at least ask.

"Ka, can I talk to you for—"

"Not that I would have anyway, but I promised Seffin I wouldn't help you with your scars." She didn't even look at her when she spoke, only disappeared through the earthen doorway.

They can't be serious. Surely, they all had to recognize the utility of helping her. She could do so much more for the Resistance if these scars were healed. Maybe Ren would see reason, he could help her convince Ka. She met him by the wall, setting his practice blade into its stand.

"Could you talk to—"

He laughed. Loudly. More of a guffaw, really. "Even if I wanted to help, neither of them would listen to me. And if I were you, I wouldn't broach the subject with Seffin. He'd rather see you dead than healed. Kent was the only real family he had, and you killed him for being *in the way*." Ren dusted his pants off and made for the doorway. "He's not going to forgive you. You wouldn't if you were in his shoes." His form disappeared into the darkness of the unlit stairwell.

It was true. In his shoes, she *wouldn't* forgive her. Forward momentum had been preserved at the cost of lives. The butler had bled out on the sacrificial altar of her revenge, piled right next to Clem and gods-only-knows how many victims from the laranee incident and the coup she unwittingly aided. No, that was a cop-out. She'd never done anything unwittingly. Maybe she hadn't known the speed with which it would all happen, but she knew Winnow would try to seize power. The cost was for others to pay, though, not her. And at the time, that's all she cared about.

Guilt is an empty emotion. Expunge it like the poison it is. For guilt brings doubt, and doubt is a paralyzing hand, dragging you to the pyre.

The Eyes' teachings sprang forward in her mind. Wise words for keeping an assassin alive, but she wasn't an assassin any longer. She abandoned those ways after her term had ended, after she met Cullen and lived a life. Brought life into the world. Nurtured life in her little town next to the sea.

If guilt is so fucking empty, why does it fill me to bursting?

Sharon willed her blunted practice blade to its stand and used kinetics to snuff the candles. Standing alone, in the middle of a room made of dirt, soundless and darker than black, she listened. She could almost hear Shorda's sailor mouth, a blonde hulk of a girl arguing with her mother as they walked up the dock of Gull Harbor for the first time. Could almost hear Connie's disappointed whining after she'd informed her that under no circumstance would she marry her father. Ren's wailing after she'd scolded him too harshly for almost killing himself with a rock. Cullen's panting breaths overtop her, his calloused hand on her cheek as he whispered, *'I love you'.*

She could almost hear it all, but for the screaming in her chest. A desperate wail from the broken woman inside her, pounding on her ribs and kicking at her spine, twisting her stomach into knots while she drowned in the blood of her victims.

Seffin

Seffin drilled elementalism with Farah in the private practice space underneath her home. Bored into the side of Brinidor, Farah and her wife, Selena, had constructed a massive, twinkling training facility, complete with an indoor outhouse—an "inhouse" Selena called it—which had a hole drilled so deep they told Seffin he'd die if he fell into it. He made a note to only use it if he absolutely had to.

Their home sat directly above a focus crystal vein. Before the coup, they smuggled bulk orders of crystals to communities that lost their Guild contracts. They were one of only two operations with focus crystals for sale outside of the Guild, and while the business kept them comfortable, they didn't make much in the way of profit. Their priority was saving lives, so they charged only a small fraction of what the Guild did. The practice room was a convenient side project facilitated by their earth elementalism mining efforts, used to help train young wielders in the wild elements, earth and wind.

"I thought you said you've done this before," Farah said, the annoyed tone in her voice failing to match the smiling mask she never seemed to drop.

"I have."

"Then why can't you lift something as small as a rock without using body movements?"

Seffin's anger flashed. "I already told you I don't know. I've only been able to do it twice."

"Right, only when you're in a real fight." Farah stood in the middle of a rock shield with her hands at her side. The only thing moving was her mouth, which did so relentlessly and provided precious little in the way of useful instruction. Both she and her wife were masters, and with Ren spending so much time with his momstrocity, Seffin wanted to see if he couldn't make progress toward mastery, to reproduce the miracle that saved him from the werewiller. So far, he hadn't made any headway, not even a little. "Well, I'm not going to fight you for real, so you're going to need better control before we can actually train how to wield without movement."

Seffin had been practicing control for hours almost every day for nigh on a year. He worked with the same little tools Ren did to achieve his superhuman proficiency, he made ever larger balls of fire to practice containing and feeding, and he followed the instructions in *The Parts of Air* to move and manipulate individual pieces in ever more complicated and taxing ways. Steadily, he improved, but apparently, that wasn't enough for the mean smiling lady. He let out a breath to calm himself. "Do you have any tips beyond 'visualize it'?"

"Unfortunately, no," Selena said, walking up to the pair. A tray hovered next to her with three steaming cups of tea. "Exerting will without using your body is completely mental, but a high level of control is necessary to even attempt it. The good news is you've done it before. Theoretically, you should be able to again."

"Theoretically," Farah emphasized, dropping her rock shield and walking over to grab a cup of tea. She took a sip before saying, "You said you're much better in a fight than you ever thought you would be. At least your instincts are good, even if you can't perform when your life isn't on the line."

That was the closest to a compliment she'd given the entire week. Normally, he'd stick to training with Ren, but he spent his days learning how to flicker from a murderer now. The hairs on Seffin's arm stood on end. She killed Kent. She catalyzed the coup. She let loose the laranee that almost killed her own son.

He wondered what kind of teacher she was, but Ren never talked about it. He always came home dead tired, ate, and then immediately started practicing again. It's not like Seffin *wanted* to discuss it, but... it's all Ren did. They barely spoke save for idle talk during supper, and then he was gone before Seffin awoke the next day.

"That's worth a shot. Seffin?" Selena's voice interrupted his thoughts.

"Yes?" He drained his teacup.

"Selena was saying that your instincts are what helped you wield without movement before. Try to recall those moments as we train." Farah walked away from them as she spoke, pieces of rock bursting from the ground and assembling themselves around her as she did.

Setting his teacup back onto Selena's floating tray he said, "I was just scared. Both times." He stepped over to the same spot he'd been training in all week, a small hole had formed from all his shuffling.

"Fear makes most people frantic, but for you, fear helps you focus. The laranee, the hoarwolves, the werewiller. These creatures would paralyze most people, but if your recounting is to be trusted, you behave like a battle-hardened veteran. Outside of life-or-death situations though, your control is a constant problem. Instead of trying to envision your body moving for the technique. Envision someone trying to kill you, or that you're back in the mouth of a hoarwolf."

A shiver went down Seffin's spine. These were some of the worst moments of his life. Almost losing Tender to a National patrol, almost dying to a werewiller.

Farah hovered a rock in front of him. For once, her smile came off genuine. "Pretend this rock is flying at you. Imagine it bursting out the back of your skull."

***

Seffin and Ren were home alone.

Ka had left to spend the night with Troy, and both Tender and Polk were working late at headquarters. It was Seffin's turn to make dinner, and he kept it simple. Seasoned vegetable mash with slices of cured beef, a modification of the fried vegetable balls he learned to love in Nari'ko. He didn't have the energy to make anything more complicated after Farah decided to lean into trauma as a training technique. Fortunately or unfortunately, it had worked. A chip in the rock was all his pain had gained him, but progress was progress.

Ren silently shoveled food into his mouth, only looking up to flash a polite smile. The same one he'd show to any stranger on the street. A smile that, Seffin had learned, conveyed as little as humanly possible. The red scarf he wore when he went out hung off the empty chair next to him. Seffin had plenty of red clothing from growing up a Rashee, but Ren's scarf is the only bit of red he kept. Always so particular about his appearance, he didn't like the way the color looked on him, so he took it off indoors.

They ate, both together and alone. Their week back in Prolivgrad had created a wedge between them. Seffin had had enough of the awkwardness, though. Today's training left him in emotional tatters, and he needed the old Ren. The one who pushed him to share his feelings. The one who forced him out into the sun when he needed it.

"How's flickering?" he started. He wanted to ask, '*How can you stomach working with a serial murderer?*' But that probably wouldn't have gone over well.

Ren swallowed his last bite of meat. "It's not, really. She won't let me enter the flicker state until I've got the third form down, and no matter what I do she keeps finding something wrong with my movements." He didn't ask about Seffin's own progress, only stood to clear the table.

"You've been spending six hours a day on one form?" Even from the dining area, Seffin could see him tense at the question. They'd been walking around these eggshells all week, and here he was stomping all over them.

"No," Ren said. "We spend most of the time on swordplay and will-blade control."

"Why? You can do that on your own." There had to be plenty of other sword masters he could learn from. The only thing special about his *mother* was flickering.

"Because according to Poppy she's the best sword master they've seen, and I'm not going to say no to—"

"You're supposed to be learning how to flicker."

"I *am* learning how to flicker, but there's only so much a person can practice one form. And flickering is honestly the least impressive thing she does. If you think my control is good you should see hers."

"I don't want to see hers. I don't want anything to do with her." Seffin shook his head, unable to comprehend why Ren would spend a minute longer with this woman than he needed to. "I thought you felt the same."

Ren stared intently at the floor. "I... do. I don't know what to say. I know she's done awful things, but I've never had a teacher that knows this much. There are so many little tricks to the will-blade I didn't know about."

If Sharon weren't his mom, he wouldn't be talking like this. "She killed Kent."

"I know."

"She killed the president."

"I know"

"We almost died because of her!"

"I know! But besides the empress, she's the first will-blade master I've ever met." Ren paused a moment, shifting his feet. "And she seems genuinely sorry."

Seffin fumed. "So, because she's sorry—"

Ren threw his hands up. "Gods, Seffin. What is it you want me to say? What are you fishing for? Do you think I *like* that she did all those things? Do you think it makes me happy? It's not my fault that she's my mom."

"That's just it. If she wasn't your mom—"

"But she *is* my mom. She didn't mean to let the laranee out. She didn't want Winnow to take over."

Seffin's face got hot. His ears buzzed and his eyes watered. "Oh, I see. So, if a stranger murders a bunch of people you boil their tongue out of their mouth and shove your sword through their neck, but if it's your *mommy* everything's forgiven. Who cares that she killed the most important person in my life for no reason? What if it was me in that house instead of Kent? Did you ever consider that? If I hadn't become a merc, that could have been my throat she slashed."

Ren's eyes went wide, and his gaze fell to the floor again. Seffin didn't know what he was thinking, he didn't read the cues. He was too angry to try.

"That's not fair," Ren said, finally. "You weren't there. Why should I consider the idea that you *might have* been?"

"If she were anyone else—"

"But she's not anyone else."

"As long as the murderer is your mom it's fine."

"Fuck you, Seffin. You have a mom!" Ren yelled. "Until a week ago, I thought mine was dead."

"And whose fault is that?" Seffin screamed back at him. "She left you!"

"Godsdamnit!" Ren stomped away before Seffin could say anything more, and then he was outside, the slam of the door echoing through the house.

Silence stretched and a too-familiar sensation of loss blossomed in his belly. He threw his remaining food away, cleaned his dish in the washbasin, tried to keep moving, tried to keep busy, tried to distract himself from his feelings. Ren had taught him that.

It didn't work.

He paced the home, pushing his palms into his eyes, and running his fingers through his hair like someone who'd gone mad. Why had he said all those things? Why had he brought up Sorca? He knew that was a soft spot for Ren. He could have stopped the argument, could have chosen not to yell, not to throw salt on a fresh wound. Sharon may be a monster, but it wasn't that simple. Seffin knew it wasn't that simple.

He stopped his pacing and leaned on an empty chair; the blood in his veins turned to ice as he looked down and saw red. Ren's scarf. He'd left it on the chair when he stormed out.

Ren

At some point during dinner, a thunderstorm rolled into Prolivgrad. Rain pelted the cobblestones in a torrent of splashes and drenched Ren mere moments after stalking out of the house. Seething, he wandered aimlessly, passing near the collapsed Lodge. Charred wood had started to rot and combined with the rain, an earthy, campfire smell permeated the area, masking the stench of the city.

Gazing over the wreckage, the placard for Mallory's, the pub inside the Lodge, swung on a single chain dangling from a blackened beam that extended out onto the street, water fell from it in a steady stream as it creaked, straining against its one remaining tether. *Seffin doesn't know what he's talking about. I don't like spending time with her.* Drawing his will-blade out he cut the chain and the placard clattered to the ground. Maybe it would make for a good keepsake.

It's just to learn flickering.

Still, he had spent the bulk of his time in the last week with his mother, remembering her tics and tells and figuring out the new ones she'd developed in their years apart. If he was honest, the last two days he'd actually been excited to see her. Eager to cross blades, hopeful for her approval. This morning, she taught him a fusion of Nashowan and Estaban styles, how to keep up to two other people on the defensive while pressing his target. He'd actually landed a hit on her with the technique. The laughter she'd erupted in was infectious, and he laughed too. Even Ka, babysitting the two of them, had quirked a smile.

"Hey, you!" A voice came from behind. Deep and authoritative.

Ren's heart raced. He touched his neck. No red scarf. *Godsdamnit.* He turned and a set of three Nationals stood twenty paces away, one held a small boy in place by his hair. He couldn't say why, but the child looked familiar somehow, his nose looked like it broke and mended wrong.

Ren's finger started itching.

The thought crossed his mind to run, but he didn't want to leave the boy to whatever fate the Nationals had in store for him. He could fight them, and he'd probably win. But after they saw his will-blade, they'd all engage, they couldn't continue restraining the boy, and who knows how that would end? The Nationals he'd met so far would slit the kid's throat before letting him go. He'd have to surrender. At least for now.

The two without a prisoner walked toward him. A blond-haired woman and a black-haired man. Even through the rain, he could see they looked at him with disgust. *How could I forget my scarf?* They each grabbed an arm and brought them behind his back.

"Where's your red?" the woman asked as she grabbed his will-blade off his hip.

It doesn't go with this jacket.

"I'm sorry, I forgot it," he said.

The other one laughed while tying his wrists. "So, you're stupid," he said, cinching the rope tight enough to dig into his skin. He called over to the one holding the boy, "The wall?"

"Wait a minute, you're going to kill me because I forgot to wear a stupid scarf?"

Ren's head exploded in pain. They'd bludgeoned him with something metal. "Don't speak," the woman said.

The man holding the boy called back, "No. Sal's first, to check with the captain. No more executions without his say-so. Someone strung up a senator's wife the other day on accident."

"Coruscare burn me," the woman said, "what happened to the ones that did it?"

"What the hells do you think?" the man said. He began walking down the street, dragging the boy with him as he went.

Ren almost lost his balance from the push the woman gave him. The rain came down in sheets as they walked. Sal's was a bar two tiers up, a hangout for the National Party even before the coup. There would be off-duty guards swarming the place along with whomever this captain was. He'd have to figure a way out of this before they made it there.

Few people were out in the rain, but the ones who were made themselves scarce at the sight of three National guards escorting prisoners. Ren's hands turned numb from the bindings. It stopped the annoying itch in his fingers, but he tested them all the same. All he achieved was tearing away a little of his skin, a stinging sensation at the edge of the numbness.

One tier up, the boy tried to slip out of the guard's hold. *Don't do that, you little idiot.* A hacking sound escaped his mouth when the guard kneed him in the stomach.

"Keep it up and I'll slit your throat," the man said.

Ren tried to focus while they walked. They'd spent the whole of the last week on flickering and swordplay, not wielding mastery, but maybe he could make an ice shard and use kinetics to cut the bindings. He concentrated like his mom had taught him, imagined his arms moving to focus, visualized the effects of his concentration...

Nope.

With the rain pounding down on him, the bindings straining his muscles, and the stress of the situation, he'd never clear his mind. He could try flickering, but his mother had said it could kill him without mastering the third form. They were planning to kill him anyway, though. At least he could save this kid before he burned himself out.

When Sal's came into view the boy started struggling in earnest. He kicked the National's shins and tugged against the man's grip on his hair. Light from the bar spilled down the street, turning the struggle into a shadow puppet play in front of them. This time, an elbow went into the kid's face and a knife flashed in the guard's hand, gleaming through the rain.

Now or never.

With his hands tied behind his back, Ren flowed into the first form as best as he could manage and put all his will into it, hoping it would be enough. Everything blurred as if behind frosted glass, and then refocused to encompass the area around him. The rain slowed so much it seemed to freeze in the air, but the now-familiar full-body burning sensation cloaked him in pain. The sound of showering rain disappeared, replaced by a slow, deep patter of drops hitting stone.

His bindings fell away with a slight tug. The woman and the black-haired man's heads collapsed as if he was punching through a pastry, the woman's left eye bulged and dislodged out of its socket. A beautiful green, even in the low light. He retrieved his blade, rushed to the final guard, and removed his head. Frantically, Ren completed the third form, finishing on the jerky movement he'd been taught.

The rain began to pour again, and the sound of four bodies thudding to the ground greeted him back into his normal state. He'd done it on the first try. It wasn't even that hard. *She's been lying to me. She knew I—*coughing sounds came from the ground. The boy lay next to the guard, his hands holding his neck, blood seeping out between his fingers and bubbling up in his mouth.

No no no no. No! Not again.

Ren dropped his blade, knelt beside the boy, and pressed his hands on his neck. The wound was too deep. Small, pleading hands reached out and grasped at his clothing. His eyes darted around confused, lost, and searching before they settled on Ren who held his fragile gaze. "It'll be ok. You'll be fine." He couldn't keep his voice from trembling. An exhale relaxed out and his breathing stopped. It was almost peaceful, like it was his own decision to fade away. To forgo a final struggle and exhale into whatever eternity had in store for him. Tendrils of blood flowed out from his body, through the rainwater, and washed down the street where it would continue down the mountain to eventually drain into one of the many lakes around Brinidor.

Ren stood, retrieved his will-blade from the dead National, and stalked toward Sal's. *She knew my form was good enough.* Cheers came from the bar; a celebration was happening. *If I had known, I could have saved him. He'd be safe at home. I'd be safe at home.* A man stepped outside. Bald, about Ren's height. He died never knowing he was in danger. *She will teach me the second form, and then I'll never speak to her again. And if she refuses...*

The warmth of the bar washed over him as he walked in, dripping water and blood in the entryway.

"Let's hear it for the new captain!" A woman wearing a red National uniform said. She held her ale aloft in the middle of a group that surrounded a man Ren knew. A man Seffin had introduced him to almost a year ago.

A man by the name of Don Rellins.

The absurdity of it all broke something inside him, and crazed laughter burst out of Ren's mouth. Everyone in the bar turned and glared, their hands reaching for their weapons. Don's eyes went wide.

"Ren," he said.

The laughing fit died almost as fast as it started. He gestured at his clothing, blood-soaked his sleeves and pants. "What's wrong? I'm wearing red."

"Ren," Don's tone was a warning. "Don't do anything stupid."

"Stupid? No. No, I've been making stupid decisions since I got here. Trusting all the wrong people. Hesitating when I shouldn't. But this? This isn't stupid. Reckless, I'll grant you, but not stupid. Tell me, how long have you been working for the Nationals? Did they actually kill your band, or was that just some really good acting when we saw you in the Pickaxe?"

Don's face twisted in anger. "Arrest him."

The four guards just in front of Ren fell over in one cut of his will-blade. The remaining twenty-or-so took a step back at the sight. *Back up all you want; it won't save you.* Their momentary hesitation passed, and a big man with a willed hammer rushed him along with two others. With quick slashes to keep pressure on all three, he took an opening and rushed the one with the hammer, pushing his blade through his torso. He extended the edge forward, skewering two unsuspecting

Nationals before he hopped backward and spun, whipping around him to bisect the other two that rushed him.

The bar stood still. Ren figured it might have something to do with watching nine of their friends die so quickly.

"What is it you want?" Don stood behind his guards.

Ren pointed to the bodies on the floor with his blade. "This. I want all of you dead."

A sharp pain lanced through his right shoulder, causing him to drop his will-blade. A woman, just outside his peripheral, had thrown a dagger while he was distracted. Don smiled, confidently stepping to the front of the crowd.

"Come with me quietly, and I'll make sure it's quick."

Ren smiled. "Stop, you're going to make me start laughing again."

Extending his left hand out, a torrent of fire burst forth, engulfing Don. He was sure the man screamed, but he didn't hear it, and he didn't wait for anyone else to get in a lucky shot. He dropped into the flicker state and started taking their lives.

Every. Single. One.

Sharon

"We should be attacking their hangouts, killing them in the street. Fear makes them desperate, and desperation leads to mistakes." Sharon paused to swallow her bite of potato before continuing to jab the air with her fork as she spoke, "Mistakes we can capitalize on."

Noah met her intensity with an affable smile. The man had no head for this type of planning, and besides, she'd scared him off from sharing his thoughts earlier. Calling him a dimwitted oaf with rocks for brains hadn't encouraged active participation in the conversation. *Maybe it was harsh, but what idiot suggests a meeting with Winnow? He'd have me filled with arrows before I even sat down.* The smile was good enough, though. She didn't need him to speak, just pretend to listen while she worked through her problems on her own.

"But no." She stabbed at a carrot. "No. They want to feed the hungry. They want to—"

"Sharon."

"—make sure people know we're friendly. We're *not* friendly. We're fighting for—"

"Sharon!"

"What?"

"There was a knock at the door."

In her ranting, she hadn't noticed. *Gods, I feel far too safe here.* A nod toward the bedroom sent Noah into hiding, the man couldn't fight to save his life. He cooked, he cleaned, and he smiled affably, but if his life needed saving, she'd be the one to do it. It was a reductive way to view him, and he'd proven far more capable than she gave him credit for in the past, but it felt comfortable to reduce him in her mind, to place him firmly below her. Snatching her will-blade from its resting place next to the door, she considered the fact she might be a bit of a bully. She locked that thought in a safe in the back of her mind, only to be opened *after* the fate of her country had been decided.

A knock sounded. The second one, apparently. She listened. Whoever they were, they were keeping very still. Other than the Resistance, the only people who had any reason to visit were Noah's working buddies, and that lot never stilled for a moment. They also wouldn't wait to knock a second time before yelling Noah's name for the whole building to hear.

Have they been trained or are they just weirdly stationary?

She'd gleaned as much info as she could out of listening, time to see who it would be. *Please just be someone from the Resistance.* She turned the knob and opened it. Every part of her that was an assassin said to run or attack, but she held back. Ren's boyfriend, Seffin, stood in front of her, dry as a bone despite the torrential downpour drowning the city outside.

Just one of the many things he could do that casually showed off the depth of his will reserves. Her body vibrated with fear. Of everyone, he had the most reasons to kill her, and the best chance of succeeding, even better than Ka. Reportedly, he could freeze an entire room in an instant, and with the rain pounding down outside, he wouldn't have to pull water from the air. He could just shatter the window and flood the room, turning her into an ice cube where she stood.

He gave her a look of suspicion and she returned the gesture. The moment stretched on too long, if he was going to attack, he would have done it by now.

"Can I help you?" she asked, a bit of irritation in her voice. If he wasn't here to kill her, then what the hells did he want?

In response, he leaned to the side and looked behind her. She stepped in his way and asked again, "*What* do you want?"

"Have you seen Ren?"

An odd question, but she couldn't sense animosity in his tone. The boy did always seem devoid of emotion in their limited interactions.

"No, why?"

"We fought. I thought he might come to you."

Boy, I am the absolute last person he would come to for support.

"Well, I haven't," she said. "Not since training today." That's when she spotted the scarf Seffin held. Ren's scarf. The only bit of red that idiot child carried with him, and he was out and about without it. Worry gripped her. "Have you checked at headquarters? Tender and that kid are there practically every night."

"Polk," he corrected.

"Sure, Polk. Tender and Polk. Have you checked with them?"

"Why aren't you teaching Ren flickering?" Again, he asked the question without emotion.

Sharon reeled at the conversational whiplash. What was he talking about? "I *am* teaching him how to flicker."

"He said you're spending most of the days on swordplay."

She was growing impatient. Her son was on the streets without any red on, a walking target, and his boyfriend wanted to know why she hadn't taught him the second form yet? *This is a conversational tactic. Say something to make the other person emotional and then assault them with seemingly unrelated questions. I'll flip the script.*

"Noah," she called into the apartment. "I'm going out for a bit." She grabbed her cloak from a nearby hook and stepped out the door.

"What? No," Seffin said. The disbelief was plain in his voice.

Ahh, some emotion. You do have feelings.

"Listen to me. You just told me my son is out on the streets, and you're holding the only bit of red he wears. Unless you plan to stop me, I'm coming with you to search."

Now who's on the back foot?

"I'm not going anywhere with a murderer." He was incredulous, which was fair. She had killed his father, but that had nothing to do with Ren. When they found her fool of a child and made sure he was safe, she would leave him alone. Until then, they were united in their cause, whether he liked it or not.

"You're right. I am a murderer. But we need to find Ren. I'm sorry about your father, but if you knew what I did—"

The punch came out of nowhere. Normally, she would have ducked out of the way, or dodged to the side, or caught it in the palm of her hand and squeezed until the bones broke. But it was so out of character, so opposite the boy's purported strengths. The split second of disbelief had been enough for it to connect, sending a shock of dull pain through her jaw. She hopped back, out of his reach.

"Ow," she said, rubbing her face where his fist connected. "What the hells?"

"I don't give a shit about my father, you prick. You killed Kent."

A shock went through her mind. That's a name she should know, but... "Who are you talking about?" Now she was the one standing there in disbelief.

Gods, I need to get better with names.

"Do you kill so often that you can't even remember them all?" *I mean... yes, actually.* "You cut his throat and left him to rot."

Shit, Ren even told me about him. An echo of regret overcame her. "That's right, the butler."

She easily dodged the second punch. A scrapper, the boy was not.

"He was more than a fucking butler!" he screamed at her.

Shit. A memory of the hulking man gazing at the family's portrait as he died came to her. Ok, now she understood.

"I'm sorry," she said. "I shouldn't have done that. If you want to kill me for it, you can take your shot later, after we find Ren."

"You're not coming with me." He stalked toward the stairwell, stomping his dissatisfaction into the floorboards. She followed.

Once outside, she found out how the boy kept dry. He diverted the rain around his body which had the unfortunate effect of drenching her with a torrent of water. She stepped clear of the deluge.

"We should check The Pickaxe first. It's on the way to headquarters," she half-shouted it to him. Hard to tell just how easily he could hear while he did whatever he did to keep the rain away from himself. He gave no sign he heard her but walked in the direction of The Pickaxe regardless.

As they walked, Sharon watched and listened for any signs of Nationals prowling around. Theoretically, they should be fine. She wore her red head wrap that covered her scars, and Seffin wore the expensive-looking red coat she'd always seen him in. But on a night with the streets mostly empty, under the cover of rain, it didn't take much imagination to picture some of the crueler Nationals using the opportunity to torment people.

Seffin didn't seem to share the worry, or at least he didn't slow down enough to exercise caution. That is, until they heard a muffled cry of pain echo out of a nearby alley.

Seffin turned to meet her eyes, the first he'd even acknowledged her presence since the apartment hallway. Sighing, she walked toward the alley with Seffin trailing behind. *Out here less than five minutes and we're already off-mission.* The thin light given off by the crystal-embedded building materials was enough to see it was Ahmad, pressed face-first up against a wall with a National twisting his arm. He let out another yelp of pain as the National made a jerky movement.

"Hey," she called over. Trying to get the attention on her instead of Ahmad. *Why the hells is he even out so late?* Setting a hand on the hilt of her will-blade, she continued, "Let him go and walk away." She hadn't decided if she would *let* him walk away yet, but whatever happened, it would go smoother with Ahmad freed.

The dummy pulled out a knife and put it to Ahmad's throat. "One step closer and I'll slit his throat!"

And here I was, thinking I might let you go.

He had fear in his eyes and desperation in his voice. A dangerous combination for a man with a hostage. Lucky for her, Ahmad moved quickly, grabbing the man's hand and twisting it. She wondered how he found himself pressed against the wall in the first place if he could move like that, but she was thankful for his sudden competence regardless. The knife clattered to the ground and he sprinted toward her. Drawing her will-blade out she threw some will into it and prepared to attack, but before she finished forming the edge on her blade, a cascade of shattering ice turned The National into a human pincushion. Spinning around, she saw Seffin with his hand in the air. The gesture was so casual, he'd turned the rain into a shower of ice needles with all the fanfare of someone sitting in class, waiting for the teacher to call on him.

Ahmad stopped next to Sharon. "Hassan didn't come home."

She looked up at the falling rain, sheets of glistening droplets glowing in the light of the city. Two people missing now.

They might have chosen a drier night to disappear.

"We're looking for Ren, have you seen him?" She gestured to the scarf in Seffin's hand. "He forgot his red."

"No, but I'll look out for him."

"No, you won't." Sharon got up close and used her mother voice. The one that both soothed and commanded. "You're heading directly home. It's dumb luck you're even alive right now. We'll look for Hassan. Do you have any idea where he might be?"

Ahmad shook his head. "After school, he'll sometimes grab some groceries." *Steal some groceries, you mean.* "Sometimes he stops by Patterson's Bakery."

Patterson's was near enough to the Pickaxe that they could take a small detour, though it would be closed by now. Maybe when the rain started the shop owners had let Hassan stay to wait it out. The Pattersons were a kindly, older couple with no love for Nationals. It was a good lead. She squeezed Ahmad's arm and gently shoved him in the direction of the lower tiers. Ahmad and Hassan had been forced to relocate to a tiny apartment in the slums after Blackbill's Brews was destroyed.

Back on the main road, feet splashing in puddles as they went, she and Seffin detoured to the Bakery. The rain stopped. It took a moment to realize it was Seffin, extending his dry zone overtop her. She intentionally kept her mouth shut. The protection from the rain was welcome and she didn't want to give him any reason to drop it.

"You saved him," he said after a few minutes.

She nodded and continued to scan the surroundings. "It's not the first time I've saved a member of that family. His brother was almost killed by a vegetable seller."

"Why?"

"He was stealing from him. I was stealing from him, too, but the boy got blamed for all of it."

Seffin shook his head. "No, why did you save him?"

The question was naïve, inspired by a black-and-white interpretation of morality. She couldn't judge him, though. The Eyes had a rigid code as well, and she'd followed that for a full decade of her life. To say nothing of the single-minded focus she kept to realize her revenge, the same single-minded focus that got his butler, his friend, killed.

"I don't kill people for the fun of it, you know."

"That's not what I asked."

They were up on the fourth tier now; ten more minutes and they'd come up on Patterson's. "When I kill, it's for a reason. Your father was the target, but your butler, Kent, wasn't exactly unassuming. I thought he might be another bodyguard, or at the least, he would give away my position. If he'd done that, it would have been me who died that day. Still, I shouldn't have done it. It was wrong."

"Is that your idea of an apology?"

"No. I already apologized to you about what I did, but if you would like another, I'll provide it." She monitored the rooflines of the buildings around them for the shadows of anyone who might be hiding up there. It was paranoia, but better to be more alert than less right now. "What I'm trying to say is that…" *What am I trying to say? That I'm not a bad person? That I'm not the monster he thinks I am? I'm both of those things.*

"It doesn't matter." He filled in the silence she'd left. "Just finish teaching Ren his flickering and leave us alone."

He shared Ren's complete disregard for how complex the technique was. Flickering is generally taught over months and takes years to master. It's not something to be compressed into a week. "We're going as fast as is safe. He's got far deeper reserves than the average flicker practitioner. Which means it's far easier for him to destroy his will pathways with the technique."

Seffin stopped and met her eyes. "What do you mean *destroy?*"

"I mean if he burns himself out enough then he'll never be able to wield again, or he'll die. It just depends on how much will he puts into the flicker state and how long he stays in it. The only reason I'm even attempting to train him is because his level of control for his age is incredible. Otherwise, it would be too dangerous, I'd just tell him to stick to your mystic bullshit. Throwing fireballs and freezing people. Honestly, I don't know why he even has a will-blade. People would kill to have the reserves he does."

Seffin started walking again. "I didn't realize it could kill him." Then he furrowed his brow and shook his head. "You really don't know why he uses a will-blade?"

The answer came to her immediately and she felt stupid. Obviously, it was because of her. Tender was an engineer and Ka's only weapons were her elementalism and her sharp tongue. The only person he'd have known to use a blade would be his mother. The one who abandoned him. She cut that line of thinking off before she let herself spiral.

Patterson's came up on the right. In lieu of answering Seffin's question, she pointed to the shop. "There. And the Pickaxe is up one level and around the corner."

The lights in the bakery were snuffed out and the door locked. The business was closed like she thought it would be. She knocked on the door loud enough to hopefully stir the Pattersons from their upstairs apartment. There was shuffling on the second level of the building in response. While the minutes passed as they waited, she considered her failures as a mother, quietly wallowing while her son's impassive boyfriend stared blankly into the bakery. The click of the lock startled them both, and Mrs. Patterson, Emma, peeked through the crack in the door with a worried look.

"Sharon?"

"Have you seen Hassan?" Sharon asked, no time for hellos and how-are-yous.

"He was here earlier when the rain started. We let him stick around to see if the storm would pass. Offered to let him stay the night when we realized it wouldn't, but he refused. Dom tried to block his way, but the boy slipped out the back." Her face dropped into a frown. "Did he not make it home?"

"We're not sure what happened, but thanks. We'll keep looking."

"I do hope he's ok."

They left her to her worried muttering and started toward The Pickaxe.

"What about Hassan?" Seffin asked.

"I'm sure he ran toward his home in the slums. He may already be there, but the Pickaxe is just around the corner anyway. We'll stop there, check for Ren, check in with Tender at headquarters, then circle back and follow the path Hassan would have taken. I'm not giving up looking, but we should be efficient."

The Pickaxe turned out to be a dead end. Inside were only blind drunk miners using the rain as an excuse to guzzle ale late into the night. The bartender, a man who flirted with every person who walked through the door, explained he would have remembered an atypically well-built, six-foot man with a will-blade on his hip. Seffin was back out the door before she could thank the bartender for his information. She walked outside to see him waiting for her in the street, impatience plain on his face.

At least he waited.

"I'm worried about Ahmad's brother," he said.

"I'm worried about my son," she said.

"Ren..." Seffin's gaze fell to the cobblestones at his feet.

"Can take care of himself," she finished his thought for him. That fact had clearly bothered him since they learned Hassan was missing. He met her eyes and they stared at each other; an understanding passed between them. The boy was right. Hassan was defenseless, Ren could handle a few guards if it came down to that. Maybe it would create problems, maybe he would blunder and create an incident that spiraled out of control, but he'd come out of any fight with a National alive. The last week had taught her that. "You're right," she relented.

"The fastest route to the slums from Patterson's Bakery would lead him right past Sal's," Seffin said.

She hadn't considered that, but Hassan was smart for his age. He should know not to walk past a National hangout, even if he *was* in a hurry, but they should still check. Going near the National hangout now, with Seffin, would be risky. Gathered together, the guards became bold and cruel, and even loyal Nationalist citizens could find themselves in The Pit or on the wall. Besides, they'd already killed one tonight. If they were forced to drop more bodies, it would undercut the efforts of Jacinda, Cal, and Tender. The Resistance was trying to have a welcoming image, and a string of murders didn't exactly support that effort.

"We can check Sal's, but we can't be conspicuous." She gestured at the dry zone Seffin kept around them. He nodded and they set off in the direction of the most dangerous place in the city.

Seffin kept glancing at her as they walked. Five minutes into their fifteen-minute trek to Sal's he finally spoke, "Why did you leave Ren for all those years?"

Sharon struggled not to explain in blunt terms just how much the answer to that question was none of his business. Instead, she took a breath. Ren had danced around the issue since he started training, wanting to press her on why revenge was more important than being a parent. The truth was that she didn't know.

"I've always been that way." She thought about her years working for The Eyes. The horrible things she did to people. "Something inside of me can't let things go. I tried to change when he was little. It almost worked, but after I killed the werewiller and saw everyone, my entire village, all the people I grew up with, dead." She looked at Seffin. The young man with his black-and-white view of the world. "They had to pay."

Sal's was just around the corner. Seffin dropped their rain protection.

The worst-case scenario was exactly what they found. Dead bodies in the street, illuminated by the light of the bar. Sharon went on high alert. An ice lance careened toward Seffin's head, and she dropped into the flicker state to cut it out of the air, the world blurred and the rain slowed to a trickle in her perception. The shadow of a mystic, red-garbed and already prepping a second lance, stood in the alleyway next to Sal's. Rushing forward, she thrust her blade through his chest and fell out of flickering. The man's own weight pulled him off her blade and he fell dead to the ground. When she turned back around, Seffin stood in the middle of the road, stunned.

"You saved me," he said.

Behind Seffin, splayed on the ground like a rag doll, lay Hassan next to three other Nationals. Another child lost to the chaos she'd caused. She walked up to the body and kneeled. Raindrops splashed in his open eyes, so she closed them. She picked him up and cradled him.

"Gods, what happened?" Seffin asked. But he wasn't talking about Hassan, dead in her arms. She followed his gaze to the windows peering into Sal's. It was a massacre. Bodies strewn everywhere, holes punched through chests, heads broken or laying haphazardly on the bar counter or the floor, one woman was pinned to the wall, her hands still gripping the sword that held her there. The scene wasn't completely unfamiliar to Sharon. She'd been the tornado that swept through places like this before, leaving nothing but bodies and questions. Before she could tell Seffin they needed to leave, he walked inside.

Stepping over the gore, he rolled over the only body wearing plate armor. It was Don Rellins, charred to a crisp.

Troy

"This is terrible news." Ka sat with her head in her hands on the edge of the bed.

Troy sat up against his headboard while lightning flashes from the storm illuminated her back. Rain slammed against the window, echoing around the room.

"If Lighton and Estaba take Winnow's side... this will get even bloodier than we thought," she said.

"Nashow is allying itself with Garvelle at least." Troy glanced over at the letter he'd received from King Edward, the ship emblem pressed into wax broke in two from opening it in haste. "The others may stay neutral." Even as he said it, he didn't believe it. "No, that's not true. Bruhier Rahal won't pass up an opportunity to inflict pain on Garvelle. He's had it out for the empress even before he became the prime minister of Estaba. And with Estaba providing the bulk of their security, Lighton will do whatever Estaba tells them to, they don't have much choice."

Another flash highlighted Ka's frame. She stood to dress, and he did the same. *This isn't even the worst news I had to give.*

He pulled up his pants and buckled them with a bit of kinetics, he'd been practicing. His shirt lay on the floor, thrown there on their way to the bed. He decided to skip it, despite the rain, the night was warm. Ka slipped her cream-colored button-up over her head instead of taking the time to undo and redo all the buttons, then turned to him with a frown, and said, "There's something else, isn't there?"

How does she always know?

"Y-Yes," he said. "A member of my team lives close to the entrance to the master pylon facility. She saw a bunch of Nationals carting in crystal dust."

Prolivgrad's master pylon was nestled in a cave on the third tier of the city. Smaller pylons encircled it, harmonizing and charging the master to project the world's largest barrier that protected Prolivgrad from the husk. Guild engineers were the only ones allowed inside, but with Winnow taking over, he could grant access to anyone he wanted.

"Please tell me you think it's for some reason *other* than holding the city hostage?"

It could be Winnow had some project with the dust that Troy wasn't privy to. Unlikely, but possible. Regardless, they should make their plans with the assumption Winnow would take the city down with him if it came to that. "I can't think of another reason."

"I have to tell Poppy," Ka said. She walked out of the room.

"What? Right now?" Troy padded after her. "It's storming. Can't it wait till morning?" She was halfway down the stairs already.

"It can't wait. They'll want to know right away," she called up the stairs at him.

His stomach turned as he stopped on the landing of the stairs. Giving Winnow the recipe for Tender's explosives had already proved a grave miscalculation. Over thirty resistance members were dead, all because of him. And now they had to worry about the pylon blowing up? *How many stupid mistakes can one person make?*

"Let me help," he said. He finished descending the stairs and turned to see Ka putting on her boots. "I caused this."

"That's not a good idea." She finished tying up one boot and started on the other. "You need to appear as if you're working on Winnow's stupid project, and you need to make sure the amalgamations are ready for binding to our mystics."

He walked over to her and knelt, trying to meet her eyes. "Ok, but why tonight? Surely you don't mean to make a move on it right now."

She shrugged her shoulders. "That's for Poppy to decide. I don't make the plans. I don't like to, and I'm not good at it."

That couldn't be further from the truth. Ka never sat idle while other people made decisions for her. That's something he did. It was part of what he liked about their relationship. He was the oaf, and she was the brains that pointed him in the right direction and gave him a shove. A spark of understanding about how unfair that arrangement might be caught flame in his mind. It didn't have long to burn before she started walking toward the door.

"Wait," he said.

She spun around, an impatient look on her face. "What is it?"

"I'm sorry."

She shook her head. "Ok? I don't know what for, but I don't have time for this." She pulled the door open. "Gods! Ren!"

Standing in the doorway, drenched, stood her younger brother. The proud posture the boy always kept was nowhere to be seen. Instead, he hunched over, gripping his shoulder and barely meeting Ka's eyes.

"I need help," he said, removing his hand from his shoulder to reveal a seeping wound.

Ka pulled him inside. In the light of the foyer, it was clear he wasn't just rain-soaked, but blood-soaked as well. Where there weren't crimson splashes on his tunic a pink tinge permeated the rest of his clothing. His sister picked a bone chip out of his hair like it was a crumb and dropped it on the floor.

"What in the name of Kohru happened?" Ka asked, her tone was accusatory, though her hand was already on the wound, knitting it back together.

He stared at the ground. "The Nationals."

Troy snapped his mouth shut upon realizing it was hanging open. *Do something. Be helpful.* The scene made him uneasy. A privileged upbringing followed by college and a cushy position as the Guild's president hadn't prepared him for all the violence of the last year. He didn't know how to react to it. How to be useful.

"Would you like—" *Don't, you idiot.* "—some tea?"

Tea calmed people. Ren was drenched, stressed, and definitely had some news to give. All the markers for the gesture of hospitality were present. In the stress of the moment his brain reached for the familiar, the polite. He felt his face get hot even before they both looked at him with dumbfounded expressions.

"Maybe some towels first," Ka said. "And yes, actually. Tea would be nice." Then she gave a small smile.

The smile was exclusively for his benefit, he knew. *Stupid. Stupid. Stupid.* He rushed off to find something to dry Ren off, and in a moment of clarity, he grabbed some of his old clothes from when he was younger and much less muscle-bound. While he hurried around the house he worried. Had Ren been followed? Did he have other injuries? Was it just a patrol?

Troy set the towels and his old clothes on the foyer bench for Ren to change into. In the kitchen, he added a bit of tinder and a fresh log to the stove before putting on the tea kettle. Then grabbed some rum and set it on the dining room table. *I'm sure someone will want some.* He eyed the bottle for a moment, then uncorked it, took a drink, and sat down. Things were moving too fast.

Ka came in and sat next to him, followed shortly by Ren wearing the dry clothes he'd laid out. An explanation followed in which the tea was forgotten. The bottle of rum drained in increments as they spoke and emptied completely when Ren got to the part where he killed Don and an entire bar filled with Nationals.

Ka massaged her temples. "This is going to have consequences for everyone in the city."

Troy didn't know much about mystics and wielding, but in speaking with Ka, he'd learned flickering ran the risk of injury. "Did you burn yourself out?" he asked.

Ren watched the floor intently. "It's not as bad as before. I can still make an edge on my will-blade, but I can't do any elementalism."

"Gods, Ren," Ka said. "I don't know whether to be mad at your recklessness, disappointed in your foolishness, happy you're alive, or thankful we discovered who the leak was."

"Can we stick with happy I'm alive, please?" He stood with visible effort. "I need to get home. Seffin'll be worried."

"I'll stop home before I go to headquarters. You're staying here. The Nationals will be on high alert looking for you by now." She examined him up and down. "Besides, you're exhausted."

Ka didn't wait for an argument. She stood, kissed Troy on the lips and Ren on the forehead, then strode toward the door. "Stay here until someone comes and tells you different." Then she was gone, out into the rainy night.

"How is she always so level-headed?" Troy asked.

Ren gave him a frown. "She's not. She's just good at acting like she is."

What's the difference?

Troy gripped Ren's shoulder and nodded toward the hallway. The spare bedroom, Sharon's room, hadn't been used since... since the betrayal. The maid had cleaned it, but other than removing dried bandages and changing the linens it hadn't been touched.

Ren hesitated before saying, "Is this..."

"Your mother lived in this room while she recovered, yes." Troy said, "I... don't have any other beds."

Ren scanned the room, his eyes seemed to stop and consider every object, what few were there. The room had always been rather bare. The whole house was rather bare, come to think of it. Ka's brother stared at the bed.

Troy saw the reticence in Ren's face. "We could double up in mine, I guess?" He couldn't keep his tone from revealing how uncomfortable that may be. It was a large bed, but he was a large man, after all, and Ren wasn't exactly small either.

"Well, goodnight," Ren said, walking into the room a few paces and standing, silhouetted by the light pushing in from the hallway.

That decided that, then.

Troy nodded, "'Night."

He couldn't fathom what the boy was going through. Didn't want to fathom it. Enough was on his plate already; keeping Winnow from breathing down their necks, trying to amalgamate enough colossi to arm the wielders in the Resistance.

Once he was back in his bedroom, he unwrapped his limb. It was always nice to have it open to air. He massaged the muscles in his forearm, they didn't ache like they used to, but it still felt good to rub it. To touch the skin he hid and ignored throughout the day.

As he lay down to sleep, his mind raced. Everything would be different tomorrow.

***

In the morning, Troy crept out of his bedroom quietly, trying not to wake Ren. At some point during the night he must have sneaked in, unable to sleep in the room his mom used to haunt. Hopefully, he could overcome that, while he wasn't a loud sleeper, he did move around a lot, and hogged the covers, and elbowed Troy in his ribs several times.

That's what I get for offering...

Troy munched on a crust of bread while he donned his shoes and jacket. Getting to the lab would be priority one for the day, and after that, he wanted to check in with Ka to see what the plan was for the master pylon. He'd decided he would help with it whether she liked the idea or not. As the Guild's president he was allowed into the facility without question. That had to be useful.

Holding the bread in his mouth he opened the door and walked out to a street overrun with red-clad Nationals harassing every citizen that went by.

"Where do you think you're going?" A woman wearing nothing but red barked at him.

"The lab," he said, flatly.

"And where's that?"

"Listen, I'm Troy Saunders, president of the Guild. Hold me up any longer and I'll make sure Winnow hears about it."

It was an empty threat. Winnow would have far more to worry about right now, but it should be enough to get this prick out of his way.

Her face cycled through anger, annoyance, and then acceptance before she finally nodded. "Carry on."

Damn right.

He walked with faux confidence as he made his way. Best to look like you belong. It worked, no one stopped him anyway, though he did see several roughed-up citizens along the streets. One bothered him, in particular. A girl with a puffy, red eye knelt over a dead dog. Her parents stood off to the side, profusely apologizing to a guard. Words like "immigrant" and "don't belong here" shot out of the guard's mouth as Troy moved past.

He let out a sigh of relief once he was safely outside the city wall. One nice thing about the lab's location was its quiet. There were no homes out here save for a few farms, the closest of which was a twenty-minute walk around the circumference of the wall. A tap on his shoulder came from Sumiko, out of breath from jogging to catch him up.

"Any idea what's got the Nationals going crazy?" she asked.

"Yes, actually. The cause is currently sleeping in my bed."

Her eyebrows raised. "How are you always at the center of every shit storm that rolls over this city?"

He shrugged. "I'll give you the details inside along with the rest of the team. I want to wait and see if Tia has any information about The Nationals' reaction first. Does your wife have any more information about the pylon facility? I'm more worried about that than anything else."

"Nationals are swarming it like flies on shit, but beyond that. Nothing."

The smell of the facility assaulted his nose the way it had every morning since Winnow fished him out of The Pit. While the smell remained, the accompanying screams from the amalgamations upon entering the lab had stopped. Their creations had noted the pattern of scientists coming in and out. That was something Troy had learned since working with the team. Amalgamations possessed a certain level of intelligence, whether technically dead or not.

He made his way up to the crystal room which he'd turned into his de facto office. It had a full view of the lab's floor while providing the comforting illusion of safety. Troy's brain knew the little hanging office wouldn't protect him long if an amalgamation got out and decided he looked tasty, but his body felt safer here, or at least it shook less.

Tia came in late, looking only slightly disheveled. Which, for her, meant all hell was breaking loose. She'd never had so much as a hair out of place in her tight bun. She reported that the Nationals had stopped her on her way to work, and she had a hard time convincing them to let her go.

Also, Winnow was on his way.

A colleague of hers, Cillian's mother, worked in the capitol building and rushed her the information this morning. The science team had planned for this, though, and even with the surprise visit, they should be able to hide what needed hiding and produce paperwork to satisfy their Dear Leader.

Troy's heart pounded against his rib cage. "Hide the gorilla. Hopefully, we get lucky and he'll forget his fixation on that thing." The lab buzzed with activity as Troy yelled orders down to the lab floor. He turned back to Tia. "Any idea what he wants?"

Sumiko responded, "The obvious answer is that he wants to rush us. We've been tasked with creating his bodyguards, and after last night, he probably feels like he's in danger."

Tia rubbed her face in exasperation. "Obviously."

Why are you always such an ass—

"He's here!" Tyler Chen shouted as he ran through the lab entrance with a look of terror on his face.

The three exchanged a wide-eyed look before running to the front to greet their unwelcome guest. Winnow always looked a little off, but this morning he looked particularly crazed. Bags under his eyes, an unkempt shirt with a loose tie and no suit jacket, hair that seemed freshly coifed from his pillow, and an angry stare, out for blood. He walked out from behind a platoon of Nationals and put a finger on Troy's chest. "I want my amalgamations, and I want them now."

Troy tried to sound as apologetic as possible. "I'm sorry, Mr. President, but the process takes time."

Winnow snapped his fingers in response and walked back to the safety of his men. Two guards came forward to grab Sumiko and Tia, they spun them around to face Troy and put knives to their throats.

This, they hadn't planned for.

Troy balled his fist, fighting the urge to grab his sword and kill the man. Archers stood with arrows drawn not fifty paces away and an unarmed man with a scar going up the left side of his face, clearly a mystic, stood just behind Winnow. Not only would he fail to reach Dear Leader in time, it would be suicide.

"Which one do you want to keep?" Winnow sounded bored.

Confidence. He doesn't know what he's talking about. Make him think he's making a mistake.

"I need both of them. Kill either and your dreams of controlling an amalgamation evaporate." Troy took a few paces forward and an arrow hissed by his ear. He stopped. "We are doing as you told us." He didn't want to lose anyone.

The moment stretched out to an eternity. Sumiko and Tia's eyes darted around, like animals caught in a trap. The air was thick with humidity from the storm the night before, making it hard to breathe. Winnow's expression shifted to one of frustration.

He's deciding if he wants to cut his losses and kill us all.

This gambit may have just lost his whole team. Rage filled his thoughts. His fingers twitched, wanting nothing more than to reach for his sword. Maybe he *could* make it to Winnow before the mystic skewered him with an ice lance, maybe his sword *would* slit Winnow's throat before the arrows could pierce his chest.

"This is the one," a voice said from behind.

A guard holding Cillian O'hare, one of the few full mystics on their team, with a knife to his throat.

Winnow smiled. "Cillian. Your mother works for me at the capitol, does she not?"

The red-haired mystic's jaw flexed. Fury twisted his face. "Yes, why?"

"We caught her giving information to the Resistance last night. I put her on the wall this morning."

Cillian screamed, struggling against his captor.

Winnow put his arms behind his back and stood as tall as he could. "That's what I thought. I trust you can respect the position this puts me in. We haven't caught *you* dealing with the Resistance, but I can't have anyone walking around with a vendetta." Then he nodded.

"No!" Troy screamed.

The cut was fast and deep. The guard dropped Cillian to the ground to bleed out, discarded like a piece of trash.

"Two weeks, Troy." And then Winnow walked away.

Sumiko and Tia were released. In less than a minute, the only evidence anything had happened was Cillian, face down in the dirt, and hatred burning a hole in Troy's chest. Transfixed on the body, Troy said, "I want to kill that man."

Tia blinked a tear out. "We... We'll need some wood to burn him."

Sumiko stalked back into the lab without a word.

No one took Troy up on his offer to take the day off. Instead, they cut some wood with their willed weapons, burned Cillian's body, and gathered on the floor of the lab.

"Klara and Sumiko need to start the binding, now," Tyler Chen said while shaking like a leaf. "We can't save them for the Resistance."

Klara, normally content to keep her opinions to herself, disagreed. "We can't use them on ourselves. Sumiko and I are the only two mystics left on the team, and we're not fighters."

Sumiko stood apart from the group, watching silently. But now she shook her head. "I don't think we have a choice. We have five ready to go, we'll bind two to me, two to Klara, and one to Tyler." She turned to Tyler. "I know you're not a mystic, but your wielding should be enough to give the amalgamations a target, and that's better than nothing." He nodded, though there was doubt in his eyes.

Sumiko walked to a table and took out a knife. "We need to rethink how we do things. Winnow doesn't value human lives. He doesn't value facts or science. He operates solely on impulse, and he'll do whatever he needs to do in the moment to achieve whatever goal he wants." She cut her finger and squeezed some blood into a beaker. Then she added a crystal powder preparation and put her hand out, charging the mixture with her will before drawing it up into a large, metal syringe.

She was going to bind herself to one right now. Troy considered stopping her. He could run to the Resistance and fetch Ka or Seffin, but they didn't have targets on their backs. His team did. Winnow knew his team. Knew their families and their routines. Knew where to find them. Their safety had to come first. Without them, there would be no amalgamations to control, and without that edge, the Resistance didn't stand much chance.

Sumiko continued, "Whenever Winnow comes back, we'll fight him. We'll dig in here and kill any National that comes near." She walked over to one of the caged laranees. They'd executed the cat and put husk in with it yesterday. Amalgamations were formed from husks fusing themselves into other husks, or in the case of wild animals, they would fuse with their corpse. Due to their size, amalgamated Colossi took an extended period of time to reanimate, though they'd made progress on speeding that timeline up. Sumiko injected the mixture into the corpse, initiating the binding, the mutation.

"What about our families?" Klara asked.

"Hide them or bring them here. There isn't a better option. What happened to Cillian could happen to any of us." She shifted her gaze toward Troy. "Let the Resistance know what we're doing and tell them they'll have their amalgamations. It will just take a little longer than we planned."

Seffin

Five days passed since the massacre at Sal's, and the city reacted in ways both expected and surprising. A spike in recruitment after the Nationals' crackdown was a fact Sharon was particularly smug about, she'd advocated for more direct methods since the beginning. But, as if to balance the scales, there was a dramatic increase in resistance members getting reported and executed, more in the last five days than the last three weeks combined.

Neighbors had begun ratting out neighbors.

Presently, the major figures of the Resistance sat in the main room at headquarters, all waiting with varying degrees of anxiety. Watching the nonverbal dance people insisted on employing exhausted Seffin, but it had proven far too useful to stop. He hoped it would eventually become natural. For now though, it took effort, and was very, very annoying. Tender bit their thumbnail while Ka scratched the back of her neck. Both were nervous. Troy was on his way, having finally agreed to meet with the Resistance, including Sharon, who sat in a chair facing the entryway, a look of boredom on her face.

Everyone was on edge except Polk, who sat next to Tender, a mask of calm next to the fretting engineer, but Seffin knew better. Polk's feet were his tell. He wiggled them when he was excited or stressed, and right now, he swayed them back and forth continuously. For a normal child, Seffin wouldn't think anything of it. Children loved being in motion, they were all energy and no control, but Polk wasn't a normal child. Not by any stretch of the imagination.

"Where in the hells is Troy?" Jacinda stood from her chair and began pacing. "He's half an hour late."

"He'll be here," Ka said.

As if summoned by invoking his name, he walked through the doorway followed closely by Cal. Troy struck an imposing, if rather frazzled, figure. He'd always been a large man, but he appeared enormous juxtaposed with Cal's aged form. Bags under his eyes only added to the determined expression he wore. Seffin couldn't help but notice his limb wasn't covered.

"Sorry I'm late," he said quickly.

"It's fine," Sharon said. "We know how difficult this meeting was for you to take. Thank you for coming."

He flashed a brief look of surprise before it turned into a scowl. Troy moved to the table they all sat around and put his hands on the sole, empty chair. "Over the next week, we'll have your amalgamations ready for binding. I need to know you have enough mystics to take them on."

"We do," Jacinda said. "And if we can help your team out in any way, please let us know."

"I want Ka," he said without hesitation. "And Seffin, if you can spare him. I'm worried Winnow will find us out and send everything he has to the lab."

"What about the master pylon?" Tender met Troy's eyes. "Has your contact learned anything else?"

"Unfortunately, no. She's been on Winnow's shit list for a while now, so she moved her wife to our lab for safety reasons. Last she checked, the Nationals were still moving in and out of the facility."

"Regardless, you don't just want Seffin and Ka. I'm told you want Ren, too," Sharon said. "What's your plan?"

He refused to make eye contact with her as he said, "Admittedly, yes. Before Winnow's deadline for the lab, I'd like to take a team to scout the master pylon facility."

"Hold on." Tender put their hand out palm forward. "We're already working on that."

"As the Guild's president, I can walk in unquestioned. You should strongly reconsider sending someone else." Troy pulled his chair out and sat in it. "My team is part of the Resistance now. It's time you start thinking of us that way, including myself."

"Oh? Are you comfortable taking orders from me?" Sharon asked with a bit of teasing condescension in her voice.

"For the sake of the city? I'd take orders from a porcine." He finally met her eyes. "But if I have to settle for you, it's what I'll do."

Sharon let out a guffaw. "Works for me." Her smile came off as... proud? But it was always hard for Seffin to tell with her. If reading Ren was like a children's book, then Sharon was like reading *The Book of Kohru* backwards and upside down.

Tender shook their head. "Regardless, you're not taking a full team into the facility. That puts too many people on the line for a simple information-gathering mission." They put their hand on Ka's shoulder before saying, "Since I'm sure I won't be able to stop her anyway, you can have Ka."

"Ren and Seffin—" Troy began.

"—will stay back at the lab. We told you we'll do whatever it takes to protect your team. Seffin and Ren can't protect anything from inside the pylon facility. Kiko should be here in a week and a half, and at that point, Garvelle can take over security."

Troy nodded. Seffin didn't know how he felt about everyone else deciding his course of action, but he hadn't seen Ren in five days. This would bring them together, a win in his book.

"I would like to be stationed at the lab as well," Polk said.

Tender frowned. "Absolutely not, you're staying with me. I promised Kiko nothing would happen to you."

Polk didn't respond, the only indication he'd heard Tender was his feet swaying more rapidly.

With the notable absence of Don, the traitor, the remainder of the meeting went as usual. It shocked Seffin how much he felt the man's absence. The one who got him his first job and ushered him into life as a merc. The man who shared stories of himself so freely and laughed so readily, who brought them into the Resistance. That was the man who fed the Nationals their hideout locations and got so many of their people killed. It didn't make sense. But the facts were the facts. He betrayed them and Ren killed him for it. Seffin tried his best to rewrite his feelings, to erase the warm, smiling face and replace it with the burnt, dead one. It worked sometimes, but other times, like now, he just felt empty.

He didn't mourn the man. He mourned his memories of the man. He mourned the idea of the man that context destroyed.

Troy stood, bringing Seffin's thoughts back to the here and now. Another good thing about this assignment was no more training with Farah. While grateful for the help, he couldn't say he'd miss spending his days reliving his worst moments. In almost a week of her torturous exercises, he'd only progressed far enough to use basic kinetics. As he left with Troy and Ka, she gave him a nod, her smile a bit dimmer than usual.

The walk to Troy's home took forever. They stopped at a fruit stand and popped into a shop, trying to keep the appearance of people out running errands. Since the night at Sal's, no one had seen Ren besides Ka and Troy. Winnow's men surveilled the home, so it was best if no one was seen visiting, not even Seffin. But this would be his last day staying there anyway, the plan for them both was to relocate to the lab indefinitely.

The last time they'd seen each other, they fought. The consequences of which were felt by the whole city. There was a lesson in there somewhere about responsibility and power, but he couldn't bring himself to care at the moment. All his thoughts were focused on seeing Ren's dimples again. The smile that melted his heart.

The night out in the rain with Sharon had been one of the hardest of his life. Worried for Ren's safety, walking around with a murderer, finding Hassan and Don's bodies. The idea that his last interaction with Ren might have been a fight gnawed at him, even after learning he was safe.

He wanted to pick their story up and start writing again. He wanted sentences and paragraphs and pages of their life to separate that night from now, but instead, he'd been subjected to five days of personal anguish, stressing over what Ren was thinking, what Ren thought he was thinking, and around, and around. Just seeing him would help.

The reunion wasn't so romantic.

Troy let Seffin into the home where Ren stood waiting. There was an embrace and a kiss, a quick smile, but on his face was resolve, not longing or relief, though he did knit his fingers with Seffin's and squeezed his hand.

"What'd they say?" Ren asked.

"It's a no," Ka said. "They want you focused on recovering at the lab. They won't even let Seffin go. He'll stay back with you."

Ren shook his head. "I want to go."

"It's a no, Ren," Troy said. "I'm not disobeying the first order they gave me, and they made good points. You're not back to normal yet, and—"

"—I'm almost there! The fireball I just made—"

"—*and* the lab needs protection, too. Even with Don gone, who knows what the Nationals know?" Troy paused and squinted his eyes. "Didn't I ask you *not* to practice your fire elementalism in my house?"

Seffin squeezed Ren's hand. "Let's talk about this at the lab."

"You two can. Troy and I will meet you there later," Ka said. "Seffin knows the way."

Ren threw his hands up. "You're going right now?"

"Yes, less time for you two to come up with some hare-brained scheme to come along, and visiting during the day is less conspicuous than visiting in the evening." Troy rushed off into his house, calling back to them as he climbed the stairs, "Can you take a few things to the lab for me?"

Ren's only response was grumbling disapproval which left Ka chuckling.

"We were right, weren't we? You would have tried to weasel your way onto the mission with or without approval?" She worded it as a question, but it sounded more like gloating. "I know you feel guilty about everything that happened."

"I don't feel guilty for killing Nationals."

"No, you feel guilty for the crackdown that happened afterward, and you feel guilty for what happened to Hassan."

Ren shook his head. "It's not about guilt. I just want them to pay."

Troy popped up from behind and set clothing and some keys in Seffin's arms. "All the more reason you shouldn't come today," he said. "You're angry and emotional, and we're not going there to pick a fight. We're going to collect information."

Ren grabbed his pack and shoved Troy's neatly folded clothes into it. "Ok, good luck I guess." He walked out the front door and closed it behind him, leaving Seffin standing in the foyer with Ka and Troy. They all exchanged expressions that conveyed both understanding and frustration.

"Seriously, though. Good luck." Seffin smiled and gave a quick hug to the two spies before leaving.

Ren sulked at the bottom of the front steps with his red scarf wrapped hastily around his neck. Seffin stopped next to him and nodded in the direction they should head. Unlike Troy or the other lab workers, they couldn't walk out the gates. Farah had made a tunnel from inside Cal and Jacinda's home for them to use.

It was an uneventful walk. Avoiding National patrols came easier to Seffin now, due in no small part to the lesson he took from Sharon. She'd insisted after their night out looking for Ren. The woman still made him uncomfortable, but he'd softened on her, if only a little. He no longer thought of her as an unhinged, toothy maw of murderous rage. Instead, she'd been demoted to a grumpy frown of homicidal impulses. Enough of a change that he was willing to accept her training on how to inconspicuously avoid guards, anyway.

Jacinda and Cal's home sat near the wall on the lowest tier of Prolivgrad. It was part of a set of drab rowhouses in a state of disrepair. Bricks were cracked everywhere, windows were smashed and boarded up, and roofs bowed like they were about to cave in. Jacinda appeared in the doorway and motioned them inside.

It was like stepping into a mansion. The rowhouses had been hollowed out and combined into one large building. People Seffin recognized as cell captains bustled back and forth, chattering at each other on their way through to some other portion of the building. Noticing their surprise, Jacinda said, "We've been treating this as a sort of backup headquarters."

"You live here?" Ren said, disbelief on his face.

Jacinda sighed as if she'd had to explain this all more times than she'd like. "Yes. As the two most prominent board members at the Lodge, we wanted to keep a low profile, especially after everything happened, that's why the outward appearance is so terrible." She casually massaged her shoulder as she spoke, rolling the joint and flexing her neck at the same time. Despite her age, her arms and shoulders were ropey with muscles. Like they were woven onto her body and plastered over with a thin layer of weathered skin. Seffin always thought Jacinda and Cal made an odd pairing. Her with her muscles and great sword, and him with his hunched, frail frame and a dueling saber. Without the saber, he'd look like just another old man.

"Were you and Cal in a band together before you became Lodge leaders?" Seffin asked, apropos of nothing. He felt his face get hot. He'd done it again. Sudden, non-sequitur questions were the old Seffin, the one without control. The new Seffin followed the flow of conversation. Listened and responded. Didn't plunge into his own world and burst from the surface with inquiries like a whale intent on disrupting every discussion in its wake.

Jacinda, gods bless her, didn't miss a beat. "No, actually. Cal was an assassin with a contract out on my head for reasons *I will not get into.* I kicked his ass and we fell in love. Part of working for The Eyes is protection for both yourself and your family, so after our marriage, they had to nullify the contract that was taken out on me. It was a loophole in their tenets they've since closed. No one foresaw an assassin marrying their mark. Anyway, our honeymoon was a trip to Estaba to kill the piece of shit who hired The Eyes to kill me. Cal finished out his term and I decided to pursue leadership with the Lodge after that."

"Honestly, that's kind of romantic," Ren said.

"It is, isn't it?" Jacinda's eyes gazed into the middle distance, and she smiled; probably thinking of their honeymoon murder. The hairs on the back of Seffin's neck stood on end. Ren may find it romantic, but it sounded gruesome. And why was she being so cagey about the reasons an assassin was sent after her?

Jacinda clapped her hands once in front of her. "Anyway, the tunnel."

They walked through the foyer into a kitchen which had a stairwell leading down to a cellar containing barrels of provisions. Pickled peppers, carrots, pickled eggs, sausages, cured meats, and dried fruits all made for a rather unappetizing fragrance. Though Seffin's stomach grumbled all the same. In the corner of the room was a shelf Jacinda pushed aside with all the effort of a bartender sliding a beer down the counter. Behind it, stairs descended into pitch darkness.

"Normally, I'd send a candle with you, but I'm sure two mystics can manage without."

Seffin made a small bead of fire in response and held it out as a light source. He took a few steps down before Jacinda said, "It's only a fifteen-minute walk. And Ren," her voice contained a warning, "thank you for following orders."

Without another word, she shifted the shelf in front of the stairwell, and they were alone. Ren scoffed, walked down to stand next to Seffin, and said, "That's getting annoying."

"What is?"

"That people don't think they can trust me."

"Be fair," Seffin said, patting him on the back with a smile. "They can't." He descended the stairs.

Ren followed after. "What's that supposed to mean?"

"Don't play stupid."

A seemingly endless hallway stretched out before them at the bottom of the stairs. After a few steps, Ren met Seffin's eyes. "You don't think I'm trustworthy?"

The answer was a resounding no, but Seffin wasn't going to say that. Besides, it was complicated. He trusted Ren to have his back, but he didn't do much to inspire confidence in his decision-making. Ignoring his penchant for thievery, he was impulsive and emotional and, Seffin was learning, vengeful. The mystic in Lanneshire and an entire bar of Nationals, both times he acted not out of necessity, but anger. It was fortunate the mystic in Lanneshire *needed* to die, and it was luck he found Don in that bar which made the resulting, city-wide shitstorm even partially worth it. Did he trust Ren? Yes. Was he trust*worthy*? No.

"I'm sorry for not trusting you with your mom." A non-answer. "I know your training is valuable. My problem was more about me than you."

"Don't apologize. You were right." The sound of hard earth crunching beneath their boots echoed behind and before them. Farah had packed the dirt in the tunnel tightly. "She was lying to me anyway. She insisted I wasn't ready even after I'd mastered the third form."

But he hadn't been ready. If he had, it wouldn't be almost a week out with his wielding still weakened. The time Seffin spent with Sharon hadn't changed his opinion of the woman too much, but it was clear she cared for Ren. In her own, warped way.

"How are you so sure she was lying to you?" he asked.

"I got out of the flicker state using the third form on the first try. It was too easy to be luck."

"Your wielding isn't back yet. Do you think maybe she was just trying to be safe?"

"My wielding isn't back yet because she didn't teach me how to properly enter the flicker state. I had to force my way in. If she'd taught me the second form earlier, Hassan would be alive."

"She couldn't have known that would happen." He hated finding himself in the position of defending Sharon. She was Kent's murderer and the woman who paved the way for Winnow—no matter how unintentional.

"She saw my stance, she saw my progress, she knew I was ready, and she refused to teach me. Probably because she wanted to keep me around longer." Ren's lips were pressed into a thin line.

Part of Seffin liked that he was still mad at Sharon. The fight they'd had was, at least in part, because Seffin felt the two were getting too close, but he knew Ren was mistaken. Sharon wouldn't withhold a technique that could keep him safe simply to spend more time with him. More likely, it was an overabundance of caution.

"I went out to search for you that night," Seffin said. "I went to her apartment to look for you."

"I'm aware."

"I told her she couldn't come with, but she wouldn't take no for an answer."

"Typical."

"Sure, but it's because she was worried about you."

"Ok? What's your point?"

"Did anyone tell you she saved Ahmad's life that night?"

Ren's eyes fell to the floor. "Hassan's older brother?"

"Yes, he was out looking for him," Seffin said. "And did you know she'd already saved Hassan's life once? Before we even got to Prolivgrad?"

"No." Ren looked confused.

"And did you know that when she saved Ahmad, she told him to go home and *volunteered* to look for Hassan?"

Ren shook his head. "What are you saying?"

"I'm saying I don't think she's any happier with how things turned out than you are. She liked Hassan. I saw the look on her face when she found his body, and it reminded me of yours, back in Lanneshire."

He didn't respond. Save for the sound of their own footfalls, silence followed them until they came to the stairs at the end of the tunnel which led to a cave that, in turn, opened onto the forested area just outside the city's wall.

Ren stopped.

"So, what? You want me to keep training with her?"

Seffin didn't know what he wanted, but he knew it wasn't his decision. "You should do what you think is best. She's *your* mom. I'm just not convinced she was trying to lie to you."

He made a groaning noise, frustrated. "Gods, I hate all of this. When did everything get so complicated?"

Seffin ignored the question. Instead, he pointed in between the trees, in the direction of the lab. Figures surrounded it, all clad in black. Garvelle's colors. But they weren't supposed to be here for another week at least.

Seffin frowned. "Speaking of complications."

Troy

Ka walked toward the master pylon facility's entrance beside Troy. She wore a green jacket over a red shirt with her usual tan pants and had her black hair pinned up in the back. Strands fanned out in an organized fashion around the top of the—ball?—of hair and swayed with each step she took. He'd never paid this close attention to any woman besides his mother, though he'd done that for different reasons. He studied his mother for survival, to warn him of danger, or to predict a need, both tasks had usually ended in disappointment or dismissal more often than not. With Ka it was fun. He liked studying her, she wasn't waiting to test him, waiting for him to fail.

The entrance to the master pylon facility was intentionally unassuming. A simple gate with two guards posted. One, a handsome woman, and the other, a pretty one. Neither had the intensity of Ka's gaze nor did they possess her strong shoulders or her commanding posture.

Perhaps I'm putting her on a pedestal...

The handsome one nodded toward them. "Move along," she commanded.

"I'm Troy Saunders, president of The Guild of Commerce. I'm here for a routine inspection."

He'd never even been in the facility. Never had any routine when it came to this branch of his organization's responsibilities, but they wouldn't know that. Or at least he counted on them not knowing. They were young and had the look of new recruits, fresh uniforms and brand-new weapons.

Despite the handsome one's forceful tone, she projected nervousness and kept looking at his unwrapped limb. Her eyes darted to Ka before settling back on him, deciding if he was who he claimed.

"Winnow said no one goes in." She held firm.

He waved his limb in her face as proof of his identity. "You know I'm telling you the truth, and you know I run this facility. Don't make this harder than it has to be. Should I fetch Winnow?"

At some point, I'm going to name-drop him and it'll fail...

The pretty one's eyes were a pleasant, pale blue which glowed against her tan skin as they widened into mortified spheres. He hoped she could convince her colleague to listen to reason. Letting them through would be the least painful option. Ka shifted her right foot back almost imperceptibly. Most would assume she was idly shifting her weight, bored with the obstacle in front of her, but Troy knew she was prepping for violence. She wouldn't kill them, just rough them up. Winnow would though, or some other jackboot underling who saw their failure as reason enough to kill them in punishment.

The guards exchanged some quiet words and opened the gate. If they were nervous about the decision, they didn't show it. The pretty one's expression shifted back into the calcified, stoic mask the National guards always kept when on duty.

Once out of earshot, Ka let out a sigh of relief. "Gods, I hate this. Those two were barely as old as Ren."

"That wasn't even the hard part."

She frowned. "This plan sucks."

Troy stopped. "You could have said something if you didn't like it."

"No thanks. Give me a husk to kill or a patient to heal. I'd rather fight five werewillers at once than organize people or come up with mission plans. I'm a blunt instrument when it comes to these things."

A chuckle slipped from his mouth. "I didn't peg you for someone afraid of responsibility."

If her eyes were daggers, he would have been stabbed full of holes after that comment. "I am plenty responsible, for myself. But everything we're doing now affects so much. If people die because of a decision I made..." Her gaze shifted to the ground. "Besides, all this sneaking around makes me nervous."

Troy reached a hand out to set it on her shoulder. She pulled away. "I'm fine," she said. "I'm your assistant, remember? Let's go."

The tunnel they stood in could have been made for colos-si, tall enough to fit a pylon and wide enough to fit a herd of porcine, and to Ka's point, a crowd of workers headed in their direction. Troy channeled the arrogance his privileged upbringing had given him, the assumption that he belonged in whatever space he walked into. It seemed to work. The men and women didn't spare a glance for them as they walked by, too focused on discussing where they were going to grab a drink after the day's labor. The conversation was so mundane, so normal, it sparked a bit of longing for pre-Winnow Proliv-grad. When the most exciting or pressing issue was where to eat and drink, and how you would make it to work in the morning with the inevitable hangover that followed.

That was a lie, though. Even back then, Prolivgrad had its problems. Miners dying. Homeless refugees begging for scraps and desperate for work. There may not have been a wall of hanged people leading to The Pit, but the city's sparkle had only ever been on its surface. Dig any deeper and it was a yawning pit of inequity and greed. Gilded shit was still shit at the end of the day.

A bend in the tunnel ran them straight into the master pylon. Troy couldn't have imagined what they found. A single crystal as large as a building hovered, glowing in the middle of the giant hollow inside Brinidor Mountain. Hoops made out of woven brass held eight smaller pylons, all orbiting in a synchronous pattern which, in turn, had smaller crystals or-biting around them, attached to yet more hoops of brass. The master pylon wasn't diamond-shaped, but a giant teardrop with thousands of facets that threw light around the room. To Troy, the truly astonishing thing was that he could actually *see* will flowing from the orbiting pylons into the central one. Focus crystals glowed when charged, but he'd never seen it flow through the air like a river the way it did here.

And he could hear it.

A hum resonated like a chorus of notes. Tender had described the sound as annoying, but right now, to him, it was sacred, holy. This room kept the whole city safe. It kept the mines safe. Its protection kept the whole world afloat. Without the mines, there were no additional pylons, no replacement for existing pylons, no cities. Only husk.

"I've never heard it before," Ka remarked, almost as transfixed as Troy felt. "It's beautiful." Shaking her head as if waking from a dream, she smiled. "Though I suppose if I heard it all day, every day it might get old. Over there." She pointed at a series of grenades strung together, tied to the base of the pylon.

After snapping back to reality, it became clear the room had been rigged to blow. If he squinted past the glow of the will rivers, his worst nightmare materialized. Every crystal in the room had enough grenades hanging off them to shatter.

Part of him had hoped there was some other reason to cart in all the crystal dust, that maybe Winnow was creating some sort of weapon or, uncharacteristically, making improvements to the pylon. But no. Their president lived up to his reputation. *Think of the worst thing he could do, and then plan for something even worse than that.*

"We should start taking these grenades off," Ka said. Wind blades hissed from her outstretched hands, cutting the ropes on the central crystal. As they fell away, she used kinetics to gently lower them to the ground.

"We're only supposed to do reconnaissance," he said.

Ka gestured broadly. Around the room were crates of crystal dust resting among other crates of reagents and bottles of catalyzing agents. A pallet of metal orbs, half empty, sat next to coils of rope. *This is not what I expected when I heard the word "facility".* The word made him think of a lab, of research and experiments and people. But other than holding the master pylon, this place was simply a big cave with a bend and a man-made hollow. No side rooms, no offices, no work areas, no tools, no equipment of any kind save for the pylon itself and, now, the strung-together grenades marring the beautiful, spinning structure before them. It also meant no employees were rushing around to maintain the area.

"There's nothing left to see. We've gathered all the info there is, and I'm not about to leave grenades tied to the most important pylon in the world."

It was a fair point. But the next batch of workers to come in would see the grenades missing, and they'd just tie more to the damn thing.

"I didn't know you were this stupid." Winnow's voice echoed into the room.

Troy couldn't fathom how he got here this fast. The facility was three tiers away from the capitol and forty-five degrees around the circumference of the mountain. The guards would have had to sprint to even arrive at the capitol by now, let alone come back. *Unless they already had a system in place to warn him, damn it.*

Troy turned around and put his hand on his sword, setting his eyes on Winnow's neck. "Why would you destroy the city? What purpose does that serve?"

"I'm not destroying the city. I have a pylon in the capitol building, and all *loyal* Egallans have been issued enough traveling crystals to keep the husk at bay. We have the wielders needed to keep everything charged long enough for us to make a new pylon network." He gestured at his throng of guards, only two of whom wore weapons, the two from the entrance. The rest must all be mystics or wielders of some sort. "A network whose charge I can control." He produced a grenade from his pocket, winding the knob on the top. "Your lab was never actually planning to make amalgamations for me, was it?" On either side of Winnow stood the two guards from the entrance, the handsome one and the pretty one.

Troy laughed. "Gods, you're such an idiot. You're not a wielder. You'll *never* be able to control an amalgamation."

"It's cute you think you know everything about me."

What's that supposed to mean?

"Drop the grenade." Ka's voice was tight.

"You don't want me to do that," Winnow said. "If I let go, this whole place goes up."

Troy's mind raced. There was no way out of this. Ka could earth slip, but they were too deep in the mountain for her to bring him along. Killing Winnow wouldn't solve anything; they'd still die, the pylon would blow up, and husk would overrun the city.

"What do you want me to do?" Troy said.

"Surrender, obviously."

"And then?"

"And then I dismantle your resistance and execute the lot of you. But, I *will* leave the master pylon standing."

"You're lying," Ka said.

"I'm not."

"I don't believe you," Troy said.

An evil little grin slipped onto Winnow's face, and then he shrugged and said, "Fine then."

Every wielder in the group standing next to Winnow placed their hands on each other. *They're combining their reserves? Oh no...* The closest wielder, a terrible scar running up the left side of his face, placed his hand on the president's shoulder just in time for him to chuck the grenade directly at them. Troy felt a tight, almost painful grip on his own shoulder, then the world fell upward as he plunged into darkness. *No. No, don't do this. We won't make it. We're too deep in the mountain.* The cacophonous rumbling above was almost an afterthought. The world was ending, and all he could think of, the only thought that surfaced, pressing itself into his heart and flooding up into his throat like acid, was that he was already dead, and Ka was committing suicide, futilely attempting to save him.

***

Troy came to in pitch darkness. A jagged rock pressed into his back while his head lay angled, resting on stone, his nose scratched up against the ceiling of whatever cave or tunnel or hole he'd found himself in. He couldn't move more than a few inches without something sharp stabbing into the flesh of his thigh or the meat of his shoulder. Breathing deeply didn't work, no room for the expansion of his chest. His knees pressed against a wall and halfway down his thigh the ground he lay on gave way, leaving his legs dangling, the edge dug into his muscle, into his bone.

A muffled cough reached his ears, vibrating through his boot. He flexed his ankle and his toe hit something not-rock.

"Troy." He felt Ka's voice more than heard it. Strained and weak. *She's alive.* His calf cramped, the pain knotting tighter with each shallow breath.

"Are you ok?" He said into the rock less than an inch from his mouth, trying to shift his head, his lips touched stone, slick with condensation from his breath. No response. He put more volume into the words, rocks stabbed at his chest in punishment for breathing deeper than he should have. "Are you ok?"

"Are you?" He barely made out the response.

Why? You should have saved yourself.

"I…" He was out of breath. "I don't know." His heart pounded. The knot in his calf grew tighter and his head fogged.

"I'm sorry," she spoke falteringly. "I couldn't get us out."

"No." Is all he could manage. Words were so hard. It took all his focus to avoid the pain of breathing deeply. His foot moved without him telling it to. The not-rock it bumped into had been Ka. Her shoulder or her head possibly, with the vibrations it might have been her chest or throat. "No." He said again.

"I'm not sure we can make it out." The words rippled through his body, up through his neck, into his ear, and then into his mind. *Sure.* He thought. *Ok, that makes sense.*

"Can you—" His head started swimming. Not enough air. "Can you… get out?"

His foot shook as whatever part of her wept against it. A sniffle and a cry shivered up from her through him and brought his own tears welling in his eyes. An unwelcome sob burst from his mouth. More pain shuddered through him. "You have to."

"I can't leave you," she whispered.

"Please." His limb scraped against wet stone, more sticky than slick. A tender burning in the flesh of his arm told him it was his blood. Breathless, he said, "You have to."

An eternity passed where all he felt was pain and all he heard was the thumping of his heart and Ka's soft breaths.

"I won't," she said, her voice a brittle promise.

You have to.

Ren

A shockwave ripping outward from Prolivgrad threw Ren and Seffin to the ground. A small yelp, almost drowned out by the force of the wave, echoed from the cave behind them. Trees shook, throwing loose leaves into the air and dropping a few unlucky squirrels from their branches. *It can't be.* Ren scrambled to his feet and leapt on a nearby boulder, trying to get a better view of the city. Jaw clenched and ears ringing, he searched the Brinidor mountainside for the source of the explosion.

Rubble where the master pylon facility used to be.

Ka. Troy.

Buildings crumbled above and below as smoke and sparkling dust snaked into the sky. A loud crack came from further clockwise around the mountain, on a lower tier where an apartment building leaned perilously. It collapsed like a tired child into a pillow of glittering cotton dust, anyone inside would have been crushed. Prolivgrad was old, and most of its buildings were constructed ages ago. They weren't built to withstand a quake.

They got out. They must have gotten out.

"What the hells are you doing here?" Seffin's voice edged into Ren's awareness.

"I want to bind an amalgamation," a familiar, high-pitched squeak said.

Ren spun around to see Seffin holding Polk by the wrist. "They're ok. They have to be ok."

"Who?" Polk cocked his head in a way Ren would normally find adorable.

"We need to check on Ka and Troy," Ren said.

Seffin shook his head. "We can't. Garvelle is here. We have to get to the lab."

"I don't care about the *fucking* lab!"

Seffin let go of Polk's arm and walked up to Ren, standing on his rock like a little king. "Whatever is going on, we can't help them right now. We don't have the luxury of running face first into a bunch of Nationals with Polk here, and we *have* to make sure the empress knows the lab's scientists are on our side."

Ren hopped off his rock. His finger itched something fierce, accompanied by a dull ache in between his shoulder blades where Ka used to massage him for comfort. *She's alive. She's alive. She's alive.* As if on its own, his right hand moved to the will-blade on his hip. The first night Troy trained with him flashed into his head. Ka resting up against the trees making snide comments as they beat the shit out of each other. Bringing his hand up, he touched the nose she broke. The nose she mended.

"Ren!" Seffin said.

He snapped out of it. "Fine. Let's go."

Tell the empress not to kill the scientists, drop Polk off at the facility, and then I'm coming. Just hold out. I'm coming.

They marched through the trees with Polk walking beside them, a worried expression on his face. The first worried expression Ren had ever seen the boy make, but if ever there was a time for worry, it was now. Prolivgrad's barrier just collapsed and Garvelle's army arrived a week early, well before the Resistance could even attempt to stabilize the city. A blood bath was being drawn.

They approached a perimeter of black-clad Garvellian soldiers who dutifully leveled their weapons at them.

"Get Kiko, now. Tell her Ren Adegast is here and wants to speak with her."

"That's not how that works, kid," one of them said, he looked like an idiot. They all looked like idiots. A bunch of stupid, dumb idiots standing in his way. The front idiot stepped forward. "We'll be taking you into custody."

Seffin moved in front of Ren and Polk. "We don't have time for this. Unless you all want to die, you'll fetch the empress." Then he produced a fireball the size of a small home above the trees, some of which smoked as their leaves began to singe. "If this explodes, we're all dead."

The soldier went wide-eyed, nodded, and ran toward the lab. The likelihood any of them had met a mystic at Seffin's level was practically zero, but the fact none of them ran in open retreat impressed him, a fireball this size would have a normal person pissing themselves, and for good reason. If Seffin let it explode, it would turn them all to ash instantly. But this was the same army that held the Gogallo hordes at bay. If any troops had the mettle to look death in the face and stand their ground, it would be them.

"Put that out, Mr. Rashee." Empress Kiko Zollinger clanged into view wearing her full suit of black armor. The fireball winked away. "You are your mother's son."

Seffin raised an eyebrow. "Excuse me?"

"You both have a flare for the dramatic. When she found out I was coming here early she stormed past my guards and demanded to know the reason, claiming I was *pointlessly putting her son at risk.'* Aisha almost lopped her fool head off. If that grumpy engineer hadn't been there to stop her, she might have."

Seffin glared. "She's not wrong, your arrival could create problems. Why *are* you here early?"

"I don't answer to you, boy. Especially after threatening to ash my best soldiers." The two closest infantry beamed at the compliment.

"I'm sorry, but we needed to make sure you knew the lab was on our side," Seffin said.

Kiko frowned. "I know I have a reputation, but slaughtering scientists on a whim is a little too ruthless, even for me."

"How was the trip?" Polk asked.

"Why is the boy out here? Shouldn't he be safe with Tender somewhere?"

Polk's face twisted into something unrecognizable, scrunched up with his brow furrowed. It took Ren a second to realize what it was... anger. "What is it with you people? I know more about how this planet works than any one of you. I know the rise and fall of every civilization in every cycle we've had. I have even deeper will reserves than Seffin. You're fools to try and lock me in a cage for protection. I can help. Bind the amalgamations to me."

Kiko arched an eyebrow and a smirk crept onto her lips. Polk craned his neck upward, meeting her gaze with a determined look. A second's consideration made it obvious how foolish they'd been to underestimate him. He was on a voluntary suicide mission, after all. Of course he wouldn't be content to sit idle while his goal, his purpose, was threatened.

"Respectfully—" Kiko began.

"—*Respectfully*, you don't get a choice in this, Empress. I tried trusting all of you and look how far that's gotten us. If we don't win this, our chances of making it into Gogallo and stopping Koth drops to zero, and you know it."

"He's right," Seffin said.

Why not put the key to saving the world front and center in a civil war? What could possibly go wrong?

Ren wasn't surprised. Seffin's affinity for insane plans was well known to him at this point. He did just threaten the

Garvelle military with a fireball on a whim, after all. Still, Polk had the right to make his own decisions.

"I agree," Ren said, though not because he wanted to. He wanted to go back in time and leave Polk in Nakonipol, safe and away from the fighting. Not here, in the middle of a disaster, preventing him from running to help his sister.

The empress pinched the bridge of her nose in the same way Ka used to. *In the same way Ka still does.* With his sister, the gesture meant she was about to cede a point or agree to something she wasn't happy about.

Kiko made a dissatisfied, grunting sound before saying, "Very well. Come, we can talk in the lab."

The line of stupid soldiers parted to allow their group access. The lab was a large, box-shaped building similar to most Guild structures. An iron door led into a hallway with the familiar, rotten smell of husk permeating throughout. A woman with a serious look on her face named Sumiko greeted them before escorting everyone upstairs, through a door to a large room containing a litany of caged amalgamations, and then up even more stairs to a hanging cage with a crystal floating in the middle.

Sumiko waited for everyone to enter the room before saying, "We have twelve hours before the city turns into a nightmare."

"It's already a nightmare," Ren said. "There's a smoking crater in the middle of it."

She shook her head. "I mean the corpses. Winnow has made a point of *not* burning the dead."

Coruscare burn me.

"You mean he planned this from the beginning?" Ren's blood boiled. How could a monster like this gain power? How were people so willing to back a man this terrible, one who would threaten the whole city? His sister—*she's alive*—was in there. Poppy was in there.

Kiko cleared her throat. "I'm afraid it's worse than that. Prolivgrad is an ancient city, and murderers don't make a habit of burning their victims' bodies. Without the barrier to prevent the corpses from turning husk, the dead will start popping up everywhere. I hesitate to say there is anywhere in the city that's safe right now."

"How long does the binding process take?" Polk asked while looking out the window, down onto the sea of caged amalgamations.

Sumiko beamed. "Actually, we have a turnaround of twenty-four hours now. That's what we've spent the majority of our time researching since we were released from The Pit."

"I'm not waiting that long to get back into the city," Ren said. He tried to keep the panic out of his voice. A calm demeanor would help him more in this situation than a desperate one, even though he *was* desperate.

Seffin put a hand on his back. "But your reserves still haven't recovered."

"I can use a will-blade just fine." *She's ok. I'm going to make sure of it.* Ka could handle herself. He knew that, intellectually. It didn't stop his body from protesting, from his stomach flipping and his heart pounding and his palms sweating and his finger itching and every inch of his skin from screaming with worry. "And anyway, like you said, my will reserves haven't recovered. I can't bind an amalgamation like this, and it's not like the lab needs any more protection than it already has."

"You're planning to go by yourself," Polk said.

Kiko squinted at him. "What is your rush to get into a city soon to be overrun by the undead?"

"Ka and Troy were headed to the master pylon facility before it exploded." A heavy hand clapped down on his shoulder and spun him around. He couldn't say when she had arrived, but Kiko's most trusted advisor, Knight Aisha Bahati, stared into his eyes with a terrifying intensity.

"You're sure? Ka was in there?"

He only nodded. She bit her cheek and turned to Kiko whose mouth had dropped open. An entire conversation took place swiftly and silently between the two before the empress nodded.

Aisha nodded back and made to leave the room. At the doorway, she paused to look at Ren, impatient. "Well? Let's go. I'm coming with you."

"I'm coming, too," Seffin said.

They'd only just reunited, but he couldn't let him come. Seffin had to bind amalgamations with Polk, and the boy needed Seffin to watch over him besides. "You have to stay." He hated saying it.

Seffin's breath hitched, he shook his head, and he stepped toward Ren, thrusting a finger into his chest. "You better not fucking die."

Ren grabbed him and pulled him close for a kiss. A frantic, desperate thing that left his eyes wet and his heart racing. "I'm sorry."

Seffin shook his head, kissed him one last time, and said, "It's ok. Go."

Then he was out the door, trailing behind Aisha who walked at a pace he had to jog to keep up with. Once outside, she started jogging, which meant he had to start running. The forest surrounding the city was peaceful, warm. Nature didn't care the world was tumbling down around him. The birds still tweeted their songs, and the flies and mosquitoes still buzzed in his ears and landed on his neck, trying for their next meal. He slapped a fly away for not recognizing the gravity of the situation, and also because it bit him.

"Tell me the state of things inside the city." Aisha didn't turn to look at him when she spoke.

"They've forced everyone to wear red, so we won't be able to tell what side anyone's on. But the guards—"

"Have sacrificed their lives. Anyone armed and wearing red will die.

"Good." *When did I become this way? Excited for murder.* "We should look out for anyone from the Resistance, too. They might know what happened."

A set of six guards stood at the entrance to the city. Before Ren could get his will-blade out, Aisha had thrown her will-spear, piercing through two of them. Their bodies hadn't even hit the ground before she pulled the spear back to herself with kinetics and sprinted forward. The archer in the group responded quickly, loosing two arrows at the knight. Momentum from the sprint allowed her to duck and slide under the first one then pop up over the second. The leap was enough to close the distance and her spear was through his head before he could knock another arrow. One guard sprinted away while the remaining two, men too young to be referred to as such, pulled out swords. *Idiots.* Walking toward them, she deflected two blows before the spear tip found the neck of the first. The surprised yelp from the second was the last sound he made, a gash going halfway through his body had him falling backward onto the street, shock frozen on his face.

A sword against a spear was already a poor matchup, but make it a will-spear wielded by someone as skilled as Aisha, and it wasn't even a match. More akin to slaughter. They should have run with their friend.

"Which way?" Aisha asked, standing in the middle of five bodies.

These corpses would turn husk if they did nothing. Ren pulled his will-blade out to quickly cut them into small pieces before jogging off in the direction of the master pylon facility. The shortest route would take them by the ruins of the Lodge. Two city tiers and three more unsuspecting, now-dead National guards later, he began to feel uneasy with the speed and callousness with which Aisha took lives. The last one looked no older than seventeen, and she'd done nothing besides try to run away. Rain-drenched bodies and the screams of the patrons at Sal's came to mind.

I'm no better.

A blast grabbed their attention on the cross street that ran next to the Lodge. Flaming bits of detritus skewered a National guard not thirty feet from their position. Near where the body lay, stood an older man holding another ball of flaming garbage in the air with kinetics. It was Professor Dunreedy, Ren's old instructor.

"I'd put that down if you want to live," Aisha said. It was the first time she'd given a warning before she went in for the kill.

"Professor!" Ren said, putting a hand on the murderous knight's arm, signaling to stand down.

The old professor dropped his kinetics and limped—*that's new*—over to them, a look of shock on his face. "Mr. Bolin, please tell me you're not the cause of all this chaos."

He probably meant it as a joke, but the presumption of guilt still needled at him, probably because he wasn't far off. The city was on edge even before the night at Sal's, but it was his actions that plunged everything into chaos. It was his fault the Nationals had their crackdown, and if he was honest with himself, he felt responsible for the master pylon as well. After all, Troy and Ka would never have been there had they not correctly assumed he'd try to force his way onto their mission.

He'd taken what little balance the city held onto and pushed it off a cliff.

Like mother, like son.

Ren shrugged uneasily. "Not exactly."

"Is this man important? We need to make haste." Aisha looked toward the street that led up to the master pylon facility with urgency.

"No one you need concern yourself with young lady." Dunreedy looked Ren up and down, probably scanning for anything red. "You've been doing resistance work?"

Does he think that's good or bad?

"Y-Yes," he said. The impulse to make a good impression on the professor came out of nowhere. Even when he attended Danvers, Ren hadn't hung his ego on the teacher's approval. But the laranee incident changed that dynamic. The old man had his respect now.

Dunreedy gave a quick nod. "Good, you wouldn't happen to know where I can speak with a representative? I'm afraid I'm a bit late to the party."

"Ren!" Aisha was getting impatient.

Trusting a man who worked for a school run by the Guild could have easily backfired, but Dunreedy was different. He'd always been different. An air of reluctance had always emanated from him whenever he pushed Ren or Seffin to sign up for the Guild, and he never brought up the academic hatred toward wild elements in his classes.

"First-level slums, all the way to the eastern edge. A set of rowhouses that look like they're about to fall down. Tell them Ren *Adegast* sent you."

Dunreedy cocked his head. "Adegast?"

"They'll know for sure it was me who sent you. I'll explain later." A grim thought occurred to him. "If we both survive, that is."

He didn't wait for a response. Aisha was halfway up the block by the time he caught her. The next right would run straight into the crater that used to house the master pylon. The crater he hoped didn't contain his sister or her lovable oaf, Troy. They were less than five minutes away.

A throng of red-clad citizens were on their knees in the middle of the street. Two dead lay next to them, one scorched and one punctured full of melting ice lances. Kaylee Sorenson, an old classmate of Ren and Seffin's back in Danvers, stood in front of them. An open forehead wound seeped blood down the right side of her face, down her neck, soaking into her blouse. Strands of long, auburn hair hung heavy with it, dripping down onto the ground. Her lips were a straight line, and her eyes met his, pain and rage furrowed her brow.

Ok, I'm getting sick of these reunions.

He'd heard she signed up with the Resistance, but she was part of a cell, not one of the leaders. Aisha looked to Ren for direction. Apparently, this scenario didn't fall under the kill-them-all-and-sort-it-out-later protocol she'd been following, and for that, Ren was grateful.

"Kaylee? What's going on."

A fireball popped into existence above her, a large one by normal mystic standards, but rather average on the Ren scale, and quite small on the Seffin scale.

"Am I killing her?" Aisha asked.

He didn't have time to consider the bizarre situation in which the second most powerful individual in the whole of the empire was taking orders from *him*, a rookie merc. "Kaylee!"

"They killed him!" Kaylee's voice was almost unrecognizable. Hoarse and scratchy, and sad. She'd always been one of his more carefree classmates.

"We didn't! I've never hurt anyone!" said a bald man wearing a red jacket. He was shaking.

"Liar! You're wearing red."

"The whole damn city wears red!"

"Who did they kill?" Ren asked, but she didn't have time to answer. A crack sounded and she fell to the ground. Knight Bahati stood there, the blunt end of her spear in the space Kaylee's head had previously occupied. Ren barely had enough time to stabilize and disperse the fireball before it exploded while all the citizens bolted away. It's lucky she was so weak, comparatively. With his will reserves still recovering, he couldn't have performed the maneuver if it were anyone stronger. The citizens took their opening and bolted.

"You killed her?"

Aisha shrugged. "I'm not sure." Her eyes fell to Kaylee. "She still breathes, so... probably not."

You are unhinged.

He considered tying Kaylee up. If she woke, she could be a danger to even more people, but leaving her tied would be a death sentence. In a few hours, husk would start popping out everywhere, and she'd be a gift-wrapped snack. Hells, she'd die anyway if she didn't wake up in time. The right thing to do would be to carry her to headquarters.

The right thing would have to wait.

The crater was in sight. They could come back for Kaylee *after* they checked on the facility. A quick jog brought them to their destination, not a National guard in sight. He couldn't tell if that was good or bad.

Aisha put her hand on the ground and closed her eyes. "What are you doing?" he asked.

"Checking to see if there are any bodies."

By feeling the cobblestones?

"How?"

Her eyes opened and she glared at him. "Do they teach you *nothing* of the wild elements here? With earth elementalism. Please be silent, I need to concentrate."

The knowledge that she was a wild wielder, and mystic level besides, shocked him. They'd only met a few times before today, but he always assumed, given her title of knight and the spear she wielded, that Aisha was a martial combatant. On the way here she only used the spear. She didn't have any of the other habits wielders had of floating small objects for convenience or adjusting the temperature of rooms for comfort. She was like him, a mystic-level wielder who used martial weapons, but she kept it a secret. *Why?*

"No!" she said. "No no no! Godsdamnit!" She pounded on the ground.

The blood in Ren's veins turned to ice. "What! What is it?"

"I can sense two bodies in a small tunnel, deep in the mountain. But..."

Acid flooded the back of his throat. "But you can't reach them. Even if you could, you couldn't slip them out, could you?"

Tears flooded her eyes. She shook her head. "No, I can't."

Sharon

Tender sat with their head in their hands across from Sharon at the table in headquarters after the master pylon facility explosion. Cal and Jacinda were absent, at home setting up their backup base. Ren and Seffin should be at the lab by now, outside the city wall, safe. But Ka had been with Troy, heading to the facility that was now a pile of rubble. To make matters worse, Polk was missing.

"The boy is with Seffin. Mark my words," Sharon said. She meant it to sound comforting, but it came out aggressive, annoyed.

Tender peeled their face from their hands, worry in every wrinkle of their skin. "Where's Farah?"

"Her emergency protocol is to shelter her students and then report here. Why?"

They stood up, towering over her. Their stature always surprised Sharon. Much too imposing for their personality. Though, she had heard tales of the engineer's participation in the Sol War. Back then, they were known as the Hammer of

Garvelle, and fun little titles like that didn't just happen out of nowhere. They'd earned it with violence.

They brought a worried hand up to their chin and squeezed, a tic she'd noticed since working with them. It meant they were unsure.

"Ka and Troy would have reported here by now if they weren't caught in the blast. If they're alive, they're buried, and Farah is the only one with the will reserves that could help."

With Ka gone, Farah is our best wild wielder. We can't spare her.

"We don't know that they're buried." She was treading carefully. "They could have been arrested. They could have gotten out and been drawn into helping people."

Tender scoffed. "I know what you're doing."

"I'm only speaking the truth."

"Ka is the best healer in the country. She might even be the best healer of our age. She's not a pawn to be sacrificed."

"I wasn't suggesting—"

"No, you weren't. Farah is part of our very limited supply of elementalists. I recognize the position you're in and I don't envy it, but we will need Ka's healing for what is to come."

They were using logic to convince her instead of emotion. That was the assumption everyone made about Sharon. That she was heartlessly driven by logic, rationality, and calculation, but rationality didn't send her on a decade-long revenge mission, and logic didn't prevent her from plunging a sword through Jessica and the country into chaos. Tender's child,

Ren's sister, was probably dead... but she might not be. They were fighting for a chance for their daughter, and Sharon couldn't say no to the person who raised her son. "Take Farah when she arrives." Before she knew what she was doing she'd rounded the table and grabbed Tender's arm. "I owe you and Ka so much. I—"

"Sharon!" Nessa burst into the room. "Garvelle is here."

"What?" *They're a week early.* "What is the empress playing at?"

"If she's here early it's for a reason. Kiko gave me her word. She wouldn't go back on it lightly." Tender said, their hand resting on Sharon's.

"Add it to the list of impossible problems that keep popping up today."

"Well, it might be a nice problem to have," Nessa replied.

Sharon narrowed her eyes. "How so?"

"The Lighton and Estaban armies have been spotted a few miles from the city's border."

That changed things. Rahal and Mitchell, the Estaban prime minister and Lighton's president respectively, hadn't responded to the Resistance when called for aid. An indication they had sided with Winnow. She had her guesses as to the purpose for their betrayal, but that didn't matter now. What mattered was killing Winnow. The Nationals worshiped him like a god. Listened to him when he made immigrants and refugees into bogeymen. Fortunately, the benefit of someone with so much ego was their tendency to make sure no one around them shined as bright. With Paul gone, there would be no one left to pick up the mantle. Washburn might have made a good replacement, but Sharon had already removed that piece from the board.

Still, a dread settled on her as if inside the toothy maw of a monster. Sharon had been an assassin, but she was only a child during the Sol War. An efficient killer she may be, but battles on the scale of the one to come were beyond her. Slinking around in the shadows didn't translate well to directing an army. Tender, on the other hand, had plenty of experience with leading soldiers in battle.

"I know I just said you can take Farah—" Sharon began.

"Kiko can lead the soldiers well enough." Tender was clinging to the idea of saving their daughter, and she couldn't blame them.

"Let me finish." Sharon looked to Nessa. "You report directly to Tender now." She walked toward the door. "I know I just said you can take Farah, but we need you to prepare the Resistance for battle. I'll find Farah, and then we'll search for Ka. If she's alive, we'll find her. Just make sure your old girlfriend doesn't raze the city in the meantime."

Tender only gave a strained nod. The idea of trusting Sharon, of all people, to save their daughter would be a bitter pill to swallow, but they didn't have much choice. They each had their expertise. Tender could lead an army, Sharon couldn't, but rescuing Ka was a singular goal, and if there was anything she was good at, it was pursuing a singular goal.

The path to Farah's led past gruesome sights. Husk had already started to animate, and the citizens were in a panic. At one corner, two husk were gnawing on the neck of a dead woman wearing a striking blue dress. She'd probably been on her way to church when the explosion happened. On another street, a Nationalist mystic burned up anyone not wearing red. It was slightly surprising, given the low number of mystics left in the city. Why would the Nationals let one of their most valuable people expose themselves like that? She lopped off their head and moved on.

Farah's home was unassuming, but honestly, most homes in the city were unassuming. Outside of the noble district, few homes were anything more than rowhouses. One of the limiting factors in building on a mountain, even one as massive as Brinidor, was that space was a commodity, and rowhouses were efficient. Farah's sat on the corner of a block, adjacent to a set of stairs connecting the tiers above and below. A line of people shuffled into the home while Farah, with her ever-present smile, waved people inside. Upon seeing Sharon, her smile took on an annoyed property.

"You know my priority is saving my students," Farah called over from her doorstep.

Sharon patted the air in a calming gesture. "That's fine. After we're done here, I have a special mission for us."

Farah shook her head and continued to shuffle the students and their families into her house, hiding them in her underground training facility. It only took another ten minutes before Farah stood in front of her, ready to hear her orders.

"We think Ka was in the master pylon facility when it exploded."

Farah's smile strained. Curses were rare. Most didn't even believe they were real, but Sharon had seen enough of the world to know they weren't only real, but equal parts bizarre and powerful. There were the ones like Tender had, causing permanent injury and pain. Ones that created a compulsion, such as Farah's smile. Then there were rumors of the ones that seemed to affect the laws of reality, like causing bad luck. From what she knew of how curses were accomplished, though, it seemed far more likely that last one was superstition. The rogue wielder who taught her about curses mentioned tying off a thread between the individual and the Sea of Intention, creating a permanent effect. But the effects had to be specific, she'd been very clear on that point.

Furthermore, curses could only be released by the one who set them. The wild wielder that cursed Farah was dead now, and as such, he was unable to reverse what he'd done. So, Farah would smile until she died, but the smile she wore now was not happy, or sad, or angry. It was panic.

Farah walked down her front steps. "If Ka's gone, we're in a lot of trouble."

"Can Selena handle things here while you're away?"

"Absolutely." Selena stood in the doorway of their home. "This was always the plan, love. Go, we'll be fine here."

A sparkling gray haze of dust and smoke had begun to settle onto the city. Beautiful floating glitter heralding the end of an era. "Ok, first thing is to check the site."

Farah jogged behind Sharon while small atrocities escorted them on their way. A man lay dead, his neck slashed, and on the wall adjacent to his body someone had painted DEATH TO REFUGEES in his own blood. She recognized the man. He'd been homeless and used to sit on her block, complimenting passersby. He was harmless. Then there was the collapsed home a woman and boy wept outside of. They stopped to see if they could help, but the father had been crushed inside. Farah gave the two directions to shelter in her home before Sharon pulled her onward.

They closed in on the crater, but a surprise awaited in the form of a spear questing for her neck. Sharon's blade was out, and deflected the spear before it could touch her skin. The woman who wielded it hopped back into a readied stance, four feet behind her stood Ren who yelled the word "stop" so forcefully Sharon might have mistaken it for a sign that he cared.

"What the hells are you doing here?" he asked.

What the hells are you doing inside the city?

"Tender is helping to ready the Resistance. I'm here as a favor to them." Sharon decided not to interrogate her son. His decisions were his, even if they were stupid.

"You're here for Ka?" His frantic eyes were searching for something to cling to, some thread of hope he could grasp.

The woman with the spear spoke up, "She's deep in the mountain, in a cave that can only be accessed with earth slipping."

"Shit," Sharon said, "is she alive?"

Farah had her palm on the ground. "I can't tell. There're two people there, but whether they are alive or dead is hard to discern."

"Who are you?" Sharon pointed her blade at the spear-wielding woman.

"Knight Aisha Bahati," Ren said. "The empress' top advisor."

"I've heard of you. Can I ask why you just tried to kill me?"

"If I had tried to kill you, you'd be dead. I was only going to question you."

"I'm Sharon, Ren's mom. You may know me by Flicker." The wide-eyed recognition was satisfying if for no other reason than to see the woman's ego deflate a bit. *'If I had tried to kill you, you'd be dead' my ass. She's lucky I didn't flicker her head off her shoulders.* "Any ideas?"

"I can make a tunnel, but it would take too long. They'll run out of air, and it'll burn through my reserves besides."

A foolish idea came to Sharon. The Pit. They needed wild wielders, and more than a few were taken into custody there. It would be heavily guarded though, especially now with the city in a state of emergency. Could the four of them make it through? With her scars still a burden, Sharon's flickering would be hindered. Ren's reserves were still recovering. Farah was strong, but they couldn't risk her right now. Then there was Bahati.

Damn it, Ka. If we save you, you're healing my scars whether you like it or not.

"The Pit. I know for a fact there are a few wild wielders in there that could help us out. Freeing the prisoners was on my list of things to do anyway." It was actually on Tender's list of things to do, but she doubted they'd complain if Sharon checked off one of their tasks while saving their daughter.

Bahati broke her readied stance and leaned against her spear. "How far is this pit?"

"Thirty-minute jog," Sharon said.

The knight knelt and touched the ground, flexing her jaw. "There isn't time."

"Their cave is small. If they are alive, they'll run out of air." Farah gave a solemn smile.

"Can you make a hole for them to breathe?" Ren asked.

Aisha gripped the back of her neck and shook her head. "They're deep in the mountain. Even that will take time and effort from both of us. We won't be able to come with you."

"We?" Sharon asked.

"Aisha is a wild wielder too," Ren said, impatient. "You two do what you can to keep them alive. We'll be back with more wild wielders."

Sharon didn't love taking orders from her son, but she also didn't disagree. Somehow, Ka had gotten both herself and Troy wedged into a small cave deep in the mountain. That meant they were alive, or at least they had been initially. Regardless, if there was a chance to save them, they'd have to leave behind their two wild wielders, leaving only one burned fighter and one burned-out fighter to jailbreak the most secure prison on the continent.

This is suicide.

Two blocks away from the crater, Sharon shed her head-wrap, rivulets of sweat poured down her cheek uncomfortably, and the hanging fabric sticking to her skin became too annoying to ignore. Besides, they were in open war with the Nationals now. No reason for the deception any longer.

"Why didn't you teach me the second form?" Ren said out of nowhere.

This again?

"You weren't ready."

"Bullshit."

The push-back shouldn't have surprised her. In the short time they'd been training, describing his learning style as oppositional would be too kind. How many times had she told him to slow down? How many times had she explained his will reserves necessitated caution? And even with that knowledge he did it anyway, and achieved exactly the result she told him he would. He burned himself out.

"It's not *bullshit,*" she said, turning the corner up to the next tier. They hadn't met a single National on their route thus far, and she started to suspect this was part of their plan. Hiding out somewhere while the husk did their dirty work.

"I popped out of flickering without issue. My problem was the amount of will I had to burn while I was in it. You could have taught me how to modify that with the second form."

Was I this arrogant as a child?

"The second form wouldn't have solved that issue by itself. You needed familiarity with your will pathways first. Familiarity that you only get from repeated practice of the first and third forms." *And had I taught you the second form, you'd have attempted it unsupervised at the soonest opportunity.* A rustling came from a nearby alleyway and they both stopped dead in the middle of the road. "It's a miracle you're even alive. Your will reserves are far too deep for safety," she whispered. A dog came trotting out holding a rat.

"Gosh, woulda been nice if you were there to tell me that when I first started doing it."

Her face got hot. *Enough of this.* "What more can I say to you? I'm sorry. I should have come back to you. I was wrong. But I lost everything. My grandfather. My husband. My best friend. I fought for that fucking village my whole damn life, Ren. I killed. I let myself become a monster. I gave everything for it. And then I watched it torn to shreds because—"

"You had me!" Ren threw his arms out as he shouted. "All you think about is what *you* lost. What happened to *you.*" He put a hand on his chest and gripped his shirt. "I lost everything too! I lost my village. I lost *my* best friend. I lost my mom." Spit flew from his mouth as he spoke. "And then a miracle happens. I meet you. And *surely* you have a good explanation—"

"Enough!" Her voice echoed off the buildings. "I know what I did. I know how it hurt you. It hurts me, too, but I can't go back in time. I want to make it right, but I can't. All I can do is what I'm doing right now." She pointed in the direction of The Pit. "Your sister and her fool of a lover are depending on us to get help." She took a breath and let it out slowly. "Let's do what we can for them. Then, if you want, I'll teach you the second form. Tonight." She walked up to him. Wet streaks under each of his eyes. She ignored the impulse to touch his cheek, the impulse to pull him in. "I'm warning you, though. Your control is barely enough to overcome the depth of your will reserves, and you haven't recovered enough to do it safely."

They jogged the rest of the way in silence. Sharon stole a few glances at her son who kept his eyes glued forward, refusing to acknowledge her.

The walled street leading to The Pit groaned with the sounds of husk. Hundreds of bodies hung rotting, and in the few hours since the barrier went down, a good number of them had reanimated, struggling against their nooses and kicking off the wall, swinging outward, only to come slamming back into the brick. One lay headless beneath their rope. It must have decapitated itself trying to struggle free.

The stench of death was overpowering, but they had to walk through it to get to the prison. From this distance, she could see there were no guards at the entrance. *Curious.* As they walked, they cut apart as many free-shambling husk as they could while keeping a forward momentum. Time was short, and the hanging husk would have to wait. At least until they reemerged from The Pit.

The empty entranceway led down to a holding area which fed into the dungeon proper. In the center of the room sat a pylon giving off a dull light and humming faintly.

"This is just like the one from the lab," Ren said. He stood a few feet from it, staring at the bracings the crystal sat in.

The thick air made breathing difficult. Sharon knew what this crystal was for. Wind rushed past them, up out of the stairwell. It smelled like sour, drunkard's breath after a night of ale. Her body stiffened. "He's mad," she said, turning toward the stairs.

"Who, Winnow?"

Air rushed through the room again, this time down *into* the stairwell. It wasn't wind. It was breath. Something was down there. Something massive.

Ren

"We need a mystic," Ren said.

Sharon stalked to the edge of the stairwell; a rush of wet, putrid wind pushed up through the room. Living in Prolivgrad most of his life gave Ren a resistance to noxious smells—fish being a notable exception—but the thick, almost viscous, air with its sewer smell brought on waves of nausea. He fought against his body's insistence he should puke.

"Gosh, would be nice if we had one of those." His mother gave him a critical look.

She didn't have to say more than that. He'd ignored her warnings about flickering and now, when they needed him at his full potential the most, he was nothing more than a man with a really sharp blade. That would be enough for most husk and amalgamations alike, but whatever was causing this rancid wind was assuredly not like *most* husk or amalgamations. The massive, flopping amalgamation outside Nari'ko came to mind. He hadn't needed elementalism to handle that. *No, just flickering. Which I also shouldn't do right now.*

Sharon pulled a torch from the wall with her will. "Grab yourself one, and let's go." She floated it without any body movement. Ren's mother had always used kinetics so casually and frequently, so precise she could even write with it. The puzzle pieces of her past began to form the picture of her present for him. Why would a mayor of a small town be a master wielder? She could turn almost any object into a weapon. You could injure her. You could catch her. But it wouldn't matter, even tied up she could kill with a pebble or murder with a pin. Skills for an assassin, not for a mayor. He understood now, she'd always straddled the line between her two jobs, but when the mayor's home was destroyed the assassin took over.

She was supposed to be my mother.

The dungeon continued its respirations as they descended, releasing the few prisoners left alive as they went. Most were business owners or low-level politicians who'd refused to fall in line with the new order. None could wield. That was expected, the more dangerous or valuable the prisoner, the lower in The Pit they would be.

The underground tower's design left much to be desired. Instead of making a single stairwell, floors had staircases on alternating sides, which meant they had to traverse a long hallway between every floor. It made escape more difficult, sure, but the amount of time a guard would've had to waste just to perform their duties must have been extreme. They lit the small torches lining the walls as they walked by, dim light danced behind them as they journeyed forward, further into the shadowy corridors.

On the sixth or seventh floor, Ren had already lost count, a low reverberation moved through. A deep, throaty sound followed by a blast of air which left their torches fluttering and the hairs on Ren's neck standing on end. Still, they saw nothing to indicate the source of the sound, only cells with sickly, weak prisoners, barely strong enough to walk their way out.

Ren's shoulders trembled. Something awaited at the bottom of the prison, something whose breath moved enough air to fill all the corridors and cells, and they were walking toward it. *Ka's in danger. She needs a wild wielder.* A grip on his shoulder halted his shaking. Was his mother actually trying to comfort him?

The grip was too tight.

He turned and the entirety of his vision became teeth as a husk came up just short on its bite, he barely pushed it back in time. It lunged at him again, he yelped, then its head fell off. The husk crumpled to the ground with a thud. His uniform said he'd been a guard in life, and judging by his badge, he was someone important. His mother had her blade out. Her eyes looked him over frantically.

"Are you ok?" she asked.

I walked through a horde for an entire day and fought an amalgamation the size of a city block by myself. Yes, I'm ok.

"How far down do we need to go?" his voice shook despite himself.

Sharon walked over, grabbed his hand, and pulled him to standing. "It's thirty floors."

"We're going all the way to the bottom?"

"Of course, the last floor will have the most valuable prisoners."

This was good news. Going through every floor meant they would save everyone. The shaking in his hands was excitement, not fear. This is what heroes did. Traversing the darkness, saving people, fighting husk, finding the beast that can shake an entire dungeon with its breath. *This is how heroes die.* Besides, the best chance at saving his sister was to make sure they found every wielder that could help... if there were any left alive.

His mother's features softened before she went on. "I won't let anything happen to you."

He believed her, but before he could respond, she turned and started trekking forward again. She couldn't have known how the words would affect him. How they brought him back to Gull Harbor, to his childhood, a fleeting memory of a time when each other was all they cared about.

They found what they came for, eventually. If his mother was to be believed, they were on floor twenty-two. Two wild wielders and a mystic were in full-body shackles, tightly pulled to the wall of their cells, all half-starved with wide, bloodshot eyes. Ren always kept some jerky on him, and so he offered it up, his mother did the same. The three freed prisoners gnawed at the rations with fervor, ripping off pieces and handing them to each other until it was all gone.

"We need a favor," his mother began. She explained the situation, how the master pylon facility was now a crater, how they believed their best healer and the president of the Guild were stuck, and how they came here specifically searching for help.

The prisoners agreed quickly, though that was expected. She *had* just saved their lives *and* promised food and shelter. They sent them on their way, reassuring them the path to the entrance was clear. When she walked toward the stairwell that led deeper into The Pit, there was only a moment of hesitation before Ren followed, continuing the journey downward again.

Eight floors left.

The walls dripped with more and more condensation as they went, and puddles started to form on the ground. Instead of getting colder the further down they went, the temperature increased with their descent. Sweat salt burned his eyes and Ren wiped it away. Another rumbling shook them, more violent than before, he had to brace up against the warm, sticky wall to keep from falling.

Three floors left.

They didn't find anyone else; every cell had been left open and empty. Breathing had become a struggle. With all the walking and the heat and the humidity, Ren was lightheaded.

Inhalation brought only putrid air and a growing impulse to turn and leave and never look back.

Bottom floor.

Finally, they stepped down onto the last floor of the prison, but it wasn't stone beneath them. Nor was it dirt or gravel or pebbles. The uneven, slick texture had some give, almost like a pillow, almost like—his mother froze, grabbed his arm, and started slowly stepping back, toward the stairs they just came down. She didn't say a word, and by the concern in her eyes and the tightness of her grip, Ren could tell he shouldn't either. That's when they heard the weeping from down the corridor. The wind, an inhalation this time, whipped past them. Something in Ren's ears went taught, like he'd swam too far underwater, it drowned out the weeping.

Part of him wanted to not care, to prioritize his own survival. *I can't save anyone if I'm dead.* Callousness, in this case, was very much in service of self-preservation. This *was* the bottom floor, though, and it had been true thus far that the further down they traveled the stronger the wielders they found.

Without a word, his mother stalked forward, gliding across—he was sure of it now—a floor made of flesh. Maybe it was cowardly, but he hung back. Whoever was at the end of the hall wouldn't need both of them and if this thing could feel them walking... on it? In it? Then better to keep it to one person instead of two.

Her torch disappeared into a cell forty or so paces in front of him. The weeping halted as an exhalation blasted through the hallway with such force Ren fell backward. He rolled onto his hands and knees, the floor was a series of tightly clustered bumps, or buds. His back, arms, and palms were enveloped in a slimy, mucous-like liquid. It clung as he stood, thick strings of it hung off him, connected to the ground.

This was saliva, the floor was a tongue.

His mother came around the corner supporting a man Ren almost didn't recognize without his crown of twigs. Sent'o's beautiful hair was matted, and the skin on his face looked draped directly over his skull. If he hadn't known better, he would have sworn the smile Sent'o flashed was nefarious, but it was just warped from malnutrition. His lips were cracked and oozed blood.

Sharon brought the Nari'ko Wilder to the steps where Ren rushed to support his other side, and they ascended together, slowly and as quietly as possible. They made it three floors before they took a break and leaned up against a wall, breathing heavily and hoping whatever slumbered at the bottom of The Pit would continue slumbering.

"I thought you were supposed to be in Estaba," Ren said after catching his breath.

Sent'o coughed. "That was a full year ago, but yes. That's where I was when the Egallan coup happened, and when I found out Rahal planned to side with Winnow, I came here to warn what was left of the Lodge." He made a weak, broad gesture at the surroundings. "This was my thanks. Ratted out by a merc I thought I could trust."

"Don?" Sharon and Ren said at the same time.

Sent'o's brow furrowed. "Just so... I knew him from before. He said he was part of the Resistance."

"Ren killed him," Sharon said, flatly. "Please tell me you're an earth elementalist."

"Hi, I'm Sent'o," he said, delicately grabbing her hand and sandwiching it between both of his. "And I am, in fact, an earth elementalist."

The gesture was intimate, but less grand than Ren was used to from him. The other two times they'd met the man was all hugs and kisses. He wondered if his mother was familiar with Nari'ko's ways.

She brought Sent'o's hands up to her lips and kissed them before cupping his cheek in her other hand. "May the will of the world guide our path."

That made sense. He knew she was well-traveled, she had to have met plenty of Nari'ko Wilders before, but she was so tender with him. It almost made Ren jealous. *Where was this soft touch when we were training?*

"Just so," Sent'o said, bowing his head.

The rest of the way went slowly. Sent'o couldn't go more than two floors without a break, and he was, unfortunately, too heavy for them to carry. Drag? Maybe. Carry? Absolutely not. The air thinned and the heat dissipated as they walked. There was very little conversation along the way, only enough to update Sent'o on the situation. He agreed to help rescue Ka without hesitation. Unbeknownst to Ren, he had been Ka's first teacher, the one who taught her healing, and he didn't like the idea of his best student dying.

On the top floor, a crowd of people awaited them. While they were in The Pit, the walls of corpses leading to the entrance had turned into walls of husk, leaping off the bricks to grab at whoever came near. As long as they stayed in the entrance to The Pit, though, they were safe. A few had made it off the wall without decapitating themselves, but the wielders and elementalists they released took care of those, their bodies lay pierced or singed outside the building they all hid inside.

"How long were we down there?" Ren asked. It couldn't have been more than a couple of hours.

Sharon poked her head out of the entryway and looked up at the sky. "Four hours. At least."

Ren pulled his will-blade out. He didn't know how long someone could survive inside a hole in a mountain, but he wanted his sister out of there, now. The street groaned and rasped a greeting at him while he went to work chopping every husk down by the neck. Sharon appeared beside him, her blade flashing toward the dangling undead. An ice lance skewered one and a wind blade hissed through another.

"Save your reserves," Ren called behind him as he separated a child husk's head from its body. His stomach knotted. If they hadn't returned his body to Ahmad, that could have been Hassan, running around among all the other dead the Nationals refused to burn. "The wild wielders will need it to help my sister, and we may need the mystics for a fight."

Sharon and Ren worked their way through the street, wet plopping sounds squelching around them as the husk fell to the ground. He regretted not taking care of this before they entered The Pit, and grimaced at the street filled with rotting corpses after they made it through. They should burn them, all it would take is a roaming husk to come and use all the dead flesh to form an amalgamation, but that would take even more time they didn't have. The few mystics in the group didn't have the reserves to light them all up without draining themselves either. *Seffin could do this with hardly any effort.*

A deep rumble and a violent quaking knocked everyone to the ground. In his periphery, Ren could hear the crumbling of buildings. More people dying. The shaking continued, rattling the teeth in his head. An earsplitting crack gave way to yet more rumbling. The entrance to The Pit tilted and jittered as if trying to keep its balance and failing miserably. Yellow teeth burst from the ground around the structure, they gave way to rotten lips and a massive tube of segmented, dull, yellow flesh that thrust upward before gravity caught up to it. A giant worm listed toward the capitol building, but it hit something and recoiled, screaming a low, throaty cry before collapsing downward against the mountain, crushing homes on the tier below. Then it stilled, hardly moving save for some undulations in its body.

Ren's itching finger hardly registered over the prickling, needling sensation that cascaded over him. Everything inside him was telling him to run, but his limbs weren't obeying. His mother had already popped up, pulling others to a standing position as fast as she could. He stared at his legs, willing them to move. The foot twitched, and then the knee bent, and then the dam broke, and he was up, grabbing as many people as he could and pulling them up too.

This was an amalgamated colossi of some creature he'd never seen. It had to be. Normal amalgamations became unwieldy blobs of flesh and hunger, they couldn't create something so structured. *No, wait... Didn't Shaia mention something about a worm?*

"A dreadworm?"

Sharon nodded. "Yes, but I don't know one got this far west."

She quickly got to business and gave their non-wielding survivors directions to headquarters, sparing the group's strongest mystic for protection. The remaining walked with them toward the crater that used to hold the Master Pylon Facility. The city had become a mosaic of disasters, and Ren had no idea what the bigger picture was supposed to be. Did Winnow *plan* all of this? Why? How?

The scene at the site was exactly as they left it, with only one exception. The two elementalists were frantic. Bahati glared at the ground and Farah's smile strained with effort.

Ren's heart pounded in his chest. "What's wrong?"

Bahati responded first. "We're not sure of anything yet."

"What happened?" Panic had him shouting now.

Farah refused to look at him directly. "We were able to get them some air, but..."

"What the *hells* happened?"

A tear slipped from Bahati's eye. "The cave they were in collapsed."

He fell to his knees. It had all been for nothing.

Seffin

"Are there any side effects to know about before we let the key to our salvation bind an undead monster to himself?" Kiko stood between Polk and Sumiko. The latter holding a small knife to draw blood from the boy.

Sumiko shrugged. "I feel nothing besides a presence in the back of my head. Tyler hates the feeling, says it whispers to him. But that could just be his shallower reserves. Jessica had said when one of her creatures died, she felt their loss, but other than that, nothing."

Seffin had already given his blood, clutching his hand with a clean towel save for the blooming red spot where it touched his finger. Polk huffed and stepped around Kiko. "This isn't your decision."

Kiko stepped in his way again and glared down at him. "I disagree. In fact, given the situation, I would say it's more our decision than it is yours."

"Empress, don't," Seffin said. "He's capable of—"

"He is a *child*."

"You have no right to treat me as such." Polk stepped into Kiko's space, throwing a threatening stare right back at her. "My entire reason for existing is to stop Koth from killing everyone, and winning this fight is a requirement for my success. Don't stand in my way."

Kiko waved her hand dismissively. "You can't be older than ten."

"So you think ten is old enough to sacrifice myself, but not old enough to fight in a battle?" Despite only coming up to her waist, the boy's presence overshadowed Kiko's. "How old was Tara when you slit her throat? How old were you?"

The empress' eyes went wide. Her mouth dropped open and her hands went immediately to her blades. "I've never told anyone about that. How could you possibly—"

A smug grin leapt onto Polk's face. "Step aside, Empress."

Her mouth snapped shut and her brows knit together. "No. First, tell me how you know about Tara."

"I was born of the Sea and I contain all its knowledge. I saw through Tara's eyes, and I saw your hands, no bigger than my own, holding the blade to her throat."

"I didn't know..." she said, but doubt slipped into her tone and her deadly stare shifted away from Polk, down to the ground. "I thought she poisoned my mother."

"I don't care, Empress. Get out of my way. Now."

Kiko stepped aside. The age lines on her face, which normally granted a distinguished look, now only accented the obvious shock. Polk stepped forward and held his hand out to Sumiko. "Take my blood."

The cut was swift and Sumiko's binding mixture was drawn into an angry-looking syringe within a minute. Since meeting, Seffin had assumed he and Polk were similar. Polk had a hard time relating to people in some of the same ways he did. But they weren't similar, at all. Polk didn't care how people reacted to him whereas Seffin spent the entirety of his first trip outside Prolivgrad wallowing in self-doubt.

There was something beneath the confidence, though. Seffin worked hard to analyze people, trying to determine how they were feeling, to figure out the dissonance between how someone behaved and what they said, and what that might mean. It was a language everyone was born with that he had to study. The studying is what led him to the flexed muscle at the corner of Polk's eyes, the lips pressed into a line, the way he gripped the hem of his tunic. Pressure is the best way he could describe it. A teapot screaming to be taken off the fire.

Seffin stepped next to him and put his hand on his back. He wanted to show him support, show him that he believed in him. Show him that the confidence he had wasn't unfounded. The boy's tension in his muscles released, ever so slightly.

Sumiko broke the silence. "I've never heard someone your age speak the way you do."

"Give me the werewiller and the laranee." Polk peered up at Seffin and then back to Sumiko. "Please."

***

The empress' about-face on Polk surprised everyone. She went from wanting to lock him away for his own safety to, within an hour, insisting he come along to meet with Rahal and Mitchell, the leaders of Estaba and Lighton. All parties promised no hostilities while they spoke. Not enough to assuage Seffin's fears, but Kiko had promised this type of thing was commonplace and, after much swearing about Rahal's status as a carrion worm, swore he wasn't so duplicitous as to ambush them during their talk.

What reassured Seffin was the fact that, between himself and Polk, any ambush they might have planned would go very poorly.

"I'm going to ask that you keep quiet as much as you can during this," Kiko said. "Feel free to answer if they address you, but please don't volunteer information they could use against us."

"Like what?" Seffin asked.

"Like the fact that we have four people with amalgamations bound to them."

"Two, for now," Polk said. "Mine and Seffin's won't be ready until tomorrow."

"Which is one of the reasons we're having this meeting. I want to delay this battle as much as possible. Even if I'd like nothing more than to twist Bruhier's head off his neck with my bare hands."

Seffin found himself wondering what happened between Kiko and Bruhier, but the empress' white-knuckled fist told him to let it be. Besides, now that he knew Polk was an *actual* know-it-all. He could just ask him about it later.

"You're planning to tell them who I am, right? That's what the meeting is about?" Polk cocked his head in an almost re-hearsed way. Done explicitly, not subconsciously. Unnatural in how reliably he performed the gesture.

Kiko grinned. "You're right. You're not like other kids, and I'm sorry for underestimating you." She ruffled his hair in a way that Seffin could only read as playful mocking. "Yes. I'm going to try and appeal to their sense of self-preservation by revealing that you're the key to stopping the hordes. Best case scenario: they relent, and we liberate Prolivgrad from Winnow. Worst case scenario: I get to punch Bruhier's heart right out of his chest." Her grin turned wolfish. "It's a win, win."

"Why don't we just kill them when we get there?" Polk asked. The innocent curiosity in his tone a stark contrast to the brutality of his inquiry.

"Because we'd rather they help us with your mission, and if we kill them. their armies won't be inclined to join up." Kiko chuckled. "I thought you were smarter than that."

The ground trembled in a wave, and they all froze. It came from the direction of Prolivgrad, glittering smoke continued to waft into the air from the crater, the haze of which dimmed the afternoon sun. No one asked the obvious question: 'What was that?' No one would know the answer anyway. Kiko was the first to move again, which prompted Seffin and Polk to do the same.

The clearing was already full of soldiers when they arrived. Half wearing the black and gold of Garvelle and the other half a mix of tans and greens for the soldiers of Estaba and Lighton. A bald man with a salt and pepper beard wearing a sand-colored breastplate stood next to a taller man wearing a green robe and a slimy smile. They each had the eyes of a predator, one a tiger and the other a snake.

The snake stepped forward, clasping his hands, and called to them from the clearing, "Kiko! I'm sorry we're meeting under such—"

"Rahal! Tell your pet to keep his mouth shut while the adults are talking. I don't trust you for a second, but I trust him less."

The snake, who at this point Seffin assumed was President Duncan Mitchell, twisted his face into an expression of offense. "I will not be spoken to—"

"Shut your mouth, Mitchell," the tiger, Prime Minister Bruhier Rahal, said. To his credit, face red with embarrassment, Duncan dutifully closed his mouth. Then the empress of Garvelle strolled into the clearing, Seffin and Polk trailing behind her. Bruhier's upper lip curled with contempt as he addressed Kiko. "Tell me the information that will save you from our armies."

Kiko put one hand on her hip and the other resting on the pommel of one of her blades and scoffed. "I'm not afraid of losing to a soft-bellied nation of farmers and their moody, older sibling. I didn't ask you here to beg for peace, I asked for this meeting to warn you. While my army is formidable, it can't be two places at once. While I crushed the two of you beneath my boot, Winnow would continue to have free rein in Prolivgrad which, as you can see—" She made a broad gesture toward Prolivgrad, a giant plume of smoke in the middle of the city billowed into the sky. "—means more meaningless deaths and more shit the rest of us will have to clean up after."

"There is no 'us' Kiko," Bruhier snarled.

"I wish there wasn't an 'us', Prime Minister. But unfortunately, you and I were born in the same age, and the gods saw fit to link our fates. Winnow must be stopped, and Jessica's plan enacted before the world is overrun by an amount of husk that would make the horde outside Nari'ko look like a little get-together."

President Mitchell's eyebrows almost reached his receding hairline. "Liar!" he shouted. "You and Saunders fabricated that whole—"

"Quiet!" Bruhier spun on the president. "Enough of your denials. How you can have a horde the size of a city in your country and still doubt the surging husk numbers is beyond me, but we won't be entertaining your conspiracy theories today. Kiko's right that the longer Winnow goes unchecked the more hollowed out Prolivgrad will become. Without the master pylon, it will be mere hours before husk start popping out of the walls. We don't have time to waste on your stupidity."

That made Seffin curious. Were they not here in support of Winnow? Or did Bruhier just have a healthy animosity toward everyone?

The prime minister turned back to Kiko. "Still, I'm not convinced we have to work with *the empire* to protect our lands."

Kiko's right eye twitched and she scratched her left index finger against the pommel of her sword. She was on edge, and looking around at the others, Seffin didn't think anyone else had noticed.

"This is Polk." Kiko gestured toward the boy and launched into an explanation of the Vessel of Koth, the series of cycles their world had gone through, and the importance of making sure Polk made it to Gogallo with enough support to take Danvers' place.

While she explained, Duncan's face kept animating into different versions of 'this is unbelievable' and 'are you actually buying this?' The man was loud even while silent.

At the end of it all, Bruhier scratched at his beard and frowned. "That explains one boy. Who's this other one?"

"Seffin Rashee," he said, afraid to say much more. The whole thing felt like a tightrope walk without a net. Kiko widened her eyes at him and Bruhier's frown deepened, apparently, they wanted more than his name. "My father was head of the research and development division at the Guild," he offered.

Kiko rolled her eyes. "And he's the most powerful mystic on record." Shooting a pointed look in his direction, she said, "*That's* why he's here."

Both Mitchell and Rahal took a step back. Rahal pointed at Kiko. "If you think killing us—"

"Relax. Unless you strike first, he won't attack you. Not even if I wanted him to." That was true. Seffin made it clear he didn't take orders from her. Especially not orders that involved unprovoked murder. A familiar, wolfish grin jumped onto her face. "But I've seen firsthand what he can do, and if you think your army could stop him, I would question your sanity."

A crack like thunder pierced their ears, followed shortly thereafter by a quake that threw everyone to the ground. The earth bucked like a horse and Seffin gripped blades of grass as if they were the reins.

"She's trying to kill us!" Duncan shouted.

"No she's not, you fool. Look!" Bruhier, lying on the ground, pointed to Prolivgrad.

Four tiers up, where The Pit used to be, a segmented cylinder of flesh towered, listing toward the Capitol building before it shuttered with a deep, pained cry, reversed direction, and collapsed onto the buildings below.

Ren and Tender were both still in the city. And Ka... Seffin got to his feet with difficulty, his body still vibrating from the quake. They had to be ok. Ever since coming back to this stupid city, it had been nothing but tragedy, betrayal, pain. He'd lost too much already. Kent and Don. He wouldn't lose Ren. He wouldn't lose his new family. Stumbling at first, he started toward Prolivgrad.

"Wait!" Polk's too-high voice pierced his panic-stricken mind. He stopped to see Polk jogging after him and Kiko standing in the clearing, looking down at the two other leaders. Polk grabbed at his hand, and if he didn't know better, Seffin could swear the wide eyes and sweaty palms indicated fear.

"Rashee, you'll want to wait a moment." Kiko's gaze didn't leave the two leaders still scrabbling to their feet. "That's a dreadworm. I have no idea how in the six hells it managed to get this far west, but it doesn't look like you two have a choice any longer. If any of us ever wants access to focus crystals again we'll have to work together."

"Dreadworms are real?" Duncan asked with a level of desperation and disbelief unbecoming of a full-grown man, let alone a world leader. Of anyone Seffin had met in his life, no one was more unimpressive. Even Tolkar.

"Gods, but you are stupid," Kiko said. "They aren't an uncommon sighting on the eastern edge of the empire, and we've killed them before. But we've never seen one west of Garvelle City. I can't fathom how it got across the Kanning Strait and onto Sol, but it doesn't matter. We need to kill it. When it's done digesting whatever it just ate it will destroy the city and anyone inside it."

"How do we know you didn't bring that thing with you?" Duncan asked.

Kiko pinched the bridge of her nose. "Honestly, who in their right mind voted you into office? Are your people really so foolish?"

"Answer him," Bruhier said, dusting himself off.

"Both of you?" Kiko appeared genuinely surprised before shaking her head and narrowing her eyes. "I should think the size of the damn thing is enough evidence to absolve me. How would I possibly transport it? Enough." She walked to join Seffin and Polk, her soldiers filing after. "If you want a chance at killing it, you'll join us. My army is the only one on Kohru that's killed one before, and we won't be sharing our techniques with enemies."

She gestured toward the city, and they left the leaders of Lighton and Estaba to make their decision.

"That man has killed a lot of people," Polk said once they were out of earshot.

"Rahal?" Seffin asked.

"No," Kiko said. "For all his bluster and hatred, Bruhier isn't a murderer. You're talking about Duncan?"

Polk kept his eyes forward. "Yes. I don't know why he acts so cowardly."

"Because he *is* a coward. A foolish coward who clings to power because the moment he slips someone will put a knife in his back. Lighton's people may be docile, but their politicians are anything but."

After a few more minutes of walking, Seffin asked, "What technique do you have for killing the dreadworm?"

"That, young Rashee, was a lie." Her lips pressed together. "We've only ever killed one, and it was only by dumb luck and Tender's inventions that we did."

Troy

Tight spaces had never bothered Troy. At least he hadn't ever given them much thought before today, but between the rock stabbing him in the chest every time he inhaled, the cramping in his calf, and the inability to adjust to get comfortable, death began to sound like a relief he longed for.

If not for Ka.

She'd saved him, at great cost. One he couldn't repay, not unless they both survived. Though, for being so smart it seemed pretty stupid to trap herself with him knowing they didn't have a way out. It was exactly the type of suicidal idiocy he would attempt to save someone he cared about. It was simple math. One dead person or two. She chose two.

The cramp in his calf knotted tighter, flexing his foot and jabbing Ka with the toe of his boot yet again. A muted '*oof*' sounded from below. The part of her he was poking had to be somewhere in the chest. Either her ribs or her breast. Asking was a waste of their limited air, and feeling around with his toe to sate his curiosity could be... misconstrued.

The air had been stale to start with and grew more and more so with each passing minute. Breathing was hard what with the stabbing rock already, but he couldn't catch his breath no matter what he did. Quick and shallow got his heart rate going and made the dizziness worse, slow and shallow only set a timer when his body would revolt, forcing a giant gulp of air which brought on the stabbing. He'd settled on four shallow and one moderate. Though sometimes it still wasn't enough, and he'd have to just cope with the rock jabbing into his chest, by now it had to have struck blood.

His cramp surged again and up came another *'oof'* from below.

"Would you stop poking my tit," Ka's weak voice still managed to carry a cartload of irritation.

Well, that answers that question.

"I..." Slow breath out, moderate breath in. "...can't help it. My calf is cramping."

"Oh." She said. A damp hand touched his leg and suddenly the pain evaporated. The stinging in his limb went away too. "Why didn't you say something earlier?" She didn't seem to have the same troubles breathing as he did.

"I didn't want you to waste-ah!" The rock pushed deeper into his flesh.

"What was that?" The hand on his leg gripped tighter. "Gods, Troy. It doesn't take much will to heal these shallow cuts, and that rock spiking into you won't take much either."

A small crack sounded next to him, and suddenly he could breathe deeply without pain. The fog that had taken up residence in his head began to clear.

"Thank you."

"I'm going to get us out of here." She let go of his calf and he immediately missed the connection. "First, we'll need some air. If we can get that, it's just a matter of time before I can drill us out of here."

"How are you going to manage that?" Speaking full sentences without pausing for breath was an indulgence after the hour of pain. "I thought it took all your will just to get us here."

"It did, but I'll have more in a bit. The makeup of Brinidor is different than other mountains. There are... soil paths through the rock. That's how I got us here. It will still eat at my reserves, but moving dirt is easier than moving rock."

Ugh, science. Troy had been forced to learn far too much of it in the last few months. Will pathways, soil pathways, amalgamation binding, crystal harmonics, focus crystal grenades. Why did *everything* have to be about science?

"How long is a bit?" he asked.

"Hard to say. Depends on what I find when I start drilling."

Great.

"I still think you should—"

"No. Not unless there's no other—did you feel that?"

The cramp started to come back, his back was starting to ache from laying at an odd angle, his nose was rubbing itself raw on the roof of the hole they were in, and the heat and humidity had triggered a profuse amount of sweating. But somehow, he didn't think she meant any of that. "No, what did you feel?"

"It's probably nothing."

The air quality improved and a hint of a breeze wafted through and then stopped. "What was that?"

"I found another pocket and made a hole for more air. It'll buy us some time."

Of all the mercs he could have been stuck with on his outing to Oleksandra's Harbor, he thanked all the gods he got Ka and her crew. "What made you take the job to escort me?"

"What makes you ask?"

"I don't know. We're stuck, there's not much else to do besides think, and I thought about that."

She made a '*hmm*' sound before saying, "Besides the ridiculous amount of coin the Guild was offering? Poppy. They knew something was suspicious about that contract. Ren thought he'd chosen it, but Poppy had it all set up for us to take from the jump." She grunted and he heard a rustling. Probably just Ka adjusting, she'd be in an uncomfortable position, just like him.

"Are all your jobs like that?"

"Any jobs I take with Poppy are, but they're always worth it. The ones I take on my own are shorter, simpler. Mostly contracts for healing or taking care of a roaming amalgamation or amalgamated colossi."

Yes, my guardian brings me on intentionally dangerous missions, but when I'm not doing that, I spend my time fighting nightmares any sane person would stay the hells away from. It chilled him how casually she spoke of putting her life at risk on someone else's whims. But he'd been placed in danger by his mother without his knowledge. At least Ka was aware and amenable to Tender's machinations.

"Did you always want to be a merc?"

She let out a long sigh. "No. I wanted to work as a researcher at the Guild. Poppy didn't like that idea, so they carted me off to Nari'ko to train as a wild wielder. When we got back, the Guild wouldn't touch me."

"Oh."

"Yeah."

Her path was set by Tender just like his had been set by his mother.

"I'm sorry."

"Don't be. I still get to do research. It's just on my own instead of in a lab, and instead of working on projects for the Guild I work on improving my healing."

That's why she carted a library around with her wherever she went.

His lower back screamed, he shifted as much as the space allowed and the scream quieted to merely a shout. The vertebrae—he'd learned that word from Ka—felt as if they were trying to tear apart from each other. He did his best to ignore it. "Still, Tender made your life into what they wanted instead of letting you decide."

Another brief gust of not-quite-fresh air pushed through. She was keeping busy while they talked. "I've given them an earful about that. It's hypocritical considering how much they hate when other people make decisions for them, but what's done is done. All I can do is try my best to live my life on my terms now. Which I do."

"Is that why you don't like being the boss?"

"The what?"

"You said earlier you don't like being the one to make big decisions."

A moment of silence passed where Troy thought he might have overstepped.

"I hadn't thought of that, but I suppose. I hate dictating what people should or shouldn't do, and outside of healing, I don't like feeling responsible for them either."

And since meeting him, their relationship had largely been shaped by her caring for him. Guilt wormed its way into his chest before a blast of air blew in, as fresh as the outside world, or at least as fresh as Prolivgrad ever came. "Good work," he said.

"That wasn't me."

"Wait, is that what you felt earlier?"

"Maybe." The word came out as a grunt as she shifted her body again. "I think... I think there's another earth elementalist out there trying to reach us."

"Thank the gods!" If someone else knew they were in here, that would increase their chances dramatically. An almost imperceptible vibration shifted the rock underneath him.

"Please tell me you felt that one."

"I did."

"Well at least I'm not going crazy."

"There's a but in there."

"… but I have no idea what's causing it."

Troy smiled. Even with the ominous vibration, the fresh air cooled his skin. For a moment he wished for some light, but then decided he was probably better off *not* seeing just how small their hole was. "All we have to do is wait now, right?" he asked. Immediately cursing himself for, again, looking to Ka to guide him out of this situation. It wasn't like he had a choice, though.

"Sure." She didn't sound sure. "I don't know what else I can do right now. I need to wait for my reserves, and the air problem is solved." She touched his calf again. "Tell me about your childhood."

"Um… why?"

"The talking helps me keep my mind off how completely fucked we are. Humor me."

"Didn't our chances just improve?"

"Moderately. But digging us out of this hole is going to take an immense amount of will. There aren't many mystic level wild wielders left in the city." She squeezed his calf a couple times. "So, humor me."

He could hear the smile in her voice, but she wasn't trying to keep her mind off the situation. She was trying to keep *his* mind off the situation. Regardless, they were stuck with nothing but time in a dank, dark hole and chattering at each other made it less miserable.

"I barely knew my dad. He died when I was five. My mom refused to tell me how."

"Sad."

"Eh, the memories I have of him are... not great. He didn't like me. Actually, my mom protected me from him." A lock box in his mind rattled back and forth. He *knew* what it contained but wouldn't acknowledge it. Best to keep it shut for now. "After he died, she sent me off to boarding school. Despite how close it was to our home, she made me stay on campus. We met once a month when she would check on my performance and plan out my class schedule. When she found out I didn't have the will reserves necessary for a wielder, I got put in business classes."

"That sounds dull."

I actually enjoyed them...

"Yeah, I wouldn't call it exciting, but I did well. The economies of the different countries are so vastly different and learning how interwoven and messy our trade agreements are with each other... I guess I'm just good at making sense of it all."

She chortled. "Troy Marcus Saunders, you nerd."

He closed his eyes and grinned. An expression lost in the pitch of their hole, but he couldn't help it. "You carry forty pounds of books around on contracts."

"That's research!"

"You're the nerd."

She laughed, which made something in his chest just a little bit lighter. "Fine. So you graduated from nerd school and your mom helped you become president of the Guild. Then what."

It sounded so much worse laid out like that. The truth is he'd been silver spooned instead of nurtured. He hadn't asked for the position; it was thrust on him. Negotiating life or death situations based on profit analyses and tangled trade agreements wasn't covered in any of his classes. Everyone needed focus crystals, but miners couldn't keep up. And the Guild mystics employed to charge outlying pylons kept quitting or requesting transfers to safer positions. Gull Harbor happened, of course, but there were towns before and after that. Hinterton, Colville, Poriah, all scrubbed from the map because of decisions he'd made.

He had been too young, too inexperienced, too dependent on his studies. Elevated beyond his capabilities. Days were spent flailing in the ocean of expectations the world had for him, and nights were spent strung out with a glass of whiskey or gin and a woman of leisure at his side. All a blur now.

"If you read the papers, you pretty much know the rest."

Ka sucked in her teeth. "Sorry. That was a thoughtless question."

An awkward silence yawned between them. Troy wondered if Ka was judging him. She *should* judge him. He wasn't innocent.

"I don't get it," she said, finally.

"What?"

"Why blow up the master pylon? Why kill the hostage before most people know you have one?"

Troy shrugged his shoulders for the benefit of absolutely no one. "Not sure. He said all the loyalists were given crystals, but I know for a fact there aren't enough for all the Nationals. The Guild has a stockpile for its own workers, but that's drained right now. We use it for pylon maintenance teams. There's no way he'd have enough to protect more than a handful of people. He had to know he'd be killing some of his own followers."

"Don't take this the wrong way, but I really miss my life from before we took your contract."

Before you met me, you mean.

She went on, "I miss not caring what makes someone like Winnow tick. I miss coming home every night and arguing with Ren and enduring Poppy's droning on and on about their inventions."

Troy didn't have anything like that to miss. There was no peaceful 'before' for him, he spent his life putting out fire after fire. "No, I... understand. It sounds dull, but in a nice way."

"Exactly. I want to be bored again."

He smiled. "Well, maybe getting stuck in this hole was just what you needed."

She stroked her hand up and down his calf. "That's not what I meant, but after the dust settles on all of this, if there is an *after*, I really do need a break. At least a few weeks. Shaia says we have years before the world ends, a few weeks of rest won't hurt."

The shake came strong and sudden, accompanied by a muffled crack. "What's happening?"

"Hold on."

The rattling continued and continued, growing stronger. There was a crunching sound and then Troy choked, dust filled his lungs. He hacked and heard Ka coughing beneath him. Another crunch and a sharp pain in his limb.

It was happening. They were going to die. Ka didn't have to though. Hours had passed, she should have enough will to get herself out. "Ka, you need to leave," he shouted.

"No."

"Ka!" he screamed this time; it brought on a coughing fit. The air was more dust than anything else at this point.

"Shut the hells up. I told you I'm not leaving you."

Why won't she listen? Why won't she save herself?

Then the air was dirt, or rather, there was no air, only dirt. A shower of pebbles and earth washed over his body, tickling and scraping and bruising. She was earth slipping them again. His ears rang after a rock collided with his head. *Just leave me here. Get out.* The quaking shook his body back and forth as they slipped, and then it stopped.

He sucked air into his lungs, Ka's face pressed up against his own as she, too, took deep, gulping breaths. Jammed together like this, they had to take turns inhaling and exhaling, there wasn't enough room for both of them to fill their lungs at the same time.

What is she thinking?

Troy lay on top of her, he brought his arms around to brace himself, so his full body weight wasn't crushing her, but there was so little room to move. She panted beneath him and shifted to the side as much as the small space allowed. He did the same, trying to shift off her so their chests weren't so aligned. It was a moderate success.

"You should have left me." His voice broke as tears formed in his eyes. The idea of her sacrificing herself was too much. "Ow!" A stinging pain lanced through his flank.

She'd pinched him. Hard.

"You are so *frustrating.* We just went through this. Stop telling me what I should or shouldn't do."

The tears in his eyes now were more from the pain than anything else. "I'm not trying to—" He paused in thought. She had a point, but he had one too. She was trying to save him, but he should have a say in whether or not someone sacrificed themselves for his sake. "I just don't want you to die."

She pinched him again, less hard but it still stung.

"Likewise, you idiot."

Breathing took precedence before they each spoke again. Troy caught his breath and the thumping of his heart slowed.

Slipping his hand into hers he knitted their fingers together. "I'm sorry," he said.

She squeezed. "That set us back. Half the pockets I sensed earlier are gone, and we're deeper into the mountain now. Closer to the mines than the surface, but after that quake it's hard to say how stable the mines are going to be."

"They weren't very safe to begin with."

"We'll make it."

"What about whoever found us before?" he asked.

"We're pretty far out of range for most wild wielders. The good news is that, between the pockets around us and our proximity to the mines, I should be able to get us out of here in a day or two."

Troy's head still rang from the rock that hit him during the slip, but that didn't sound like quite the *good news* she was making it out to be.

Sharon

The city sparkled beautifully despite everything. The sun only shone dimly through the haze, but it didn't stop the rubble glinting. It didn't stop the city's insistence on catching Sharon's eye with flashes of light no matter where she looked.

She hated it.

In a situation like this, the lights set her on edge. The flash of a sword and the gleam of an ice lance may be distinctly different than the glimmer of focus crystals, but her reflexes hadn't gotten the memo. She fought the urge to go for her will-blade, attempting to parry threats that weren't there.

She was jumpy. Ren's scream at learning his sister had been crushed to death was so sudden it almost ended with a wild wielder in two pieces. Sharon's hand gripped the hilt of her will-blade for only a moment, but it was enough to spook those around her. Everyone took a few steps back, granting a wide berth.

"Are you sure she's dead?" Sharon asked. "She slipped out of danger once."

"No. We're not sure of anything. We're not even sure it was her in that hole to begin with." Farah's smile was straining, desperately trying to turn into a frown.

"She's not dead," Sent'o said. His voice was still weak from his time in The Pit, but it had confidence.

Aisha's eyes snapped to him. "Explain."

Sent'o had his hand on the ground, eyes shut tight. "I'm telling you there's two people. Deep in the mountain. At least, if I'm reading the vibrations correctly. It's not easy at this distance."

"She's alive?" Ren jumped to his feet. "We need to get her out of there."

"It will take weeks." Sent'o wobbled as he stood. "She won't survive that long."

"What are you saying?" Ren turned on the Nari'ko Wilder, almost accusatory. "That we shouldn't even try?"

"Ren, settle down." Sharon gave him her mom voice. "Sent'o, do you have any ideas?"

"Several, but none of them are great." He rubbed his bloodshot eyes. He'd been through so much, and here they were, leaning on him, demanding more of him. "Option one: We rely on Ka to get out on her own. I'm confident she'll be fine as long as there are no more quakes, but with the dreadworm that's unlikely."

"So, we kill the dreadworm." Ren couldn't seem to stop himself.

He needs to learn to exercise calm in these situations.

"Dreadworms don't die in one hit, boy. And I don't know if I've ever met a creature that lets you carve into it without fighting for its life." Aisha's annoyance with her son was both obvious and justified. "Let the wild wielder finish."

"Option two: We go into the mines. I sensed a shaft that leads close enough to Ka. I should be able to get her out with an hour or so of work."

"With all the quakes, the mines are the worst place to be right now. Not to mention husk have started to pop up everywhere, and I'm sure the mines won't be spared their presence," Farah said.

"Let's go to the mines." Ren started walking away.

No one followed.

Sharon ignored her son's frantic behavior. *Don't criticize. Lead by example.* "Do we have a way to kill the dreadworm without creating too much of a quake?"

"Tender would be the one to ask," Aisha said. "It was before my time, but I'm told they are the only person to ever kill one."

It rankled her, the idea of going back to Tender having failed their one and only request they'd ever made of her, but dreadworms weren't a part of the request when they made it. Sharon knew what had to be done. "We'll do both. Sent'o, go with Ren. Save your will reserves and let him handle any husk you come across. The rest of us are going to headquarters to see if we can't make sure that dreadworm never moves again."

Ren had already stopped walking away once he'd seen no one was following. "You're not coming with?"

She fought an overwhelming impulse to tell him yes, yes she would go with him. She would never leave him again. After their decade apart, she would always be there for him now, but that wouldn't help. She was needed elsewhere and her presence in the mines wouldn't help anyone.

"I wouldn't increase the likelihood of success in the crystal mines. I stand a better chance of helping with the dreadworm problem."

She didn't mention the rest of the cold calculus she'd just done. The mines would be dangerous and unstable, and risking the Resistance's two strongest martial combatants and a slew of newly recruited wielders wasn't worth one healer, no matter how much of a prodigy she was. Two people should be enough to get the job done, adding more added nothing but risk. The look of disappointment on his face only lingered for a moment before he set his jaw and nodded.

"Be careful," she said as Sent'o trundled over to him. "And look out for Sent'o."

Then she turned back to the odd group she'd assembled and signaled them to follow. She moved quickly toward headquarters, before her instincts convinced her to stay with her son.

There was something more she wanted to talk to Tender about, too. Something even more concerning than the dreadworm. They hadn't seen more than a handful of Nationals since the explosion, and not a single one since that creature swallowed the entirety of The Pit. Where were they, and what did they have to do with the worm?

***

"We can't touch it until Ka's free." Tender's face drooped. Their intimidating stature reduced to an exhausted, slumped over creature sitting at a table in the common room at headquarters. "The last one I killed flailed wildly before we finished it off. This one should remain dormant for at least a day while it digests. We leave it until I can prepare."

Noah pressed his thumbs into a knot in Sharon's shoulder while they spoke. The man's grip was like iron, and Sharon loved the way he destroyed her back with his massages. "Ok, so we wait," she said, "but when we're done waiting is there a way to prevent it from flailing? If it does what you say, it could—ah!" Noah's thumb dug underneath her shoulder blade. "—destroy the whole city."

The newly released prisoners sat around in headquarters sipping ales and shoving food in their mouths. Farah had vouched for the structural stability of the underground hideout. She spent months ensuring the soil was packed tight enough to weather something like this, which was an odd thing to prepare for. The woman was almost as paranoid as Sharon.

"How in the hells did it even get here?" Tender stared up at the ceiling. "The wall of pylons on the eastern edge of Garvelle should keep them confined to the eastern edge of the empire."

"A worm *could* dig deep enough to get under the pylon barrier," Aisha offered, her mouth full of jerky.

Tender waved their hand dismissively. "They wouldn't do that. They eat husk, primarily, and there's plenty of those shambling about on the border of Gogallo. They wouldn't drill through rock when they have everything they need right in front of them."

Sharon had heard of dreadworms before. She'd even seen one, briefly, on a mission that led her to Garvelle's eastern front. But she'd never heard of an amalgamation that ate other amalgamations. Husk combined with each other, or they combined with and reanimated the bodies of other dead creatures. They didn't *eat* each other though. They always went after living things, things with will, humans in particular.

"What do you mean they eat husk?" she asked, wincing at another knot Noah found in her neck.

"Dreadworms aren't amalgamations, or husk really." Tender scratched at their chin. "Or, I mean, they are, but they're... different. They're not colossi that's been taken over by husk. They're born amalgamated. They have a life cycle."

Sharon waved Noah off from the massage, giving him a quick peck for his trouble. "How did you kill the first one. Let's start there."

Tender shrugged. "We used a focus crystal infused cord, wrapped it around the body, and tightened it until we cut the head off, but—" *Gods, why is there a but?* "—that doesn't kill them. They're worms. They'll just grow a new head. So, we brought a pylon overtop the body while it was trying to recover, and it eventually burned away. The problem with that, though—"

"Is that it flailed around the whole time, didn't it?" Sharon rubbed her temple and squeezed her eyes shut, thinking. They couldn't use that method; it would destroy the whole city. She bit into a dried piece of pineapple Aisha had given her. It felt stupid to say it, but screw it, they needed ideas. "What about a net?"

The old engineer frowned. "I considered that, but we have a day to make the tools we need. We won't have time to weave a net."

"Your grenades?" She was just shouting ideas now.

Tender's eyes got wide. "There's an idea."

"You seriously didn't think of grenades before I said something?"

"Of course I did," they said, "but we could combine the ideas. Anchor the cords into the ground and pin the worm down. Increase the tension on all the ropes and cut it into segments."

"What about the part of it that's left in the ground, won't it grow back?"

"That's what the grenades are for."

Sharon nodded. "So, that's the plan for the worm. What about the Nationals?"

"Yes, since Ren and I came into the city we've barely seen any." Aisha stood by the stairway leading out of the hideout. "It's strange they're not even trying to maintain order."

"It's not," Tender said. "This was their plan all along. Destroy the master pylon and let the husk kill everyone, then use their own pylon to ash all the husk and retake the city. I can't fathom what the worm is for, though. It just creates an even bigger mess for them to clean up afterward."

"Are we sure the worm is their doing?" Farah asked.

"Yes." A voice from the stairwell drew everyone's attention. The clanking of plate armor heralded the empress of Garvelle as she stepped down. She walked into the light of the room and the gold accents flashed, drawing attention to the Garvelle lion carved into her breastplate. "That worm doesn't belong here. It was compelled to come."

"Kiko. You're early," Tender said. Sharon couldn't tell whether they were happy or annoyed at seeing the empress. They had history, everyone knew it, but that greeting hadn't been overly warm.

"And it's a good thing. I solved your Estaba and Lighton problem." The monarch had a smug smile on her lips as she spoke.

Tender's face turned to shock. "You defeated their armies already?"

"Not exactly." Polk appeared, flanked by a visibly worried Seffin. "We're pretty sure they're going to help us fight the worm."

"Unnecessary," Tender said, "we can manage the worm." They walked over to Polk and knelt down to his level. "Don't you ever leave without saying something again."

"The troops will help with keeping the husk off our workers, and if Kiko is right, we'll need help against the Nationals, too." The boy met Tender's eyes with a resolute glare.

Is this a staring contest?

Sharon cleared her throat to draw attention. "Do you have evidence that they brought the worm here, or is that just a hunch?"

"I have a loose theory. It's also a bold claim, and not one I'm willing to make at the moment. Regardless, I think it best if we assume the worm is theirs." Kiko's smile thinned as she spoke. The woman was intimidating in her plate armor with blades on either hip. Sharon had never met Garvelle's empress before, but she knew her reputation. If rumors were true, she knew of Sharon as well. It's amazing how small the world seemed when so many major players gathered in one place. "Where is King Edward in all of this?"

"He was supposed to arrive with troops from Nashow next week." Tender broke their stare off with Polk and peered at the empress directly. "They planned to arrive at the same time as you, so as not to alert The Nationals of our alliances prematurely."

"Lay off it, Tender. I was worried."

They pointed an accusatory finger. "I had hoped you had a good reason to come early, but no, you're just impatient."

"Where's Ren?" Seffin finally asked.

On a suicide mission. I should be there with him.

"In the mines," Sharon said. "He's there with a wild wielder named Sent'o trying to save Ka. Or at least we hope it's her that's stuck in there."

"It's Ka," Tender said. "No one else could earth slip two people that distance by themselves, not without combining will reserves with someone else. Anyway, if you want to help, I need mystics and engineers working on my ropes and winches. I pulled out my old designs for the rope, but the winches will have to be..."

The empress chuckled. "Tenderized?"

Tender cringed.

"Oh, come on. It's just like old times." Kiko slapped the elderly engineer on their shoulder.

"I was going to say *improvised,* and I didn't miss your bad jokes."

The empress glanced at the papers strewn across the top of the table Tender sat at. She snatched up two pages with crude drawings of a winch, lines and labels going every which way on the page. "Aisha." The knight snapped to attention. "Brooks and Ariel are upstairs. Give them this and tell them to get to work on assembling the winches, have them bring any questions to Tender. Then get me Soren, Bray, and Cai. We'll use them to help charge and weave the focus crystal infused rope. Assign a wielder to accompany any team that goes into the city, tell them no one goes out alone. Between the husk and the Nationals, we don't need to take any chances." Aisha nodded and left. The empress pointed at another page on the tabletop. "I assume you have all the necessary components?"

Tender gave an exhausted nod. "This warehouse we're under is drowning in rope and Farah has a stockpile of crystal dust stored up." They set a hand on Seffin's shoulder and leveled a somber gaze. "I know you're worried, but in all likelihood, Ren would be done by the time you even reached the entrance to the mines. I won't stop you from going, but I don't think it's wise."

"He'll be fine," Sharon said. *He has to be.*

A vibration, so small she almost missed it, shook the room. Glass bottles behind the bar counter made a soft clinking. Everyone in the room braced themselves. For a moment, that was all that happened. A small shake, nothing serious. Then the floor jerked sideways, and everyone fell to the ground. Mugs filled with ale splashed to the ground, liquor bottles fell and shattered behind the counter, chairs tipped, spilling their occupants down with them. Sharon curled into the fetal position, wrapped her hands around her head, and swore she would kill that damnable worm...

And the monster that brought it here.

Troy

Either an hour or a day had passed, Troy wasn't sure. The darkness and silence warped his sense of time to a maddening degree. All he could be sure of was that time was, in fact, passing. His heart was beating, Ka's breaths came at regular intervals, and the smell grew steadily worse as their breath and other bodily functions transformed the earthy dust smell into a school changing room reminiscent of unwashed teens.

Ka had connected three other pockets to their own, each one granting a small relief of fresh air. But she waited now, filling her reserves. A little more time, she said, and they'd be out of their pocket and into the mines. Out of the frying pan and into the fire. Whatever force collapsed the pockets would have wrought havoc on the man-made, poorly regulated mines. A crumbling path out was still a path out, though, and they had to try.

"Oh," Ka said, breaking a long silence.

Troy looked toward the sound of her voice expectantly. Nothing but void stared back. He never realized just how much he relied on visual cues to conduct conversations. "Oh, what?" he asked.

"I think someone is there."

"Where?"

The hushed shifting of fabric on rock filled their small cave as she moved.

"Where?" he repeated.

"Shh, be quiet," she hissed, then added, "In the mines, I think."

"They found us?"

"Be quiet!"

He didn't want to be quiet. He wanted to keep asking questions, to seek solace in knowing, in understanding. The last year had taught him half of terror was ignorance, and right now he'd had his fill of being in the dark. Trauma was easier to digest if he knew the why, even if the why was simple cruelty. At least then he could file it away and lock it in the same part of his brain he kept the memories of his father.

Twenty-three breaths later he figured enough time had passed. He reached over, fumbling for Ka, wanting to rest a hand on her to indicate he was trying his best to be patient, but it was time to give him something other than silence to ruminate on.

"Ow! That's my eye."

"Sorry."

Again, he gave the darkness an expectant look, and again, it responded with nothing in return. Until Ka sighed, and said,

"Someone's definitely down there. Two someones, and one of them is an earth elementalist."

Yes!

"That's good, right?" he asked.

"Yes. They're strong, they're digging us out."

"How long?"

He heard either a chuckle or a cry. "They're... almost done. Get ready to crawl."

The suddenness rattled him. An eternity in darkness, and now, in moments, they would crawl to freedom. A tear reached his eye and he fought against the impulse to weep.

Crumbling, shifting earth accompanied a blast of air. The sound of Ka's scrabbling was easy enough to follow, not that there was any risk of getting lost. The tunnel they crawled through held no branching paths. It was a steady decline, punctuated by nerve-wracking, steep drop-offs. Whoever had made the tunnel didn't waste time on making sure it was safe, but what were a few scratches on his face compared to freedom?

Several harrowing drop-offs later, he tumbled into a mine tunnel. Ren stood over him holding a blindingly bright torch in one hand while he gripped his sister in a hug with the other. A gaunt person with a serene face held their hand out to help him up. He took it. Just the simple act of standing felt amazing after all that time spent in a hole. How many days had they been in there? He was starving.

"Seven hours stuck inside a mountain during with all those quakes and you survived?" the serene person said. "I'm so proud of you, Ka."

Troy reconciled his perception with reality. He should be better at judging time based on how well he did it in The Pit.

Ka and Ren's embrace made his heart sing. Against all odds, they had made it. He needed to put his emotions somewhere, he needed to hug someone. Reaching for the closest person, he pulled in the gaunt individual and wept. They were kind enough to return his embrace, patting him on the back. He felt more hands and arms wrap around him, the siblings had joined in.

Then the floor ripped out from beneath them, throwing everyone to the ground. Ren's torch clattered onto the cave floor and threw shadows everywhere. The rumbling of rocks falling echoed in the distance.

From the ground, Ka threw her hands up, her arms jerking around with the shakes that kept coming. The quaking around them dulled. "Any help, Sent'o?" She spoke to the person on the ground as she shifted to her knees, barely heard through gritted teeth.

They shook their head. "I'm all out. It took everything just to get you out of the mountain."

They say running will reserves dry is uncomfortable, exhausting. Ka was on her knees now, and in the flickering light, the effects of it were clear. Twice in the last day, she'd used up everything to keep him safe, and now she was doing it again.

Her face and shoulders drooped, she struggled to keep her arms aloft, her eyes were bloodshot, sweat pasted her hair to her neck. She was gorgeous. His savior.

His goddess.

This woman had no obligation to him. Yet here she was, risking her life for a man she'd known for less than a year. A man whose stupidity granted Winnow the tools he used to kill people. What did she gain by saving him again and again? He'd been nothing but a burden to her.

Whatever the answer, it didn't matter. His life was hers now. Every breath, every beat of his heart, every movement would be for her. Not because she saved him, but because she wanted him saved. Because of her frustration at his insistence she save herself. Because, never in his life, had he felt this... this...

Oh, gods. I love her. And she loves me.

The quaking stopped and Ka's arms fell to her side, she tipped precariously. Troy scrambled to her side to catch her. "Are you ok?" he asked.

Her eyes lolled open and met his own. "My hero."

You're the hero.

"We need to go, now." Ren was on his feet already, his torch in-hand.

"I don't think she can walk right now," Troy said. Ka was in his lap, dazed. She shook her head.

"I can walk." A pitiful attempt at sitting up was followed by collapsing backward.

Sent'o stood and ambled over to them. "She's completely drained her reserves; you'll have to carry her."

I'll carry her out of this cave. Up a mountain. Over a river. To the ends of the world.

He stood with Ka in his arms. She was light enough, after all, and what else did he need all these big muscles for but to carry the one person who cared about him to safety.

"It's quite a ways," Ren said.

"I'll be fine." Troy cradled his savior, holding her close. "Lead the way."

The tunnels winded and branched, but Sent'o led them through smoothly. Around collapsed paths when possible and through unstable-but-still-holding paths when necessary. It was a strange thing to notice, but the mine didn't twinkle. The walls were all browns and blacks and greys, but no glint of focus crystals, no glittering facets dancing in his vision. It was odd. In his head, the mines were all tunnels made of stars, but of course that wasn't true. They were *mines.* They plucked out all the stars and embedded them in their city. Installed them in town centers and carried them around for protection. That was the whole point.

"I have had enough of being in poorly lit tunnels to last me a lifetime." Ren started complaining, which meant he'd started to relax. It was like a beacon of hope, whining their way to safety.

At first, Troy thought the stench meant they were getting close to the exit. But the stink had a different quality to it than the Prolivgrad he knew, less refuse and more rot. Then he saw the bodies of husk laying in pieces, strewn across the floor of the tunnel. The mine itself hadn't been the only dangerous part of saving them.

Ka nestled into his chest, somehow oblivious or unbothered by any of the smells around them, including his own. Troy couldn't smell himself through all the decaying corpses, but he knew he couldn't smell good. Regardless, she pushed her face into his chest like he was the most comfortable pillow, and he gripped her tighter. Nothing bad would happen to her as long as he lived.

Before long, a thin light shone ahead. A cold, faded white contrasted to the warm, fluttering yellow of the torch Ren held. They were almost out. Husk peppered the ground so thoroughly it was hard to find a place to put his feet.

How many did they have to kill to get to us?

The entrance to the mine had a wooden fence surrounding a large staging area for crystals. Pallets and carts sat unused. The only thing on the pallets now were pieces of husk, a pair of legs dangled off a wagon sitting next to the gate. Troy must have been making a face because Sent'o touched his shoulder. "Ren is very skilled. You're in good hands."

Troy nodded. Getting to headquarters was all that mattered now. He made for the gateway...

What in the six hells?

A giant... tube? ... of rotting flesh lay across the city. It came out near the capitol, exactly where The Pit used to be.

"What? What is that?" Troy asked.

"That is a dreadworm," Sent'o said. "Before we came here, we climbed out of its throat."

The world had never been kind. Kinder to Troy than most others, but life, generally, was cruel. With the existence of the husk, few people could claim to have lived a peaceful life. This though, *this,* was too far. This was a nightmare.

"Is that what caused the quakes."

"Yes," Ren answered quickly. "My mom is working with Poppy to figure out what to do about it. We should get back to headquarters, she'll be worried about us."

Really? Sharon sent him?

The streets were empty. Save for a few husk shambling around, begging for Ren to cut them down, they saw no one. It was almost nice, not having to worry about National patrols. Not having to worry about acting patriotic or thinking up plausible lies to explain exactly why you were on the street, simply existing.

"Ren!" A throaty scream echoed off the buildings. A girl no older than Ren stepped around the corner, her blonde hair hung heavy with blood and sweat.

"Kaylee! What are you doing out here? You should be at a safe house."

"You let them go."

"Ren," Troy said, worried.

Ka's brother frowned with the sort of grim solemnity of a mourner. Whoever this person was, they were about to meet a version of Ren that hadn't existed more than a week ago, before he cut down every single National in a pub over a kid he'd never even met. Ka rested in Troy's arms, still unconscious.

"Kaylee. I'm glad you're alive. I didn't—"

"You. Let them. Go. They offered him up on a platter to the Nationals, and you let them go."

Ren fell into an Estaban readied posture, one of the stances Troy taught him. "Kaylee, I don't know what you're talking about, but if they are guilty, we will find them and bring them to justice."

"He was from Vicksbough. He was an Egallan, born and bred, and they still killed him."

"Then we'll make them pay, but you need to let us through, and you need to report in."

I was wrong. This isn't Ren, the butcher. He's trying to save her.

"I was making them pay when you stopped me. You won't stop me again."

Two ice lances sped through the air, but Ren cut them down before running straight for her. He had to. He'd burned himself out, couldn't flicker, and couldn't use elementalism. A will-blade was all he had, all that protected them from this mystic.

An orb of fire careened in their direction, it wasn't near the size Seffin could produce, or even the size Ren could when he was at his best, but it would kill their little group easily.

She'd made a grave error.

Ren altered the trajectory of the fireball then he threw his blade at her. An ice wall burst out of thin air to block, but it immediately started sliding in half. Not only were her reactions too slow, they didn't take into account a will-blade's edge. The fireball missed them, detonating in an explosion twenty paces down the street, but Kaylee was dead, lying in two pieces. With a faraway look in his eyes, Ren made sure she couldn't turn husk, and then they were on their way again.

Troy decided not to ask who she was. If they survived, maybe they could talk about it over drinks. Maybe he could thank him for saving their lives. But not right now. Right now, a person Ren knew was dead, and Ren was the one made to kill them. Best not to linger on it.

Moving up two tiers to the level of the warehouse that held headquarters, Troy finally got a real look at the city. Prolivgrad, as he knew it, was gone. Any building over three stories had toppled and turned to rubble. Even the capitol, barely in view from this angle, was smoking, half the building lay in pieces. Below, in the residential areas, people milled about, but their movements were jerky, and they stumbled more than walked.

Not people, husk.

Ka stirred as the warehouse came into view. She made a series of faces ranging from 'what's going on' to 'oh, we're safe' and then finally to a scrunched-up expression that clearly meant 'put me down!'

He did.

She dusted herself off and began walking, wobbly at first. A resistance guard stood at the entrance, he had a fresh cut on his chin and brilliant blue eyes which darted around nervously. On recognizing Ka, he let them pass into the mess that was the warehouse. Gone were the organized shelves of Nationalist paraphernalia, replaced by mounds of supplies splashed with red. A pathway through the debris had been made. Lining the walls of the building were black clad Garvellian soldiers, and in the back office a few mystics sat with their hands hovering over piles and piles of reflective rope.

When did they all get here?

They all stopped at seeing the group. One of the mystics, she was clearly the eldest, became misty eyed before sniffling and getting back to work, doing whatever it was that they were doing with the rope. The stairwell down sat open now, no longer hidden behind a shelf. No need to hide, after all. Winnow's actions meant they were in open hostilities.

They descended into the common room which exploded in cheers at the sight of them, even Polk cracked a smile. Tender, Ka, Ren and Seffin hugged and wept. Troy took a step backward to give them some space, but as he did, Ka's hand shot out, grabbed his shirt, and yanked him into the embrace. He blushed and didn't know what to do with his hand, which was silly, it was a hug. He reached as far around their little cluster as he could and squeezed. A sense of belonging came cloaked in awkwardness. Open affection was unfamiliar to him, but it was also comforting and welcoming and warm.

In the middle of the hug, Troy caught Sharon's eye as she sat on a bar stool with a look of satisfaction on her face. He would never forgive her, but he was grateful she sent Ren for them. They were all together despite everything, even with a giant worm trying to bring the mountain down on them. That brought on another thought.

"The rope has something to do with the worm?"

Kiko sat over a mug of ale as she responded, "We thought we had till tomorrow to finish it, but with that last quake—"

"It was just a shift. It's digesting an entire building, it might not even be the last time it does it," Tender said.

Aisha walked into the room and exchanged a nod with Kiko. The empress stood and drained her mug of ale. "Well, its *shifting* is getting a lot of people killed. If we can move up the timeline, we should."

Sent'o, mouth full of carrots and jerky, said, "We fould weigh unfil morring, ah leaft."

"Our wielders are mostly dry or exhausted." Tender backed Sent'o up. "It would be unwise to make our move while we're weakened."

"With Estaba and Lighton backing us up we should be fine." Kiko strolled over to the bar and set her mug down. Noah grabbed it, dutifully, and started a refill.

"Actually, Your Majesty," Aisha said. "I have some bad news regarding that."

Kiko's mouth dropped open. "Don't tell me they still plan to attack us."

"No." Aisha met her eyes. "They won't attack, but they *are* refusing to help."

Kiko's hand slapped the countertop. "Vultures!"

"They plan to wait and see who wins. Then ally with the victor?" Polk asked, his voice as piercing as ever.

"Worse than that," Tender pulled out a chair and fell into it. "If he thinks he has a chance at success, Bruhier will try to take over Prolivgrad."

"That would be foolish," Polk said. "Didn't you just get done saying that King Edward from Nashow would be here within the week?"

"I did," Tender said, "but Bruhier is an opportunist. An honorable one, if you can believe it, but he views this as a war now and in war the rules of honor are different. If he thinks he can occupy the city and dig in enough to repel Nashow, he will."

"What about the amalgamation bindings?" Kiko turned back to Aisha.

"About that." The knight had a grim look on her face. "Tyler Chen's mental state degraded. We killed the creature bound to him, and that seems to have helped. But that's one less asset we have."

Troy snapped out of the whirlwind of revelations he was hearing. "What do you mean his mental state degraded? Is he ok?" His team had been through enough. *Tyler, has been through enough.* If amalgamation binding was causing mental symptoms...

"He was breathing when I left. That's all I can confirm." She addressed Kiko. "We'll have to exercise caution with the binding going forward. Sumiko says no one less than mystic level should undergo the process. We have a few mystics binding right now, but that will use up all of the available amalgamations for the moment."

Tyler's will reserves weren't mystic level, but he was only bound to one amalgamation. *Please be ok.* Could it affect mystic level wielders if they bound to too many? "What were the symptoms?" Troy asked to a woman that shouldn't be here for a week yet.

"He was hearing a voice." Aisha's tone became curt, but he brushed it off, this was important.

"Just one voice?" he pressed.

She frowned. "Yes."

"You're sure?"

"No. I'm not sure. I'm not him, and he wasn't exactly talkative when I left."

The worm.

It was a leap, but it was worth mentioning. "What if the voice he's hearing was Koth's?"

Sent'o coughed while eating a potato. "What makes you say that?"

Yes, what did make him say that? His mother's actions that led to her death were erratic, at least for her. The attempted assassination on Winnow came out of nowhere. Even Tia had been surprised and appalled. Then on the night of the coup—Troy glanced at Sharon—she'd been drinking. His mother *rarely* drank, and when she did, it was ritualistic. Only one and usually accompanied by a brief smoke. She didn't like losing her mental acuities. Sharon even commented that night how easy it was... how his mother hadn't seemed as sharp as she was led to believe.

Now, Tyler binds to an amalgamation and needs to have it put down before he loses his mind. Then there was Winnow, an unstable individual by anyone's standards, but he'd always been reliably selfish. His actions since the coup had been increasingly nonsensical. Cruelty for cruelty's sake. Starving his own citizens, increasing the prices on the crystal trade to a prohibitive degree. It's as if he was trying to destroy the city. Trying to draw the ire of surrounding countries. A selfish person wouldn't provoke their neighbors in the needless way Winnow did. Not unless they thought they could get something out of it, and what was there to gain by hoarding the focus crystals? Nothing.

"The worm," he said. "It shouldn't be here."

The empress' voice dripped with condescension. "Thank you for that brilliant observation—"

"Auntie Kiko, let him speak." Ka touched his shoulder.

"What if Winnow is bound to the worm?"

"O.. kay?" Kiko said.

Troy went on, "I mean, what if he bound himself to the worm and that's what's making him behave this way? It explains why the worm would come here."

She shook her head. "We know from Jessica and Pulpin that the binding has to be done at a specific time during the amalgamation process. Dreadworms are born amalgamated."

"What happens if you bind too late?" Troy asked. "Did you ask? I never did."

"Husk are beings filled with Koth's will. Their only drive is to bring more will into Koth's portion of the Sea of Intention." Polk spoke to a room now filled with confused faces, but not Troy. He'd been listening when Ka explained the Sea of Intention to him.

"So, if someone was bound to an amalgamation already filled with Koth's will—" Kiko started.

"They'd be bound to Koth himself," Tender finished.

Ren's eyes got big. "Sorca," he said. "Sorca was a researcher on Pulpin's team before he tried to take over Lanneshire."

Was everyone who bound themselves to an amalgamation destined for madness?

"While this is important information, it doesn't change anything," Kiko said. "The bindings are already done; it would be a waste not to use them. We still have to kill the dreadworm and we still have to remove Winnow from power."

Troy shook his head, appalled. "At what cost?"

Kiko's glare froze the blood in his veins. "Any cost, Mr. Saunders."

Seffin

Morning came and Ren lay next to Seffin with his eyes open, staring up at the ceiling of the tent. Thin light peered in through an open flap which caught an early breeze, lazily floating back and forth. Seffin put a hand on his chest. "What is it?"

Ren turned his head, giving a determined look which Seffin read as faux confidence. "I'm sure it's fine." Rolling onto his side, he set a hand on Seffin's cheek, thumbing just underneath his ear, the same one that used to be a nub.

"You're worried about the binding," Seffin said. "You think I'm losing my mind?" He smiled and flexed his fingers, making his hand a claw and lightly scratching at Ren's chest, pretending to be a monster.

Ren only frowned. "Sorca did."

"I'm not Sorca, and according to Troy, he was one of the earliest researchers on my father's team. If someone was going to go mad from Koth's influence it's probably the guy who was there from the beginning, when they didn't have the process nailed down yet."

"But you said you can feel something." The worry in his eyes made a pit in Seffin's chest, but there was more to it. Ren already hadn't handled the situation with Sorca well, but now they both knew Sorca's impulses hadn't been his own. He'd been corrupted, almost as much a victim as the people he killed.

Seffin's only side effect from the binding process was a small presence in the back of his mind. Barely even there. If Polk's theory was correct, even that would go away once the amalgamations died.

"If the amalgamations don't die, I'll kill them myself after the battle." Win or lose, there would be no point in keeping around the rafadon and laranee he'd been bound to. He wouldn't become another Sorca.

Ren wrapped his arms around Seffin and pulled him into an embrace, nestling his head into the crook of his neck. The sleepy warmth and relaxed intimacy threatened to lull him to sleep again, and that couldn't happen, even if they had only gotten five hours of rest. He started to pry Ren's arms off him. "We should get up."

Ren held tight. "No, I'm good."

Seffin smacked his shoulder. "Get off."

"Fine! You go then!" Ren spun around and curled into a fetal position, baring his back. Seffin put his palm on it, feeling his warmth. The man was like a stove when he slept. Seffin ran his fingers down Ren's spine, out over the muscles and over his side, then wrapped his arm around, gripping his soft belly and pulling him close.

"I thought we had to get up," Ren said.

"We do." Seffin gave him a squeeze, kissed the back of his neck, and untangled himself from the sheets before standing.

Last night, Tender and Kiko sent all the captains back to their resistance cells to gather and prepare. All mystics and wielders had strict orders to rest, *actually* rest, while anyone else with shallow will reserves spent the night making rope or constructing winches. Scouts confirmed The Nationals were hiding behind a pylon barrier at the capitol building. The cowards were going to watch their fellow countrymen eaten alive and turned husk while they hid.

For safety, Kiko made the Garvelle military camp open to all Prolivgradian citizens. The worm made the city a dangerous place to linger at the moment. Troops escorted as many people as they could to this location. The only downside was that, with so much movement, the pop-up base made for a restless night's sleep. Twice, Ren and Seffin were interrupted by someone walking into their tent, confused about where to go, where to lay their head.

Seffin put on the green jacket the Nari'ko people had made for him and tossed Ren his blue one. "Get up or I'll fetch Ka."

Ren spun to face Seffin, scandalized. "You wouldn't."

"I would. Up. Now."

Ren groaned and got to his feet, donned his jacket, and pulled on his immaculately clean combat boots, grumbling all the while. This ritual had played out countless times on the road. Pestering Ren to get a move on was a morning chore just like breaking down the tents or packing up camp. Which is perhaps the exact reason he was acting out the part of the reluctant participant, Seffin couldn't tell, but he had to admit it made the start of the day less tense.

They left the nostalgia and comfort of the morning ritual in their tent as they stepped out into the bustling camp. Ka, still smudged with dirt from her time spent inside Brinidor, stalked toward them. Seffin knew the look on her face, they were late getting up and she was on her way to perform her sacred, sisterly duty of dousing Ren with water until he roused. Upon seeing them she smiled, though there was a bit of disappointment in it.

"I still think I should be up there helping with the worm," she said as they approached.

Seffin stopped in front of her. "You and Sent'o are our best healers, and I doubt you've fully recovered anyway."

"Ren hasn't recovered, and he'll be up there," she said.

She sounded... a lot like Ren, actually. Which made it all the more comical when it was Ren who said, "Are you... whining? Is that *whining* I hear?"

"Oh, gods." She pinched the bridge of her nose. "I'm turning into you."

Ren smiled. "There are worse things."

"No, there aren't." She shook her head and turned to Seffin. "Polk is waiting for you at the winch wagons."

"Where's Troy?" The man hadn't taken yesterday's revelations well, making it odd he wasn't attached to Ka at the hip in this moment.

"He's with Sumiko and Tia, making sure all the bindings are going well. He's... actually quite knowledgeable about it." Ka's tone was a mix of disbelief and pride. "He said if they won't kill the amalgamations then he'll at least make sure everyone bound to one is doing it as safely as possible."

"Speaking of: mine and Polk's are..." Seffin cast his eyes about, searching for his rotting turtle and decaying cat.

"At the winch wagons already, you can find them by the smell." Ka frowned. "Gods, I should be up there with you."

"We'll be fine!" Ren said. "We'll be back before noon with the worm dead and the city liberated."

Ka grabbed them both in turn and kissed them each on the forehead, then looked to Seffin. "Let's hope any injury he gets leaves him mute."

"I don't know. I think I'd miss the endless complaints about fish." Seffin joked, but he worried terribly. People were going to die today. Lots of people. All it would take is for the worm to roll over when they weren't ready, or for a National to get a lucky shot off.

Ren sighed. "Enough you two. We need to get going."

A brief, tight hug and they separated. Ka toward the medical tents and Seffin and Ren toward the unpleasant odor of the winch wagons.

They arrived to find Tender climbing into the back of one, underneath the winch's drum. A cavalcade of swearing and clanging poured out. The engineer wasn't satisfied with the quality of work, but what could they expect with machines made in less than twenty-four hours?

Polk stood nearby, transfixed on the four bound amalgamations: two laranees, a werewiller, and a rafadon. They were easy to control. All Seffin had to do was imagine what he wanted them to do in his mind, put some will into the thought, and the creatures performed it perfectly. Intentioned will was supposed to be difficult to master, but this barely took any effort at all, at least for him.

"Are you alright?" Seffin approached and put his hand on the boy's back.

He broke off his stare and looked up at Seffin. "For now."

An ominous answer, but he frequently said ominous things and navigating the maze that was Polk's communication style took time Seffin didn't have right now. Polk went back to staring at the amalgamations and Ren shot Seffin a look which he deciphered to mean 'what in the hells is wrong with that child?'

A few loud clangs followed by a click rang out of the wagon, and Tender shimmied their massive form out the back. "That's as good as it's gonna get."

"Good morning," Ren said.

Tender responded with a disgruntled grumble. "Good isn't the word I'd use." They frowned. "We're behind. We need to get going."

The "winch wagons" had actually been a single winch wagon by the time they arrived, the rest had gone ahead. "This will work," Seffin said. "And there's always the backup plan."

Tender shook their head. "I usually like your crazy plans, but if you don't mind me saying so, this one sucks. It'll likely get you killed."

"Hopefully not," he said.

"What plan?" Ren's mask of confidence slipped.

Seffin put a hand on his shoulder. "It doesn't matter. The winches will work."

"Let's go," Polk said, and walked toward the gates of Prolivgrad. Tender pushed the wagon in the back and Seffin and Ren took the front, pulling and steering their way into the glimmering, crumbling city they called home.

***

The winches didn't work.

From the start, the earth elementalists couldn't anchor the wagons properly. The wagons themselves had to be kinetically lifted to their locations where they would use spikes driven into the mountain to secure them. The problem was that the city had become rubble which shifted frequently, fraying the cables meant to keep the wagons in place, many snapped even before they had a chance to put the crystal-infused ropes in place.

To make matters worse, the ropes weren't supposed to touch the worm until all winches had been secured, but a plan made in the dead of night and put in place in the early morning was destined for poor implementation. Mystics were supposed to keep the ropes aloft, over the worm, while everyone else prepared to tighten the winches. Unfortunately, due to mis-communication, ignorance, or simple human error, one of the ropes brushed the worm prematurely. The thrashing began mid-morning, and the Nationals surged in shortly thereafter to put a stop to the mischief Garvelle and the Resistance were up to.

Ren risked his life on the front line, closest to the capitol building. Seffin wasn't overjoyed with that knowledge, but he was grateful his lover wasn't here. If Ren knew what he was about to do he may have stopped him, dooming everyone.

An arrow hissed passed Seffin's head. The sharp impact of metal on stone was almost anticlimactic, improper given how dead he would have been had it struck true. Tender and Polk crouched nearby. Polk held his eyes closed, no doubt giving orders to his amalgamations despite his inability to use inten-tioned will. Brute force through his deep reserves was appar-ently enough to direct the monsters bound to him. Tender stared wide-eyed at Seffin after the arrow missed. The old en-gineer worried over him like he was one of their own. Seffin had the rafadon lumber over, making a barrier between Seffin's group and the army of Nationals, he'd sent the laranee to the front line with the simple instruction to attack anything wearing red.

Polk's eyes shot open. He met Seffin's gaze and nodded, he was ready. Seffin created a sphere of stone around himself with holes punched large enough for him to see, but small enough it would be unlikely for an arrow to get through. Polk raised it into the air. The ride wasn't exactly smooth, but Polk's kinetic control had improved since turning trees into splinters with a wave of his hand.

Arrows and ice lances pelted the protective sphere. A fireball careened in Seffin's direction, so he sent out his own to collide with it, detonating it before it could reach him. That would be the most dangerous part. The ball of stone could only protect him so much, and once he started wielding it would be difficult to split his focus.

Below him was an ocean of violence. Waves of men and monsters crashed against each other. Polk's laranee worked in tandem with Seffin's, jittering through enemy lines and spraying blood every which way. The werewiller shunted rocks and devoured red-clad morsels, a pocket of deadly silence in the chaos. The rafadon fell during Seffin's ascent, but not before the explosion from its shell left the surrounding troops in pieces. It functioned as a simple wall now, an obstacle between their little team and the rest of the battle. The amalgamations wouldn't last much longer, though. The Nationals were already forming teams of mystics to take them down at range. Seffin would have to finish the worm off before that happened, or every mystic the Nationals had would turn their attention to his floating rock.

The plan was simple but dangerous. Brute force. Tender had set aside infused ropes which Seffin floated into the air. With a full view of the worm, he wrapped the ropes around the gargantuan creature and began to cinch them tight. Its skin smoked where the rope touched and a scream, deep and pained and angry, exploded out of it. It ceased its thrashing and erected itself, an undulating tower amid a broken city.

Then it did something Seffin did not expect, it faced him. As if it knew exactly the cause of its pain. He threw will into the rope, cinching it tighter. His ball of stone would not help him if the worm lunged, but how fast could something that size actually be?

Weightlessness came on suddenly and stopped just as fast. He lost his balance, slamming into the bottom of the sphere. He regained his footing and created a small window to look down at Polk, below his feet. A husk had gotten to him, but Tender stood next to it with a bloody hammer. Seffin refocused on his task and gasped. With the new angle, the worm didn't need to lunge to reach him, it only needed to fall in his direction, which it was already doing, but it wouldn't just crush him, it would crush Tender and Polk too.

He cinched the rope again, throwing everything he could into it. Another fireball shot in his direction; he barely registered the mid-air ice wall he made for it to crash into. With only a whisper of thought, he let the ice wall drop and made pillars of stone beneath the worm, to slow its descent. Ice lances meant for him were redirected into the creature's flesh automatically, instinctively, as natural as breathing. The rope was halfway through the creature's body, only a little more. He pulled it tighter, breaking the dam he'd constructed to control his will reserves. He let everything flow into raw kinetics. No technique. Only power.

The whip-crack of the rope snapping through the worm's body broke his concentration. He saw its head falling, but he was falling too. His body slammed into the floor of the sphere which exploded. The ground bounced him back into the air as a shockwave ripped passed, kicking up dust and debris, throwing him. He couldn't breathe, the world was spinning, and then...

Darkness.

Ren

The Nationals had prepared.

Late morning, after the first rope brushed the worm, red-clad National guards appeared as if by magic. Popping out of alleyways and buildings and streaming down roads like surging rivers of blood. It was silly to think this all might have gone smoothly, and naive to think a will-blade would grant him all the advantages he was used to.

This wasn't a mystic, or a husk, or an amalgamation. This was an army fully equipped with willed weapons and backed up by mystics itching to skewer him with ice lances or reduce him to ash. The husk were there, sprinting around and sinking their teeth into anyone not paying close enough attention, but they were a nuisance. Humans were the real problem. They fought fiercely, with desperation and panic. They fought as if they had nothing to lose.

Only their lives.

Lives Empress Kiko Zollinger was all too happy to take. The Lion of Garvelle was a black and gold tornado, dripping in blood. Ren kept his distance. The ground around her was littered with pieces of people, she snaked her will-blades between her enemy's own willed weapons and took them apart before they could get close. She parried a woman wielding a spear and had her head off in the same breath. Another soldier with a will-blade deflected a slash only to have his legs cut cleanly at the knees. She swiped an arrow out of the air with one blade while extending the tip of her other through someone's chest. She was mesmerizing and terrifying, a true monster.

A snapping sound next to his ear brought Ren's attention to his mother. She'd cut an arrow out of the air meant for him. *I should learn how to do that.* "Stop gawping," she commanded. "You need to keep moving or you're an easy target." She pointed up the hill, toward the capitol. "Winnow is up there. I don't know what the fool is doing standing outside, exposed with his troops, but he looks different, crazed."

They ducked behind a pile of rubble that used to be a clothing shop. "You didn't kill him?"

"He has an earth elementalist with him. I can't get close."

A husk leapt over their rubble pile only for Ren to cut it in two. "How did he convince a wild wielder to work with him?"

She gave a withering look. "Questions we can seek answers to *afterward*. For now, we need to focus on getting up there. Have you seen Farah and Nessa? Or that professor you recruited? I have an idea."

"Nessa took one look at the empress and left to another street. Said she wasn't suicidal and that, if I were smart, I'd find somewhere else to be. I haven't seen Farah nor Dunreedy, but that doesn't surprise me. They're not martial combatants, they'd be in the back lines."

She made a frustrated *'tch'* sound. "Do you think you can flicker?"

No. He wanted to say. *You're the one who told me I shouldn't.* "Why?" he asked.

"I can get the wild wielder, but I'll need help. You only need to pop in the flicker state for a moment. Do you think you can handle it?" She peaked around the edge of their rubble pile and ducked back in just as an ice lance shattered by her head. "They know we're here. Gotta move."

Ren got into a crouching position to run with his mother. "I don't know the second form. We didn't have time—"

"I'm going to take out the mystic that's targeting us. Watch me."

Starting with the final stance of the first form she brought her limbs together, close to her body. Then, almost faster than Ren could follow, she was up the street, her will-blade dripping with the mystic's blood as he crumpled to the ground. She'd dropped out of the flicker state, but the soldiers around the mystic didn't have time to act surprised before she cut them down.

She's almost out of will. Mystic level wild wielders took a lot of effort to fight if they got their rock shield up. That's why she needed help with this one.

Ren pictured his mother's movements, practiced them in his mind, internalized them as best he could. He wouldn't know how it felt, though, until he did it. The point of the second form was to get into the state in a controlled way, but how would that feel, how would he control it? His mother beckoned and he sprinted over.

He felt for his reserves, the emptiness he'd had in his chest for the last week had lessened. Maybe he wasn't back to normal yet, but... "I should have enough will to flicker."

"Did you see my movements?"

"Yes, but I don't know how to—"

"The intensity you go into it with is what sets your speed. Try not to throw everything you have at it, but... also don't do too little or you won't move fast enough."

"Just be perfect the first time?"

"Exactly."

"Great, what's the plan?"

"You're going to be bait."

"Not great."

"Do as I tell you and you'll be fine. The wild wielder specializes in earth. You can recognize him by the scar on his neck. He has four boulders floating in the air, and a—" A husk lunged out from an alleyway. She shattered its skull with her fist, and it flopped to the ground. That, too, was a version of flickering, but how she concentrated it to one part of her body he hadn't puzzled out. "—a rock shield surrounding him," she finished.

"You need to get him to throw one of the rocks in his shield at you and then dodge it."

"That's it?"

"No. The technique is to angle their rock so that you dodge into the path of one of his boulders, then, faster than you can physically respond, he'll slam the boulder down on you. Bait him by starting with the first form and dodge into the second, then flicker away from the boulder. Get to safety and drop out of the flicker state. I'll handle the rest."

Perfectly dodge into a form I've never done before, not too much will into it, or I'll burn myself out, but too little and I won't be fast enough, and if I fail, I'll be crushed.

"Got it. Why do I have to do this?"

"Because if he sees me coming, he'll throw his whole shield at me, and I don't have the reserves left to dodge it. I need to get close enough to reach him with my extended blade."

The sounds of people fighting for their lives clamored around them. Despite Garvelle's numbers advantage, The Nationals were winning. The enemy's back line sat safely behind a barrier while the entirety of the Resistance had to contend with the husk and the worm. Ren did his best not to think about the worm. He saw the winches fail and didn't *want* to know Seffin's plan. It was surely dangerous, probably reckless, but it would most likely work.

He'd better be ok.

"It's a short run up," she said. "Give me five minutes and I'll be in position. As soon as he sees you, he'll shunt a rock in your direction. Are you ready?"

The rest of the army was already putting everything on the line. It was his turn. He nodded. The frown she made was a surprise, so were the tears, and so too was the frantic hug and hurried kiss on his forehead. "I wish there was another way, but..."

"It's dangerous for you, too, and you trust me. I get it." He reached out and touched her cheek, the burned one. "Afterward, can we talk about speeding up my training."

She chuckled and wiped the tears away with her sleeve. "Deal."

They sprinted up a side alley, hopped a crumbling brick wall, and dispatched a set of three husk. One was a child, the indentation around her neck an explanation for how she'd died. A fury brewed in Ren's chest. Winnow was a monster, but it was his followers that did this. Weak-willed, fearful wretches seeking a strongman to protect them.

The path his mother took deposited them behind the barrier. She put a finger to her mouth to indicate silence, and then pointed forward, toward the street. He'd be on his own now.

The wild wielder would be around the corner with Winnow nearby, overlooking the battle. He braved a peak to spy the wild wielder. They had short, black hair and an angry scar running up the left side of their neck and head. The moment he stepped onto the street; they would notice him. He ran through the second form in his head again.

I can do this.

Five minutes passed; his mother should be in position. The paving stones vibrated as he ran toward the road. By the time he got there, the ground shook violently. He was out in the open, in the direct line of sight of the wild wielder, but they didn't see him. Instead, they stared, transfixed, down the mountain.

The worm.

Ren followed their sight line. The worm was lunging at a small ball of dirt suspended in the air. The top section of its body was cinched, billowing smoke. The ball plummeted downward. *Seffin!* Then it stopped suddenly, hanging in the air again. The worm's lunge turned into a fall; it was going to crush the ball. The crack of the rope going taught echoed through the air, then, unable to do anything, unable to save the person he cared most about, Ren watched the worm's head fall.

The cobblestones bucked, throwing him down. A boulder the size of a horse bolted in his direction. This was it. This was where he'd die, but the boulder exploded, his mother knelt beside him, dust and pebbles raining down around them, and then she was on the ground, small dots of red peppering her body. He sat up. The wild wielder threw their hand out, the hiss of a wind blade darted in his direction. A blast of wind buffeted his body, not from the direction of the wild wielder, but from the alleyway he'd come from, sending both him and his mother tumbling.

She shouldn't be here.

By the time he stabilized himself and made it to his feet, Ka had engaged with the wild wielder. Her hands were everywhere, hissing with each gesture. The scarred wielder dodged frantically. He shunted his rock shield at her. She batted it away. The three remaining boulders careened in her direction, they collided on her, shaking the ground. *Ka, Seffin, Mom...*

Ren clenched his jaw. Fury brought him to standing, and rage brought him through the first form, but as he started the second, the wielder popped into the air, limbs flailing around like a doll tossed off a cliff. As he fell back to the ground his body separated first into two, then four, then eight, and then Ren couldn't keep track any longer. A crunching, wet thud was all that was left of the wild wielder. Ka's body poked halfway out of the ground ten paces from the boulder impact, she ejected herself out of the cobblestones in the same way Ren normally found so annoying.

She sprinted toward him, then past him, and kneeled next to his mother. The puncture wounds began to close when she placed her hands on her chest and neck.

"Why are you here?" Ren asked.

"We need to go," she said without looking at him. "That wielder wasn't the only person protecting Winnow. There's more soldiers on the way."

Ren glanced back up the mountain. Winnow was running for the capitol building while eight soldiers ran toward him, one nocked an arrow. Dropping into the second form, he felt it, it was like setting a running pace. The world turned to frosted glass, and he tasted the stench of the battle, the metallic smell of blood invaded his nose.

It was amazing.

The itch that normally cascaded over his body was nothing more than a tingle, there was no pain, no burning, only the smells and the tastes and the cloudy vision that somehow brought the world into focus despite the blur. The soldier loosed their arrow, but Ren could see it swimming through the air. He cut it down before it could reach its target.

The soldiers couldn't react. They moved around as if stuck in syrup. What he was about to do to them brought on a fleeting pang of guilt, but he could process that later. For now, he had to keep his mom and his sister safe. In a flurry of swipes, he cut through their chests, where their hearts would be, hoping their deaths would be swift to spare them pain. The archer was last, and as Ren dropped out of the flicker state, he heard the clatter of their remaining arrows hit the stones.

"Ren!" Ka supported his mom on one side. She beckoned him over with her free hand.

He shook his head and pointed his sword toward the capitol building. "I'm going after him."

"Not by yourself." Ka made for the alleyway, though she kept her eyes on him.

"I have to." An image of the worm falling flashed through his mind. Maybe he made it, maybe they'd all beat the odds today, but enough people hadn't. Winnow needed to die, and he needed to die now, before anything worse happened. Before another worm burst from the mountainside and finished them all off.

He didn't wait for a response. He sprinted in the direction of the capitol, his sister's voice screaming behind him. *She'll forgive me, or I'll die and it won't matter.*

Ren had at least one flicker left in him, and only two soldiers had escorted the president into the building. He could do it. He could end it.

Both soldiers lay dead just inside the entrance. He turned them over. Terror twisted their faces, but nothing else indicated what killed them. No blood, no cuts, no punctures, no limbs twisting in unnatural directions, no broken bones. Just two soldiers who ended their lives in agony.

A warm draft with the smell of rot drifted through. Emanating from deeper inside. *Did he actually succeed in binding an amalgamation?* Ren made his way over broken columns and through giant cracks in walls that shouldn't be there—the quakes had done a number on the place—always toward the odor, toward the sickening heat of the breeze.

The path led him by portraits of past Nationalist presidents, now their frames were in pieces, strewn about the hallways and rooms he stepped through. Chairs of red velvet tipped over or broken, tables crushed under the weight of stones fallen from the floor above. Official looking papers rustled as he stepped past.

The importance of this building hadn't hit him before, not like it did now. His country was in ruins. Anyone that knew how to run things was either already dead or still fought in battle while the symbols of their freedom, their sovereignty, crumbled. And now he walked toward the man, the creature, that had caused it all.

Ren would remove him from power with violence.

Egal had turned out no better than Kelsig, with their barbaric ways of deciding their leaders. But Kelsig chose to rule by blood, Winnow had thrust this on their country, fed everyone a diet of fear, made reason impractical. That wasn't fair, though. Paul Winnow was one man, he couldn't have done it on his own. The truth was, Egal *did* choose this. The people, by their ignorance and apathy or hatred and zeal, brought this on.

The smell led Ren to the senate chambers where mounds and mounds of crystal dust lined the room, piled halfway up the walls. In the center, by the dais, a pylon spun lazily while Winnow sat leaning up against the base. His mother had been right, the president did look different. His skin was a foul gray, and even from this distance, Ren could see his eyes were yellowed.

"Don't," the president said to himself, a conversation with no one. "It hurts." He doubled over with a pained grunt, and then reached a smoking hand out toward the pylon. "It's been so long. Our fates aren't so dissimilar, you and I, both locked away, both struggling to survive." His hand caressed the pylon crystal and smoke billowed out before he pulled it away.

Ren dropped into the first form.

"Stop." The voice coming out of Winnow wasn't his. It was deeper, filled with malice. "I was wondering if it would be you or your awful mother."

Something tugged at the back of Ren's mind, a tickle, where spine met skull. He stood. The impulse to drop his blade came on strong, but the itch in his finger, normally a simple nuisance, lanced pain up his hand, through his arm.

What the hells was that?

"I didn't expect so much resistance." The voice coming out of Winnow sounded amused. Tendrils of smoke emanated from his body. "No matter," he said.

"Who *are* you?"

A cruel laugh came in answer, followed by a toothy smile. "Exactly who you think I am."

That shouldn't be possible. Koth was locked inside Lana Danvers. He shouldn't be able to take another vessel. "How?"

"What does it matter? You won."

Another tickle at the back of his head, another lancing pain. "Stop it!"

Koth grumbled. "Your defect is protecting you."

"How are you doing that?"

He sighed and smiled again; a faint sizzling sound came from his position. "I was hoping to kill both of them, but that stupid engineer."

"What are you talking about?"

"Seffin," he said. "And Kohru's little pet." Winnow raised his hands up, gesturing broadly. "This was all for them. I almost had it, too. We could have ended this stalemate today, but alas... I was too eager."

He knows about Seffin... Wait, almost? Seffin's alive!

"Don't get too excited." He pulled a grenade out of his pocket. "You're not going to see them again."

Ren dropped into the first form, but pain shot up his arm again and then out to his whole body.

"Ah ah, you're not going anywhere." He brought his hands together, gripping the small sphere. His smile widened. "What Kohru has made on this planet is an abomination. You'll die here. I don't need you meddling any more than you already have." Then he shook his head and gripped his face. "Stop it! Stop it!" It was Winnow's voice, his real one.

Ren took the opening. First form, second form, frosted glass, and he was sprinting for Winnow. The smell coming off Winnow's body was unbearable, he thrust the blade through his chest. Winnow fell back slowly while the grenade hit the ground with a low thud.

A deep, slow clockwork tick reached his ears.

Still flickering, and with all the strength he could muster, Ren bolted from the room. He leapt over piles of rubble and broken furniture, he fought against time, the air itself was trying to hold him back. A shockwave shifted everything around him, he stumbled, glittering particles of crystal dust pushed past him leaving trails of smoke. The powder was about to turn his entire world into an inferno. The door was just up ahead, everything behind him was swallowed, replaced by brilliant, sparkling flames.

Out the door, out the capitol gate. His reserves were almost dry. This would have to be it. He snapped into the third form and the world was engulfed in flame. He shielded his face with his coat.

Flaming debris rained down around him, slamming into buildings and tumbling through lines of troops down the mountain. Everyone went for cover. Ren ducked into the alleyway, and the ground rumbled yet again, but this time it was followed by distant cheers. It took him a moment to realize what had happened.

They finished the worm off!

Tears flowed from his eyes as he smiled, it was over.

Sharon

Dried flakes of blood fell from Sharon's jaw as she scratched at the freshly healed wound. Bits of umber red peppered the blanket on her lap while Ka sat next to her in the healing tent, her hand on the back of Sharon's neck, her will flowing through her body.

In the cot to the left lay Ahmad, clearly alive but seemingly sorry for the fact. He stared at the ceiling of the tent, blinking only now and then, as if it took an effort to perform the task. Sharon recognized the all too familiar signs of grief. After Hassan's death, Ahmad lived and breathed the Resistance. He threw himself at the cause, at a purpose. Now that purpose was over, and he was left alone in a healer's tent with no one to live for but himself. She made the decision then and there to help him. After things settled a bit, she'd make sure he had the means to land on his feet. A house maybe, or money enough to build one. That wouldn't fix it, nothing but time would soften his hurt, but he'd have one less thing to worry about.

What he really needs is a friend, but the gods know I can't fill that role.

"How do you feel?" Ka asked.

Breathing came easier, now that she'd coughed up all the blood left in her lungs, but with her life saved and the battle over, exhaustion crept in, nestling behind her eyes and weighing down her limbs. *There's something I wanted to say.*

"Thank you."

The cold smile was expected. Sharon had abandoned her own son, framed Troy for the death of his mother, murdered Seffin's friend—his name was Kent—and paved a path for Winnow's rise to power. None of those things had been done *to* Ka, but they hurt her just the same. Sharon didn't expect forgiveness, didn't deserve it. Still, she needed Ka to know.

"Not for saving me," Sharon clarified. "For watching after Ren." She coughed out a chuckle. "He has a knack for putting himself in danger, I'm sure he'd be dead if not for you."

Ka let go of Sharon's neck and wiped her hands on a towel. "Of all of them, Seffin is the one to worry about." She stood and surveyed the tent while she wiped strands of hair out of her face.

"I worry about him, too, funny enough," Sharon said. "I'm glad he survived."

A flash of surprise on Ka's face was quickly replaced with the stony mask she'd kept since carrying Sharon to the tent. That was fair. To be honest, she surprised herself with how much she worried for them, her son's little family.

"How did you end up at the front line? If you don't mind my asking."

"I'm not great at following orders, and I wasn't about to sit back and watch while my whole family risked their lives." She gave Sharon's arm a squeeze. "I heard what you did for me while I was stuck in the mountain, how you saved Sent'o. Thank you." Then she walked in the direction of a man groaning on the ground.

I'm sorry you had to take on my responsibility. I'm grateful for the space you made for my son. I'm disappointed in myself for being so blinded by anger.

I wish I wasn't this way.

Ka wouldn't want to hear that, though. The woman was wise beyond her years because she had to be. Far more than just a sister to Ren, she cared for him, watched over him, guided him. But her wisdom had come at the cost of her adolescence, and Sharon was partially to blame for that.

That's what she had done *to* Ka.

Her eyes felt heavy, and exhaustion won its battle. Sleep took her as her head hit the pillow, its scratchy fabric smelled of sweat and blood, struggle and strife.

***

"But how?" Sharon asked, frustrated. "Binding requires a person's blood, doesn't it?"

"We'd have to ask Sumiko if there's another way." Cal sat next to Jacinda at the table in headquarters which, impossibly, hadn't experienced much, if any, damage from the worm's quakes. Other than broken bottles and toppled furniture, their hideout was in pristine condition. His eye squinted at Ren. "Are you sure the worm was taking orders from him?"

Ren shrugged. "I don't know if it was taking orders, but they were connected. I'm sure of it." Seffin sat next to him, close. If she looked under the table, Sharon was sure she'd find them holding hands. They'd been like this since the battle, and although young love was sweet, it was also cloying. Still, it had her thinking of Noah over by the bar, and the unspeakable things they were going to do to each other after this meeting. Last night she'd slept in the healer's tent, but tonight she didn't plan on sleeping. After the debrief, she and Noah would drink themselves stupid in celebration, and rut till the sun came up in whatever tent or alleyway they could find some privacy. Noah caught her eye and grinned.

Patience.

"Maybe we're thinking about it wrong," Seffin said. "What if Winnow didn't bind the worm. What if the worm bound him?" It was miraculous what an hour with Ka could do for the mortally wounded. When they found Seffin on the way out of the city his legs had been crushed. Delirious, he'd mumbled something about Polk needing to live his life. Not to throw it away. Tender had carried him while Ka carried Sharon back to the tent with Polk on lookout.

Troy scratched at his chin, blond stubble showing after a day without his typical, time-consuming grooming routine. Every morning during the months she lived with him, he would take up the bathroom for hours, shaving and plucking and doing gods only knows what else in there. Whatever he did it worked. He was the prettiest man she ever saw. "I think that could be a possibility," he said, settling his gaze on Polk. "It makes sense, doesn't it? We bind amalgamations by taking over creatures influenced by Koth when they're at their weakest, during the amalgamation process. Well, I can tell you from personal experience that Winnow had some of the shallowest will reserves I've ever seen. We did tests with him when he wanted to bind an amalgamation. He could barely move a pebble. Do you think Koth could take over someone if they had shallow enough reserves?"

When the hells did he get so smart?

Polk looked down in thought. "I... I'm not sure. It hasn't happened before, as far as I know. But you're describing intentioned will, and there *have* been incidents where a wielder with deep enough reserves has influenced, and even controlled, someone with shallow reserves. It takes an extreme amount of will to do that though."

"Werewillers can wield," Ren said. "Can dreadworms?"

"Yes, actually," Tender said. "They expend most of it on moving through the ground."

"Winnow was desperate to bind an amalgamation. It wouldn't surprise me in the least if he tried to bind the dreadworm." Troy took a sip of his ale and set the cup down with a clunk. "Or maybe he's been puppeted by Koth the whole time?"

Ok, not that smart.

"Doubtful," Sharon said. "If that were the case, he'd have shown signs far earlier. Whatever happened to him it happened after the coup."

"There was a dead zone set up in The Pit. I can't think of any reason to do that other than to make sure he had access to the worm," Ren said.

"But how would he know about the worm in the first place?" Troy asked.

Tender frowned and said, "This might be a crazy idea, but I'll say it anyway. Dreadworms have immense will reserves, but they're base creatures. They use their will on instinct to move... to the best of our knowledge anyway. Is it possible Koth took direct control of the dreadworm and used intentioned will to convince Winnow into binding it?"

"Anything is possible," Polk said. "Koth's core is still imprisoned within Lana. We know that because if Koth were freed the husk wouldn't increase at a steady rate, they'd explode in numbers. But we're near the end of a cycle, when he's at his most powerful. That might grant him more direct influence. It would explain the horde outside Nari'ko."

"If that's true, what's to stop another worm from coming here, taking over someone else?" Jacinda asked.

Tender shook their head. "For one, there are only a handful of dreadworms that exist, less than fifty that we know of. For two, we don't know the manner in which Winnow was bound to the worm, we can't assume it's the same process we use. And for three, Winnow was in an exploitable position. He had convinced his followers to kill anyone who so much as disagreed with him. If Koth took over any of the other world leaders, he'd have a hard time convincing their citizens to do what he wanted, especially if one of the side effects is turning into a living husk. It would be obvious they were controlled."

This is getting us nowhere, it's all theoretical. We should move on for now.

"What are we doing with the remaining Nationals?" Sharon asked.

"The ones we rescued from Empress Zollinger?" Jacinda scowled. "They're being held in our hideouts, guarded by resistance members. It would be easier if we could make a camp outside the walls for them and guard that, but with the Garvelle army right there, I don't trust her to leave it alone."

The empress had taken it upon herself to issue a death sentence to every single National still left standing at the end of the fighting. Including the noncombatants. It was cold, even for Sharon's taste. Many of them were more gullible than evil. They deserved punishment, many even deserved death, but Kiko would butcher them all regardless of circumstance.

During her time with The Eyes, the few pockets of anti-imperialists Sharon met had always confused her. Garvelle's cities had far less poverty, far fewer murders, and far better living conditions than anywhere in Egal. But she hadn't lived there, only visited. Perhaps she should have listened more closely, opened her eyes wider to what life was really like under Empress Zollinger's rule. It wasn't her country though. Wasn't her problem. She had her family to worry about, her little town by the sea.

"Can Farah and Selena make some secure holding cells?" Sharon asked.

"It'll take a few days, but yes. Though I'd rather someone else be the one to ask her." Jacinda shot a look back at Sharon.

Despite her repeated statements claiming so, the Resistance did *not* think of Farah as a glorified shovel. It just so happened she was very good at digging out structurally sound rooms. The base they all sat in was evidence of her skills. Were they supposed to ignore her talents? If Farah didn't feel it was fair to ask her to dig so much, she might have chosen to specialize in another element. Despite how justified they were, Sharon had no intention of delivering the order. She'd had enough tongue lashings and heard enough indignant monologues from the wild wielder for a lifetime.

Sharon stared right back at Jacinda. "As our soon-to-be elected leader, I feel it only fair you be the one to tell her, Jacinda. Delegation is part of the job, after all."

I did my part. We beat Winnow. Lean on someone else.

The room looked on at the exchange with amusement. Nobody wanted to be here right now, and nobody wanted to run the necessary errands or do the necessary chores. They wanted to celebrate. To drink and dance and make love and fall asleep secure in the knowledge they would wake up in the morning.

"But this *is* delegation." Jacinda cracked a mischievous smile.

"Let me rephrase," Sharon said. "No."

"Ugh, fine. I'll be the one to tell her if you stop by our hideouts and let the guards know they'll need to continue their rotations for a few days before we can relieve them."

Godsmotherfuckingdamnit!

That was manipulative. Jacinda would make a great politician. "I'd be happy to," Sharon said and put a forced smile on her lips. She knew this game, any more arguing and she'd get a worse task, it's how she managed Ren as a child. She'd just been mothered, but the epiphany faded behind the anticipation of pinning Noah to a wall and having her way with him.

"We have ten days to get the city into some semblance of order before our meeting with the other nations," Tender said. "It's important that we appear to know what we're doing."

"The Guild will handle repairing and restarting the mines. Though, ten days is far too short a time span to produce results," Troy said.

Jacinda stood from the table. "Let's call it there for the day. No need to get bogged down in long-term planning the day after we won the city. Handle your assignments and I'll see you all in Garvelle's camp for the festivities this evening."

Seffin and Ren leapt out of their chairs and made for the exit. She knew exactly what they were off to do. Noah sidled up beside her. "I got us a tent in Garvelle's camp tonight. Traded a soldier a bottle of vodka and some porcine chops to let us use it." Their building had collapsed in the quakes, robbing them of a private place to have their way with each other, but Sharon lamented the loss of the little cafe on the ground floor far more than their apartment.

"Does the soldier understand what state they'll find the tent in when they return?" she replied.

He squeezed her ass and she shoved him off, laughing.

"Ahh, to be young again," Cal said.

Sharon shot him a glare. "Oh, hush."

Troy tapped her on the shoulder. "Can I have a word?"

This is the first he'd voluntarily spoken to her outside of a formal meeting. "Of course."

They stepped to the end of the bar. He tapped his finger on the bar top, which was nervous energy, the man was impossible to keep still when he was thinking hard about something. "I told the science team everything."

Wow, he truly is smarter than he used to be.

It was the one thing she told him not to do in order to keep his life, but Tender, Jacinda, and Cal were here. Even if Sharon wanted to make good on her promise to kill him, she'd die in the attempt.

"That's fine, Troy. Though I'd ask that you refrain from spreading that information any further. I'd like to continue helping with the rebuilding efforts, and I doubt the citizens would let me if they knew the truth of everything."

"So, you're not going to try and kill me?"

"I've done enough to you, don't you think?"

"I'd say so."

"Good, that settles that. Now you can go back to being surly every time I'm in the room, and I can go back to pretending like I don't care."

"*Pretending* you don't care?"

Sharon put a hand on his shoulder. He winced, but she squeezed anyway. Then she ducked behind the counter. Eight bottles of vodka and two bottles of whiskey found their way into her satchel.

"What do you think you're doing?" Jacinda asked.

Sharon raised the satchel up. "Gifts for the guards who can't attend tonight. If we don't give them alcohol, they'll find it from somewhere else anyway, and this way my news will go down easier."

Jacinda considered a moment. "Hand me one for Farah, would you?"

Sharon tossed her the last bottle of gin, Farah's preferred liquor. She walked for the exit but made sure to pull Noah in for a kiss before she left. "I'll see *you* at the party."

***

Sharon sat in a cot next to a snoozing Noah, rolling a coin over her knuckles—eye open on one side, eye closed on the other.

It had been in the pile of wild wielder Ka left behind during her daring rescue. At the time, the metallic tinkling barely registered over the sloppy plops of chopped up elementalist hitting cobblestones, but yesterday afternoon she remembered the sound and it stuck in her ears. A ringing note, too familiar to be coincidence.

The noise could have been the wielder's jewelry, though it wouldn't have the same, tinny quality.

They could have carried any number of coins on them, as many people do, but it was only one coin she heard, one sound.

It could have been the sound of sword's clashing in the battle, but the coin bounced and came to a stop in a way only coins do, rolling over onto its flat surface with rapid, staccato notes as it settled.

Still, none of those sounds would have put a splinter in her brain on their own, but The Coin of Eyes was heavier than normal currency, and had a unique, deeper tone. A tone Sharon—Flicker—knew intimately after ten years of fiddling with her own coins on contracts. It was unmistakable, and its presence meant Winnow had been working with The Eyes.

Sharon expected there was something going on with her former employer for some time now. They had tenets they followed religiously, and one of those tenets was not to interfere in matters of war. They would gladly cause one, but once the conflict was formalized, The Eyes were supposed to avert their gaze. The organization didn't want to draw the attention of full armies, nor did they wish their members to take sides. The rule was a closely held secret, one they didn't want the different nations' leaders to know.

However...

Assassins had been popping up in odd locations since Sharon's return to the city. Eyes were trained to kill, deliver their coin, and leave. Cara Soledar's undercover position in the Guild had always been odd for an eye, and the cost of assassinating a popular politician was exorbitant, did Jessica actually have the money to hire one to kill Winnow? Now, there's one protecting the president in the middle of a battle for the city.

Noah's own drunken snoring woke him up and he sleepily found the object Sharon sat obsessing over. "What's that you got there?"

"A problem," she said. She let herself ignore it overnight, allowed herself the break after her brush with death, but the longer she waited the more the splinter lanced into her brain.

She threw on her smallclothes and began to lace up her britches.

"Whoa, you're leaving?"

"I have a hunch. I need to check something." She leaned down and kissed him on the forehead. "I should be back before lunch. If I'm not... well, take care of yourself."

"What's that supposed to mean?" But she was already gone. She couldn't answer without lying or agreeing to bring him with, and she wasn't about to do either.

If they still follow the old ways, I should be able to find them.

Assassin dens moved with regularity, but abandoned dens always held a code instructing any eyes where the next den would be. It would involve bouncing around the city, but she could follow the trail of dens in Prolivgrad from the time she left until now, provided the worm hadn't destroyed them.

The first was under a gaming parlor, not crushed, luckily, but very much abandoned. The slip of paper hidden under a floorboard was old, and time hadn't been kind to the ink. The dots and arrows were decipherable though. The dots were stars, the reader was meant to line up the depicted constellation and follow the arrows to the next den. Assassins were required to commit the night sky to memory, and so she faced the direction where the constellation would have been and followed the arrows.

So it went, all morning. Each den brought her closer to the current one. Closer to a possible conclusion she didn't know if she was ready for. She'd just gotten Ren back. They'd just won the city. Here she was, throwing her life away following a trail to a bunch of killers on a hunch.

The papers she found became less aged and the ink less faded, and finally she came upon what had to be a recently abandoned den. In the middle of the room lay a body, it was cut to pieces, decayed and crumbling into the cracks of the floorboards. *Ominous.* Its right hand rested ten feet from the corpse, still clutching a note. She pried it from whoever-the-hell's dead fingers and gasped at what she saw.

It was the symbol of their order, The Eyes of Koth, but it had been modified. Instead of one open eye and one closed, both were wide, glaring back at her. This person had been a member of the Cult of Koth, and they'd somehow made it into The Eyes' den.

Directions to the next hideout were hidden in a moldering book on a shelf, disguised as a lazy bookmark. Sharon's body vibrated. What was she about to find? The constellation guided her to a simple home near Prolivgrad's wall, small and in disrepair. The entrance hadn't been trapped so she walked in to find a not-so-secret door by a bookshelf left wide open, the pungent decay of husk wafted out, accompanied by raspy groans.

She took her will-blade out, walked through the door, and descended a flight of stairs into a moderately sized room. She used kinetics to light the candles and dropped her blade in shock.

Pinned with daggers and writhing on the back wall were two assassins turned husk. The leaders, the left and right eye of the order, identifiable by brands on their shoulders, one closed eye and one open. On the wall above them a message was written in blood, candlelight licking at the letters.

KOTH SEES CLEAR. KOTH SEES THE TRUTH. KOTH SEES ALL.

Then a glint caught Sharon's attention. The assassins' eyes. They'd been carved out and replaced with open eye coins, all staring at her, wide and angry.

Troy

Kiko never planned to let Prolivgrad slip from her grasp. She explained her reasoning with gentle words, phrasing the annexation as if she was doing Egal a favor, but everyone at the summit knew this had been her plan from the start. The toughest part of it all was Troy couldn't disagree with her. Egal *had* put all the other nations in danger. With Egal's population reduced to almost half of what it used to be, they would need assistance and capable leadership to recover in time to help Polk with his mission.

Duncan Mitchell sat with atypical quietude, almost serene, while Bruhier fumed next to him at their corner of the table. His medium brown skin shifted to the color of a tomato as Kiko laid out her offer, her mandate. Even Tender looked appalled.

"You can't lay claim to an entire country," they said. "The citizens must have a say."

"Then vote," she said. "If it makes you feel better about the whole thing, but the fact is, at least for now, we're going to manage Egal like any other territory in the empire, Prolivgrad especially. We can talk about your ability to self-govern *after* we stop the husk. I won't leave the fate of the world up to chance any longer."

King Edward sat next to her, nodding along. Nashow's economy was tied heavily to Garvelle, if these talks soured, Troy had no question what side he'd land on.

"Empress," Ka said, though Troy had never heard her address her as anything other than 'Kiko' or 'auntie' or some variation thereof. "We've spoken to community leaders, captains, and heads of the Resistance, and they all agree. Egal wants to clean up its own mess. Jacinda and Cal—"

"Are not elected to anything," she said.

"It's been less than two weeks, Kiko," Tender said. There hadn't been enough time to organize candidates, let alone an election.

And we've spent the bulk of the time erecting makeshift pylons and killing husk. "You aren't elected either," Troy said. "You were given your empire and now you're forcing us into it."

The empress shot him a dangerous look. "Careful, Mr. Saunders. I was not *given* anything. Regardless, your capital city sits atop the only source of focus crystals in the world. We need the mines up and running again. Now." She took her pointer finger and jabbed it down on the table. "If you think the loss of life in Egal dramatic you should see the number of settlements we've lost in the empire because of this."

Not a fair comparison. The empire is over five times the size of Egal, but she knows that. She's baiting me into comparing death tolls as if it's a contest.

"No one knows how to get the mines up and running better than our own citizens, and no one knows how to distribute crystals better than me," he said. "I can promise you'll have your crystals."

"You're not in charge, Mr. Saunders," she said.

Tender cleared their throat. "Neither are you."

Kiko frowned. Whatever the two's shared history, this disagreement was forming a wedge between them.

"Estaba won't accept Garvellian rule of Mount Brinidor," Bruhier finally said. "You already trampled over half the world. We fought a whole war over it, and if I recall correctly, the deal was for you to stay on your own half. You will honor that agreement or by the gods—"

"No," Tender said. "No, Rahal, no threats of war. We *will not* survive another one."

"So you're going to let her take over your country? Do you have no pride?"

None of this is helping.

"We're not *letting* anyone take over anything," Troy said, "but the people have been through enough. They're exhausted. We're *all* exhausted." Underneath the table, Ka set her hand on his and squeezed. She came today because he wanted her there. If it were up to her, she'd be out killing husk, helping to rebuild the Lodge, or working through the never-ending list of those who needed healing. This was exactly the type of thing she loathed. Making decisions for other people. Forcing her will on others. Troy was beginning to think she had a point.

This sucked.

"Exactly. We've all been through enough. Let us help you," The empress said, a vulture circling.

The proposition wasn't without merit. The empire relied on the crystals from Mount Brinidor the same way everyone else did, to leave control of the only source to another country required trust, and Egal hadn't exactly been the most trust-worthy of stewards, even before Winnow took over.

A woman with a tray of teas entered the tent, Knight Bahati stood next to the entrance and eyed her as she set a cup down in front of each guest. Then she refilled their waters and stood in the corner with the pitcher, dutifully.

A smile slipped onto Duncan Mitchell's face. "This is sun-sap tea," he said. "Brewed from a flower that only blooms once per year." He took a sip and made a show out of it. "It's a delicacy in Lighton."

"I prefer bloodleaf," Kiko said.

Duncan deflated.

Tender shook their head. "Your help comes with hooks, Kiko. I would rather we manage this ourselves. If we can get you the crystals the empire needs will that satisfy you?"

"No," she said, "I'm afraid the rest of the world has been at the mercy of Egal for too long already. As I said, we can discuss Egal's ability to self-govern *after* the husk are taken care of."

We need to come back to this later. Everyone is too dug in.

"Speaking of the husk," Troy said. "Has everyone heard Ren's report on Winnow?"

Kiko scoffed. "Who cares? Even *if* it's true that Koth influenced Winnow, it changes nothing."

Duncan shifted in his chair uncomfortably. *That's right, he never did believe the husk were growing in number.*

"You don't find it important that our enemy took over an entire nation?" Troy said.

"Not my nation," Kiko said. "Not his." She pointed at Bruhier. "Or his." She pointed at King Edward. "And even if he was being influenced by a binding like your scientist, what was his name?"

"Tyler Chen," Troy said through gritted teeth. Luckily, the man's symptoms had cleared, but he went through hell to try and help gain this victory. The least she could do was remember his name.

"Right, Tyler. If someone becomes corrupted, like Tyler, then we kill the amalgamation and cut off the connection, right? A simple solution."

Troy felt his face get hot. Winnow may have been unique in how simultaneously stupid and ambitious he was, but they hadn't discovered *how* Koth came to control him. He wouldn't have bound an amalgamation the same way the Guild did. That mattered, and instead of acknowledging the fact, she was taking cheap shots.

Duncan interjected. "Everyone, the tea is getting cold."

Kiko shot him a withering look and he flinched like she was about to leap over the table and rip his head off. From the moment the meeting began it was clear how much she despised him. She grabbed her water glass and took a sip of that, instead. Duncan slumped in his chair. As petty as the gesture was, the tent truly was too hot for tea.

"Besides," Kiko said, "who knows what Ren saw? I struggle to believe Koth took control of a living person. There's nothing recorded in our history books of something like that happening. Hells, Polk himself even said it hasn't happened before."

"He never said it wasn't possible," Tender said. They took a sip of the sunsap tea and flashed a mollifying smile in Duncan's direction.

Kiko shook her head. "I'm being forced to repeat myself. It does not matter. It doesn't change what we need to do."

"Sharon seems to believe him," Troy said. "She even confirmed his report that Winnow looked grey, like a living husk."

Kiko paused and pinched the bridge of her nose. "Fine," she said. "It *would* be disastrous if this happened again. We can assign a team to look into it."

Finally, we gained some ground. Troy nodded. "Now, about Sharon's report regarding The Eyes—"

Choking sounds came from Troy's left. Tender's hands were on their throat. Ka was out of her chair and next to them in a moment, hands on their chest.

What are they choking on?

High-pitched squeaking and wheezing turned into crashing as they fell to the floor, silent now except for their boots kicking at the ground. Troy looked around the room frantically. Everyone's faces were masks of terror. Clangs came from the other side of the table with more choking sounds. The empress had fallen over as well. Aisha rushed to her side.

"Sunback venom," Ka said. Tears were in her eyes. "Hold on, Poppy. Just hold on."

Seconds felt like an eternity as Ka's hands glowed against Tender's skin. In all the times he'd seen Ka's healing, her hands never glowed. The clanging on the other side of the table continued. Aisha, sobbing and frantic, yelled over. "Ka, help me! She's dying!"

Ka only shook her head and kept her hands on Tender.

"What the hells did you do!" Bruhier jumped up and pointed a curved dagger at Duncan.

Troy's heart raced. The server who filled their waters started for the exit. "Hey! Don't move!" He rushed to intercept her. A knife flashed in her hand, and she thrust it at his neck. On instinct, he brought his hand up to block. The knife sunk through his palm, and he fought her as she continued to push it toward his throat. Through the explosion of pain, he shoved her backward to the ground. Without another hand he couldn't pull the knife out. He gripped down onto the blade shoved through his palm, red with his own blood. The server jumped to her feet, but before she could spring away, he slammed the knife into her skull.

Her body went limp with the knife still lodged in; she brought Troy down with her as she fell. He was stuck.

"What the fuck did you do!" Bruhier's voice boomed.

"W-W-Without the empress and without Tender we can take Egal, y-y-you said it yourself!"

Kiko's legs were kicking, Aisha sobbed while she held her hand and brushed hair out of her face.

Tender had stopped moving and Ka lay over their chest, still. *Ka! No!*

Coughing sounded from Bruhier's side of the table and Duncan fell to the ground, bright red blood streaming out a deep cut in his neck, his eyes already staring at nothing, lost.

"Ka!" Troy yelled. "Ka! Say something!"

Where are the rest of the guards? Did the assassin kill them?

Then Bruhier was standing over him, frowning at the scene. Without a word he grabbed the dagger, pried it from the assassin's skull, and slipped it out of Troy's hand. The pain was nothing. Troy rushed to Ka, grabbed her shoulder, rolled her over, blood dripping all over her clothes.

The tent was silent.

Her breaths came quietly, but she was alive. Beneath her, Tender's chest rose and fell in a steady rhythm.

Wailing erupted from the other side of the room.

"No! Gods, no! Your Majesty! Kiko!" Aisha's pained voice filled the air. "You can't die. Not now."

King Edward stood in a corner of the tent like a scared mouse trying its best to avoid notice. Troy pulled Ka off Tender and stared at each of their chests. They had to keep breathing. Bruhier knelt down beside him and grabbed at his hand. He pulled away on reflex, but the Estaban prime minister's grip was strong.

"Fucking hold still," he said, wrapping Troy's hand with some cloth torn from the dead assassin's shirt. When he finished, he stood up and sighed. "Duncan, you godsdamned fool."

Aisha's sobs turned into soft, hitched breathing as Troy sat silently, putting pressure on his wound while his eyes remained fixed on Ka's chest, ensuring it continued to rise and fall, rise and fall.

***

"Absolutely not," Ka said, still wearing her mourning whites from the empress' funeral.

Knight Aisha Bahati, already back in her armor after the funeral, knelt in front of Troy, Seffin, Polk, and the Bolin family in their living room.

Tender could barely contain their outrage. "We had a deal."

Aisha looked up at them, meek. An unfortunate messenger. "Forgive me, Your Majesty, but—"

"I am *not* Your Majesty," Ka said, then turned to Tender, "and when were *you* going to tell me Kiko was my birth mother?"

Tender glared at Aisha. "Never. Because Kiko wanted nothing to do with raising a child. Which was perfectly fine with me, since I wanted nothing to do with running an empire. That was the deal."

"Gods, Poppy, you can be such a hypocrite. Aren't you the one that's always on about making your own choices? Does that philosophy only apply to you, personally? You get the freedom to choose and everyone else gets the freedom to deal with the consequences, is that it?"

Tender's gaze found the floor, but they said nothing, no explanation for their behavior.

"Find someone else," Troy said to Aisha. "Why don't *you* take the throne?"

She met his eyes and spoke through gritted teeth, "If I were the only one who knew, I would. Gladly. But it's on record. All ranking officers in the military are aware of Ka's lineage." She bowed her head back down. "The empress wouldn't budge. She wanted the throne to go to her only living relative."

"I refuse. I'll abdicate," Ka said.

"There is no such thing in Garvelle. Abdication means execution," Aisha said, still staring at the ground.

Ka scoffed. "What kind of monster made that law?"

"Your great grandfather," Polk said. "He was—"

"A monster," Tender said. "No use explaining further."

"Fine, the territories can run themselves. I'll dissolve the empire," she said.

"No," Aisha, Polk, Troy, and Tender all said at once.

"We need to be united right now more than anything. We can't waste our time and resources on restructuring half the world's government," Tender shook their head as they spoke.

Time and distance to process the assassination might have made this conversation less hostile. But the empress only died two days ago, and despite Ka's anger at who she now knew was her mother, she hadn't any time to mourn the loss. Instead, she would have to reconcile 'Auntie Kiko' as not only her birth mother, but also the type of person that would annex a sovereign nation, the type of person to burden her with a throne she didn't want.

Ka fell into a nearby chair. "I can't."

"You must," Aisha stood. "I will be there to guide you."

"Then I'm dissolving the empire as soon as Polk is installed as Koth's vessel."

Aisha sucked in her teeth. "If that is your wish, but as monstrous as Cedric Zollinger was, the only reason the eastern front bordering Gogallo hasn't fallen is because the empire united to stop it. Those countries were on the verge of being overrun, and the husk aren't going away completely even *if* we succeed."

"That is the one and only nice thing anyone can say about him," Tender said.

Even with that, he killed the king of Teveen after he surrendered.

"So, you're saying if I dissolve the empire, people will die. If I abdicate, I'll die." Ka looked defeated.

Aisha stared at her for a moment, likely weighing her words. "I'm sorry, Your Majesty."

"Stop calling me that!"

Tender placed a hand on Ka's shoulder. "I think what my daughter is trying to say is: we have a lot to discuss, could you please give us some time?"

"Of course." Aisha, looking grateful for an exit to the conversation, bowed and walked out the front door.

"I'm grabbing some water, would Your Majesty like a glass?" Ren grinned from ear to ear.

Not helping.

"While you're in there, why don't you get everyone some water. I'm parched," Troy said. Ren's grin turned to a frown and he stalked off. *That's what you get for being a little shit.* He turned to Ka. "There has to be some way out of this."

Ka shook her head, but it was Tender who said, "There isn't. Maybe if I'd gotten anything in writing, but I stupidly thought Kiko would keep her word."

"If the law was made by the emperor, then I should be able to change it if I take up the throne, shouldn't I?" Ka's eyes were desperate.

"No," Polk said. "The empress has final say on any new laws, but any change to an existing law directly affecting the throne must be approved by each territory's minister."

"Let's do that then," Ka said.

That would be a mess.

As if reading his thoughts, Ka sighed before saying, "Never mind, that would just cause a war."

"Gods, I could kill her all over again," Tender said. "If I had known—"

"If *I* had known." Ka glared at her parent. "Then I could have talked to her. I could have explained to her what a mistake this is."

"It wouldn't have done any good," Seffin said. "She never intended to give the throne to anyone but you, and Kiko was stubborn." Troy nodded. The boy wasn't wrong, at some point between leaving for Nari'ko and returning to Prolivgrad he'd become an expert judge of character.

Ka threw up her hands. "So what? I'm stuck?"

Ren returned with a tray of waters and began handing them out with a pleasant, though smug, smile. "Here you go. Is there anything else I can do for you, Empress?"

"You might not want to antagonize her. She could have you executed with a word," Troy said.

He rolled his eyes. "I don't see what the big deal is. Just have Aisha do everything."

"It's not that simple," Troy said. "Garvelle's army answers to the empress alone, there's also the matter of preparing for our push on Gogallo, not to mention disputes between territories. The ministers aren't going to be content with a counselor settling their differences. Don't even get me started on the mess that is Garvelle's trade agreements. Aisha can't handle it all on her own. No one can."

Ka put her head in her hands. "There is one silver lining," she said to the floor. "I'm not Kiko. I'm not about to annex my home. Egal will be able to rule itself now."

Troy's heart broke. If she left Egal to run itself, he couldn't go with her. He'd have to stay back to help rebuild, she couldn't assign an emergency minister to take over and run everything. There would have to be elections, the Guild would have to get back on its feet, the mines would have to reopen. Tender would have to stay to help rebuild the Lodge. Ren and Seffin would stay for the same reason, and Polk would do whatever Seffin did.

She'll be alone and ruling an entire empire. This is her worst nightmare.

He walked over to where she sat, bent down, and grabbed her hand. "I'm sorry."

Tears filled her eyes as she smiled at him, and his heart shattered into even smaller pieces. "Gods, what am I going to do?"

She'd done so much for all of them, and now they had to watch her leave, on her own, when she needed them most. He squeezed her hand.

I'll join you as soon as I can.

Epilogue

Garvelle City always left Kulelika Bolin unsettled. The black and white marble used to construct most of the city's major structures made for an ominous appearance, and the tall, thin spires turned the skyline prickly, uninviting. Gazing out her balcony from the castle, she could imagine the city itself poking her eye out.

Six years.

Empress for six years and she still couldn't calm her nerves. The time may have flown by, but it did so with violence and loneliness. Six years of ceding border settlements to the husk. Six years of listening to Knight Bahati's insistence on a firm hand when Ka never wanted her hands anywhere near the throne in the first place. She'd ruled on land disputes. She'd ruined merchant's lives with her decrees.

She'd issued executions.

The marble railing was cold and wet from the rain this morning. She leaned on it anyway. Despite the view, it was the most peaceful place she'd found in this building since her accession, and she liked looking down at the city below more than she liked dry sleeves. The people, her subjects, appeared as ants, milling about the palace grounds and in and out of the gates. All with their own little jobs. All with their own little lives. Lives she would upend to a staggering degree in short order.

Garvelle City would soon host the largest army ever assembled in all of history, at least in this cycle. In the coming months, her ants would have to make space for soldiers from across the world. Something, her counselors had explained repeatedly, they were loath to do. Garvelle City was as deep into the empire as one could get, and its people didn't enjoy visitors. They didn't enjoy much, to be frank. Of every culture Empress Kulelika had come in contact with, her own people took first place in the wet blanket contest. Joyless, self-righteous, stoic, and harsh, they were in no way prepared for the amount of color the other nations would infuse into their black-and-white landscape.

"Peering down on the commoners, Your Majesty?" Troy's voice had a smile in it like it had since he arrived two months ago. The Guild needed a representative in the army, and no one could perform the duty better than him. Or he told himself that anyway. Since his arrival, he'd done little else besides fawn over her in between sparse meetings with her generals.

"Stop teasing. I'm Ka to you, and you know it." His bulky frame approached wearing nothing but a pair of loose-fitting, linen pants. He wrapped her in his big arms, and she leaned into his chest.

"Only a few more months," he said. "Then we get the band back together."

A smile slipped onto her lips at the thought, but guilt and dread slapped it off. The excitement she had for seeing her family was spoiled by the reason for their visit.

The final push into Gogallo.

They'd delayed long enough. Time was needed to recover from the destruction of Prolivgrad, to repair their relationship with Lighton after Bruhier killed their president in cold blood, to hopefully, if Ren and Seffin were successful, convince Karm to join in the fight. The island nation to the northeast of the empire was even more isolationist than Kelsig. Her younger brother and his husband insisted Polk could convince Karm to join them, so she'd granted them a ship and a crew and sent them on their fool's mission.

Everything hinged on Polk. Ren couldn't be trusted to convince a dog to eat table scraps, and Seffin, gods bless his progress, didn't fare much better in matters of diplomacy. Everything *always* hinged on Polk. The poor boy, teen now, took on his responsibilities knowing full well he wouldn't be around to enjoy the fruits of his labor. His dedication never wavered.

It would have been better if Poppy had gone along, but they were on some mission with Sent'o and Sharon into Northern Gogallo. What they planned to do there, they wouldn't say, but once Poppy dug their heels in, they were immovable. It would be suicide for most people, but Sharon, Sent'o, and

Poppy were not most people. If anyone could journey into Gogallo and come out alive, it would be them. At least that's what she told herself in order to sleep at night.

Ka sighed. "We lost another pylon yesterday."

"That's three in as many weeks," he said. "Are you sure it's not a dreadworm?"

"I've learned far more about dreadworms than I care to repeat, and I can safely say it's not. They can't be compelled to come into contact with a barrier. This is either sabotage by Koth cultists or the pylons are simply being overrun by the sheer number of husk." Empress Kulelika patted her Troy on his chest and pulled away. "We need to figure out which, and we need to figure it out before the armies arrive."

Koth cultists were an unwelcome surprise to Kulelika when she took the throne. She'd heard of them before, and even killed a few with Poppy during her time as a merc. But the cult had increased its presence in all portions of the world ever since the fight for Prolivgrad, ever since Sharon discovered The Eyes of Koth were no more. And where they remained secretive on the continent of Sol, they acted more openly in the eastern portion of the empire. A constant thorn in her side.

The castle rumbled. A memory of complete darkness bubbled up in her mind before Troy's arms were around her once again.

Kohru's light, what in the hells was that?

She pulled out of Troy's embrace to look out over the city. The courthouse, with its two spires, had gone missing. There was nothing but a hole in the ground where it once stood.

Troy gasped. "Where... where in the hells did it go?"

In the hole, obviously.

But she held her tongue. Troy had a way of asking questions he already knew the answers to and calling him on it only made everything take longer. "We need to get—"

Knight Bahati burst into the bedroom behind them. "Your Majesty!"

"I saw," Empress Kulelika said. "Do I need to ask who did it?"

Bahati shook her head. "I already sent scouts to confirm, but the Church of Koth—"

"They're cultists. Don't legitimize them."

They're scum that would destroy the world for the empty promises of their evil god...

...

How in the hells did she have the time to send scouts already?

"I think the *cult* is responsible, yes. No one else has the organization to pull this off." Bahati looked Troy up and down with a disappointed look. She'd never really liked him, and Empress Kulelika never bothered to figure out why. A monarch didn't need an adviser's approval on who they took to bed, and if Polk became the new vessel for Koth, she wouldn't need an adviser's approval for anything before long.

Despite protestations from Bahati, Ka planned to stick to her word and dissolve the empire after the battle.

"Gather the counsel and get me a report on who we lost. I doubt they targeted the courthouse for the symbolism alone. Oh, and have Farah sent to the site, maybe she can sense some tunnels, or at least shed some light on how they managed this. We need to find where they're hiding and smoke them out."

Before she could destroy her own empire, she'd have to save it first.

Thank you for reading!

Did you like this story? Please consider leaving a review. They are more vital to a new author's success than most people realize, and golly, I sure would appreciate it.

Want more from the world of Kohru? A free short story will be released in conjunction with each of my first three novels. *The Eye*, and *The Princess* are already available if you subscribe to my newsletter at mjlindemann.com. Make sure to whitelist me so you can keep up to date on new releases, as well as pictures of the cutest dogs you've ever seen in your entire life. Not that I'm biased or anything...

You may enjoy my other works set in the world of Kohru, here is a complete list in reading order:

The Eye
The Will of the World
The Princess
An Eager God
The Engineer

The Lies of the Heavens